DIFFERENT
DAUGHTERS

DIFFERENT DAUGHTERS

——A HISTORY OF THE——

DAUGHTERS OF BILITIS

AND THE RISE OF THE

LESBIAN RIGHTS MOVEMENT

MARCIA M. GALLO

CARROLL & GRAF PUBLISHERS
NEW YORK

Different Daughters
A History of the Daughters of Bilitis and the Rise of the Lesbian Rights Movement

Carroll & Graf Publishers
An Imprint of Avalon Publishing Group, Inc.
245 West 17th Street, 11th Floor
New York, NY 10011

AVALON
publishing group incorporated

First Carroll & Graf edition 2006

"Who Said It Was Simple" by Audre Lorde © 1982, 1973, Audre Lorde Estate. Published by permission of the Charlotte Sheedy Literary Agency, Inc.

All photos from the author's private collection unless otherwise noted. The author wishes to acknowledge Beth Elliott, Lynn Fonfa, Barbara Gittings, Barbara Grier, P. D. Griffin, Bev Hickok, Nina Kaiser, Shirley Kelly, Kay Lahusen, Phyllis Lyon, and Stella Rush for permission to use photographs and images; and thanks the unnamed cover artists for *The Ladder, Mattachine Review*, and *ONE*, whose work is reproduced here.

All cover art from *The Ladder* © 1956, 1957, 1960, 1964, 1966, 1969, 1970, Daughters of Bilitis, Inc.

Photograph of Lisa Ben courtesy of West Coast Women's Collection (now the June L. Mazer Lesbian Archives).

Library of Congress Cataloging-in-Publication Data is available.

ISBN-13: 978-0-78671-634-0
ISBN-10: 0-7867-1634-7

9 8 7 6 5 4 3 2 1

Interior design by Maria E. Torres
Printed in the United States of America
Distributed by Publishers Group West

For Anni, with love and thanks.

Contents

Acknowledgments

My greatest thanks go to the women of the Daughters of Bilitis for their courage and candor, then and now, especially Barbara Gittings, Kay Lahusen, Phyllis Lyon, Del Martin, and Stella Rush. I am grateful as well to the nearly three dozen women with whom I've talked over the last six years. Many of them—including Ada Bello, Clara Brock, Jeanne Cordova, Beth Elliott, Barbara Grier and Donna McBride, Bev Hickok, Lois Johnson and Shari Barden, Nina Kaiser, Sue Handley, the "Mama Bears" women (Natalie Lando, Shirley Kelly, and Carol Vorvolakis), Martha Shelley, and Billye Talmadge—opened their homes, their files, their photo albums, and their hearts to me; many others met me for coffee and shared their most intimate memories. I also thank former Mattachine Midwest leader William Kelley for his help. Their trust in me was validated by a 2005–2006 publication grant from the American Association of University Women, which offered much-needed financial assistance. I thank AAUW for its support.

A number of people took time from their own busy lives to provide direction as "Different Daughters" was born, grew up, and came out. In particular, I am indebted to Martin Duberman. Over the last decade, he not only guided my research but also generously and

consistently shared his knowledge of history and politics, his understanding of the workings of academia and publishing, and his personal support. He has taught me more about scholarship and
friendship than he will ever know, and I am very grateful.

I also thank Bonnie Anderson, who read numerous drafts of the
manuscript and always provided useful criticism and assistance, as well
as lively dinner conversations. Blanche Wiesen Cook shared her abun-
dant passions and insights about love, peace, justice, activism, and
how to tell a good story. Diane Bernard, Clare Coss, Sandi Cooper,
Deborah Cox, Elaine Elinson, Lynn Fonfa, Joshua Freeman, Adrian
Jones, Angela Moreno, Alisa Solomon, and Eli Zal all helped "Different Daughters" develop, and I am very appreciative of their
efforts. In addition, friends Amber Hollibaugh helped me find the
confidence in myself to write, Achebe Powell soothed my fears about
surviving in academia, Leisa Meyers gave me concrete ways to share
my scholarship, and Rhonda Copelon provided a Sag Harbor "study
hall" at a crucial moment in the summer of 2005.

This book was motivated by what I couldn't find in most libraries:
the story of a small group of ordinary lesbians who helped change the
world. Unlike many of my colleagues in the Ph.D. program in History at the City University of New York, I started classes in September 1995 knowing exactly what I wanted to research. What I
didn't know is how much the CUNY experience would change my
life. There I found superlative professors, helpful staff, and good
friends. I am grateful for my associations with the late Phillip Can-
nistraro, Thomas Kessner, Gerry Markowitz, David Nasaw, Randolph
Trumbach, and Barbara Welter; Department Secretary Betty Ein-
erman; and colleagues Kelly Anderson, Marcella Bencivenni, Harry
Lirtzman, and Christolyn Williams. Because of all of them, my professional training was more like joining a guild than navigating a huge
public institution in the midst of New York City, one that, despite

being constantly under-funded and under political attack, provided excellent schooling to me, and thousands more like me, for whom a graduate degree often seemed a distant dream.

One of the exciting realities at the CUNY Graduate Center is the Center for Lesbian and Gay Studies (CLAGS), founded in 1991 by Martin Duberman. I benefited greatly from its free programs, publications, and visionary leaders, from Duberman to Jill Dolan, Alisa Solomon, and Paisley Currah. Through CLAGS I also met my editor, Don Weise, who has been a great source of friendship and support. As an international network of activists and intellectuals, CLAGS made the world of queer inquiry accessible. It helped bring me closer to the work of women's and feminist scholars like the late Gloria Anzaldua, Cheryl Clarke, Lillian Faderman, Estelle Freedman, Elizabeth L. Kennedy and Madeline Davis, Cherrie Moraga, Joanne Meyerowitz, Esther Newton, Gayle Rubin, Leila Rupp, Barbara Smith, Carroll Smith-Rosenberg, Jennifer Terry, Carol Vance, Martha Vicinus, and E. Frances White, among others. All of them stirred my soul and motivated me to write about lesbian lives. Allan Berube, Jonathan Ned Katz, and especially John D'Emilio, provided me with inspiration and encouragement: their pioneering gay and lesbian histories established models of engaged scholarship, rooted in our diverse communities, that still resonate more than twenty years later.

Without fail, it has been in our various communities that I have found the most helpful people and inspiring stories. Lesbian and LGBT community-based archives provided "homes away from home" for me during the last decade, beginning with the Gay, Lesbian, Bisexual, Transgender Historical Society in San Francisco. My thanks to Daniel Bao, Paula Jabloner, Terence Kissack, Kim Klausner, Martin Meeker, and the late William Walker, all of whom consistently provided assistance and encouragement. In Brooklyn, many women at the Lesbian Herstory Archives accommodated my weekend schedules and gave me access to the treasure trove of DOB materials there; my thanks to Deb Edel, Maxine Wolfe, and especially Manuela Soares, Sara Yeager, Kelly Anderson, and Trista Sordillo for the extremely valuable Daughters of Bilitis Videotape Project. In Chicago, it was great to work with Karen Sendziak at the Gerber/Hart Library and in West Hollywood, I enjoyed the time I spent with the women at the June Mazer Lesbian Collections. Steve Capsuto shared his knowledge of lesbian and gay media images and "hooked me up" with audiotapes from the William Way GLBT Center in Philadelphia. All of them—and hundreds more—do the vital, unglamorous, often underpaid or volunteer work of preserving the untold stories of sexually nonconforming women and men, in communities around the country and throughout the world, who would otherwise remain invisible.

In addition to creating community institutions, sexual nonconformists also have shown the world new ways to construct family. My bicoastal orientation the last decade means that there are a number of people to thank, east and west. The Maggitti clan in "A Place to Be Somebody"—Wilmington, Delaware—helped me go home. My love and thanks to Mom, Ed, Mike and Shelley, Matthew and The Twins (Mark and Melissa). I wish that Dad could celebrate this achievement with me; I know he's very proud. Tara Dunion and her family (Gary, Nate and Kyle Guggolz) have brought me unexpected and uncommon joy. Dear Mary Klein still is very dear, after all these decades, and Rose Carter is, too. In New York, I am blessed with tremendously supportive in-laws or, more correctly, "in-loves:" in addition to those mentioned earlier, I thank Howard and Myrna Allen; Dee Battistella; John Cammett; Lisa Cammett; Melani Cammett and Angelo, Alex, and Lena Manioudakis; Joanne Hansen; and Anita Jones.

On the left coast, a big chunk of my heart still lives in San Francisco. I owe a great debt to my ACLU of Northern California comrades, old friends and fellow travelers Mila de Guzman and Leni Marin, Dorothy Ehrlich and Gary Sowards, Elaine Elinson and Rene Cruz, Dick Grosboll, Donna Hitchens and Nancy Davis, Sandy Holmes and Kate Kendell, Happy Hyder, Terry Kay and Daisy Santos, Esta Soler and Chris Cleary. My dear friends Lynn Fonfa and Blue Walcer generously provided much more than housing; they offered me second homes, on Castro Street and at La Casita de Nevada. All of my San Francisco family provided good food, celebrations and shoulders to cry on. My only regret is that Doug Warner was absent from Dorothy's dining-room table when we ate, drank, laughed and reminisced about our adventures in San Francisco since the late '70s.

Above all, there has been the strength and support I found in Fort Greene, Brooklyn. In 1999, toward the middle of "the DOB project," I fell madly in love with a handsome, talented, opinionated, sensual and sweet artist and lawyer who has become my best friend as well as my partner. This book is dedicated to her. She and her amazing daughter have put up with a lot of my *agita* with humor, grace, space, home-cooked meals and take-out Chinese. Thank you, Anni and Mena Cammett. I love you both very much.

A Note About Naming

In researching and writing about the women and men who were homophile activists in the 1950s and 1960s, I found myself immediately confronting the issue of anonymity. Many people who were members of the Daughters of Bilitis, Mattachine Society, or ONE, Inc., utilized pseudonyms, especially in their published writings. Some of them have discarded their "pen names" in the more open atmosphere of the last thirty years; however, some have not. In addition, many archival collections restrict or prohibit researchers from using real or birth-names unless explicit authorization is given to do so.

I received permission from all of the women interviewed for *Different Daughters* to refer to them by their DOB names as well as their real names. However, there are three women who are integral to the story that I could not interview and for whom, therefore, only their DOB names are used: Ernestine Eckstein, Del Shearer, and Lisa Ben. I cannot locate either Eckstein or Shearer and have no current information on either woman. Although my research has revealed Eckstein's familial surname, I will respect what I assume would be her wishes and use "Eckstein" as her surname. I do not know whether "Del Shearer" was a pseudonym but am treating it as such. Lisa Ben has refused recent requests for interviews because her confidentiality has been violated in the past, when some writers have used her real name despite her objections. In deference to her wishes, I will refer to her as Lisa Ben.

One of the most unsettling things I learned as I met with former DOBers around the country is the new form of imposed anonymity that some feel they must accept. As they age and become more dependent on caretakers, or live in assisted living centers and nursing homes where heterosexuality is assumed, some Daughters who had been proudly "out" in the past are reluctant to reveal their lesbianism today. For those with financial resources and mobility, some gay, lesbian, and women's retirement communities are now a reality; for others, however, the pressure to conform in exchange for safety and services is, again, overwhelming.

Prologue

When the package marked "FBI" finally arrived in April 1981 at their home in San Francisco, Phyllis Lyon and Del Martin wondered what on earth it could contain. They pulled out sixty-four sheets of paper, many of which resembled abstract black and white checkerboards. The envelope was filled with page after page on which heavy dark ink obscured typewritten words, two or three lines of print, and whole sections of reports. They saw scribbled notes on faded lists of names, time-worn announcements and flyers, and barely legible copies of terse government memoranda.

Their first reaction was amazement, quickly followed by outrage. "I think it's incredible that the government would waste so much money on such nonsense," Martin said. It had taken over a year for them to receive the materials the U.S. government had gathered about the Daughters of Bilitis (DOB), the lesbian group they helped organize a quarter century earlier.

By the mid-1970s, the widespread and illegal government surveillance and disruption of peaceful domestic U.S. organizations—a counterintelligence program known by its acronym, COINTELPRO—was big news. From fabricating stories of marital infidelity to framing activist leaders for murder, the misdeeds of J. Edgar Hoover's FBI, in concert with the CIA and various branches of the U.S. military, validated what many activists had long thought might have been going on. Americans who believed that "we" would never spy on U.S. citizens engaged in lawful social and political activities were in for a rude awakening.[1]

The thought that the Daughters had been infiltrated first occurred to Lyon and Martin in 1977, when a *San Francisco Examiner* story revealed that a CIA agent had secretly attended the group's first national convention. It was hard for them to believe that any of DOB's educational or organizing efforts—derisively characterized as "conservative" by so many gay liberationists then and since—could have been considered in any way threatening to the authorities. However, Dr. David Rhodes admitted in testimony before a Senate subcommittee investigating covert government activities that he had attended their conference in San Francisco in 1960. Rhodes said that he had gone to interview lesbians and test CIA theories about how different kinds of people react differently to the same situations. He admitted that the experiment was a flop: few women were interested in talking with him and he "didn't learn much."[2]

Lyon remembered Rhodes immediately; he had come to the conference with one of DOB's invited speakers, a professor from the University of California at Berkeley who studied homosexuality in nature. She didn't think much of it at the time; quite a few men were invited as speakers or observers. "We were surprised that they stayed all day," Lyon said recently. "They went to the banquet and everything."[3]

The Rhodes revelation motivated Martin to write to Washington. She started with the CIA, asking for any and all files related to herself or to the Daughters of Bilitis. She wondered whether it was the picnics, parties, and "Gab 'n' Java" discussion sessions, or the public meetings with researchers and psychologists, that the federal agencies had been worried about.

What they learned was that the FBI had been keeping tabs on the Daughters of Bilitis from the beginning. Reports were filed throughout the late 1950s and 1960s, starting with a long memorandum from 1956. It contained pages of materials on the Mattachine Society, the "subject organization" of the memo. A special section follows with the misspelled heading "DAUGHTERS OF BELITAS." The unnamed agent reported, "according to information received in March 1956, the above organization is in the formative stage, with headquarters in San Francisco, California. It is composed of women whose aim is to solve the many problems of the lesbian and the 'lesbian mother.'" After that, the memo misidentified DOB as a subsidiary— or "ladies' auxiliary"—of the Mattachine Society. Clearly, the informant failed to recognize the Daughters of Bilitis as a fiercely independent, freestanding organization by and for women.

Next among the photocopied pages is a memo to "Director, FBI" from "SAC, Phoenix" and other local agencies. It noted that Martin made reservations for a breakfast meeting at the Clark Hotel in Los Angeles in 1957. "That was our first attempt to form a chapter in L.A.," she remembered. The meeting, of course, had been announced publicly in DOB's monthly magazine, *The Ladder*. There were also copies of pamphlets produced by the East Coast Homophile Organizations, or ECHO. They distributed leaflets such as "What To Do In Case of Arrest" in the wake of bar raids and routine police harassment in the mid-1960s. "The most hilarious part was that this same material had been sent directly to the director of the FBI by the Mattachine Society of Washington [D.C.]," Martin remembered. "They invited Hoover to discuss the federal government's policies." He never responded.[4]

Incredulous, Lyon and Martin read on. They then learned about the "tip" the FBI had received from women who were part of the Cleveland chapter of Citizens for Decent Literature in 1964. They had written to J. Edgar Hoover to share the news that a national convention for lesbians would be held at the Hotel New Yorker in Manhattan that year. The DOB's biennial meeting—reported in the *New York Times*—was actually held at the Barbizon-Plaza because the New Yorker had reneged on the promise of rental space. At the time, the management kept coming up with one nonsensical requirement or irritating delay after another; the Daughters thought that they were just nervous about having so many lesbians on their premises. But the files revealed that when the FBI got the Cleveland ladies' letter, an agent visited the Hotel New Yorker to urge them not to rent space to DOB. Frustrated but undeterred by the hotel's reluctance to host them, the Daughters secured space at the Barbizon-Plaza and the convention took place as planned. There is no evidence that any Citizen for Decent Literature attended.[5]

The material in DOB's FBI files, while largely innocuous and sometimes comical, reveals a pattern of regular official surveillance and intermittent interference. The question remains: why would the U.S. government waste taxpayers' dollars on a small lesbian organization that advocated integration into society? Who—or what—were they afraid of?

Started by four female couples—including Phyllis Lyon and Del Martin—in 1955, the Daughters of Bilitis was formed as the modern U.S. civil rights movement gained momentum and was reaching widespread popular consciousness. Lyon and Martin were "New Dealers" who had come of age at the end of the Depression, optimists who shared President Franklin Delano Roosevelt's vision. They heeded his admonishment that "the only thing we have to fear is fear itself." They read Eleanor Roosevelt's "My Day" columns and were inspired by her intelligence, courage, and commitment to social action.[6]

The first Daughters thought that their new group would provide a nice place for lesbians to meet; soon they added a newsletter that grew into an internationally known magazine. In 1958, they began to organize a network of local chapters. Starting in 1960, and continuing for the next decade, they sponsored public biennial conventions on issues of importance to lesbians and gay men. Through the publicity their conferences generated, they began, carefully at first and then with increasing candor, to talk with newspaper reporters, radio producers, and television talk-show hosts about the reality of their relatively ordinary existences. The Daughters slowly lifted the veil of secrecy that surrounded lesbians' daily lives in mid-twentieth-century America.

The story of the DOB is important and illuminating for a number of reasons. Despite the availability of lesbian and gay history today, there has been relatively little written about lesbians in general, and even less about the Daughters of Bilitis specifically. Many works have downplayed their contributions to the movements for sexual and gender freedom in the U.S. in the 1950s, 1960s, and 1970s—from the homophile and gay civil rights movements to women's liberation and the creation of lesbian-feminism. This may be a reflection of sexism in the gay movement as well as in society at large; an example would be the persistent mischaracterization of DOB as nothing more than an assimilationist little "ladies' auxiliary" of the mostly male Mattachine Society.[7]

Whatever the reasons, many of DOB's former leaders either react wearily or shrug as if to say, "So what?" As New York Daughter Kay (Tobin) Lahusen put it, "I wonder what today's activists would do if they had to confront what we did back then?"[8]

The Daughters of Bilitis also was unique in that, at a time of intense racial segregation in the U.S., it provided opportunities for women of color and white women to socialize and work together.

"Unlike many other groups in the 1950s," remembers Billye Talmadge, an early activist, "there were no color bars in DOB." She emphasized that "there were not just African-Americans, but Asians, Latinas . . . the driving force was that we were gay women." While the organization's membership was overwhelmingly white, it was not exclusively so.

DOB's 1956 Articles of Incorporation stated that they welcomed all women, "regardless of race, color, or creed." This declaration did not just gather dust in organizational files. There were two women of color, a Chicana and a Filipina, among the initial eight organizers. In addition, Cleo (Glenn) Bonner, DOB's national president from 1963 to 1966, was the first African-American lesbian to head a national gay or lesbian rights organization. At the local level, some black and Latina lesbians assumed positions of leadership within the organization from the mid-1950s through the 1970s, and a few Asian-American and Native American women contributed their skills to DOB and its magazine, *The Ladder,* as well.[9]

But DOB was a product of its times. Its commitment to nondiscrimination notwithstanding, the separate-and-unequal practices that walled off segments of U.S. society also limited its ability to implement its principles. At least one longtime DOB leader remembers that there were varying degrees of difficulties in addressing racial differences among some chapter members, particularly those Daughters from the southern United States. "Racism was often very present, and very difficult to deal with—at times it threatened to tear us apart," LA DOB co-founder Stella Rush remembers. "But at least we tried." And it wasn't just white southerners who could make potential black DOB members uncomfortable. As Martin Duberman recounted in *Stonewall,* "Once, in the early sixties, Yvonne (Maua Flowers) had gone with another black woman to a DOB meeting on Manhattan's Lower East Side, and had been repelled by it. The white women reacted to the black women's presence first with shock, then with a supercilious casualness that was at least as offensive. Yvonne never returned. 'I can't be here,' she decided, 'with all these white girls.'"[10] Yet the centuries of struggles for racial and gender equality in the U.S. provided crucial inspiration to many women in the 1940s who would soon become the first "Different Daughters." One of them learned a painful lesson about the cost of being different while still in high school.

Los Angeles, April 1942. Seventeen-year-old Stella Rush heard the incredible news first thing Monday morning when she got to school. Her good friend Jane Kubota was leaving, just two months before the end of their junior year.

As soon as possible, Rush found Kubota and asked her to talk about what was happening. Visibly shaken, the normally calm Kubota reminded her that it was wartime; she then told Rush about the black-and-white military notices that were tacked up on telephone poles and displayed in the post offices all over Los Angeles. Four months after the surprise attack by the Japanese military on the U.S. naval forces in Honolulu, the American government issued an order requiring all Japanese families to report to local military authorities by the end of April. They could bring only clothing and bedding, a bit of food for their uncharted journey, whatever they could carry. No pets allowed. The entire Kubota family was being sent somewhere, Jane didn't really know where.

Rush couldn't believe what she was hearing. First came the sense of shock, then grief at the loss of her friend. They spent as much time together as they could before the Kubotas' departure; within weeks, Jane and her family were gone. They had to leave behind their car, their home, their friends, most of their money, and Mr. Kubota's job. Rush finally learned that they had been imprisoned in something

called a "relocation" camp, one of which was located at the abandoned Santa Anita racetrack. Despite having been accused of no
crime, the Kubotas were interned there; they, along with other
Japanese families in their area and over one hundred thousand more
from neighboring regions along the West Coast, lived in the former
horse stalls at Santa Anita and several other abandoned sites, scattered
throughout the West and the South, for the next three years.[11]

Devastated and depressed, Rush wrote letters to Kubota but felt
she wasn't doing enough. She turned to their social studies teacher.
Mrs. Hughes suggested that they organize a trip to bring school
materials to their friends at the camp so they wouldn't fall behind in
their studies. Delighted by the idea, Rush began gathering books and
supplies.

At the last minute, her teacher canceled the trip; she gave no explanation that made any sense to the few students who were eager to go.
Rush convinced her reluctant mother to take her, and the two of
them traveled to Santa Anita, bringing books and magazines for her
friend that were subsequently "lost" by the guards. Jane's parents and
two of her classmates were very disappointed that Mrs. Hughes was
too frightened to keep her promise; today Rush reasons that her
teacher's inability to help her students may have been rooted in
her need to protect not only her job but her son's Conscientious
Objector status.

Rush saw her friend Jane Kubota only once after that, but the
experience stayed with her for the rest of her life. "It was the first time
that I was really aware of the cost of being different, even in this great
country of ours. I wondered, how could this be happening to natural-
born citizens in the land of the free?"[12]

Just a few years later, in 1945, the end of World War II—achieved by
unleashing an awesome and potentially uncontrollable American

atomic power—also unleashed an emotional mix of pride and anxiety that saturated society. The "good guys" had won "The Good War," but the reality of the A-bomb infused and distorted postwar stability. A weapon so vast and destructive could boomerang, and the relatively swift Soviet replication of the atom bomb, as well as the "loss" of China to a Communist-led revolution in 1949, spoiled the victory party for America's leaders. It led to an official policy of containment, marked by the need to further delineate "us" and "them." U.S. opinion makers emphasized a climate of fear, a "Cold War" that created larger-than-life enemies, both internally and externally.[13]

One personification of the fear mongering of the early 1950s is the *Invasion of the Body Snatchers* syndrome: the fantastic imagery of a wave of seemingly innocuous people morphing into monsters poised to destroy "the American way." The nation's headlines, comics, movies, and radio broadcasts trumpeted warnings about all sorts of scary invaders-from-within—aliens, mutants, juvenile delinquents, sex perverts, and above all else, Communists—on the move from Hollywood to Main Street. The message was clear: you couldn't be too careful, and you couldn't trust any strangers. Home, family, and private life became the refuge from all of the uncertainty outside, further fueling a sense of isolation and seclusion. As protection, many people retreated into what seemed safe and familiar, wearing the armor of conformity when venturing outside.[14]

Conformity was proving effective in the political arena as well. The Republican Party in 1950 was desperate to reclaim the White House after eighteen years of Democratic rule. Their campaign strategy was simple: in order to discredit New Deal programs, they would discredit New Dealers, seizing on the American fear of sexual, social, and political vulnerability. Republican Senator and Minority Whip Kenneth Wherry of Nebraska was a key fund-raiser for the Republicans. A public relations wizard, he initiated a hate-the-homosexual campaign and equated deviant sexuality with anti-Americanism, claiming that it was impossible to "separate homosexuals from subversives." Wherry called for measures that would protect "seaports and major cities" against the "conspiracy of subversives and moral perverts."[15]

Wherry was extremely successful in reaching his targets: the Republican Party saw its donations increase and a mainstream reiteration of their homos-as-homewreckers theme became a political mantra during the early 1950s. The *New York Daily News* warned about the "all-powerful, super-secret, inner circle of highly educated . . . sexual misfits in the State Department . . . [who were] all highly susceptible to blandishments by homosexuals in foreign nations." Established religious leaders helped the hysteria along. The popular evangelist preacher Billy Graham praised the vigilant Americans who were busy "exposing the pinks, the lavenders, and the reds who have sought refuge beneath the wings of the American Eagle."[16]

Thomas Corber, a Cold War–era film scholar, writes that "the discourses of national security tried to exploit fears that there was no way to tell homosexuals from heterosexuals." Initally, they succeeded. "The total number of men and women affected by the anti-homosexual purge is incalculable. Many agencies did not keep records of such dismissals . . . nevertheless, some published figures give a sense of the scale," David Johnson wrote in *The Lavender Scare: The Cold War Persecution of Gays and Lesbians in the Federal Government*. "As many as five thousand suspected gay or lesbian employees may have lost their jobs with the federal government during the early days of the Cold War." Johnson asserts that in the 1950s, far more homosexuals than Communists were trapped by government regulations and dismissed from their jobs with the various agencies of the federal bureaucracy.[17]

As the political scientist James Morone has written, "The red scare compounded anxiety about America's moral strength. When investigations turned up 'unsuitable' gays, the inquisitors expanded the scope of their outrage." Despite the fact that this infamous period often is named after him, Senator Joseph McCarthy of Wisconsin was a relative latecomer to the witchhunt. McCarthy was in many ways most useful in playing the vicious attack dog, helping to popularize the conflation of "security" with "loyalty," "disloyalty" with "nonconformist," "unconventional" with "Commie," and "Red" with "queer."[18]

A cruel irony could be found in the widely whispered rumors that circulated about the private life of McCarthy's top aide, Roy Cohn, who died of complications due to AIDS in 1986. Cohn was an extremely closeted "fellow traveler" in the homosexual subculture but, riding high during the period the writer Lillian Hellman labeled "Scoundrel Time," he assisted his boss in persecuting hundreds of gay and lesbian workers in Washington and elsewhere, and successfully intimidated thousands more from even applying for federal employment.[19]

Nora Sayre has written about the response two respected journalists, Joseph and Stewart Alsop, received in 1950 when they published a piece in the *Saturday Evening Post* criticizing Senator Wherry's equation of homosexuality with risks to national security. McCarthy himself replied in two threatening letters to the editors of the *Post*, hinting that Joseph Alsop, who was single, was himself homosexual. McCarthy also threatened that "anyone" who got in the way of "cleaning the Communists out of government" was in danger. The bullying strategy worked. Sayre notes that "during the four years that followed that warning, the Alsops wanted to write more pieces opposing McCarthy for the *Post*. But the magazine ran no subsequent articles about him by anyone." If a respected national magazine could be intimidated into silence in this way, what chance did the average U.S. citizen have against the government and "the Committee?"[20]

In 1952, the nation's war hero, General Dwight D. Eisenhower, was elected president on the Republican ticket. Within the first year of his first term in office, Eisenhower granted the federal Civil Service Commission a power he could never bring himself to enforce while a commander in the U.S. Army: the power to deny employment to women and men in all U.S. government jobs on the grounds of "sexual perversion." By signing Executive Order 10450 in 1953, Eisenhower set in motion the official exclusion of gay men and lesbians from federal employment, an exclusion that would last for more than twenty years. Never before had so many Americans had to swear to their heterosexuality in order to get or keep their jobs.

In the documentary film *Before Stonewall,* released in 1986, Johnnie Phelps, a former Women's Air Command (WAC) service member, told the story of being ordered to compile a list of all the lesbians in the service during the postwar occupation of Europe. "There were lesbians all over the place. My Commander General was Eisenhower and he said one day, 'It's come to my attention that there are lesbians in the WACs, we need to ferret them out. . . .' I looked at him, looked at the secretary who was there with us, and said, 'If the General pleases, sir, I'll be happy to do that, but the first name on the list will be mine.'" Phelps paused. "And the secretary said, 'if the General pleases, sir, my name will be first and hers will be second.'" Phelps then told Eisenhower, "Sir, you're right, there are lesbians in the WACs—and if you want to replace all the file clerks, section commanders, drivers, every woman in the WAC detachment, I will be happy to make that list. But you must know, sir, that they are the most decorated group . . . there have been no illegal pregnancies, no AWOLs, no charges of misconduct." After a moment, "Eisenhower said, 'Forget the order' and I said, 'Yes sir, sir.'"[21]

Eisenhower's 1953 Executive Order stands in bold relief against his 1947 refusal to "ferret out" suspected lesbians from the military.

It is a measure of how much changed in U.S. political life in just a few years: from wartime heroism to postwar mediocrity.

Despite this, examples of social activism could be found. The black lesbian feminist poet and teacher Audre Lorde wrote about hearing some incredible news when she was living in Mexico in 1954. "That spring, McCarthy was censured. The Supreme Court decision on the desegregation of schools was announced in the English newspaper, and for a while all of us seemed to go crazy with hope for another kind of America."[22]

One year later, after National Association for the Advancement of Colored People (NAACP) activist Rosa Parks refused to move to the back of the bus after a long workday, African Americans proudly walked the streets of Montgomery, Alabama, for more than a year rather than accept a segregated transit system. It was the first large-scale boycott against state-sanctioned discrimination since World War II. Grassroots organizing was happening in a variety of places and on many issues. For example, in Washington state, Oregon, and California, Japanese and Japanese-American women and men began challenging laws that prohibited them from owning property and started reclaiming the resources and respectability stolen from them in the internment camps. Farmworker organizers fanned throughout the fields of the Southwest to help Chicano, Filipino, black, and white people form unions and cooperatives, launching their decades-long fight to improve their working and living conditions. Courageous activists led demonstrations against the anti-Communist witchhunt and mounted campaigns to support the outspoken artist and critic of U.S. imperialism Paul Robeson and the suspected spies Julius and Ethel Rosenberg. "Ban the Bomb" signs and buttons surfaced from coast to coast despite the dominance of Cold War rhetoric, and New York housewives began to organize a national network of women against war.[23]

Even gay men and lesbians began to quietly question their demonization in American culture. Accounts of gay activism that assume it
all started in June 1969 at the Stonewall Inn antipolice riots in New
York ignore the deep roots planted by 1950s organizers; they have
been enriched by more recent investigations and new evidence.
Similarly, accurate descriptions of the resurgence of the women's
movement in the latter part of the twentieth century must include
the importance of "the decade of domesticity" that supposedly
defines the 1950s.[24]

As the historian Elaine Tyler May has written, "Signs of stirring
were evident beneath the surface of postwar complacency. While
most women experienced discontent in isolation, as exhausted housewives or underpaid and exploited workers, a few groups did begin to
organize on their own behalf." She also points out that the widely
trumpeted "domesticity" of the times was racialized as well as
gendered: "In the postwar years, white women faced pressure to
become full-time homemakers . . . black women faced no such
stigma." Due to racism and economic necessity, African-American
women usually had to combine paid work with domestic responsibilities, as did most women of color; but the black press, unlike its white
counterparts, presented female workers, who were also wives and
mothers, as heroines to be admired and emulated. It also celebrated
some of the women who were organizing for civil rights, one of the
very few political arenas at that time in which black women were the
majority of activists.[25]

Further, feminism, although dormant as a mass movement, was
certainly not dead as an ideology, especially not for women who loved
women. As Lillian Faderman argues in her 1999 work *To Believe in
Women,* devoted female same-sex couples, whether or not they
referred to themselves as "lesbians," dedicated themselves to
expanding women's possibilities in the first half of the twentieth

century. They worked as educators, social reformers, attorneys, and physicians, creating homes together and networks of female friends in the interwar years that sustained them in the Cold War era.[26]

Although relatively unknown today, Dr. Jeannette Howard Foster is an example of someone who spent her life radically "expanding women's possibilities." Her experiences as a college student at Rockford University in Illinois in 1917 motivated her to undertake a landmark lesbian research project. During her junior year, she was called on as a member of the student council to discipline two other female students in a "morals case." Foster realized that she first had to figure out what a "morals case" was. She started digging and found scientific writings, beginning with Havelock Ellis's *Studies in the Psychology of Sex,* on same-sex attraction.

Continuing to be fascinated by the topic, personally and professionally, she kept reading; each new reference to romantic relationships between women led her to others, in poetry and literature, and she began compiling lists of information.

Foster's pursuit of her pet project coincided with her own pursuit of education and career options in the early decades of the twentieth century. A strong, self-directed white woman, her travels took her to many parts of the country during a time when few women had such opportunities. After graduating from Rockford, she received her master's degree at the University of Chicago in 1922, worked as a writing teacher in Minnesota for nearly a decade, then returned to school, earning another master's from Emory University in Atlanta in 1932 and a doctorate from the University of Chicago in 1935, both in library science. When she was offered a professorship in her field at the Drexel Institute in Philadelphia in 1937, she accepted readily, in part because she knew that at Drexel she could devote a good deal of her time and energy to her research on "female variants." She had access to more extensive collections of rare literary works featuring female same-sex desire in Philadelphia and at other eastern sites.

But an offer to work with Dr. Alfred Kinsey and his sex research team at the University of Indiana in Bloomington was even more compelling, especially with all of the excitement generated by their 1948 report, *Sexual Behavior in the Human Male*. Now they were compiling a second research study—on women. Foster and her lover Dr. Hazel Tolliver agreed to join the project, convinced it would help minimize public ignorance about homosexuality.[27]

For many lesbians and gay men in the late 1940s, the cost of being true to their desires was shame and a constant fear of exposure. It coexisted, however, with the shadowy excitement of developing new and different lives and loves in a handful of major metropolitan areas. There, down dark streets in the warehouse district behind unmarked doors, tucked in alleyways near derelict buildings, or way out near the beach in shacks hardly anyone but the vice squad noticed, gay women and men could experience a secret, sexually charged world hidden from the rest of society.

The discovery and acceptance of one's homosexuality put gay men and lesbians in de facto positions of defiance—of prevailing social norms, of religious teachings, of traditional family values. For many, the possibility of ostracism and punishment meant that they had no choice but to live in two worlds—"normal" and "deviant"—and become adept at negotiating both while maintaining strict segregation between them.

"Lisa Ben" is a celebrated postwar lesbian activist who still does not allow her real name to be used publicly. Tiny and energetic, a white woman with light brown, wavy hair and a wide smile, she discovered gay life in Southern California when she left her family home in the farmlands near San Francisco Bay and relocated to Los

Angeles in 1945. Within two years, she was introduced to the homosexual scene by a female friend who asked her if she was gay. Ben thought her friend wanted to know if she was a happy person, and, generally pleased with her new life in L.A., she enthusiastically said, "Yes!"

Her friend smiled broadly and promptly invited her to a local bar. It was most probably a bar unlike any Ben had ever seen. For one thing, it would have been very dimly lit, with wall sconces and table candles providing an otherworldly glow. For another, while there were quite a few men and women there, they congregated in different parts of the room. By the time the third or fourth cute, tomboyish girl had come over and exchanged a few words, asking if she wanted a drink or what her name was, Ben would have gotten wise to what was going on. So this was what being "gay" meant![28]

Ben became a regular at the bar, known as the If Club; her easygoing personality and keen wit made her a favorite among the women who gathered there night after night, and especially on weekends. At twenty-six, she loved to dance and sing; she was writing essays, poems, and short stories while working as a typist for the Hollywood movie studio RKO. She was excited about being a small part of the growing entertainment industry but found that she had a great deal of free time on her hands at work. Her boss told her that the important thing was to "look busy." An avid reader, she had observed on L.A.'s newsstands what seemed to be magazines available for almost every hobby or avocation. Why not one for gay women?

She got to work creating a newsletter, and in June 1947, *VICE VERSA* made its debut, subtitled "America's Gayest Magazine." Ben has said that she named it such as a play on society's views of gay life as a vice. She also utilized it to mock society's notion that heterosexuality was "normal" and therefore good, while homosexuality was "abnormal" and bad. With *VICE VERSA,* she proudly claimed nonconformity.[29]

However, her fears of being found out were so great that not only did she write and publish *VICE VERSA* anonymously, she typed two sets of originals with five carbon copies of each, making a total of twelve copies, rather than use the still laborious but much faster mimeographing process, which would leave behind evidence. Not trusting the mail initially, she handed out copies to friends and friends of friends at the gay bars. It was a great conversation starter, but she learned quickly that some women were too nervous to accept a copy of anything that appeared deviant.

In the inaugural issue, Ben boldly announced that *VICE VERSA* was "a magazine dedicated, in all seriousness, to those of us who will never quite be able to adapt ourselves to the iron-bound rules of Convention." She had a hit on her hands, but Lisa Ben only produced *VICE VERSA* until February 1948; the Valentine's Day issue that year is the last. She was writing most of the copy herself or retyping material she found elsewhere. Each issue contained a variety of information, from show business news and reviews to political commentary and poetry. Despite a positive response from the women who received it, she felt she just couldn't keep it going.

Over the last fifty years, the little magazine and its creator have attained near-mythic status in the lesbian and gay movements. Most stories of Lisa Ben's life attribute the demise of *VICE VERSA* to the tediousness and isolation of the work. Lisa Ben also has said that she lost her job at RKO and the resources and privacy it provided her. All this may be true, but what rings truest is that the magazine had introduced her to dozens and dozens of lesbians. She was enjoying her new life so much that, as she has admitted, "I wanted to live it rather than write about it." In 1948, Lisa Ben was a lively newcomer to a small world of women: "They took me to their collective bosoms and boy, was it fun!" She filed away her extra copies of *VICE VERSA* for the time being.[30]

That same summer, also in Los Angeles, a handsome, young radical activist named Henry (or Harry) Hay walked the beaches with his male lover, distributing flyers announcing a new group, Bachelors for Wallace. While his efforts yielded little in the way of immediate recruitment or votes for the progressive presidential candidate, Hay didn't give up the idea of organizing a group of men dedicated to social action. Two years later, Hay and four other white gay men—Rudi Gernreich, Bob Hull, Chuck Rowland, and Dale Jennings—founded the Mattachine Society in Los Angeles on November 11, 1950. The name they gave their new group came from Hay's study of secret all-male fraternities; they fashioned themselves in the image of a brotherhood of masked men who performed at medieval festivals, "court jesters who were privileged to tell the king the truth from behind their masks," as former Daughter Barbara Gittings has described them.[31]

Hay was one of the first to argue that homosexual men and women constituted a minority group. An active member of the Communist Party until 1951, he gave up his affiliation due to his increasing inability to reconcile his sexual orientation with party prohibitions on homosexuality. But he brought his training as an organizer to the new arena for activism. Hay and the other founders carefully expanded Mattachine's discussion groups and leadership circles. They were aided by the publication in 1951 of a groundbreaking new book: Donald Webster Cory's *The Homosexual in America,* a first-person account of gay life from a deeply closeted, married man whose real name was Edward Sagarin. Cory's book advanced the then radical idea that gay men and lesbians deserved all of the rights and protections offered other minority groups in the United States.[32]

By 1952, a small group of Mattachine activists split off to publish a newspaper and named themselves after a Thomas Carlyle passage, "a mystic bond of brotherhood makes all men one." ONE, Inc., was the first to establish educational programs on gay issues, from monthly discussions to annual Midwinter Institutes. They also created the first known publicly sold magazine produced by and for gay people. *ONE* magazine, edited by Dale Jennings, appeared in January 1953; it attracted a number of talented gay men and a handful of women, including Ann Carll (Corki) Reid and "Eve Elloree" (Joan Corbin), the staff artist. Reid was a short, athletic white woman. Corbin was delicate, pale, and pretty. Many women fell in love with her—including Reid. And, eventually, so did "Sten Russell" (Stella Rush).[33]

The twenty-eight-year-old Rush found Corki and Joan, and the small group of gay and lesbian activists in L.A., soon after *ONE* magazine was launched. Born on April 30, 1925, she was the only child of a troubled marriage, the dutiful daughter of a matrilineal white Kentucky family. Her father died when she was eighteen months old. Throughout Rush's childhood and adolescence, her mother moved them back and forth between her family's home in Richmond, Kentucky, and Los Angeles.

From an early age Rush was intellectually curious and a dedicated student. She also says she understood very young that being a female meant that she was not allowed to participate in some of the most appealing aspects of life. "I remember being in a rage as a child because in Kentucky my boy cousin could go off to a tobacco staving party and I couldn't. The men would use a long wooden pole—a stave—to spear and dry the tobacco leaves. It seemed exciting: all the men were there, drinking and cussing and telling stories. No girls allowed. And I wanted desperately to go along." In addition, witnessing the unfairness of her friend Jane Kubota's persecution as a racial minority only deepened her awareness of discrimination.[34]

After graduating from high school in Los Angeles in 1943, Rush got a trainee drafting job at North American Aviation and worked there for two years to save money for college. She was then able to attend the University of California at Berkeley, and it was here that she first encountered Phyllis Lyon. "She was a 'wheel'—a junior and an editor of the *Daily Californian*. I remember being at a meeting with her, sitting across the table from her. She didn't notice me at all." Rush also joined the off-campus Unitarian Church, which was known as a center for progressive political and spiritual people. She remembers that time of her life as a rich, rewarding one; she felt that she had found a community of like-minded women and men.

By 1947, despite two scholarships, Rush's savings ran out and she had to leave Berkeley. After she completed her third year of college at UCLA in 1948, she went to work for Firestone Tire and Rubber. She also continued her involvement in the Unitarian Church. After choir practice, she'd join other church members for a beer at the If Club, the bar right around the corner that also happened to be a favorite spot of Lisa Ben's.[35]

The lesbian and gay subculture that existed in postwar Southern California and in other major metropolitan areas was centered in a handful of bars and "explained" in a few books—paperback novels with lurid covers and a handful of scientific studies—about homosexuality. The novels were titillating but didn't always ring true; the nonfiction works were hard to find and usually depressing. And the bars: although the If Club was an exception, the clubs that welcomed gay people were often dilapidated and dingy; all of them were prone to police raids.

Rush's firsthand experience of a bar raid in 1949 underscored her sense of secrecy and futility. "[A]ll of a sudden the police were there and made all of us go outside. The raid seemed to be aiming mainly at the guys, although if a woman gave them lip she could also go to jail. The police were very democratic about that." Rush's involvement with the activist Unitarian Church came in handy in this situation.

"We'd had some counseling to give only our name and address when we were asked—don't tell them where you work. Let them think you are unemployed so you don't end up on the front page and they don't alert your boss."[36]

In 1953, Bea Blanton, a recent ex-partner, took Rush to a party where she met Corki and Joan and learned more about the gay magazine they both worked on. Rush was impressed by them—especially Corki—and by *ONE*. Earlier that year, as a way of sorting out her feelings, she had written a cautionary essay about her experiences in L.A.'s gay bar scene; when her new friends read it, they urged her to let them print it. She reluctantly agreed but, like them, she created a pen name to protect herself from any job loss. Her article, "Letter to a Newcomer," signed by "Sten Russell," appeared in *ONE* magazine early in 1954. Soon she was "on the inside," writing reviews and reports on conferences. Rush had joined the few women and men working for recognition and acceptance of homosexuals, a newcomer to a new cause.[37]

Because the available literature on gay men and lesbians was so sparse and generally so negative, everyone Rush knew at *ONE* was reading and talking about a new book. The thick, boring-looking tome on the taboo subject of female sexuality became a publishing bombshell in 1953; once again, the Kinsey team from Indiana shook American notions of normality.

Working under the direction of Alfred Kinsey, Drs. Wardell Pomeroy, Clyde Martin, and Paul Gebhard compiled data on 5,940 white American women throughout the 1940s. They questioned their subjects extensively about their sexual beliefs and practices in the same way they interviewed men for their first report in 1948. In *Sexual Behavior in the Human Female*, Kinsey and his team again shifted the sexologists' research focus from seeking causes of vice and abnormality to providing honest information about everyday behavior; this time, however, they were writing about sex as practiced by average white American women. In addition to questioning the then prevalent belief in vaginal orgasm as the main source of women's sexual pleasure, their findings directly challenged the popular views of some sex practices—such as masturbation or homosexuality—as "abnormal." Released the same year as President Eisenhower's Executive Order banning anyone showing signs of "sexual perversion" from federal employment, Kinsey's second study caused even more of a furor than the first one had. It also cost Kinsey his financial backing and brought him under congressional scrutiny.[38]

In all the hoopla, however, what was not publicized was that Kinsey's research librarians were a lesbian couple, both of whom had contributed their own sexual histories for inclusion in the report on women. Jeannette Howard Foster and Hazel Tolliver were the only openly gay, long-term couple at the Institute, and they labored diligently to track down and translate historic references to lesbian love. Although mostly they enjoyed the work—despite some disputes between Kinsey and Foster, both of whom were very strong and opinionated personalities—Foster's main focus was on completion of her lesbian bibliography. Soon, the two women decided to relocate to Kansas City, Kansas, where Foster joined the library staff at the University of Kansas City.

In 1954, she finished her life's work. At the age of sixty and after decades of research, she knew that her opus was groundbreaking. Going beyond the Kinsey team's study of contemporary female sexuality, she had carefully chronicled every literary reference to women who loved women that she could find throughout history. Unlike the notoriety accorded Kinsey's work, however, hers would be ignored by almost everyone. Her audience did not yet exist, except in the handful of lesbian and gay bars in places like San Francisco.[39]

• • •

In the early 1950s in the City by the Bay, gay and lesbian nightlife flourished despite regular law enforcement crackdowns usually timed to coincide with city elections. According to the historian Nan Boyd in *Wide Open Town,* the years between 1951 and 1955 were a "heyday" for San Francisco's lesbian bar scene due to the numbers of women-owned, and lesbian-friendly, bars in the City.[40]

Nightclubs, restaurants, saloons, and cafes managed and frequented by gay people were also somewhat protected from raids at that time due to a landmark 1951 legal decision, *Stoumen v. Reilly.* In *Stoumen,* the California Supreme Court ordered the reinstatement of the liquor license of one of San Francisco's most popular gay bars, the Black Cat, persuaded by the First Amendment arguments of the San Francisco attorney Morris Lowenthal. The Black Cat's victory in *Stoumen* established the right for gay men and lesbians in California to assemble in a public establishment, as long as there was no "illegal or immoral conduct on the premises." For a time, local authorities and state Board of Equalization officials, charged with policing the provision of alcoholic beverages, stopped targeting gay and lesbian bars. However, the protection provided by *Stoumen* began to crumble when a 1955 state statute allowed revocation of liquor licenses on premises that were "resorts for sex perverts."[41]

By the mid-1950s, the cultural and political tolerance for San Francisco's lesbian clubs and homosexual hangouts began to be tested by some local luminaries. According to Boyd, "the seeds of change were planted in 1954 when William Randolph Hearst's daily, the *San Francisco Examiner,* called upon Mayor Robinson to clean up the city." Hearst's propaganda coincided with, and helped magnify, an increasingly shrill political rhetoric connecting homosexuality to violent crimes. Further, local police as well as the head of the FBI were making links between homosexuality, juvenile delinquency, and corruption of minors, urging parents to police their own children carefully for any signs of "degeneracy," such as possessing pornography, frequenting Lovers' Lanes, or any other "unsavory" habits.[42]

After a series of articles appeared in the *Examiner* in the early summer of 1954 alleging a "marked influx recently of homosexuals," an infamous bar raid took place on September 8, 1954, insuring weeks of headlines in San Francisco's newspapers and instilling a renewed sense of fear among the City's gay men and lesbians. San Francisco police arrested the owners of the lesbian bar Tommy's Place after their five-month investigation allegedly revealed it as a favorite haunt of a handful of "sexually rebellious" teenage girls. "The public trial of Tommy's Place sparked a citywide panic and intensified a police crackdown against homosexuals," Boyd asserts. It was followed in October by a U.S. Senate subcommittee hearing on juvenile delinquency, held in San Francisco as part of a nationwide tour, that emphasized the ties between teenage misbehavior and sexual deviancy.[43]

At the time of the raid on Tommy's Place, Phyllis Lyon had been looking forward to celebrating her thirtieth birthday on November 10. Now she and her lover might reconsider whether going out to one of the women's bars was a good idea. Despite the climate for gay people, Lyon loved San Francisco; she always claimed the city as her home even though she was born in Tulsa, Oklahoma. The daughter of a Southern belle, Lyon grew up to be a quick-witted, adventurous young white woman with a statuesque figure, big brown eyes, a broad smile, and a decidedly flirtatious style. Her family moved many times during her youth because of her father's job as a traveling salesman for the U.S. Gypsum Company. Lyon attended schools in three different parts of California and graduated from Sacramento High School in 1943; several years later, her family settled in San Francisco. She went off to the University of California at Berkeley in the fall of '43, where she majored in journalism. She became an editor—"a wheel," as Rush remembered her—of the school's prestigious student newspaper, the *Daily Californian.*

Graduation in 1947 meant looking for work. By 1949, despite a reporting job in Chico that enabled her to interview one of her idols, Eleanor Roosevelt, Lyon tired of small-town life. She decided to move to Seattle for a position as associate editor of *Pacific Builder and Engineer* magazine. There she met Del Martin.[44]

Born on May 5, 1921, Dorothy Erma Corn, later known as Del, grew up in San Francisco. She graduated from George Washington High School after attending Presidio Junior High with the shy young Judy— soon to be "Lana"—Turner. After one year at the University of California at Berkeley, Dorothy Corn transferred to San Francisco State College (now San Francisco State University) to eliminate the commute to and from the East Bay. She studied journalism there for two years and worked on the school paper. At nineteen, Dorothy married a college classmate, James Martin, and two years later gave birth to their daughter Kendra. But after her husband discovered love letters revealing her crush on a female neighbor, he filed for divorce. However, the judge hearing the case wouldn't allow the letters to be used as evidence, and Dorothy Martin received custody of their daughter.

Several years later, James remarried. "He and his new wife thought they couldn't have children and James asked for Kendra, indicating that a mom and dad were the ideal way to raise a kid," Martin remembers. As a single working mother who was also trying to come to terms with her feelings for other women and figure out who she was, Martin was doing the best she could but it wasn't easy. She finally agreed that Jim and his new wife could have Kendra live with them with the understanding that she would visit regularly.

Deliberate, intelligent, and inquisitive, Martin was a good-looking young white woman who favored tailored women's clothing and supported herself by working at odd jobs in the San Francisco Bay Area, including as a reporter for *Pacific Builder* in San Francisco. In 1950, she accepted a job in Seattle as editor of the *Daily Construction Reports,* the sister publication of *Pacific Builder and Engineer.* Excited by the promotion, she prepared to move north; perhaps, she told herself, she had a chance to create a new life.[45]

Lyon has often described meeting Martin in Seattle—"she was the first woman I'd ever seen carrying a briefcase!"—and starting a friendship with her. Lyon threw a party to welcome Martin to town, and the two became buddies. But after two-plus years of being "her good straight friend," Lyon let Martin know that her feelings were growing beyond friendship. "Del made the first move one evening in my apartment," Lyon remembers. "It was rather a tentative move—a half move—and I made the other half. We had sex but made no commitment." Lyon returned to San Francisco in 1952 to go on an automobile tour of the country with her sister Patricia, but their plans were interrupted when they reached New Orleans and Tricia fell ill. She had contracted polio en route. "We were there for a month and then returned to San Francisco, where our parents were," Lyon explains. She called Martin ("collect!") repeatedly throughout the trip, and when she got back to San Francisco, they made plans for Martin to join her. Lyon located an apartment on Castro Street in what was then known as Eureka Valley and, near midnight on Valentine's Day 1953, they began their life together, close to family and a few old friends.[46]

Lyon found work in an import-export firm; Martin was a bookkeeper for Mayflower Moving and Storage. They applied for and received a mortgage on a small house perched on a hillside overlooking the Valley, with a big front window and a great view of San Francisco, and bought a car. Like many couples, they had a rough first year; at times it seemed they were staying together mainly because, as Lyon remembers, "it would have been too difficult to figure out who would get the cat." Martin's young daughter was living with them, which was fine, but Lyon's entanglement with a former boyfriend wasn't. Their love for one another, and their shared passion for books and politics as well as parties, kept them going.

They knew that part of the problem was their isolation from other women. Lyon and Martin socialized with a few heterosexual couples and became business partners in a short-lived restaurant venture with two gay male friends, but they were continually frustrated that they had not met many lesbians. The bars were the only place where they could find them and, Lyon remembers, "we were too shy" to approach the small cliques of close friends who gathered at the Paper Doll or other gay places. More important, by May 1955 a new statewide alcohol enforcement agency—the Department of Alcoholic Beverage Control—had been created by the California legislature. Within its first few months in existence, San Franciscans were told that the ABC "Fights Bar Hangouts of Deviates."[47]

From then on, there was an official policy of regular surveillance of, and frequent raids on, San Francisco's gay and lesbian nightspots that would continue through the end of the decade. Given the hazards of a night on the town in 1955, private social clubs were an attractive alternative. So when a new friend suggested they join her and some other women to talk about starting a club for lesbians, Lyon and Martin thought it sounded like a great idea.

CHAPTER ONE

"Qui vive"

Starting the group was Rose Bamberger's idea, but no one is sure who came up with the name. Phyllis Lyon vividly remembers the phone call from Rose in September 1955, "when she said, 'Would you like to be a part of the group of six of us that are putting together a secret society for lesbians?'" Lyon raises her voice as she tells the story. "We said, 'YES!!' Because we would immediately know five more lesbians and we did, which was . . . AMAZING." Lyon and her lover Del Martin had been "desperately seeking" other lesbians for two years, looking for friends. They were in their early thirties, attractive and well read. They liked to drink, laugh, and have a good time, but they also cared about social issues. Surely there were other women in San Francisco who shared some of their interests.[1]

Lyon remembers that toward the end of the summer of 1955, two good friends, a gay male couple, had responded to their constant complaints about "where are the lesbians?" by introducing Lyon and Martin to Rose Bamberger. Rose was a young Filipina who believed it was possible to create a safe place for lesbians to have fun. Lyon explains, "She wanted it to be in people's homes and she wanted it to be so we'd be able to dance . . . so that we wouldn't get caught up in police raids and we wouldn't be stared at by tourists and so on.

You couldn't dance in the bars in those days. And she loved to dance. That was the whole idea behind it."

Soon she had recruited eight lesbians—four couples—who were willing to get together to talk about starting a club. At their first meeting, someone suggested they consider naming themselves Daughters of Bilitis. Afterward, "Del and I went to the library to look up 'Bilitis,'" Lyon remembers, "and of course found nothing. They had said it would be a great name because no one would know what it meant."[2]

It was a perfect name for the 1950s: clever and suggestive. Its sly mystery was its appeal. The Daughters were inspired by the work of the nineteenth-century poet Pierre Louys, whose *Songs of Bilitis* celebrated lesbian love. The sensual—some said pornographic—poems were included in *The Collected Works of Pierre Louys,* which had been published in paperback in 1955. It was enjoying some popularity among readers of books—both paperback and hard-back—with homosexual content, including the women gathered at Rose's home. Daughters of Bilitis was a vague enough name, they agreed, that if asked about it, members could claim to belong to something as benign as a women's lodge or a Greek poetry club. Only the enlightened or those already "in the life" would know about Louys's invention of Bilitis, a mythical female who seduced the celebrated Sappho.

A legendary ancient Greek poet and teacher, and lover of women as well as men, Sappho was one of the few icons available to lesbians in the 1950s. Her very name defined female same-sex love in the eighteenth and nineteenth centuries, when women who loved women were called Sapphists; by the mid-twentieth-century, it was Sappho's friends and students on the Isle of Lesbos who were beginning to serve as venerated ancestors and literary role models for some gay women. At the least, the island's inhabitants provided an alternative way of naming same-sex desire. Some gay women—like Phyllis Lyon and Del Martin—were starting to call themselves "Lesbian" despite its ugly associations in popular culture with deviance and danger. The L-word was used as a dirty curse in the '50s, but some saw that it might be reclaimed as symbolic of an erudite, celebrated, woman-centered past.[3]

At their second gathering, everyone agreed to adopt the name Daughters of Bilitis. There is no recorded debate over its pronunciation, but "Bill-EE-tis" is correct, according to former members. "Bill-EYE-tis sounded like a disease," Phyllis Lyon insists. "Later, when we acquired a copy of the recording of *Songs of Bilitis*, we found this to be the correct pronunciation."[4]

They knew that, as descendants of Sappho's "friend," the new group would be shielded from unwanted public attention while subtly signaling its link to lesbian sexuality. It was to be the first—and only—unanimous decision the four founding couples would make.

The women who accepted Rose Bamberger's invitation knew that they had at least two things in common: one, they were lesbians, and two, they all wanted to find places where they could gather with friends, unafraid of arrest or harassment. The bars in San Francisco and other parts of the Bay Area that welcomed gay people were fine, within limits; what was intriguing was the possibility of creating their own private group. They envisioned a comfortable environment in which they could talk, drink, dance, and dine, without paying high prices for watered-down cocktails or worrying about whether this was the night ABC or the vice squad would arrive, sending everyone into a panic.

Mary and Noni, June and Marcia, and Phyllis and Del joined Rose and Rosemary after work on Friday night, September 21. Over drinks and dinner, the four couples began to make plans. Someone volunteered to take notes, and produced a one-page typed account, recording their earliest concerns and decisions. From the beginning, "social" did not necessarily mean "casual" to DOB's founders.

The name for the new club came first. They considered a number of possibilities, all of them creatively noncommittal: Musketeers, Plus Two, Habeas Corpus, Qui Vive, Two Plus, Amazon, Vaisya, Geminii, and Chameleon, in addition to Daughters of Bilitis. They also came up with a way to visibly identify themselves to one another. "It was decided the club should have colors and an insignia, both to be displayed in the form of a pin to be worn by all members."[5]

The eight women approached the new club as they would a business enterprise. At thirty-one and thirty-four, Lyon and Martin were the oldest members of the group; the others often deferred to them and generally accepted their ideas. However, it was obvious from the beginning that there could be conflicts about the group's purpose and structure, with some of the women wanting strict guidelines for new members and others feeling they'd welcome anyone interested who was vouched for by someone already in the group.

They reached agreement on the number and titles of officers, who would serve for six-month terms, and they scheduled business meetings for the first Wednesday of each month at 8 P.M. They then turned their attention to constructing rules and regulations for their new group and created an application card, which included a "space for talent." To protect themselves against any possible charges that they were contributing to the delinquency of minors, the founders instituted a requirement that any new member had to be over twenty-one ("and prove it"); it was also noted for the record that any new member must be a "Gay girl of good moral character." The foundation for the new club was in place.[6]

On October 5, they got back together again at the home Rose shared with Rosemary Sliepen. The members of the new Daughters of Bilitis chose as their club motto the French phrase "Qui vive," which they defined as meaning "on the alert or on guard." They selected club colors ("sapphire blue and gold") and an insignia, "in the shape of a triangle," unwittingly choosing a symbol used by the Nazis to identify homosexuals in the concentration camps.[7] They approved a constitution and by-laws after adding language insuring that the group would be for women but hospitable to males on specific occasions.

The Daughters then elected their first leaders: "President – Del Martin; Vice President—Noni Frey; Secretary—Phyllis Lyon; Treasurer—Rosemary Sliepen; Trustee—Marcia Foster." And everyone received a food assignment for the next meeting: "Rosemary and Rose (Fried Chicken)," "Mary and Noni (Baked Beans)," "June and Marcia (Potatoe [sic] Salad)," "Phyl and Del (Salad, hors d'oevures [sic] and miscellaneous items)."[8]

On October 19, 1955, the eight cofounders hosted "the first meeting of the Daughters of Bilitis" at June and Marcia's home. Guests included newcomers "Bobbie, Toni, and Gwenn, sponsored by Del and Phyl; and Elizabeth, sponsored by Noni and Mary." They agreed to write to the two homophile groups then in existence, the Mattachine Society and ONE, Inc., subscribe to both of their publications, and contact the National Association for Sexual Research in San Francisco and the Cory Book Service in New York, thereby exhausting all resources then available for same-sex organizing. Their announcements about the new club—and their active efforts to recruit friends and friends-of-friends—had had the intended effect; word about the new group was spreading, if slowly. From the beginning, however, there were awkward situations and uncomfortable moments among the founders. The Daughters were aware that creating a lesbian social club meant that they, as the organizers, had to be open to welcoming strangers into their homes; what was becoming increasing clear was that new members could be women with whom they might have little or nothing in common but their sexuality.[9]

There were already racial, ethnic, and class differences among the eight of them: Rose was Filipina, Mary was Chicana, and both were involved in relationships with white women. Two founders had children, two worked in typically "blue-collar" trades and two held "white-collar" administrative positions. Some of them wanted only to have a place to socialize with other lesbians; others wanted to mix socializing with social action. It often seemed as though none of them was quite ready to deal with the various and sundry styles, opinions, and needs of lesbians that their club would attract.[10]

At the October 19 meeting, three unknown women arrived dressed in men's clothing. "Noni and the others busied themselves in the kitchen, making coffee, and taking a very long time to return. So Del and I were left to entertain them," Lyon remembers. "And it wasn't easy." One of the women subsequently opened Peg's Place, a San Francisco lesbian bar popular in the 1960s and 1970s. But in 1955, according to Lyon, she looked "rough and tumble" and didn't seem to have much to offer the new group. "She just sat there," Lyon says. "She didn't say much of anything all night long, except that she certainly wouldn't be willing to carry a DOB membership card. She thought that if she did, someone would find out she was a lesbian. As if it wasn't obvious!" The butch and her friends never returned to a DOB meeting after their first visit. The concerns they had voiced about exposure, however, lingered: they quickly proved to be ones the Daughters would hear repeatedly from women too frightened of being found out to give their name, much less join a lesbian club.[11]

Given the unwillingness on the part of so many women to identify themselves as members of a group "interested in . . . sex variants," the Daughters realized that they needed to create a club that would be even more nonthreatening. A "SPECIAL MEETING" was called for November 9, 1955, to "re-define the purpose of the Daughters of Bilitis," and to solidify the group's mission. They also decided to institute a rule that "If slacks are worn they must be women's slacks"—most likely a direct result of the visit from the three butches—and one declaring that no meetings would be held at non-members' homes.

"RULES FOR CANDIDATES FOR MEMBERSHIP IN DAUGHTERS OF BILITIS" are dated November 16, 1955; for the first time, they opened membership to all women who were "interested in promoting an educational program on the subject of sex variation, and for sex variants." The Daughters of Bilitis now had eleven members.[12]

A turning point came late in January 1956. After reading an article in the *Mattachine Review* about a lobbying campaign to change California's "sex laws," DOB voted to ask members to "write their legislators regarding changes in the law." They were also beginning to share ideas with their fellow homophile organizers. After an ugly internal coup in 1953 ousted its radical founders and abolished its original organizational structure, the Mattachine Foundation changed its name to Mattachine Society and moved its national office to San Francisco. The Daughters were impressed by the careful approach to organizing favored then by Mattachine's leaders. "Mattachine, in its 5 years of existence, has found it much better to grow gradually, to look for quality in members rather than quantity."

After a helpful mid-month brunch meeting with local Mattachine activists, Lyon and Martin decided to attend a ONE, Inc., Midwinter Institute in Los Angeles, representing DOB. There they were welcomed into the homophile fold by the small group of gay men and women—including Stella Rush—who were writing for *ONE* magazine and organizing educational programs on homosexuality. Lyon and Martin returned home full of enthusiasm and encouragement from their colleagues to the south. The mix of social activities and social action in the programs of the homophile groups inspired them, and they planned to provide both.[13]

But the tensions sharpened between those who wanted DOB to be a secret lesbian social club and those who wanted to be more connected to the activities of the new homophile movement. In January, Rosemary and Gwenn agreed to explore the possibilities of club members going bowling, horseback riding, and on other outings; they were less and less interested in redrafting the club constitution, challenging state laws, or going to homophile conferences with gay men. The January 4 meeting was Rosemary's last, and DOB lost Rose, then, too; Gwenn would stick around only a bit longer.

By the spring of 1956, disagreements among the original organizers over the DOB's purpose and constituency continued to plague the still-small club. There were regular disputes about whether DOB's priority should be organizing private social activities or public programs; they also argued about whether attendance at DOB business and membership meetings should be limited to lesbians.

"We thought that creating a *women's* educational organization would encourage more lesbians to come forward," Del Martin said, as the stigma of belonging to a specifically lesbian group would be removed. They also saw the potential for creating allies among heterosexual women, like Phyllis's sister Patricia. Further, after meeting some of the men involved in the Los Angeles and San Francisco groups, they believed that working collaboratively yet strategically with the other homophile activists made sense. But they couldn't convince the others.

Their disputes reached the boiling point by early summer. Half of the original founders had decided they didn't want to stay involved with DOB. Two of the core activists, June and Marcia, moved to Redding, three hours north of San Francisco, for better-paying jobs. Noni Frey stayed involved for a few more months but then left to start first one, then another, lesbian sorority in San Francisco. The tiny group of Daughters was in danger.[14]

Lyon and Martin rallied their allies. Billye Talmadge was one of them, although she also remembers the fear that was so prevalent among lesbians at that time and the extraordinary caution many women had about any involvement with organized groups, including DOB. And for good reason: Talmadge says that "there were 27 reasons why you could lose your teacher's license in California at this time, above all if you were a card-carrying Communist or a suspected homosexual." She and her lover Jaye Bell met Phyllis Lyon and Del Martin in 1956 shortly after they arrived in the Bay Area. "I was a public school teacher and Jaye Bell (nicknamed 'Shorty' because she was so tall) was my partner." The two women met in Seattle after Bell received a dishonorable discharge from the military. "She was accused of being 'homosexual' and decided to find out what that was." Both of them attended DOB socials and meetings; by early summer 1956, Talmadge remembered, "Del and Phyllis were frustrated but they decided to throw a party to give DOB one more try."[15]

By the next monthly discussion meeting on June 14, the members were able to welcome newcomers "Carla," Brian (O'Brien), Pat (Hamilton), and Griff (P. D. Griffin), all of whom took on specific assignments for the group. Sandy (Helen Sandoz) had joined the Daughters, too, after breaking up with her lover.

"Sandy was one of the only lesbians we knew in San Francisco when we moved here from Seattle in 1953," remembers Phyllis Lyon. "Del knew Sandy beforehand, when she was with a woman everybody called 'Bridge.' We visited them and Sandy's partner wanted nothing to do with DOB. When they broke up in 1956, we got Sandy."

Born on November 2, 1920, near Eugene, Oregon, Sandy was the only daughter of a Swedish immigrant mother who worked as a maid for a well-to-do family. Her mother was ill and often hospitalized throughout Sandoz's youth; she didn't meet her father until she was eighteen years old. Sandoz attended Reed College in Portland in the early 1940s, earning a degree in psychology. After graduation, she went to Alaska on a civil service assignment. She returned to the Northwest—first to Washington, and then back to Oregon—and worked in personnel management. In 1953, she was in a serious traffic accident. Sandoz spent a year in a full-body cast; the injury left her unable to sit for long periods of time for the rest of her life. Looking for a new career that might utilize her interests in art and graphic design, she learned sign printing. By the mid-1950s, Sandoz had found her way to San Francisco and was working at Macy's. After she and her lover separated, she also found new friends in DOB.[16]

In June 1956, in addition to welcoming a handful of new members, the Daughters took a bold step—an irrevocable move away from the secret lesbian social club that had originally been envisioned. The new core group decided to create more effective ways to recruit members, and they decided to embark on an "all-out publicity campaign" as well as to publish a newsletter. "An article will appear in M. Review and also ONE will give us space." As they created their first press release, some members suggested a statement that "we are against communism" be added to their printed material. The strong civil liberties beliefs of many of them, however, prevailed over the climate of fear that permeated the mid-1950s, and no such statement was included.[17]

The Daughters then agreed on their Statement of Purpose and outlined the steps they would take to advance social change for "the homosexual."

DAUGHTERS OF BILITIS—PURPOSE

A women's organization for the purpose of promoting the integration of the homosexual into society by:

(1) Education of the variant, with particular emphasis on the psychological, physiological and sociological aspects, to enable her to understand herself and make her adjustment to society in all its social, civic, and economic implications— this to be accomplished by establishing and maintaining as complete a library as possible of both fiction and non-fiction literature on the sex deviant theme; by sponsoring public discussions on pertinent subjects to be conducted by leading members of the legal, psychiatric, religious and other professions; by advocating a mode of behavior and dress acceptable to society.

(2) Education of the public at large through acceptance first of the individual, leading to an eventual breakdown of erroneous taboos and prejudices; through public discussion meetings aforementioned; through dissemination of educational literature on the homosexual theme.

(3) Participation in research projects by duly authorized and responsible psychologists, sociologists and other such experts directed towards further knowledge of the homosexual.

(4) Investigation of the penal code as it pertains to the homosexual, proposal of changes to provide an equitable handling of cases involving this minority group, and promotion of these changes through due process of law in the state legislatures.

From the beginning, however, there was an essential contradiction: the very subject matter at the heart of DOB's Statement of Purpose meant that their appeal would be limited. The responsible, professional women they hoped to attract would often be too fearful to participate. Most family members and employers wouldn't approve of too much openness about one's private life, particularly if that private life was widely viewed as deviant. In addition, many lesbians, like Martin, were responsible for the care and well-being of their children.

But a hardy few responded eagerly. Barbara Gittings remembers her first DOB meeting in San Francisco in the summer of 1956. "There were about a dozen women in the room and I thought— wow! All these lesbians together in one place! I had never seen anything like it." Imagine: a group of intelligent, articulate gay women committed to socializing and social action. Gittings returned to New York excited by the newsletter the group was planning.[18]

Born on July 31, 1932, in Vienna, Austria, Gittings was a much-traveled daughter of a white U.S. diplomat and his wife. Her parents settled in Wilmington, Delaware, where Gittings was an excellent student who loved drama, music, and singing. Even as a teenager, she was aware of her attraction to other girls and, evidently, didn't hide it too well. She first heard "the word" in her last year of high school. She had qualified for the National Honor Society but was rejected on grounds of "character": one of Gittings's teachers took her aside and explained that the rejection was based on Barbara's "homosexual inclinations."

Not sure what "homosexual inclinations" were, Gittings started doing research. While attending Northwestern University in Evanston, Illinois, for a year, she found descriptions in psychological textbooks and studies that didn't match who she felt herself to be. In secondhand bookstores, she found more comfort in gay and lesbian fiction, including the sensational 1928 novel *The Well of Loneliness*, by Radclyffe Hall. While living back at home with a strict Catholic father, she had to hide her forbidden books or face recriminations. Gittings left home for Philadelphia in 1950, at age eighteen, and started her quest for "my people." Another book brought her to them.[19]

Gittings discovered Donald Webster Cory's *The Homosexual in America* in 1955 and arranged to meet him in New York. He told her about ONE, Inc., in Los Angeles and Gittings made California her vacation destination in 1956. Her pilgrimage led her to ONE's office, then to the headquarters of the Mattachine Society in San Francisco. They referred her to the Daughters of Bilitis. Although she didn't join immediately, she gave them her name and address and they put her on their mailing list for future reference. They were slowly building an organization.[20]

Each of DOB's stated goals—self-knowledge and self-acceptance; public education; involvement in research; and lobbying to change the laws criminalizing homosexuality—reflected the members' beliefs that a conscious, carefully constructed program of discussion, information, and outreach to sympathetic professionals would best advance the nascent movement for gay and lesbian rights. In this way, they mirrored the objectives of the two other homophile groups then in existence, both of whom had similar mission statements.

But given the bar raids that could and did erupt at any time—the emotional equivalent of tremors along the San Andreas Fault for gay and lesbian San Franciscans—the DOB invited Ernest Besig to address their July 5, 1956, meeting. Besig was the executive director of the San Francisco branch of the American Civil Liberties Union (ACLU) and was one of the first "guest speakers" invited to a DOB gathering. That night, he emphasized that merely *being* homosexual was not illegal. He also encouraged DOB members to educate themselves and their friends about their constitutional rights when dealing with the government, particularly the police.[21]

This signaled the start of a long and productive professional association between DOB and local branches of the ACLU, an association that grew over the years and was nurtured by the Mattachine Society and ONE, Inc., as well, in Chicago, Denver, Los Angeles, New York, San Francisco, Washington, and other cities throughout the United States. The ACLU was one of the very few established civil rights organizations whose local leadership was willing to work with homophile activists.

Despite significant legal challenges to government censorship of artistic works with homosexual themes or content from the 1930s through the 1950s, the official position of the ACLU in 1957 was that there was no constitutional basis on which to challenge felony arrests for homosexual acts. However, the Union's leaders asserted "homosexuals, like members of other socially heretical or deviant groups, are more vulnerable than others to official persecution, denial of due process in prosecution, and entrapment." Such matters were deemed to be "of proper concern to the Union." Local laws requiring the registration of people convicted of homosexual acts were condemned as unconstitutional.

However, the ACLU affirmed its previous policy, and that of President Eisenhower's Executive Order 10450, that the use of homosexuality as a factor in determining federal government security clearances was valid but, the Union cautioned, "only when there is evidence of other acts which come within valid security criteria."[22] This rather tepid statement on the rights of homosexuals was met with thanks from many homophile activists, including the DOB, who saw in it an opening to work with the organization.

Many homophile movement activists were also involved with their local ACLU, like researcher Vern Bullough and the Los Angeles branch; some, like Franklin Kameny in Washington, D.C., helped establish an affiliate and were elected to its board of directors. In San

Francisco, in addition to nearly a decade of cooperation and alliance between DOB, Mattachine, and the local ACLU, the harassing behavior of the police at the 1965 New Year's Ball for the newly established Council on Religion and the Homosexual brought the ACLU of Northern California into active defense of those arrested.[23]

These changes, in turn, helped influence the national board, and by 1966 the ACLU formally endorsed the principle of gay rights. In 1973, the national organization formed the Sexual Privacy Project. In addition to litigation and lobbying, they addressed gay issues internally with education and policy debates. Today, the ACLU's Gay and Lesbian Rights and AIDS Projects house one of the largest LGBT advocacy and legal programs in the world.[24]

DOB's strategic meeting with Besig within the first year of the group's founding is also one concrete early example of what would become their organizing style. By inviting him to speak to their meeting, they established a connection with the leading civil liberties group in the City and helped start a dialogue with those who could advocate on their behalf. They educated themselves and informed the ACLU of the very real social and legal constraints endured by lesbians and gay men.

In the mid-1950s, every one of the forty-eight states in the U.S. had laws on the books criminalizing "sodomy," usually defined as any sexual act except male-female intercourse. Oral as well as anal sex, whether practiced by homosexuals or heterosexuals, brought punishments of up to fourteen years in prison in states like California. Regardless of how the laws were written, however, they were almost always used to punish male homosexual acts. Such "perverse" sex acts were routinely viewed as legally equivalent to bestiality and incest.

Despite the fact that far fewer women than men were actually arrested and charged under such laws, early DOB activists agreed to join with gay men to remove the legal weapons used against them.

However, not all Daughters agreed; some lesbians wanted to avoid the issue while others insisted it was important to *all* gay people to challenge the laws that criminalized homosexuality.

"You see, not only did the lesbian not exist—psychologically or historically or whatever—in the minds of the general public, there was also a tremendous division between gay men and women. . . . There was a lot of animosity and resentment over the fact that it was the gay guys who were creating such havoc with the police—the raids, the indiscriminate sex, their bathroom habits, and everything else," remembered Billye Talmadge. Her comments reflect the very real feelings on the part of some lesbians that gay men's sexual practices were as much a problem as society's condemnation of homosexuality. Some lesbians thought that aspects of gay male eroticism, from public sex to promiscuity, helped fuel antihomosexual sentiment that hurt all of them, women and men.[25]

Lyon and Martin, among others, believed strongly in working with their gay brothers to challenge unjust criminal laws. They never adopted an official "blame the victim" stance when it came to policies on homosexuals and homosexual behavior, even if some of the behaviors in question were not ones they, as lesbians, engaged in or approved of. They would debate the issues and air dissenting views from members, but they did not alter their commitment to changing criminal codes. Their solidarity with gay men on this issue was more important than their personal attitudes about appropriate sexual practices. "We wanted to change the sex laws that made people felons," Lyon says. "We thought that there would come a time, hopefully, when there wouldn't be any laws against our sexuality and we'd be accepted as people by the outside community."[26]

Where DOB differed from the mostly male homophile groups was in their emphasis on reaching the individual lesbian—"the variant"—first and foremost. They recognized that many women felt shame about their sexual desires and were afraid to admit them. They knew instinctively that, without support to develop the self-confidence necessary to advocate for one's rights, no social change would be possible for lesbians. It is this emphasis that distinguishes them from the other gay groups at the time and it is a difference they would continually reassert. The prescient "the personal is political" feminism of Lyon and Martin shaped the organization's priorities from its beginnings, and it was articulated ten years before the resurgence of the women's movement. Educating women to question the limitations imposed by gender and sexuality in Cold War America was challenging enough; to do so openly, as an organization dealing with lesbianism in the cultural climate of the 1950s, was unheard of.

At the end of the summer of 1956, the Daughters—all sixteen of them—were focused on creating something that would appeal to lesbians who wanted more than a nice place to go on Saturday nights. DOB had lost most of its original members, regrouped, recruited new women, and, perhaps most important, come to a consensus on a mission for the group. They would provide both social and political opportunities for their members, and sponsor parties and discussions, picnics and business meetings. The secret lesbian social club was now an organization that prioritized integration into society.

Their alliances with heterosexual women on the basis of gender, as well as their solidarity with gay men based on shared same-sex eroticism, meant that they would always negotiate the connections and fissures between gender and sexuality in fighting lesbian oppression. The founders' establishment of the Daughters as a membership organization to which only women could belong gave them the psychic and physical space to define themselves and their goals, organize social services and activities, and debate strategies and tactics for social change from their experiences and perspectives *as women*.

The Daughters charted a difficult course. Pioneers and activists, they navigated the norms of acceptability in post–World War II America. "Integration" may have been the buzzword but, throughout the United States, segregation was the daily reality for blacks, Latinos, Asians, Native Americans, Jews, immigrants, and poor people; demonization was the norm for leftists, intellectuals, lesbians, and gay men. The women who were active in DOB wanted the paper promises of American equality to be made real, and they were willing to accommodate themselves to many if not most of the prevailing social mores to reach their goal. In return, they wanted recognition that they were just as "normal" as anyone else. They wanted acceptance as well as an end to harassment and discrimination.[27]

DOB's belief that lesbians needed to adapt to societal norms while trying to reform social policies and practices is reminiscent of the early years of the black women's club movement between 1880 and 1920. In addition to their strong belief in appropriate representation of the lesbian, the very name DOB activists chose for their newsletter one year after the organization was created—*The Ladder*—shows a clear if unintentional correlation to the "uplift ideology" of early twentieth-century black women. Their newsletter was intended as a vehicle for the individual lesbian to elevate herself, out of the depths of self-hatred and social strictures. By her actions, she would enable others to do the same.

According to the historian Paula Giddings, "Black women activists believed that their efforts were essential for reform and progress, and that their moral standing was a steady rock upon which the race could lean. . . ." Like the well-educated, segregationist white women who formed local, national, and international women's clubs and organizations in the nineteenth and early twentieth centuries, the founders of the black women's club movement were mostly middle-class and Christian, married, and devoted to notions of reform, not revolution.

Above all, they were respectable. "The ideology of respectability is one of a number of strategies that African Americans have developed to create unity," E. Frances White wrote in *Dark Continent of Our Bodies: Black Feminism and the Politics of Respectability.* "To be positioned outside the 'protection' of womanhood was to be labeled unrespectable. Black feminists of the first wave understood the costs of this label to all black women."[28] Reviewing three works of African-American women's history in 2003, Paisley Harris noted, "Respectability was one of the primary bases upon which African Americans claimed equal status and citizenship during the Progressive era. Defined more expansively, it continued to be an influential basis for claiming rights through the civil rights era and beyond."[29]

"Our woman's movement is a woman's movement in that it is led and directed by women," announced Josephine St. Pierre Ruffin at the Boston national convention of the National Association of Colored Women. From 1896 until it was supplanted by the National Council of Negro Women in 1935, the NACW brought tens of thousands of black women throughout the United States into local and regional clubs which worked to care for the poor, the aged, the sick and disabled, and the young in their communities, as well as to agitate for national antilynching legislation and for women's suffrage. It provided real experience in organizing and management skills for the women involved and created an important platform for Progressive policies and campaigns. "Such leaders of the movement as Mary Church Terrell and Ida B. Wells saw the clubs as a way to mobilize black women to uplift the entire race," White summarizes, but "they struggled to have black women reclassified as good women rather than expose the bankruptcy of the entire system."[30]

The instincts and organizational impulses and attitudes of many of the early organizers of DOB echo similar themes. Their efforts to counter the prevailing images of lesbians as immoral, their commitment to being a strong women's organization rather than an auxiliary of one of the predominantly male homophile groups, and their belief that true social change can come about only when stigmatized individuals can claim a sense of entitlement and self-esteem are reminiscent of the tenets of the black women's clubs which predated the Daughters by half a century. So, too, is their unwillingness to present consistently a critique of U.S. society and the prevalent "good woman/bad girl dichotomy" that was used so forcefully against them.

In 1955, DOB's founders were balancing safety with visibility. With the mask provided by their name and their program of education and research, they "could have been a society for raising cats," as their lawyer Kenneth Zwerin commented after finishing DOB's application for incorporation as a tax-exempt, not-for-profit organization in California in 1957. But Lyon, Martin, and the other early Daughters also boldly advertised their interest in female homosexuality. For many of them, the tightrope act was extremely difficult but essential.[31]

CHAPTER TWO

Climbing *The Ladder*

The four-page, single-spaced, typed letter arrived at DOB's post office box in late April 1957. It contained not only a much-needed financial contribution but, even more important, words of encouragement for the Daughters and their new publication. "Please find enclosed a money order for $2.00. I should like to receive as many of your back issues as that amount will cover. In the event $2.00 is in excess of the cost of six issues—well, fine. Those few cents may stand as a mere downpayment toward sizeable (for me, that is) donations I know already that I shall be sending you."[1]

The author, a young female playwright, did not reveal how she first found out about the Daughters of Bilitis or their new magazine. But she made it clear that she appreciated their efforts. "I'm glad as heck that you exist. You are obviously serious people and I feel that women, without wishing to foster any strict *separatist* notions, homo or hetero, indeed have a need for their own publications and organizations." Phyllis Lyon, the editor, was so delighted she went on to print the entire missive, taking up nearly four of the issue's twenty pages to do so. "Women, like other oppressed groups of one kind or another, have particularly had to pay a price for the intellectual impoverishment that the second class status imposed on us for centuries created and sustained. Thus, I feel that THE LADDER is a fine, elementary step in a rewarding direction." As was customary in *The Ladder's* "Readers Respond" column, the letter was signed only with the initials "L.H.N." and her location, "New York, N.Y."[2]

"L.H.N." also voiced her strong support for at least outward conformity for homosexual women and men. "As one raised in a cultural experience (I am a Negro) where those within were and are forever lecturing to their fellows about how to appear acceptable to the dominant social group, I know something about the shallowness of such a view as an end in itself . . . [O]ne is oppressed or discriminated against because one is different, not 'wrong' or 'bad' somehow." She insisted, however, "as a matter of facility, of expediency, one has to take a critical view of revolutionary attitudes which in spite of the BASIC truth I have mentioned above, may tend to aggravate the problems of the group." The writer admitted that she had learned to ignore feelings of discomfort "at the sight of an ill-dressed or illiterate Negro. Social awareness has taught me where to lay the blame." She went on to imagine a time in the future when "the 'discreet' Lesbian will not turn her head on the streets at the sight of the 'butch' strolling hand in hand with her friend in their trousers and definitive haircuts" and added, "[B]ut for the moment, it still disturbs." Her concerns seemed to be mostly with the best way to change opinions and attitudes about homosexuality among "one's most enlightened" heterosexual friends.[3]

"L.H.N.," or Lorraine Hansberry Nemiroff, was one of the first *Ladder* readers to address the issues of positive lesbian representation. In doing so, she articulated her understanding of the sorts of social strictures operating for sexual, as well as racial, minorities in the United States in the late 1950s. Hansberry, the award-winning author of *A Raisin in the Sun,* became one of the youngest playwrights, and the first African-American woman, to have a drama performed on the Broadway stage. Born in Chicago to a middle-class family, Hansberry had moved to New York in 1950 and found work with Paul Robeson's newspaper *Freedom*. Three years later, she married a white male friend, Robert Nemiroff, and began writing for the stage.

Hansberry was an early subscriber to *The Ladder* and was also familiar with the other homophile groups and their publications. "Just a little afterthought," she added to her May 1957 letter to DOB, "considering Mattachine; Bilitis; ONE; all seem to be cropping up on the West Coast rather than here where a vigorous and active gay set almost bump one another off the streets—what is it in the air out there? Pioneers still? Or a tougher circumstance which inspires battle? Would love to hear speculation, light-hearted or otherwise."[4]

The "speculation" on dress and behavior that Hansberry sparked, however, would not be light-hearted. She had started a heated debate over the formation of a new lesbian identity, one that would circulate throughout the next ten years among lesbian as well as gay male activists. An article, "Transvestism—A Cross-Cultural Survey" by "Barbara Stephens," was printed in the June 1957 *Ladder*. It drew responses that show the diversity of opinion among DOB members and *Ladder* readers on the organization's "dress code."

One letter, signed by "A.C., New York, N.Y.," offers congratulations and support to the new organization and its newsletter but then states, "I consider myself (and my roommate also considers herself) a mild transvestite—that is, we wear slacks almost always on our off-work hours. We are comfortable in them and we have no problem adjusting to the stares of passersby." A. C. then proclaimed dresses, high heels, and "stocking holders"—the confining and much-hated girdles and garter-belts—"the most uncomfortable contraptions men have invented to restrict the movements of women."[5] Despite the dictates of fashion in 1957, a feminist awareness of the limitations of women's clothing, stretching back to the days of the mid-nineteenth-century reformer Molly Bloomer, still prevailed for some lesbians. As

A. C. enumerated, ladies' garments often restricted freedom: women wearing them "cannot walk very far, lift many things, or sit with their legs apart in warm weather." Another Daughter wrote with ferocity: "Of all the intellectual rubbish in the history of mankind, none has been more voluminous than the conventions and taboos of dress." She insisted that "the cult of conformity" must end.[6]

The lengths to which a lesbian would go for societal acceptance was a contested issue from the beginning in the Daughters of Bilitis. DOB championed outward conformity to achieve integration, primarily through the provision in its Statement of Purpose that required members' adoption of a "mode of dress and behavior acceptable to society." Despite this, the organization's leaders and members included many dissenters. "Sheesh! Was that ever enforced?" Stella Rush responded when reminded about DOB's "dress code." Another Daughter remembered early meetings where "everyone" was in blue jeans. Billye Talmadge added that the jeans were probably men's, "because those were the only jeans we wore in the 1950s."[7] The debate over outward conformity would continue for years, helped along by the Daughters' new publication. It provided a forum for lesbians to debate questions of how much, when, and where to assimilate to the dominant culture.

By the end of the summer of 1956, Lyon, as "Ann Ferguson," was named editor of *The Ladder,* with Noni Frey ("Tori Fry") as assistant editor, "BOB" (a woman named Brian O'Brien) as art director, and Barbara Deming ("Bobbi Deering") in charge of mailing. (Deming, a San Francisco woman who was one of the five original cosigners of DOB's Articles of Incorporation and remained involved with the local chapter for many years, is not to be confused with the New York–based peace activist also named Barbara Deming.)

In addition to advertising their upcoming programs, the Daughters decided they would use the newsletter to print a series of articles on the many manifestations of "fear": "fear of a group, ridicule, what people will say, job, public opinion, the law, involvement with a possibly communistic or radical group, and ostracism." Using the facetious in-group shorthand "homos" to describe themselves and their male allies, the Daughters agreed on pragmatic solutions to counter the fears they believed robbed gay men and lesbians of self-esteem. One of the first things they would publish would be "an article on how the homo, by his or her own self-consciousness, makes himself more miserable than need be."[8]

Despite the use of "homo" in an internal document, their public use of language to describe themselves was changing. Although the Daughters' earliest written records refer to the "gay woman," from the first issue of *The Ladder* on, their preferred term was "Lesbian" and it was usually capitalized. They also adopted "homophile," denoting love of same, which began to be widely used by the 1950s gay and lesbian organizers mid-decade. They quoted Basil Vaerlen, a San Francisco psychotherapist: "It was felt that the use of the word 'homophile' would produce a more favorable and constructive reaction from the general public; that as soon as 'homosexual' is used there is a marked reaction of a negative tone." Dr. Vaerlen delivered one of the earliest talks on "Is a Homophile Marriage Possible?" to DOB in June 1957. (His answer: "Any marriage is possible between any two people if they want to grow up—and it is nobody's business but their own.")[9]

The first issue of *The Ladder* appeared as a mimeographed twelve-page newsletter early in October 1956. It looks homespun, in part because of O'Brien's hand-drawn cover. She portrayed two slender women dressed in tailored slacks and blouses at the foot of a ladder, which reaches into the billowing clouds above it. The slogan "from the city of many moods . . ." decorates the back cover, along with DOB's organizational coat of arms and motto, "Qui vive." The newsletter's name was taken from the image she presented.

Inside, and underneath a list of officers and staff (most of whom used pseudonyms or slightly altered their first or last names), they printed a brief explanation and the first of many regular requests for money. "We are sending this first issue to you with our compliments in order to acquaint you with our organization and the work we are doing. However, in order to help defray publishing expenses we are asking for donation of $1.00 for one year of THE LADDER. If you wish to receive future issues and to help the cause please send in the questionnaire on page 12."

On page 2, editor Ann Ferguson explained, "Just one year ago the Daughters of Bilitis was formed. Eight women gathered together with a vague idea about the problems of Lesbians, both within their own group and with the public. The original idea was mainly that of providing an outlet for social activities, but with discussion came broader purposes and the club was formed with a much wider scope than that originally envisioned."

Ferguson emphasized that DOB was a women's organization: "This membership is open to all women over 21 who have a genuine interest in the problems of the female homophile and the related problems of other minorities." Women could join as either active ("$5.00 initiation fee") or associate ($2.50) members, "with monthly dues of $1 for the former and 50 cents for the latter." The group's monthly program of public discussion meetings, also started in 1956, featured local speakers from "business, professional, and medical fields." After DOB's Statement of Purpose they added the disclaimer: "The Daughters of Bilitis is not now, and never has been, affiliated with any other organization, political, social or otherwise."

A CALENDAR OF EVENTS listed a September 30 picnic as well as bowling at the Sports Center at Thirtieth & Mission streets in San Francisco, on October 13: "Meet at the coffee counter." The first in a series of discussions on lesbians' fears—"both real and

imaginary"—was set for October 23. There was also notice of a "Hal-
loween Party at 651 Duncan St." on October 27. "$1.50 per person.
Refreshments provided. Phone your reservation (VAlencia 4-2790)
by Friday night, Oct. 26."

But editor Ferguson made it clear that social events were only one
aspect of DOB's work. "It is to be hoped that our venture will
encourage the women to take an ever-increasing part in the steadily-
growing fight for understanding of the homophile minority." The
President's Message, written and signed by Del Martin, further underscored DOB's particular role in the homophile movement: "While
women may not have so much difficulty with law enforcement, their
problems are none the less real—family, sometimes children, employment, social acceptance." Martin made a passionate plea for involvement in the Daughters of Bilitis, and in the homophile movement
generally, primarily on the basis of gender identification, not sexual
orientation: "Women have taken a beating through the centuries. It
has been only in this 20th, through the courageous crusade of the
Suffragettes and the influx of women into the business world, that
woman has become an independent entity, an individual with the
right to vote and the right to a job and economic security." Her
staunchly feminist orientation—whether or not the explicit terminology of feminism was used—was clear from the first newsletter. It
marked DOB as a group committed not only to socializing but to
social change. Martin's beliefs in women's activism are still inspiring:
"It took women with foresight and determination to attain this heritage which is now ours. . . . Nothing was ever accomplished by hiding
in a dark corner. Why not discard the hermitage for the heritage that
awaits any red-blooded American woman who dares to claim it?"[10]

The *Ladder*'s first issue also included a tribute to the pioneering
sex researcher Dr. Alfred Kinsey, recently deceased, written by Dr.
Harry Benjamin of San Francisco in a letter to the editor of the *San*

Francisco Examiner: "In the passing of Dr. Alfred Kinsey the world has lost an outstanding scientist and a champion of human freedom and happiness. . . . Kinsey's work will go on under the guidance of his able associates." The Daughters added that they invited "any professional people" and "researchers planning projects, or with projects underway" to contact them. "We wish to cooperate in any way possible to further knowledge of the Lesbian."

A QUESTIONNAIRE was printed on the back page of the first issue and included four questions:

1. How can our organization help you?

2. Are you primarily interested in discussion meetings, publications, social services, social functions, sports?

3. On what topics would you like to hear leaders in the fields of psychiatry, law, psychology, sociology, business and the clergy speak?

4. Have you any suggestions as to whom we should get as speakers?

A coupon completed the page:

I wish to join the Daughters of Bilitis____
Enclosed is $1.00 for 1 year of THE LADDER____
I am 21 years of age or over____

Signed _____
Address_____
Phone _____

The Daughters' timing—in launching their newsletter as well as expanding their public programs—was fortuitous. Weeks before *The Ladder*'s debut, a new crisis had hit Bay Area lesbians. On Friday, September 21, 1956, police raided the Alamo Club (popularly known as Kelly's) in San Francisco. As reported in the second issue, "[h]auled into the city jail and booked on the charge of frequenting a house of ill repute were a reported 36 women. At the hearing the following Monday we understand only four of those arrested pleaded not guilty. We feel that this was not due to actual guilt on the part of those so pleading but to an appalling lack of knowledge of the rights of a citizen in such a case." The Daughters announced that a local attorney, Benjamin M. Davis, had volunteered to speak. "He will discuss 'The Lesbian and The Law,' with special emphasis on a citizen's rights in case of arrest." They also announced that they would be printing a guide, "What To Do In Case of Arrest," which appeared in the next issue. "'Never Plead Guilty'" is more than the title of [the San Francisco criminal defense attorney] Jake Ehrlich's book; it is advice to be remembered," they added as a postscript to *The Ladder*'s coverage of the raid.[11]

An editorial written by Martin and titled "The Positive Approach" observed that due to the raid, "[a] paralyzing fear has been heaped upon an ever-present dread of detection. The persecuted are seeking cover once again. The innocent are convinced of their guilt. The tolerant become intolerant of their fellows. Growth is stultified by a sludge of misunderstanding."[12]

As if to counter the resurgence of fear, the same issue contained an article headlined "Your Name Is Safe!" signed by editor Ferguson. She assured *Ladder* readers that their donations to DOB for *The Ladder* would not expose them to harm. "Your name on our mailing list is as inviolate as the provisions of the Constitution of the United States can make it," she stated, and quoted a 1953 U.S. Supreme

Court ruling in *U.S. v. Rumely* upholding the right of a citizen to refuse to reveal readers' names to a congressional committee. She quoted Justice William O. Douglas: "Once the Government can demand of a publisher the names of the purchasers of his publications, the free press as we know it disappears. Then the specter of a Government agent will look over the shoulder of everyone who reads." Ferguson concluded, "This Supreme Court decision points the way to even stronger safeguards of a free press, a freedom which is a basic necessity of the democratic way. The decision also guarantees that your name is safe!"[13]

With their second issue, in addition to civil liberties education, the Daughters began to use *The Ladder* to provide concrete alternatives to negative professional attitudes about homosexuality. They printed an account of a Los Angeles lecture by a leading San Francisco psychiatrist, Dr. Norman Reider, who "declared his belief that modern laws against homosexuals are largely unfair, unjustified, and ineffective." Professional critiques of antihomosexual attitudes and policies, particularly from maverick medical and mental health practitioners, would become a valuable part of each monthly newsletter.

So too would the section entitled Readers Respond, which featured portions of selected letters the Daughters received. Among the first was one from a member of Dr. Kinsey's team, Paul Gebhard, executive director of the Institute for Sex Research at Indiana University: "Thank you for Volume 1, Number 1 of The Ladder. It is a welcome addition to our library and we are interested in receiving all subsequent issues."

Their emphasis on confronting fear was validated by many readers. A letter from "J. M., Cleveland, Ohio" expressed what the Daughters assumed many lesbians felt.

"I cannot tell you what a source of both inspiration and pleasure *The Ladder* contained for me within its pages. I, as an invert, can only know of what momentous importance such a movement as yours can mean, for the ultimate good of all of us. One of the insertions in *The Ladder* caught my attention and I could not help but muse over it with some irony. The part about 'Come out of hiding.' What a delicious invitation, but oh, so impractical. I should lose my job, a marvelous heterosexual roommate, and all chance of finding work. . . . I would be blackballed all over the city."[14]

The next issue—December 1956—featured a new assistant to the editor, "Helen Sanders," the named used by Helen Sandoz in her DOB activities. Noni Frey, the former assistant who was also the last member of the original founders besides Phyllis Lyon and Del Martin, had left DOB the month before. The president was now D. Griffin (P. D. Griffin), with Martin serving as second-in-command.

Many of the women involved in DOB in 1957, like Phyllis Lyon and Helen Sandoz, protected their identities by using pseudonyms or "pen names" in the newsletter's list of officers and staff. As "J. M." from Cleveland described, being honest about one's homosexuality at that time could expose a lesbian or gay man to possible dismissal from employment, loss of family and friends, or worse. For the first few years of *The Ladder*, the leaders of DOB would continually reassure their readers that involvement in the organization would help, not harm, them. As Martin exhorted her readers in the first issue: "What will be the lot of the future Lesbian? Fear? Scorn? This need not be—IF lethargy is supplanted by an energized constructive program, if cowardice gives way to the solidarity of a cooperative front, if the 'let Georgia do it' attitude is replaced by the realization of individual responsibility in thwarting the evils of ignorance, superstition, prejudice, and bigotry."

In addition to a Schedule of Events that included the "Daughters' annual New Year's Eve Party" at 651 Duncan Street, was a long review of a book published by ONE, Inc. *Homosexuals Today—1956* included descriptions of roughly two dozen homophile social, political, and service groups around the world. "To read of the work and progress of these organizations . . . should be truly enlightening to those readers of *The Ladder* who still have doubts and reservations concerning the time and the wisdom of pursuing the fight for full citizenship for members of the homosexual minority." They highlighted the book's inclusion of Lisa Ben's magazine *VICE VERSA* and noted that the Daughters of Bilitis was advertised as well.[15]

The new year started with a small recognition of DOB and their new newsletter in the media: the editor proudly announced their first citation in a monthly New York newspaper, *The Independent*. The newspaper's mention of the Daughters was appreciated, but a new book by the Manhattan psychoanalyst Edmund Bergler was not. *The Ladder* summarized a review in *Time* magazine (December 10, 1956) of Bergler's recent work, *Homosexuality: Disease or Way of Life?* An excellent example of negative psychiatric thinking about homosexuality, Bergler's comments were harsh: "The full grown homosexual wallows in self pity and continually provokes hostility to ensure himself more opportunities for self pity; he collects injustices—sometimes real, often fancied; he is full of defensive malice and flippancy, covering his depression and guilt with extreme narcissism and superciliousness." *Ladder* editor Lyon noted, "If you are curious about the book, we do not suggest your buying it. Try to borrow it . . . and read the full review in TIME." She also urged readers to consider Bergler's ideas very critically and ended the review with a defiant "We don't think Dr. Bergler's ideas are acceptable to us or to a vast majority of people in the psychiatric field."[16]

The following month, Lyon proudly announced, "For those who doubted our legality or our permanency we can only say 'See, we're incorporated and we're here to stay.'" Working with a local attorney,

Kenneth Zwerin, who was referred to them by Mattachine members, the Daughters of Bilitis incorporated as a not-for-profit organization in California. Lyon also noted the establishment of DOB's first office, a desk in a suite of rooms rented by Mattachine at 693 Mission Street. "For the present you can reach us via EXbrook 7-0773, the phone number of the Mattachine Society. . . . Our own private phone is still a future project. Phones cost money, you know."

A thorough review of ONE's Midwinter Institute, held the month before in Los Angeles, filled six pages and featured notes on a talk given by Dr. Albert Ellis, "New York psychologist," as they described him, on how best to combat the antihomosexual culture of the United States. There was also a glowing summary of a talk given by "Henry Hay, Los Angeles folklore specialist." Hay, known more often as Harry in the homophile movement, had left the Mattachine Society and was pursuing his passion for knowledge about gay cultures; at the 1957 Midwinter Institute, the largest known gathering of gay and lesbian activists up until that time with perhaps fifty participants, he "sketched the history of homophile life from the dawn of history to the present time" and helped create an interest in gay history. The Daughters announced also the tentative program being developed by the ONE Institute for undergraduate and graduate study of homosexuality. And a talk given by Blanche M. Baker, a San Francisco psychiatrist, to Institute participants helped cement what would become an important relationship between "Doc" Baker and the Daughters. Baker's presentation on "The Circle of Sex" challenged rigid societal notions of "the male and female concept." She was quoted as saying that "[t]here is a growing awareness of the mixture of the male and female components in each of us. . . . Nature does not work in straight rigid lines, but rather in cycles or circles."[17]

The Ladder announced a new forum on "How Secure is Your Job?" for February 26, "when a panel of experts in the field takes over to answer the question." The panel included DOB's Helen Sandoz, listed as "Sanders"; the moderator would be Dr. Vera Plunkett, a San Francisco chiropractor and an early heterosexual friend to the homophile movement. Most of the discussion centered on ways the gay man or lesbian could behave either in a job interview or as part of the office staff to "fit in" and be accepted. The following month's upbeat report on the panel, however, prompted a letter of dissent from "B.D.H., Washington, D.C.," who wrote in May 1957 that "so much adverse publicity has been given homosexuals by the newspapers and Congressmen" that he did not share the optimism of the speakers at the February forum. "I know of a homosexual who lost his Government position a year ago and who since then has been unable to obtain employment. He seems to have developed a 'mental block' and so great is the fear which grips him because of this misfortune that he cannot bring himself to make the final step in approaching a prospective employer for an interview." The writer provided two more examples of gay people whose lives had been ruined by loss of employment due to blackmail or arrest. He noted that most employers did not want to hire gay men and lesbians due to "the prevailing mores and the stigma which attaches to the employer" simply because of the presence of homosexuals in the office.[18]

Given the continuing impact of federal regulations barring their employment by the government, it is no wonder that lesbians and gay men in the nation's capital were feeling far less optimistic about employment prospects than those attending a job forum three thousand miles away in San Francisco. The reach of *The Ladder* was already increasing information about the daily lives and regular concerns of lesbians and gay men throughout the country.

"Why a Chapter in Your Area?" headlined an article encouraging the formation of DOB groups beyond San Francisco in 1957. The idea of organizing local chapters came up almost as soon as *The Ladder* started arriving in women's mailboxes. Letters of interest arrived at the Daughters' San Francisco post office box from lesbians who wanted to form groups in their areas, but there were some nay-sayers as well. One subscriber wrote, "If an L.A. chapter were to be formed in this area, what would be its main activities? I think your publication is a great thing, but I do wonder about these meetings you hold. It seems that those attending and listening to a discussion are the very ones who would least benefit from hearing what is said. Other than the social aspect of the group, I don't yet see the purpose."

Del Martin explained the need for local DOB groups early in 1957. "Letters received by the Daughters from points far and wide certainly indicate a basic need for 'someone to talk to.' . . . Perhaps some individuals are able to cope with the problem alone. We doubt that this holds true for very many." In that same issue, *The Ladder* reported that "sixteen people attended a get-acquainted brunch of the Daughters of Bilitis in The English Room of the New Clark Hotel in Los Angeles on Sunday, January 27." Enough Southland lesbians responded positively to DOB's mission that the group's leaders in San Francisco announced that "immediate steps will be taken to start a provisional chapter in the Los Angeles area."[19]

One of the "immediate steps" that aided the development of the Los Angeles DOB was basic human connection: Helen Sandoz and Stella Rush met at the ONE, Inc., meeting in Los Angeles early in 1957 and were immediately attracted to one another. "I was asked by Del and Phyllis to keep an eye on her," Rush remembers. "Make sure she got to the sessions, didn't just check out. She was very smart and got bored easily. And I found her at the bar in the hotel where the meeting was being held, we started talking, and that was that."

As "Sten Russell, Los Angeles Reporter," Stella Rush wrote about many of the earliest homophile meetings and programs for *The*

Ladder, beginning in April 1957, while maintaining her connections to *ONE*. Despite (or perhaps because of) the difficulties of managing a brand-new, red-hot, long-distance lesbian relationship, Sandoz decided to move from the Bay Area to Los Angeles by year's end and begin a new life there with Rush.[20]

By the summer of 1957, another important DOB relationship was formed. "As promised, THE LADDER begins with this issue its running bibliography of Lesbian literature (fiction, non-fiction, drama, poetry)," Lyon wrote in the March 1957 issue. The first column carried capsule summaries of *The Collected Works of Pierre Louÿs; The Well of Loneliness; Wind Woman,* by Carol Hales; and *Claudine at School,* by Colette. In August 1957, a letter from "G.D., Kansas City, Kansas" commended the editor for the "Lesbiana" feature and enclosed "a few additions." Lyon responded, "Also would like to ask G.D. to send along a sentence or two about the book as well as title, author, publisher, year, etc."

Their correspondence began a fifteen-year tradition of the Daughters presenting "Gene Damon" (Barbara Grier) and her concise, subjective, and sometimes controversial reviews of lesbian-themed writings in *The Ladder.* Each month, she analyzed four to ten books dealing with lesbians and homosexuality, from pulp fiction to serious literature, by female and male authors. One of the first books she reviewed when she took over the column in September 1957 was Thomas Hardy's *Desperate Remedies;* she also reviewed *The Dark Island,* by Vita Sackville-West.

The daughter of a physician and a secretary, Barbara Grier realized at age twelve that she was "a superior being" and a homosexual. Born on November 4, 1933, in Cleveland, Ohio, Grier spent most of her life as a Midwesterner before relocating to Florida in 1980. She described growing up in an Anglo-American family of "eccentric, theatrical" people that included a Mormon iconoclast (James Jesse

Strang) and the British actor David Niven. Her family moved around a good deal in the 1930s but settled in Kansas City, Kansas, when she was in high school.

Grier made Kansas City her home. Her passion for books drove her to work in libraries for much of her life, and she befriended such women as the science fiction writer Marion Zimmer Bradley and the bibliographer Jeannette Howard Foster. Foster had moved to Kansas City with her lover after they left Kinsey's team of sex researchers. In 1956, Grier—a twenty-three-year-old lesbian bibliophile amassing her first collection of gay literature—contacted Foster at Bradley's suggestion. It was also through Bradley that Grier learned about DOB.[21]

Bradley and Foster had become friends and colleagues by the early 1950s, sharing ideas and encouragement mainly through correspondence, and Bradley reviewed Foster's *Sex Variant Women in Literature* for the May 1957 issue of *The Ladder*. "To the collector of Lesbian literature the work is invaluable, listing as it does every major work and many minor ones." But Bradley's review was critical in part: "I confess myself somewhat exasperated by the chapter devoted to biographical conjecture about Emily Brontë. Granting that Miss Brontë may well have been a Lesbian—the lady has been dead for enough years that this posthumous identification is apt to soothe the vanity of many Lesbians and cast no aspersions on her family—her work certainly contains no reflection of this aspect of her character, and Miss Foster's 'proofs,' frankly, do not convince me at all."

Foreshadowing later debates over claiming that historical figures had been "in the life," Bradley thundered: "Even more eyebrow-lifting is the chapter which includes the Biblical BOOK OF RUTH. . . . I am fairly sure that a scholar of Biblical history, or one of Jewish mores, however open-minded, would reject the theory, not as offensive but as absurd." She concluded, however, that Foster's book was "a major milestone in the literature of homosexuality in general and female variance in particular." The 400-plus-page bibliography exhaustively catalogued poetic and literary references to Western lesbians and bisexual women in literature, with 324 titles. Foster created sections beginning with "The Ancient Record," "The Dark Ages to the Age of Reason," "Romantics to the Modern," "Later Nineteenth Century," "Conjectural Retrospect" (in which she discussed major lesbian writers of the past), and "Twentieth Century Poetry" and fiction up until 1954.[22]

Foster's voluminous research only became available because she was determined that it not be suppressed: in 1956, no one wanted to publish a bibliography of works on "the female sex variant," so she paid Vantage Press to issue the book. The public response at the time was so minimal as to be mute. As soon as she learned of the new lesbian club and its newsletter, however, Foster wrote to *The Ladder*'s editor and sent a copy of her book. She had found her audience.

CHAPTER THREE

Some Facts About Lesbians

Natalie Lando hurried up Market Street as the Ferry Building clock showed 6 P.M. She wrapped her raincoat closer to her body to keep out the wet chill of the November night and the mist of the fog blanketing the streets and buildings. She had promised to lend a hand at the DOB office to get the magazine ready and, even though she'd much rather be heading home, she was committed. There were at least three new articles to prepare, probably requiring at least half a dozen stencils, and she was already weary from a full day at the typewriter.

She knew that being tired when you were typing *The Ladder* usually meant that you made mistakes. Mistakes meant delicately lifting up the thin top layer of the stencil, dotting a drop of smelly correction fluid onto the mistyped letter, then putting another drop on the thicker sheet, underneath. It sometimes helped to blow softly on the sheets so that the fluid would dry more quickly. After a minute, she'd have to carefully reposition the sheets in the holder so that the typewriter key would strike the corrected spot with precision. Each letter of the word typed in error had to be lined up exactly. Then she'd strike with a firm finger on the correct key and pray that the cranky old Underwood wouldn't misfire.

But first she had to get to the office. Market Street after dark was a bit grim. Once she reached the three-story concrete block building, she'd enter and climb the dark stairs inside, moving quickly down the hushed corridor, alone. "I don't mean to make it sound sinister, because it wasn't, really, but I was very young and very scared."[1]

For the women who subscribed to *The Ladder*, the magazine was a monthly link to a larger world. "I have been receiving THE LADDER and have been a member of the Daughters of Bilitis for more than a year now. The day my copy arrives I sit and read it from cover to cover," wrote "G.M." from Orange, New Jersey, toward the end of 1957. "If only there was a chapter here in New York or New Jersey I would be the first to join."[2]

"Like many another LADDER reader, I am always thoroughly delighted with your magazine and all too seldom write to tell you so," confessed "C.H., Pasadena, California" in the March 1958 issue. "I wish I were blessed with financial means, talented with writing ability, or in some other way qualified to make more of a contribution to DOB than I can, but as I am not I join the ranks of those quiet followers who find you a light in the dark night and a warm fire for alien souls."[3]

These two letters and dozens, then hundreds, more arrived at DOB's San Francisco office in 1957 and 1958, written by women living in big cities as well as small towns; from Portland, Oregon, to Huntington, West Virginia; from Paris, France, to Winnipeg, Manitoba, Canada. For DOB members who lived in the Bay Area and could help create *The Ladder*, like Natalie Lando, the magazine consumed hundreds of women-hours for every issue produced. The unglamorous, unacknowledged nitty-gritty work for the magazine included typing articles and address labels, preparing layout and paste-up, and negotiating with the printer. DOB members sorted, stapled, and inserted each copy into plain manila envelopes and sent it out to friends and subscribers across the country and around the world. In the October 1959 issue, editor Phyllis Lyon wrote about the extensive processes involved for each monthly issue, all done by volunteers. "Many women work one night a week at the office—but just before LADDER deadline it usually is every night of the week."[4]

The letters they received made the work seem worthwhile. For the individual women who somehow found a copy, *The Ladder* was a means of sharing otherwise private thoughts and feelings, connecting across miles, and breaking through isolation and fear. For those women, married or single, who relied on the U.S. mail to receive their copies in rural as well as metropolitan areas in the latter part of the 1950s, it was a radical departure from what had been available. Finally there was something more than sorrowful stories about elite misfits, paperback novels with tragic endings, psychological treatises about depravity and illness.

Women found out about DOB's magazine through friends; at leftist or alternative newsstands and bookstores; near college and university campuses; and at the bars. It was surreptitiously handed around at work, and sometimes the very professionals whose opinions DOB was hoping to change would recommend it to their clients and colleagues.

The little magazine also provided a way for women outside DOB's chapter cities to be involved in the lesbian movement, and it attracted many writers, editors, artists, and intellectuals who wished to express their ideas to a nascent lesbian community.

Beyond receiving their monthly magazine, however, many *Ladder* letter writers wanted a way to meet other lesbians. Local organizing was a priority for DOB, and in 1958, just three years after the club was first formed, the number of DOB groups tripled. Within a month of one another, in New York and Los Angeles, DOB leaders Barbara

Gittings and Marion Glass, as well as Helen Sandoz and Stella Rush, organized local DOB and Mattachine members into monthly parties, outings, and discussions.[5]

Gittings first found DOB in 1956 on a vacation to the West Coast and wrote a few letters to the editor of *The Ladder.* In 1958, because she lived in Philadelphia and they had met her two years earlier, she was asked by Lyon and Martin to convene the first East Coast DOB group. "Barbara was always going back and forth to New York, to concerts or plays or something," Kay Lahusen remembers. Lyon and Martin entrusted her with the small mailing list of area members and, working with another local Daughter, Marion Glass, Gittings called an organizing meeting: "Mattachine notified the handful of women on its mailing list, DOB in San Francisco notified its few *Ladder* subscribers on the East Coast, and with no more than ten women in attendance, DOB's New York Chapter got started."[6]

Glass, a young white woman who worked as a statistician for the state of New York, used the pseudonym Meredith Grey in her DOB work. Lahusen describes her as "very nervous but very bright." She was eager to help Gittings get a New York chapter going, in part because "she had a crush on Barbara."[7] Gittings didn't encourage a romance but recognized that the two women worked well together; they began to plan activities to recruit potential Daughters in the New York area. *The Ladder* letter writer quoted above, "G.M." from Orange, New Jersey, surely received an invitation to the local organizing meetings; what we don't know is whether she had the courage to attend.

In November 1958, Lyon and Martin took their first cross-country trip to promote DOB and meet East Coast supporters. They took advantage of the New York visit to enjoy themselves and play tourist—"we went in search of the perfect martini!" Lyon remembers—as well as to take care of DOB business. The journey itself was an adventure; neither one of them had ever experienced air travel. And on arrival, they were set to meet with one of *The Ladder's* earliest correspondents: before leaving San Francisco, Lyon wrote to Lorraine Hansberry about their trip and she invited them to her home in Greenwich Village. They telephoned her on the appointed day. "She said it was obvious we weren't New Yorkers because New Yorkers don't get up that early," Lyon said about their initial conversation; in their eagerness, they had neglected to consider the schedule of a busy playwright and called Hansberry at 7 A.M. Regardless of the hour, and the fact that she was preparing her play *Raisin in the Sun* for its opening on Broadway just a few months later, Hansberry agreed to see them that morning. They were nervous about meeting her—"we didn't know any real celebrities"—and were somewhat in awe of the young woman who was causing a sensation with her searing commentary on American race relations. Martin described Hansberry as smart, pretty, and gracious. "She was very nice to us but said that she just couldn't get more involved" with the Daughters.[8]

But a few New York area women did volunteer to get involved; early members of DOB there included Bea and Millie, who hosted DOB gatherings and "Gab 'n' Java" all-women discussion sessions at their home in New Jersey, and Vanessa, a young black woman who attended meetings and mailing parties regularly in the early days. Gus Kaufman was another founding NY DOB member; she offered her Manhattan apartment for meetings. And, despite being married with children, Jody Shotwell helped get the local group started and contributed a number of her writings to *The Ladder*. Within a year, the New York Daughters opened an office—a tiny space shared with the local Mattachine Society at 1133 Broadway, in the theater district—and began to produce its own local newsletter. By November 1959, they proudly announced that "the only older group [of DOB] is in San Francisco where the Daughters of Bilitis was founded in 1955";

they invited readers to "send us a card and a few words of greeting—or gift yourself or a friend with a subscription to *The Ladder*, the D.O.B. monthly magazine ($4.00 yearly)."[9]

On the West Coast, DOB was expanding as well. In Los Angeles in 1958, a few months after they started living together, Helen Sandoz and Stella Rush called an organizing meeting of local DOB members and *Ladder* subscribers. It was held at the home of one of Sandy's friends, a woman named Barbara Brown who lived in a wealthy part of Los Angeles. After the first meeting, the group convened regularly at Sandoz and Rush's home on Waterloo Street in the Silverlake area, "a dear little house which cost $150 a month at that time." Rush served as treasurer for LA DOB when the chapter began, a position she would hold for the next six years. "We were doing things to bring in money to help support *The Ladder*. We would have a speakers meeting but if it was a male speaker, half of the women wouldn't come."[10] Given Rush's longstanding relationships with local ONE and Mattachine activists, the L.A. chapter began by cosponsoring local homophile forums and meetings with the better-established groups. Sandoz and Rush were mainstays of the new chapter; *VICE VERSA* creator Lisa Ben was an early member, as was Venice Ostwald (or Vostwald).

From the beginning, Ostwald and Sandoz clashed. "They were both very forward, very outspoken and they crossed swords," Rush remembers. But Ostwald continued to attend meetings and soon was chapter president. "I got divorced after my husband came back from Korea in 1958," Venice Ostwald explained. "I met Del and Phyl at a ONE meeting; I also met my lover-to-be." Ostwald, a tall white woman with a big smile who used the name "Val Vanderwood" in her DOB work, remembered that a group of women talked then about organizing a local chapter of DOB, but it took another year for a group to gel.[11]

In January 1958, Ostwald (listed using "Mrs. V. C. Vostwald," and "graduate student, ONE Institute") was one of the debaters at the ONE Midwinter Institute on whether "Heterosexual Living Is Better Than Homosexual." Stella Rush reported in her *Ladder* review of the program, "Vostwald said that it could be conceded that heterosexuality was better for heterosexuals, but certainly not for homosexuals."[12]

A few months later, she was one of the first LA Daughters. "It was a broad-based group—there was a real cross-section of people— colored people, white people, poor people, professionals—but it was always a very small group." She led the local DOB for the next few years and then moved to Northern California—first to Hillsborough, a suburb south of San Francisco, then to San Jose—to teach at local colleges. It was while she was living there that she became friends with another early DOB activist, Florence "Conrad" Jaffy.[13]

"Florence and Venice had a lot in common," Phyllis Lyon remembers. "They were both into the academic thing." Jaffy, who always used the name Florence Conrad in her DOB activities, taught economics at the College of San Mateo, south of San Francisco. Small and wiry, a white woman with thick, short-cropped hair, she joined DOB in 1957 after moving from Chicago. Jaffy believed passionately that the Daughters would make an important contribution to "the cause" if it could provide a voice for "Lesbians who probably do not otherwise come to the attention of the public or of researchers." As research director, she shaped the research efforts that DOB initiated. "She was responsible for getting DOB members to participate as guinea pigs in research projects in the late 50s and early 60s," Lyon and Martin wrote about Jaffy upon her death in 1986. "She carefully screened researchers who approached DOB to check their credentials, hypotheses and biases. She was determined that it was possible to refute negative psychological theories about Lesbians and homosexuality."[14]

Jaffy was convinced that if "the experts"—researchers and "professionals"—had more information about homosexuals, they would learn that gay women and men were no more abnormal than anyone else—a radical concept in those days. She believed it was vital to provide data showing that it was societal strictures and stigma that created homosexual neurosis. That information, in turn, could help change public opinion. She argued that valid scientific studies were necessary and important tools in dismantling prejudice and discrimination against homosexuals.

In 1958, "in an effort to make a small beginning in the collection of descriptive data on Lesbians," Jaffy led the DOB's first forays into sociological and psychological research efforts. As the women's studies scholar Jennifer Terry has argued, "The movement's embrace of social science promoted two main points. First, it sought to argue that homosexuals were not, by definition, sick, stressing instead that homosexuals were average people, just like everyone else. Secondly, homophile activists' interest in scientifically generated statistical surveys was related to their arguing that homosexuals represented a minority, but a substantial one, worthy of respect for its social and cultural contributions. Scientific surveys became a strategy for visibility."[15]

In DOB's Statement of Purpose, the first two goals listed ways of educating "the variant" as well as the public. The third goal focused on research, which they viewed as an essential tool in expanding the public's knowledge of gay men and lesbians, a tool to advance social change.

Until 1958, only Alfred Kinsey, a zoologist, and his colleagues at the Institute for Sex Research in Indiana treated homosexuality as anything other than a serious illness. No mainstream religious institution, university, or government agency gave any credence to the idea that gay men and lesbians were productive, stable people who contributed a great deal to society. No public library openly displayed books with homosexual themes or information. Even if one knew they existed, any available literature, medical treatises, and psychological case studies had to be specifically requested or read surreptitiously in the racks. Popular films or books that featured gay men and lesbians generally portrayed them as miserable, tormented human beings or showed their salvation at the hands of science, medicine, or their conversion to heterosexual love. Culturally speaking, gay men and lesbians in the postwar period might be portrayed as bright and beautiful but they were always fundamentally flawed. "From the beginning of the '50s, popular fiction increasingly reflected the hypocrisy of the times," the writer Michael Bronski asserts.[16]

The media images that included them simply reproduced the dominant stereotypes of the day. The Daughters were determined to present new, more accurate sources of information. Most of the early DOB activists enthusiastically read the 1953 Kinsey Report on women and discussed its importance for lesbians. But they believed that research by lesbians about their own lives would prove even more valuable. Within its first three years, DOB twice launched efforts to learn more about their members. Their first survey, printed on the back page of the premiere issue of their newsletter in 1956, resulted in only a handful of responses.

They then decided to conduct a "sociological survey" of their readership, and Jaffy guided their efforts. This was a big undertaking for the tiny group. The 1958 DOB Questionnaire not only marks the first time that a survey of lesbian life was done by lesbians themselves, it was one of a handful of data collection efforts focusing specifically on lesbians, especially "normal" ones—women not in mental hospitals, prisons, or under intensive psychiatric care.

Unknown to them at the time was the work decades earlier of a pioneering lesbian researcher, Mildred (Berry) Berryman. Berryman and her life partner, Ruth Uckerman, opened their Salt Lake City home to local lesbians and to many gay visitors to the area. "They were accepted in their community as eccentrics," said Uckerman's son-in-law Vern Bullough, a heterosexual scholar and one of the earliest homophile activists in Los Angeles. In an effort to counter the largely negative research findings then available on homosexuality, Berryman interviewed her lesbian and gay friends in the 1920s and 1930s. She began to write summaries of her case studies while working for the American Red Cross in 1940 but never completed the project; her partner Ruth preserved her notes. After her death in 1972, Bullough and his wife Bonnie Uckerman, Ruth's daughter, completed Berryman's research and in 1977 published it as "Lesbianism in the 1920's and 1930's: A Newfound Study." Berryman's work still provides valuable first-person information about pre–World War II lesbian friendship circles, particularly those found in smaller U.S. cities far from the coasts. It also hints at the importance some lesbians placed on compiling information about their lives to challenge the experts who studied them.[17]

The Daughters modestly announced their research results in *The Ladder* in 1959 under the headline "DOB Questionnaire Reveals Some Facts About Lesbians." In the Introduction, Jaffy noted that she and her "research team" mailed a four-page survey to all *Ladder* subscribers; they asked for current demographic information as well as personal and family history. "Of the more than 500 questionnaires sent out, 160 completed replies were received over the following 12 months, of which 157 were considered usable."

The results of the DOB Questionnaire, although "disappointingly small," were nonetheless revealing, both in terms of the questions the DOB activists asked of their readers and the responses they received. In her analysis of the data, Jaffy insisted that their intention had not been to test any particular hypothesis or theory of homosexuality. She went on to carefully qualify the results: "Even in the case of questions such as these, however, the smallness of the sample, and the absence of any 'control' group, would make it impossible to rigorously prove or disprove any particular proposition about Lesbians." Despite this, Jaffy knew the study was important. "We believe that a description of this group, however imperfect it may be, is not without interest . . . As will be seen, it is a quite different type of group from that usually studied by doctors and criminologists."[18]

Jaffy wrote up her summary of the more salient results for *The Ladder*, noting the higher-than-average levels of education, income, and professional occupations among the respondents. Their property and home ownership, as well as voter registration, also surpassed that of the general population of white women according to Census Bureau figures for 1957. Above all, Jaffy emphasized the relative stability of lesbian lives and loves.

After discarding the few male entries received, Jaffy described how she and her team tallied up the responses from women who were 98 percent white (they used the term "Caucasian") U.S. citizens who hailed from many parts of the country and world: the women reported having been born or raised in forty states and ten countries. Their ages ranged from nineteen to sixty-two, with a median age of thirty-two; nearly three-fourths of the respondents came from urban backgrounds. Despite their median age, which made many of them eligible for military service during World War II, only eighteen percent of the women had served in the armed forces and none of the respondents was currently enlisted.[19]

In one of the most striking findings, Jaffy reported that 82 percent of the women had completed four years of high school and almost half had finished four years of college. Over two-thirds of the Daughters had had some college education and 16 percent reported advanced degrees. Jaffy noted the "high educational level of our group" and that Census Bureau figures for 1957 reported "only 45% of white females over 25 for the U.S. as a whole had completed four years of high school, and only 6% four years of college." Further, she reported that income for the group was well above average. "The median monthly wage of those reporting specific income figures is $350, or $4200 annually. This compares with a 1957 median annual income for white income-earning females over 14, nation-wide, of only $1310." A variety of occupations were listed: professional, semi-professional, managerial and official, clerical, students, trades, sales, housewife, and "others." "The professional group is more numerous than any other (38% of the total; semi-professionals were 6.4%); while clerical workers are second with 33% of the total . . ." Again, Jaffy emphasized the higher numbers of Daughters in the "professional" category compared to the general population of employed white women. "In 1958 [Census Bureau data] professional and semiprofessional workers amounted to only 13% of white employed females, compared with 44% in our group." DOB leaders used "professional" as code in reporting the survey's results; a majority of the respondents actually reported being employed as teachers. Paul Gebhard, one of Kinsey's researchers, had advised Jaffy and other DOB leaders not to specify this fact because of the witchhunts against homosexual educators in the 1950s.[20]

Another area of difference was regarding military service. "While no member of the group is presently in the armed services, about 18% have at one time been a member," the DOB report noted. "Although we have no directly comparable figures for the female population in general, this appears to be a high proportion: in 1945, at the peak of military strength, only 1/2 of 1% of the total female population 21 years of age or over was on active duty in the military services. Since that time the percentage has dropped to a mere 0.06%."

Religious background revealed some interesting nonconformity. While half of the women answering the survey reported being Protestant, the next highest category of respondents—23 percent—said they had no religion or were agnostic. Catholicism was claimed by 19 percent, and 2 percent of the lesbians said they were Jewish.

Under "General Impressions," Jaffy drew the outline of a group of lesbians that complicated, but did not completely refute, many of the myths then prevalent about them. "One individual has been a prostitute; two are reformed users of narcotics; four report themselves as reformed alcoholics and one as presently so." Although the purpose of DOB's survey was to counter the prevailing notion of homosexuality as sickness, Jaffy felt compelled to report data that was not in accord with their goals: she added that eleven women had at one time been committed to mental hospitals, mostly for brief periods, and that nineteen of them had been arrested, "most commonly for drunkenness and traffic violations." But she highlighted the fact that "family history material shows some, but surprisingly little, of the disturbance usually thought to be associated with deviant personality development."[21]

Nearly one-fourth of the Daughters were currently married or had been previously. "Along the same line, while 100 persons count themselves as exclusive homosexuals, as many as 98 reported some heterosexual relationships. These 98 must, and do, include a number of persons rated as exclusive homosexuals." Jaffy admitted that the use of the word "relationship" in the survey had been "ambiguous," and she wondered if the replies received "overstate the number of relationships involving actual sexual intercourse."

Further, confronting common assumptions about lesbians and gay men as clannish and alcoholic, the DOB Questionnaire also asked respondents about friends and fellow workers ("the largest number— 50%—have friends about evenly balanced between homosexuals and heterosexuals"); frequency of drinking; and frequency of patronizing homosexual bars. The largest number of Daughters reported drinking "socially"—once or twice per month. In an interesting twist, Jaffy speculated that geographic locale might have more to do with heavy alcohol consumption than sexual orientation. "A geographical breakdown, not possible with our present data, might perhaps indicate that the heavy-drinking stereotype is more nearly approximated in some sections of the country." Jaffy didn't go on to say which sections those might be. But she asked, "[W]here homosexuals drink heavily, do they do so for social rather than psychological reasons?" She also reported that more than half of the 157 respondents said that they went to gay bars but that "the largest group of those who go at all attend once or twice a month . . . Here again a geographic breakdown would be interesting."[22]

Under "Sexual Life," Jaffy wrote, "[t]he vast majority of the group has had homosexual experience—there are only four (possibly five) exceptions," but did not provide more detail. She again admitted problems in the survey with using the word "experience," which "may be broad enough to mean to some people emotional relations with no physical contact, or varying degrees of contact." In trying to gather information about actual sexual practices and feelings rather than how each woman defined herself sexually, DOB's survey reflected both the methodology of the Kinsey researchers and the lack of a strong lesbian, bisexual, or transgender identity in the late 1950s. Further, foreshadowing later debates within lesbian feminism about whether "woman-loving women" who did not have sex with females could be considered lesbians, Jaffy reported that Daughters' experiences of same-sex "intimate physical contact" varied greatly.

A number of tables were included in this section, with information on age of first lesbian experience and age of first awareness of homosexual tendencies. There was considerable emphasis on lesbian relationships. "A large majority of the group (72%) is presently engaged in a homosexual relationship," she noted. The majority of relationships lasted from one to three years, except for women over thirty-five—most of them reported relationships of a decade or more. Jaffy concluded that "lasting homosexual relationships, though not universal in the group, are not only possible but by no means rare."[23]

The Questionnaire also tackled butch and femme identifications but did not explain their resilience. Under "Sex Role Varies," Jaffy reported that more than one-third of the Daughters "refused either label" when asked "Do you consider yourself predominantly feminine, masculine, or neither?" She downplayed the fact that another one-third of her respondents chose "masculine" and one-fourth selected "feminine," reflecting the recurring debates within DOB over the popularity of the gender-based roles for lesbians. Instead, presaging the privileging of androgyny that would erupt among lesbian feminists in the 1970s, she emphasized the "number of persons [who] indicated specifically that they recognized both 'masculine' and 'feminine' elements in themselves. It is probable that a large majority of persons, Lesbian and otherwise, have such a mixture of elements, but that awareness of this mixture, as well as the mixture itself, varies from person to person."[24]

Jaffy concluded the Questionnaire's findings by noting that Daughters' family backgrounds were "fairly conventional . . . 30% of respondents counted their adolescence as 'average' in happiness"—about the same as those who rated theirs "unhappy." She emphasized that "a large majority have not had, and do not want, psychotherapy" and admitted reluctantly that while DOB's survey showed that their members did not conform to popular assumptions about lesbians' heavy drinking and continuous attendance at gay bars, it did lend support to "the stereotyped 'butch' picture."[25]

Within the next year, Jaffy worked with Mattachine members in

San Francisco to compare the results of the DOB survey with one undertaken of their male members. Approximately one hundred Mattachine men participated; what was most surprising was not their findings but Jaffy's concluding statements.

While uncritically accepting the then prevalent belief that men were intrinsically and "constitutionally" more sexual than women, Jaffy explained that male homosexuals' lower economic and cultural status in society (and thus their greater "adjustment difficulties") was due to "a reverse reflection of the high prestige of masculinity in our culture." In other words, even without adopting "feminine" characteristics or labels, gay men's rejection of traditional male values and roles (as husband, father) brought with it lowered social status. At the same time, she asserted that when lesbians rejected the "traditional" role of women in society (as wife, mother), they were in some ways gaining privilege. "In a society that is male-oriented and where masculine values have higher prestige, the lot of any male who rejects these values in any way is difficult," she stated. "Lesbians, on the other hand, when they reject the traditional role of women, may be harmonizing their behavior not only with their own inclinations but also with the really dominant values of society."[26] By assuming that all lesbians "reject the traditional role of women"—which DOB's own Questionnaire data did not support—Jaffy unwittingly betrayed her own biases about femme lesbians and lesbian mothers. She also assumed that society would reward, rather than punish, unconventional women.

The research project's emphasis on proving lesbian normality drew some sharp retorts from DOB members. It added fuel to the debates over DOB's emphasis on integration, which some Daughters felt implied conformity and acceptance of the status quo, as exemplified by the following eloquent protest: "Every cover-to-cover reading of *The Ladder* leaves me with a nagging in my brain that all is not right with the endeavors of the DOB. Now, to my satisfaction, I have put the finger on the cause of my disquiet." The writer, "R.L., California," went on to offer another perspective. "I prefer to see the problem of the Lesbian as an aspect of the larger problem of society today: Conformity—the neglect of the individualistic impulse that alone leads to creativity and the ultimate enrichment of culture." She or he boldly proclaimed pride in oneself, experts be damned. "What at one time to most of us seemed a curse is perhaps a blessing to all. Perhaps instead of pleading, 'Please, world, accept us—we're really very nice and not a bit different,' we should say, 'Look, world, we understand the agony of losing what each of you finds best in yourself and we can help you to be unafraid of your uniqueness!'"[27]

This letter, printed in *The Ladder* in November 1960, is a perfect reflection of a time when being "unafraid of your uniqueness" was gaining popularity. In 1960, the virtue of nonconformity was slowly spreading beyond bohemian enclaves; it could be seen in such disparate cultural influences as the sudden rise in popularity of folk music or the razor-sharp humor of Dick Gregory. It inspired new ways of fighting for justice and peace—such as the sit-ins against Jim Crow laws organized by young black students of North Carolina A&T at Greensboro lunch counters that spread like wildfire throughout the South. A new generation of activists was determined to push beyond the boundaries set by both U.S. society and their parents' beliefs and traditions. As the youngest U.S. president in history, John F. Kennedy and his rhetorical New Frontier ideas generated fresh excitement and a growing belief in both personal and institutional change. The importance of individual conscience meant, for many Daughters, that each person would be valued for who she was, not how she fit in or what she owned. They believed that the new decade required goals of "creativity and the ultimate enrichment of culture" rather than the old pursuit of accommodation and acquiescence.

CHAPTER FOUR

A Look at the Lesbian

It could have been at a gathering like this one that Clara Brock learned how to play chess. Dubby was always having the girls over to her apartment, friends from DOB and other parts of her world. Draped over chairs and relaxing on the couch, they often played 45s, drank highballs, and munched chips. Cigarette smoke scented the air. Sometimes a couple would start dancing, soon joined by others. But Dubby's attention would have been on the chess pieces in front of her. She would have caressed the square tops of her set, reached over to rub the other set of rounded chess pieces, and noticed for the thousandth time how good they felt in her fingers.

Dubby thought their lessons were going well; Brock was a willing student and soon she'd be a worthy opponent. But that night, she was unsure of herself. As Brock tells the story, Dubby noticed that, after her first move, Brock hesitated. She then reached for her knight and moved it across the board. After Brock placed the piece in its new position, Dubby reached out, put her hand on the knight, and said, "I don't think you want to do that." Brock looked at her, took another look at the board, and admitted, "Yeah, you're right—I don't think I want to do that." Despite the coaching, Dubby won the game within fifteen minutes.

Outside, the San Francisco sky would have been striped pink, deep purple and darkening by the moment. One of the girls, yelling to make herself heard over six women singing, "I found my thri-ill," and six pairs of loafers stepping in unison across the wood floor to Fats Domino's "Blueberry Hill," called out, "Dubby, don't you think we should turn on some lights?" Dubby would have yelled back, "Oh yeah, I always forget that you people need them."[1]

Pat Walker—or "Dubby," as she was known to her DOB friends— was born on February 18, 1939, in Los Angeles. "When I was about eleven or twelve, my mother told me about gayness, about *The Well of Loneliness*," she remembered in a 1988 interview. "My mother had gay friends, and my sister is also gay. At fourteen I realized I liked girls—I never felt bad about myself because of it." Walker, who died in 1999, was a short black woman with close-cropped hair. "The thing everybody always commented on was that I stood breast-high to the world."[2]

Walker was partially blind from birth, and she lost her eyesight completely in her teens. "I went to the Oakland [California] Orientation Center for the Blind in 1958—I was nineteen. Somebody came from a class at San Francisco State to observe people at the Center, which was made up of blind or newly blinded people. She picked me out as gay. She started taking me to different things." Walker's new friendship with DOB activist Billye Talmadge introduced her to a circle of lesbians who became friends. "All the women were really nice—I was a new experience for them, and they were a new experience for me."

"It was the first place I felt warm and accepted," she remembered. "There were parties, picnics, getting together to work on the magazine . . . everyone would help. But there were also disagreements, about politics. That was stressful, to disagree with people you really cared about. It was like a family in that way."[3]

Walker was a small businesswoman in Berkeley—she ran the concession stand, selling cigarettes, candy, and gum, in the lobby of an office building downtown. She volunteered with San Francisco Suicide Prevention in addition to spending many nights on DOB projects. She had an active love life—in fact, at one point she was like a one-woman DOB recruiting machine, bringing at least two if not three of her girlfriends into the group (all at different times, mercifully). Friends and loved ones mattered most to her; she also was passionate about music.

Pat Walker became president of DOB's San Francisco chapter in 1960, when former chapter leader Jaye Bell was elected national president. "People suggested I run for office, and I didn't have the courage to say no. I didn't feel that I knew enough or had enough experience. It was a gesture." Del Martin remembers her as "a strong leader who had no trouble delegating authority."[4]

DOB groups included an assortment of women: working class and professional, young, middle-aged, older; a mix of racial, ethnic, religious backgrounds. Walker said in 1988, "I didn't think about being black that much, until it was brought up. I think that [my] being blind was more of an issue." She remembered that only one other black woman was involved then in San Francisco, Cleo (Glenn) Bonner. Bonner met Phyllis Lyon and Del Martin in 1960, when they were invited to speak to a small, select gathering of lesbians in Oakland and she was the only one who responded to their invitation to get involved in DOB. Bonner worked at Pacific Bell, the local telephone company, and was raising a son; she was in a committed relationship with a white woman. Bonner chose to use the pseudonym "Glenn" in her DOB work to protect herself and her family.[5]

As one of their first DOB assignments, "Cleo and Cush," as Bonner and her partner Helen Cushman were known, organized DOB's new Book and Record Service. It was a tedious job that demanded accuracy and commitment, and they shared the work for the next two years. Jeannette Howard Foster's *Sex Variant Women in Literature*—$5.00 and "autographed by the author"—was one of the first books offered through the new service when it was launched in May 1960. Other titles included *Odd Girl* and *The Third Sex,* by Artemis Smith (35 cents)—"two novels on Lesbian life, well-written and ending happily," and *Christ and the Homosexual* by Rev. Robert Wood, who DOB heralded as "the first American to tackle the subject of the homophile and the church openly and forthrightly." Rounding out their list was the *Complete Cumulative Checklist of Lesbian Literature,* compiled by Marion Zimmer Bradley ($1.50). Soon they would also offer Lisa Ben's 45 rpm recording of the "Gayest Songs on Wax" for $1.98.[6]

Orders began coming in from women throughout the country and around the world. The Daughters reasoned that the Book and Record Service would provide hard-to-find resources to their supporters as well as revenue for their treasury—they asked 10 or 20 cents per title for "handling"—as authors like Donald Webster Cory and the other homophile groups had shown was possible through their experiences managing book services in the 1950s. Many women in DOB's network in 1960 still had limited access to gay-themed information and entertainment, so DOB discreetly provided it for the next few years, courtesy of the U.S. mail.

Throughout the winter of 1959 and into the following spring, Lyon, Martin, Bonner, Walker, Brock, and the DOB's other San Francisco leaders were in a frenzy of activity and excitement. Another unprecedented experience was in the planning stages for women who lived in Northern California or were willing to travel to San Francisco for a short holiday: the DOB was planning a lesbian convention for the last weekend in May. They had arranged to rent the main meeting room of the Hotel Whitcomb, at 1231 Market Street, for Memorial Day weekend, and they spent months planning every detail. DOB's first convention, titled "A Look at the Lesbian" and advertised as an opportunity to enjoy both the scheduled program and San Francisco's much-vaunted scenic and social pleasures, was historic and they knew it. The Daughters were well aware that this was the first large public gathering of lesbians in America, and they worked hard to see that it would be successful, but the response they received far exceeded their hopes.

The press releases they sent out to local radio and print media definitely helped. In the March issue of *The Ladder*, the Daughters announced that they had received typically irreverent notice from the popular local columnist Herb Caen in the *San Francisco Chronicle* when he wrote: "Russ Wolden, if nobody else, will be interested to learn that the Daughters of Bilitis will hold their nat'l convention here May 27–30. They're the female counterparts of the Mattachine Society—and one of the convention highlights will be an address by Atty. Morris Lowenthal titled 'The Gay Bar in the Courts.' Oh brother. I mean sister. Come to think of it, I don't know what I mean." The next month, in an unsigned article headlined "DOB Convention Highlights," the Daughters admitted, "It may seem that we're bugging you about DOB's first national convention—and we are. We believe you will be missing a great deal if you pass up this gathering—the first we know of to concentrate on the Lesbian and her problems."[7]

Finally, after months of planning and promotion, the conference weekend arrived. Two hundred women had registered to attend, many of them consciously using a conference focusing on "the Lesbian and her problems" to take a significant step toward openly embracing a new identity and rejecting the stigma of deviance. The gathering at the Hotel Whitcomb did not disappoint the planners:

it turned out to be a challenging mix of socializing and sermo-
nizing. It also started a tradition of biennial lesbian conventions,
organized by DOB and open to the public, which continued for the
next decade.

A registration fee of $12.50 included a Friday night cocktail party
at Martin and Lyon's home, panels of speakers, a luncheon, and a
cocktail reception and banquet on Saturday at the hotel. On Sunday
there was a business meeting during the day and a Dutch-treat dinner
for members and guests ("women only") at Charlotte Coleman's gay
bar, The Front.

"Probably the casual on-looker would not have known just what
sort of convention this was. We don't mind," wrote Helen Sandoz.
She and Stella Rush came up from Los Angeles for the event; Sandoz
had the job of preparing an account for the next issue of *The Ladder*.
The excitement of so many women together in one place was conta-
gious, and the jam-packed party at Del and Phyllis's home on Friday
night went on until the early hours of the next morning. Despite
their lack of sleep, DOB organizers got to the hotel early on Saturday
to check on arrangements and greet their guests—including some
they hadn't expected.

"The cops were the Homosexual Detail—Rudy Nieto and Dick
Castro—and they showed up just as lunch was going to start," Phyllis
Lyon remembers. The police had come to investigate whether there
were women wearing men's clothes. They encountered Del Martin at
the door and asked her about the nature of the event; she suggested
they take a good look at the attendees. Every woman there was
dressed in her best dress or skirt and blouse, stockings, and heels. In
an attempt to defuse any possible problems, Martin invited the
policemen to step into the meeting room "and see for themselves if
anything out of the ordinary was going on." They looked inside but
said nothing more. Martin even offered to speak with them by

telephone later that evening. After they left, she thought to herself, "I just gave the police my home phone number. Now why on earth did I do that?" The officers attended the Saturday afternoon debate on gay bars but didn't contact her or return to the convention site after that—at least not in uniform.[8]

While the Daughters were prepared to do their best to minimize disruptions throughout the weekend, they were unable to control the audience reaction to some of their invited speakers. "Saturday was a day to remember. We started out with the usual panel . . . the pat on the head . . . the understanding . . . the backup by professionals," Sandoz reported. "Then lunchtime came. An Episcopal minister served up our dessert with damnation." Stella Rush remembers first the stunned silence, then the feeling of growing rage in the audience as their luncheon speaker, the Rev. Fordyce Eastburn, blithely noted the doomed spiritual condition of homosexuals. Despite their anger, however, the crowd remained polite and bit their tongues.[9]

In *Lesbian/Woman*, Del Martin and Phyllis Lyon wrote about their choice of Rev. Eastburn as the luncheon speaker for their first conference. "[T]he church was at the core of all our problems, and there had to be some way, somehow to reach the church. We were determined to have an official representative from some particular denomination."[10] They got the official representative of the California Episcopal Diocese, who gave gays who wanted to be accepted by the church two choices: change or be celibate. "We look at it this way: we've opened a door to communication with the church. And that's what we were looking for," Martin remembered. Other Daughters seated in the audience during Eastburn's tirade, such as Rush, emphasized his impact on participants. "It was awful—once more we were being told we were sinners." She remembered, "the men and women activists held up well, for they had come to accept themselves. But a gay boy I knew in L.A., who had no ties or experience in ONE, Inc., or the Mattachine and had come at my invitation, was harmed rather than helped. I lost his friendship over it."[11]

Sandoz noted that, after Eastburn, "we managed to recover during a pleasant interlude with an ACLU speaker" but it didn't last long. A heated exchange between two opposing lawyers in a recent gay bar case not only sent shockwaves through DOB's convention but made headlines in the San Francisco papers. "The speakers were admirable in their vehemence. The audience rumbled but had the good sense not to erupt. What could have been violent was constructive," she wrote in *The Ladder*.[12] Morris Lowenthal, who represented gay bar owners in a number of cases, and Sidney Feinberg, a lawyer with the state's Department of Alcoholic Beverage Control, had faced each other in court over the right of gay people to congregate in bars and nightclubs; Feinberg defended the state's statute that banned such places as "resorts for sex perverts."

Rush emphasizes that "the only thing that saved part of the audience from erupting into a riot and taking the rest of us with them, were Del Martin's uncommon leadership abilities and her appealing to our highest state of mind—pouring oil on troubled waters, as it were."[13] The Daughters saw the gay bar issue as paramount. While they had organized DOB as an alternative to the bars, they continued to patronize them and believed they had a basic right to socialize wherever they chose. In DOB's early days, its members spent a considerable amount of time advising women of their legal rights in case of arrest and finding lawyers for victims of police raids. They had also supplied evidence in an important Bay Area lawsuit. "*The Ladder* had the distinction of having its September and October 1958 issues filed with the District Court of Appeals along with an *amicus curiae* brief by Lowenthal and Associates in the case of an Oakland Lesbian bar called Mary's First and Last Chance," Martin and Lyon noted in

1972.[14] Although Lowenthal's brief asserted a dichotomy between the members of DOB and the lesbians who patronized bars, many Daughters were regular customers of the numerous nightspots catering to gay men and lesbians in the San Francisco area. DOB's program for their first convention included not just a debate on the "gay bar question" but a gay bar tour for out-of-town visitors, complete with map and annotated comments provided by local Daughters.[15]

For a lesbian conference, the day's program had featured a mostly male roster of speakers; there also were several men among the attendees, including the undercover CIA agent David Rhodes. "We had a hell of a time finding women to be on the panel," Phyllis Lyon remembers. "Most of the ones we contacted were afraid people would think they were Lesbians. That is why my sister was on the opening panel. The men weren't afraid of being thought a Lesbian!" For the most part, however, men's active participation in the Daughters' first national gathering was not commented on—until Saturday night's banquet. With a sly wink at the sometimes contentious interactions between gay men and lesbians, the Daughters used their centerpiece event to publicly name their favorite "S.O.B.s."[16]

Surprised San Franciscans Kenneth Zwerin, DOB's attorney; photographer Jeff Wiener; and local Mattachine activists Hal Call, Don Lucas, and Steve Kellogg were each called to the podium and presented with a "Sons of Bilitis" award. The Daughters also applauded "S.O.B.s" Art Maule from New York Mattachine and Carl Harding of Denver Mattachine; ONE, Inc., activists Dorr Legg, Don Slater, and Jim Kepner; and Jack Fox, "Compleat Carpenter," from Los Angeles. Their celebration of their male allies—which became a regular feature of DOB's national conventions—showed that, despite many Daughters' struggles against male domination, they appreciated the support they had received from many men since DOB's founding.[17]

By Sunday night, the feelings of euphoria overwhelmed their exhaustion. "Those of us who attended will never forget the excitement, the living proof of our worth. It was a timely shot in the arm when so much is adverse in so many areas," Helen Sandoz ended her *Ladder* report. She put another spin on the convention theme of "A Look at the Lesbian" by astutely naming the many people who were there to observe them, whether they had been invited to attend or not. "Thank you, DOB; ABC [State of California Department of Alcoholic Beverage Control]; Vice Squad, professional folk . . . thank you all for letting us see you and letting you see us."[18]

That summer of 1960, the high-energy days and nights of pre-convention planning were followed by weeks of feverish post-convention production of *The Ladder*, complete with detailed coverage of the speeches and debates. There also was a change in *Ladder* leadership: Phyllis Lyon announced that she would step down as editor. "I believe that four years of a one-woman editorship is enough. New ideas and a fresh slant on the problems involved are necessary if THE LADDER is to continue to be what we wish it to be," she wrote in "Au Revoir" in the June 1960 issue. However, she was full of praise for her successor. "Not only does she have a journalistic background, but also a DOB background as one of the founding members of this group. But more importantly, she has the unqualified enthusiasm needed for a job which more often than not devolves into the sheer drudgery of proofreading, typing stencils, etc., rather than just sitting at a desk and 'editing.' . . . Your new editor is a woman with the combined attributes of creativeness, business sense, warmth of feeling toward human problems and frailties, humor and just all-round competence—Del Martin."[19]

An obvious attribute Lyon neglected to add in describing her colleague and lover was "unafraid of controversy." One of the first things Martin did when she became editor of *The Ladder* was to take on one of the most popular lesbian authors, "Ann Aldrich." She printed two critical reviews of *Carol in a Thousand Cities*, the most recent best-selling paperback "tell-all" of lesbian life written by Marijane Meaker using her Ann Aldrich pseudonym. Meaker explained recently that she was inspired to begin writing her Aldrich series in the mid-1950s by Donald Webster Cory. "His book was mostly about the men. I wanted to do the same thing for the women." Meaker had already made a splash with her 1951 novel *Spring Fire*, published under the pseudonym Vin Packer.

A talented writer, she was in the right place at the right time: in the early 1950s, Meaker began working as a reader at Fawcett Publishing in New York, which had just started a new division for paperback originals. She became close friends and drinking buddies with a Fawcett editor, Dick Carroll, who one night encouraged her to write a novel for the new division. When she said she wanted to tell a story about a lesbian love affair at a boarding school, "he said it was a very interesting idea but that I had to put the story in a college setting, to make it more appealing. . . . I called it 'Sorority Girls.' Dick didn't think it would sell with a title like that so he changed it to 'Spring Fire.' Well, 'Spring Fire' came out and it sold like crazy."[20]

It was one of the first paperback originals with overtly lesbian content and, despite its unhappy ending, was hugely popular with gay women. Meaker remembers, "[A]t that time, the postal regulations governed the content of paperback originals—they were shipped via the post office, all in one big box; one of them could cause the whole shipment to be refused and returned. So you couldn't have anything that might be labeled obscene—which meant that the lesbian stories couldn't have a happy ending; we had to make sure to have a girl going crazy or realize she wasn't really gay. But by 1954 or 1955, the regulations had begun to relax and we could have happy endings." She created Ann Aldrich—an "all-American" author—and in 1957 published *We Walk Alone* as a groundbreaking personal narrative of lesbian life. "It too sold like crazy. Again, I received cartons of mail, including one letter from Ann Holmquist of Bala Cynwyd, Pennsylvania. She was married, with a couple of kids. She wanted to know how to write about her fantasies of lesbian love." Ann Holmquist would soon begin publishing lesbian paperbacks under the pseudonym Ann Bannon.[21]

Despite her popularity, however, to many DOB members Aldrich's largely negative portraits of lesbians were difficult to accept, as they contradicted the Daughters' quest for self-esteem and positive representations. In April 1958, *The Ladder* featured an "Open Letter to Ann Aldrich" written by Del Martin. In it, she criticized *We Walk Alone* and Aldrich's second book, *We Too Must Love,* and accused Aldrich of perpetuating stereotypes. "You have glossed over that segment of the Lesbian population which we consider to be the 'majority' of this minority group. We refer to those who have made an adjustment to self and society and who are leading constructive, useful lives in the community in which they live." DOB then gave Aldrich a free year's subscription to *The Ladder*.

Perhaps in retaliation, her next book, *Carol in a Thousand Cities,* savagely attacked DOB. Aldrich went after the content and appearance of *The Ladder* in 1958, dismissing it as amateurish and taking the magazine apart, "Rung by Rung." As Meaker commented in 2005, "I hated their fiction—I tracked it for a year. I hated their presentation of us. I hated the way they acted like we hated men, I hated their butch-femme stuff, I did not like their ignorance . . . but I did like one cover. It was a Christmas issue and showed a drawing of a tree. Under the tree were two presents: one was neatly wrapped, the other was a mess. I thought that was a cute way of showing butch and femme." She added, "I used to fight with Lorraine Hansberry about them and *The Ladder* . . . she said she understood my criticisms but appreciated what they were trying to do."[22]

In 1960, in her *Ladder* review of Aldrich's *Carol in a Thousand Cities*, Barbara Grier (as Gene Damon) wrote, "With her witty knife ever in hand, she slashes to ribbons every story without exception that appeared in THE LADDER during the year 1958 (including two written by this reviewer). In sum total the book is about half for and half against Lesbianism. One wonders how Miss Aldrich feels way up there judging and defiling her people."[23]

Jeannette Howard Foster went even further. She wryly noted in her withering *Ladder* article on Aldrich's work, "Ann of 10,000 Words Plus," "Miss Aldrich doesn't admit to writing fiction herself. Even if her three volumes on gay life in NYC read a good deal like it, they are sufficiently literal reportage to have got her boycotted by several gay bars in that city—the patrons don't care to be used as copy." Taking aim at Aldrich's popularity and productivity, Foster dismissed her by charging, "[W]hat these reveal is superlative early training in Writing to Sell, and something like diarrhea of the pen." Foster wondered whether Aldrich had undergone "self-analysis" and quit being "emotionally arrested," (i.e., was cured of lesbianism) and counseled sarcastically, "[F]or my money someone's not sure just who she is. People Who Live in Glass Houses Should Undress in the Dark."[24]

Ultimately, Aldrich's negative comments actually helped DOB. She fostered knowledge about the organization and its magazine in the very audience DOB was trying to reach: lesbian or questioning women who were buying books about gay people. By October 1960 Martin printed a letter thanking Aldrich: "Your slap at THE LADDER has boomeranged! Aside from the mail you yourself have received and graciously forwarded, letters and subscriptions have been pouring into the DOB office. One letter addressed simply to "Daughters of Bilitis, San Francisco, California" reached us. Another queried the San Francisco Chamber of Commerce for our address."[25]

Delighted by the publicity her book had generated, the Daughters nonetheless continued to pursue a strategy of positive representation and felt that "kiss and tell" writers like Aldrich did more harm than good. They determined that *The Ladder* would be the one source where women (and men) could find portrayals of lesbians that showed them as normal human beings who had families, jobs, went to school, fell in love, suffered heartbreaks, and survived. They wanted to provide an antidote to the humiliation and harassment that was increasing throughout the country as gay visibility was building.

In 1961, the largest gay bar raid in San Francisco history resulted in nearly 100 people arrested, 14 of them women, further fueling debates in DOB about conformity. "One municipal judge called the city a 'Parisian pansy's paradise' and threatened stiff penalties for any homosexuals brought before him."[26] Soon after the raid, owners of the City's gay bars formed the Tavern Guild and vowed to fight back. DOB welcomed the new group into the homophile fold.

Although bars were still the main public venues in which gay men and lesbians congregated, it was becoming increasingly dangerous to go out for a drink with friends. Police raids were trapping women in cities like Chicago as well as San Francisco. "On February 17, [1961] shortly before midnight, the police arrested some 52 people, herded them off to a Chicago jail, and charged them with presence in a disorderly house. . . . At the station those women wearing 'fly fronts,' regardless of whether they wore lipstick, long hair, or earrings, were made partially to undress in order to determine whether they wore jockey shorts," wrote "Del Shearer" to *The Ladder* in March 1961. "Though I do not wish to go into the details of their fifteen-hour detention period, I will say that the conditions of the lockup itself, as well as their treatment, violated more than a few Illinois laws. . . . If we ever hope to win our battle, we must fight. First, we must unshackle ourselves from fear, for it alone is our omni-present enemy . . ."27

Despite the fact that Illinois was the first state in the U.S. to reform its penal code, removing old statutes on sex offenses in 1961, homophile activism was slow to take hold in the Windy City. A Mattachine group had been started in the mid-1950s, fell apart when its membership dropped off, and was revived in the early 1960s. Del Shearer began to organize DOB's Chicago chapter in late 1961. Close cooperation with other local homophile activists—such as the pioneering civil rights attorney Pearl Hart—were a hallmark of the group, as was its conscious outreach to black communities and news-papers. Early Chicago DOB members included the noted lesbian poet and paperback novel writer Valerie Taylor ("Velma Tate"), a fre-quent contributor to *The Ladder*.28

Unlike "Ann Aldrich," Taylor was one of the few lesbian paper-back writers who was also an early homophile activist and DOB member. Born Velma Nacella Young in Aurora, Illinois, in 1913, Taylor developed scoliosis in her youth that led to lifelong disability; it also gave her a sense of herself as unattractive and instilled in her an early appreciation for the underdog. As a child growing up on a struggling farm in rural Illinois, reading and writing poetry became her lifeline. Taylor continued to write at Blackburn College in Illi-nois in the mid-1930s and during her marriage, in 1939, to William Tate. Her first poem—a prayer—was published in 1935; in 1946, when her children were young, she resumed writing, and published as "Nacella Young."

In the 1950s, Taylor's poetry appeared in the *Ladies' Home Journal, Good Housekeeping,* and the *New York Herald-Tribune.* The sale of her first novel, *Hired Girl,* for $500 in 1952 enabled her to divorce her increasingly abusive husband. She also began writing for the original paperback novel market. When Jeannette Howard

Foster's pioneering bibliography on lesbians was published in 1956, Taylor contacted her and the two women started a life-long friendship. She learned about *The Ladder* from Foster and published poems, essays, and short stories in it from 1961 to 1965.[29]

Between 1957 and 1964, Taylor published seven lesbian novels: *Whisper Their Love, The Girls in 3-B, Stranger on Lesbos, Return to Lesbos, Unlike Others, A World Without Men,* and *Journey to Fulfillment.* "Along with Ann Bannon, Taylor was one of the most popular authors writing about lesbian lives for mass market paperback publications," according to the artist and author Tee Corinne, her literary executor. Taylor created complicated lesbian characters. One is Erika Frohmann, a young Jewish survivor of a Nazi concentration camp. In *Journey to Fulfillment* she is relocated to an unnamed Midwestern town in the United States and amazingly finds herself in the middle of a lusty, barely submerged teenage Isle of Lesbos—almost all the perky young female coeds in the middle-class suburb she now calls home are bedding each other. Readers explore postwar American society, as well as the passion Erika felt for her new friend Judy, right along with her as Erika discovered these strange new worlds. Taylor's talent for telling a scintillating lesbian love story made her a paperback success; she used her success to popularize her expansive, and progressive, worldview.[30]

Inexpensive paperback novels were one of the primary cultural arenas for the expression of a 1950s "fixation" on homosexuality in the United States.[31] Starting in the late 1930s, government-issued Armed Forces Editions offered a broad range of literature—one example is Pearl S. Buck's *The Good Earth*—and were designed to fit into the pockets of uniforms. Their sales skyrocketed in the decade after the war, in part due to the popularity of fiction with lesbian content. Although the paperbacks presented cover images of lesbians that were contrived and almost comically inaccurate for most "real" lesbians, their value was in their display and discussion of female-to-female sexuality. For the first time, inexpensive information about lesbianism was widely available to men and women of all orientations.[32]

A man looking for cheap thrills, or a young woman wondering about her "feelings" for a female friend, could find in "the pocket books" a world of forbidden romance, a subterranean world full of pleasure and danger. Young women and men seeking to enter gay life could find virtual maps and descriptions of the cities, and neighborhoods, where it could be found. For some women, such as Ann Holmquist Weldy ("Ann Bannon"), Marion Zimmer Bradley ("Miriam Gardner"), Patricia Highsmith ("Claire Morgan"), Marijane Meaker, Artemis Smith, and Valerie Taylor, the lesbian novels were also their livelihood. All the above writers' works, and many others, were avidly reviewed and promoted by the Daughters through *The Ladder*. They were not only fun to read; they were one of the few places to find passionate lesbian sex and attractive lesbian characters, regardless of whether the stories were wildly exaggerated or comfortably recognizable.

But despite the increased visibility of lesbians through the paperback novels, DOB's leaders pursued their goal of social acceptability as the route to integration. In the fall of 1961, on DOB's sixth anniversary, President Jaye Bell again pleaded the case for the Daughters' strategy: "Perhaps some may feel we are advocating conformity," she stated. "We are, when it comes to common courtesy to those who are yet so uneducated that homosexuals strike as much fear in them as do child molesters, dope addicts, the mentally ill, etc." She argued for pragmatism. "This is outward conformity, the same outward conformity demanded of numerous groups of people who are in positions foreign to the public at large. For instance, the ex-convict, the alcoholic, or the conscientious objector . . . To do other than conform outwardly would hurt them personally and be of no avail until the public is better informed." Bell proudly reported in *The Ladder* on the many responses to DOB's research efforts from professionals. She described Dr. Ralph H. Gundlach, a New York psychologist, and encouraged DOB members' cooperation with Gundlach's new project, "a study on the Lesbians not under therapy." She noted that DOB was helping design the questionnaire Gundlach could use.[33]

As if to underscore the increasing public relations work facing the organization as it entered its seventh year, *The Ladder* reported on a radio program, "How Normal Are Lesbians?" featuring DOB's Research Director, Florence Jaffy. The program was significant because it was one of the first radio talk shows to rely on a lesbian rather than a medical professional or other authority figure to discuss female same-sex desire. It was part of the WEVD "University of the Air" series directed by "Mrs. Lee Steiner, psychologist and marriage counselor," a friend to the homophile movement in New York. Jaffy joined Steiner and "Mrs. Elsie Carlton, housewife," on the show and discussed the findings of the Daughters' 1959 research into members' backgrounds and lives.[34] She utilized the opportunity to speak honestly about lesbians' experiences. The planning and analysis she had done with the DOB questionnaire helped her make the reality of their lives more visible to the public.

To the world at large, DOB actively promoted a view of the lesbian as average, wholesome, and nonthreatening; she also was a member of a minority group persecuted as a result of ignorance and intolerance despite her desire for acceptance by society. However, personal connection was still one of the most significant benefits DOB provided its members six years after it started. Nearly all of the women who would be the mainstays of DOB leadership and innovation in the 1960s—Phyllis Lyon and Del Martin, Stella Rush and

Helen Sandoz, and Barbara Gittings and Kay Lahusen—met or worked together in DOB and shaped its growth as they nurtured their own relationships. Lyon and Martin were founders of the Daughters of Bilitis in San Francisco in 1955, two years after they became a couple; Rush and Sandoz met through DOB in 1957 and the following year started the Los Angeles chapter, which they guided for the next decade. Gittings—the first organizer of lesbians on the East Coast—and Lahusen met at a DOB party in Rhode Island, fell in love, helped lead the New York chapter for nearly a decade, and created a life devoted to the gay cause.

Kay Lahusen first contacted DOB in 1961. She began by attending meetings, then planned programs and helped with the chapter's newsletter; when she began getting credits in *The Ladder* in 1963, she picked "Tobin" out of the phonebook to use as her DOB name. Besides, she insists, "Lahusen is too hard to pronounce!"

Lahusen was born on January 5, 1930, and raised in Cincinnati, Ohio, by her grandparents. She is a small, delicately-featured white woman who came to terms with her love for another young woman as a teenager. "I decided that I was right and the world was wrong and that there couldn't be anything wrong with this kind of love." After the devastating breakup of a college love affair, she moved to Boston to work for the *Christian Science Monitor* in the reference library, where "they filed homosexuality under *Vice.*" In 1961, Lahusen contacted Richard Robertiello, a New York psychiatrist, after reading his book *Voyage to Lesbos: The Psychoanalysis of a Female Homosexual.* It was a smart move on her part. She wanted to learn about where to find other lesbians; he told her about the Daughters of Bilitis and gave her a copy of *The Ladder.* "So I wrote to DOB and who got my letter but Barbara." They met that same year and quickly became lovers. Soon they radically transformed DOB's organizing and public relations strategies, ushering in a new era of visible homophile activism.[35]

CHAPTER FIVE

Removing the Mask

She was no longer certain who she was or what she might hope to become, but she certainly didn't intend to spend the rest of her life pretending to be Mrs. William Ollenfeld, that smug little housewife. She didn't even like the way the woman did her hair.

She ran a wet comb through the lacquered curls, smacked down the resulting fuzz with a brush dipped in Bill's hair stuff, and caught the subdued ends in a barrette. The plain styling brought out the oval shape of her face and the winged eyebrows, her only beauty . . . Now she was beginning to look like herself again.

She ran downstairs, relishing the freedom of bare legs and old shapeless loafers.

Valerie Taylor, *Return to Lesbos,* 1963[1]

By the summer of 1962, the Daughters had attracted the attention of increasing numbers of researchers. Psychologists and sociologists from around the country were discovering the wealth of material to be gained in interviewing and analyzing the women who were its

77

members. When DOB's second national convention took place in Hollywood that year, the program included two reports from sociologists who were researching lesbian life, including one on lesbian couples by a married heterosexual woman. Stella Rush remembers the woman researcher's active involvement in local chapter gatherings. "She came to everything, really got involved." By the time of her presentation at the Hollywood Inn to the hundred women and men gathered to hear her report, however, it was clear that her interest in the organization was more than academic. While reading DOB materials, attending meetings and parties, and interviewing some of the Daughters in the Los Angeles area, Rush remembers, she "fell in love with one of our members and left her husband!"[2]

In addition to the drama of lesbian love affairs, planning for the convention was plagued by another controversy. It started with a feud between the San Francisco and Los Angeles groups. LA DOB president Jean Nathan was furious when Del Martin stepped on local toes and independently extended an invitation to Thane Walker, founder and spiritual leader of the Prosperos Society, based in Southern California, to be their banquet speaker. Stella Rush and Helen Sandoz heard all about it directly from Jean. "She was steamed," Stella remembers. "She didn't appreciate the interference from San Francisco." They knew they had to try to keep the peace and not let emotions get too out of hand; they had to convince Jean that if Del thought enough of the man to ask him to address their meeting, he must have something worthwhile to say. "We told Del she might have to call him and withdraw the invitation." But before they did that, Rush and Sandoz located the headquarters of Walker's group in Culver City. One spring Saturday in 1962, they drove over to hear him speak. Rush and Sandoz were immediately enthralled by what they heard. "It was Thane's sex lecture that got us to join."[3]

Named after the magician in Shakespeare's *The Tempest*, the Prosperos Society was founded in 1956 in Florida by Walker, a handsome, charismatic man who claimed to have studied with the Russian spiritualist Gurdjieff. Walker was based in Hawaii but taught classes in Southern California as well. The Prosperos Society, still active in 2006, is an ontological group who believe in the healing power of intellect and consciousness; the group attracted some of the California women and men who were leaders in the homophile movement in the 1950s and 1960s. Its leader was by all accounts charming, witty, and extremely accepting of gay men and lesbians. "He'd send these beautiful women to our meetings, to get us to join—he knew what he was doing," Rush explained. "He pursued us." Walker drew freely from many religious and spiritual teachings— "I've milked many cows but the butter's my own" was the way he put it. He taught that the spiritual identity of everyone ("beingness") is both male and female, and he believed that God, "as male and female beingness," was present in each person. The Prosperos experience takes place in lectures, classes in "Translation" and "Releasing the Hidden Splendor," and intensive individual sessions. The central relationship is that between teacher and student within a community of believers.[4]

DOB leaders Billye Talmadge, Pat Walker, Stella Rush, and Helen Sandoz, as well as Del Martin and Phyllis Lyon, joined Prosperos in the early 1960s; other homophile leaders like Hal Call had joined even earlier. Walker's luncheon keynote speech at the 1962 DOB convention introduced his philosophies to many of the Daughters who had not yet experienced them. However, some of DOB's East Coast sisters—like Barbara Gittings and Kay Lahusen—were not impressed. "We couldn't get over all these lesbians flocking to listen to this man," Lahusen said in a recent conversation. "He didn't move us at all."[5]

Despite the disputes over Walker, DOB's second national convention opened as planned on Saturday morning, June 23. Jean Nathan proudly welcomed the attendees; Jaye Bell, DOB's national president, followed Nathan at the lectern on opening day. Bell used her remarks to emphasize again DOB's belief in integration: she insisted that society had nothing to fear from homosexuals and pointed out that the vice squad and homosexual details of police departments in the big cities, even though they regularly engaged in "peephole and entrapment" activity, rarely came up with charges other than solicitation and vagrancy. "The Bill of Rights in this country applies to the homosexual as well," Bell pointed out. She cited this as one of the reasons for organizations such as DOB to exist: to advocate for "the cause" on behalf of those who couldn't afford to fight for their rights.[6]

Religion continued to be an important topic for the Daughters and their guests. In addition to Walker's luncheon speech, a star attraction at the Convention was Saturday morning's panel on "Religion and Mental Health," moderated by the pioneering homophile psychologist and researcher Dr. Evelyn Hooker. They also discussed legislation. Given the slow but positive revisions to laws against homosexuality taking place in a number of states, such as Illinois, there was a session on the American Law Institute's Model Penal Code and on the advocacy campaigns under way to encourage state legislatures to adopt it.

Going beyond religion and law, however, the Daughters for the first time focused specifically on media representations of lesbians. A panel with the writer Jess Stearn (author of nonfiction accounts of gay life *The Sixth Man,* on male homosexuals, and *The Grapevine,* about lesbians) took on the timely question of "Is the Lesbian Being Portrayed Realistically by the Mass Media?" The answer, predictably, was "NO!" In fact, the most significant result of the DOB's 1962 National Convention in Los Angeles was that it provided them with an exceptional public relations opportunity: a Daughter was featured in the first nationwide broadcast of a television show that included a woman who identified herself as a lesbian.[7]

Paul Coates interviewed "Terry," president-elect of the L.A. chapter, as part of his syndicated show *Confidential File,* a tabloid-style television series known for its exploration and exploitation of titillating topics. As Stella Rush reported in the July 1962 issue of *The Ladder,* "Coates seemed intrigued that such a group [as DOB] would dare to put on a convention. 'Aren't you inviting disturbance?' he asked and seemed surprised that the organization was receiving official recognition from law enforcement officers and professional people."

Rush went on to note that DOB's representative, the pseudonymous Terry, had "described herself as a 38-year-old college graduate who is presently running a poodle grooming parlor." Rush reported that "Terry," being self-employed, could appear on the program both because she believed in the organization and "because I'm the least vulnerable." She gave background on the Daughters, their convention, and recent controversies over the legality of lesbian and gay bars. Terry estimated DOB's current membership to be between 125 and 150. "Coates asked if she hadn't meant to add the word 'thousand,'" Rush noted, and went on to emphasize that Terry had been introduced to "some twelve million viewers."[8]

This was a first not just for Terry but for the Daughters of Bilitis as well. The publicity the nationally televised interview created meant that the Daughters started receiving even more mail from women eager to find someone who might understand what it was to be a lesbian. For example, from *The Ladder,* November 1962:

Thank you a thousand times over for your publication! How elated I am to know that such a magazine exists. I can't begin to tell you how lonely it is walking alone . . . I have an intense longing to communicate with other persons like myself, who live on the outside.

L.L., California[9]

By the next year, many new women joined DOB and some who had been active assumed different roles in the organization. An important change in leadership took place in New York in 1963. That spring, Barbara Gittings edited her first issue of *The Ladder.* She had been asked by DOB national officers in 1962 to take over the editorship of *The Ladder* from Del Martin "temporarily." She agreed, reluctantly. But she took the job as a way to continue working in the organization, having spent five years "worrying about who was bringing what to the covered dish supper," as her partner Kay Lahusen put it: organizing local parties, attending meetings, and printing the chapter's newsletter. She was ready to take on national responsibilities.[10]

Besides, DOB's New York chapter was in strong hands: Shirley Willer became president in 1963. Born on September 26, 1922, Willer joined the Daughters in 1962. A large white woman from Chicago who dressed in men's clothes whenever she could ("they are cheap and fit better"), it was in nursing school that she became aware that her desires for other women meant she was a lesbian.

"When I finished reading *The Well* [*of Loneliness*], I started looking up words in the dictionary and the encyclopedia. I didn't find very pleasant descriptions." Willer moved to California during World War II but returned to Chicago when the postwar recession eliminated her job and made finding a new one difficult. In Chicago, she met other gay women, including Pearl Hart. Willer and a few friends talked about starting an organization for lesbians, but Hart's discouragement—"it's too dangerous"—dissuaded them. When she learned about DOB in the early 1960s, Willer headed to New York and wrote to the chapter there. Marion Glass answered her letter, and the two became lovers and colleagues. In 1963, they willingly took up the challenges of leading DOB's only chapter on the East Coast, delighted that Barbara Gittings, the cofounder, would now be editing *The Ladder.*

Willer brought more than experience to her leadership of DOB. She had a wealthy friend, an "angel" who wanted to secretly finance DOB's operations and improve its public image. Over the next five years, "Pennsylvania," as she was nicknamed by Martin and Lyon, contributed approximately $100,000 to the DOB in checks of $3,000, written to a different Daughter each time. The named recipient would sign the check over to the organization. Lyon remembers meeting their major donor once. "She came through San Francisco and we met her for drinks. She was so nervous when we started talking about lesbians . . . up until then, she had been very poised and sophisticated, but when we started talking about lesbians she couldn't even look at us. She started blushing and fidgeting." The daughter of a prominent East Coast family, who also supported organizations like Planned Parenthood, the woman donor never allowed her name to be recorded nor her contributions to DOB acknowledged. The regular donations she gave DOB, however, provided the necessary means to put their new emphasis on visibility and publicity into action.[11]

In addition to presenting reports, fiction and poetry, nonfiction essays, and, increasingly, international news, *The Ladder* also began to promote a new DOB project, one which represented a fairly bold step for a lesbian organization. They established a national Daughters of Bilitis scholarship program for women in honor of Dr. Blanche M. Baker, a San Francisco psychiatrist and friend of the homophile movement. After "Doc" died in 1960, Del Martin and Billye Talmadge planned a way for the Daughters to keep her spirit and her belief in education alive, then proposed it to DOB leaders. They suggested scholarships named for the well-schooled, witty San Francisco woman who was one of the first professionals to publicly advocate the mental health of gay men and lesbians. At the business meeting held during the 1962 convention in Los Angeles, the national board ratified the plan. There would be two annual scholarships. One—open to all women—was to be used "for furtherance of higher education for a full time woman student attending a recognized college or university." The other was specifically for "the Lesbian, enabling her to better her earning power," including any vocational or trade school. Some Daughters wondered how many women would dare to apply, given the negative stereotypes still so prevalent about lesbians. The DOB's governing board voted to proceed despite the uncertainties; the scholarships, they hoped, would promote the organization in academic and scholastic circles as well as provide a way for DOB to make concrete contributions to the education of individual women. All the chapters agreed to collect funds and advertise for applicants in their areas.[12]

Baker's death was a blow to the homophile movement. Because she was a San Franciscan, Lyon and Martin had lost a friend as well as a colleague. She had been a rare woman, pushing in the 1950s for the recognition of gay people as healthy and whole by the medical establishment; when she died nearly a decade later she was still one of only a handful of respected professionals who promoted this view. The harsh political climate in San Francisco in the early 1960s made her death an especially significant loss.

It seemed to homophile activists that for every positive newspaper story or professional speech, there were many more negative ones. Continued harassment and raids had led the owners of San Francisco's gay bars to organize the Tavern Guild in 1961. Now there were three homophile groups in the City, each working to organize their particular constituencies. One of the first things the new Guild members did after they formed was to approach DOB and Mattachine activists in San Francisco. Inspired by examples of legislative changes in other states, they suggested a lobbying campaign to revise California's laws. The homophile leaders agreed; the first step was to request a meeting with their local state assembly members. "We first met [Phillip] Burton through 'the Bobs,' two gay men who were our neighbors," Phyllis Lyon says. "They had been active in Democratic Party politics and knew Phil Burton. So they introduced us to him." A small group of gay activists then met with California Assembly members Burton and John A. O'Connell in 1962. They were told bluntly that the two legislators, though sympathetic to their cause, "didn't have even a remote chance" of success at getting an antidiscrimination bill passed at that time. Burton and O'Connell suggested to the assembled lesbians and gay men that they get church leaders to support changing the laws.[13]

"We thought, 'That'll be the day,'" Martin remembers. But then they met Ted McIlvenna, a Methodist minister who worked with young runaways and street people through the Glide Memorial Methodist Church. They were pleasantly surprised. Working in the Tenderloin, one of San Francisco's poorest neighborhoods and the center for X-rated entertainment of all sorts, McIlvenna was not only open to them but interested in doing something to reach his colleagues. He had a number of gay kids in his ministry, he said, and thought it was wrong that they couldn't find comfort and acceptance in the church. After the damnation offered by religious leaders like Rev. Fordyce Eastburn just two years earlier, Lyon and Martin were given a sense of hope by meeting McIlvenna and starting discussions with him. Perhaps the more open ecumenical spirit of the times and the increasing involvement of activist clergy and laity in civil rights struggles would extend to homosexuals.[14]

The fall of 1963 followed a long, hot Freedom Summer of increasingly violent reactions to civil rights struggles at home—including the murders of the NAACP activist Medgar Evers in Jackson, Mississippi, and four girls at the 16th Street Baptist Church in Birmingham, Alabama: Addie Mae Collins, Carole Robertson, and Cynthia Wesley, age fourteen, and Denise McNair, eleven. Although nonviolence was the mantra of the movement, especially as preached by Rev. Martin Luther King, Jr., to more than 250,000 at the Lincoln Memorial in August, other voices—notably that of the scorching, savvy Minister Malcolm X in Harlem—were questioning whether it was possible to make significant change through nonviolent direct action and passive resistance. As historian John D'Emilio has detailed, Bayard Rustin was the Gandhian architect of nonviolent protest in the United States and the brilliant organizer of the 1963 March on Washington. He lived his life caught between two worlds, that of the largely heterosexual black ministers and politicians leading the struggle for racial equality and that of his own private same-sex passions. They collided during a vicious public attack by the staunch segregationist Strom Thurmond on the floor of the U.S. Senate; Thurmond used Rustin's arrest ten years earlier on a "morals charge" in Los Angeles to discredit him just days before the August 29 mass rally in the nation's capital. Rustin was shunned by some of the leaders of the civil rights movement he helped create. The tiny homophile movement couldn't come to his aid, nor is it likely that he would have welcomed it. His exposure was further proof of what the cost of their homosexuality could be for activists.[15]

But inspired by the organizing strategies of the black civil rights movement, four East Coast homophile groups saw strength in numbers and created a "loosely structured coalition" early in 1963. Started by the Mattachine Society of New York, the Mattachine Society of Washington, D.C., the Janus Society of Philadelphia, and the New York chapter of the Daughters of Bilitis, their goal was to encourage discussion and cooperation among them. Barbara Gittings and Kay Lahusen were very enthusiastic about the possibilities of the new East Coast Homophile Organizations (ECHO) and used *The Ladder* to promote it; Shirley Willer and Marion Glass eagerly represented the Daughters within the new group.[16]

ECHO's first conference was scheduled to coincide with the American Psychological Association's annual meeting in Philadelphia in the fall of 1963. It was during the meeting that one of the first public reactions to an expert's descriptions of homosexual "sickness" was made. As the psychologist Albert Ellis expounded his view of "the exclusive homosexual as psychopath" to the largely gay audience, a caustic comment caused uproarious applause: "Any homosexual who would come to you for treatment, Dr. Ellis, would *have* to be a psychopath!"

Polite silence began to give way to more assertive methods of organizing, and the omnipotent status of psychiatrists and psychologists in setting mental health standards for sexuality was beginning to be questioned among some homophile activists. They had read too many books, listened to many speeches, about their "sickness." Some felt that it was time to respond more aggressively to the research findings; others wanted to work in collaboration only with carefully screened professionals. Florence Jaffy, DOB's Research Director, planned to exert more control while still encouraging Daughters to join selected projects. In June 1963, she announced "New Research on Lesbians to Begin This Fall!" and urged all *Ladder* readers to complete the questionnaire being prepared. "By collecting accurate information on the lives and backgrounds of Lesbians, and by analyzing and reporting this objectively, such a study can advance the cause of genuine understanding of the Lesbian." She promised anonymity and emphasized that the researcher, Dr. Ralph Gundlach, "is not a psychiatrist" but rather a social psychologist.[17]

In September 1963, the "Gundlach-Riess Study of Lesbians" was announced in *The Ladder* with a coupon inviting readers to participate. An article by Gundlach, "Why is a Lesbian?" accompanied the invitation. DOB's Research Committee had met with Gundlach the previous summer and was involved in formulating the study's procedures and the questionnaire to be used. Gundlach and his colleague Bernard Riess were interested in examining the human behavior of lesbians. In "Why is a Lesbian?" he said, "Our question is, why are some adult persons a-sexual, some heterosexual, some homosexual, some bi-sexual, and some other-sexual? Essentially, WHY is a Lesbian? What determined the basis for choosing?" He asked, "How can we get beyond just re-stating our own beliefs with vigor and emotion? How can we get beyond prejudice, superstition, gossip, convention, and doctrine, to some sub-strata of fact?" Gundlach's answer was exploration: "We are trying to discover from a number of unique persons, some things that are common to most or to some small groups and clusters, about their family relations in childhood; their feelings and remembrances about brothers and sisters, and school mates; their relations to teachers and other adults; their induction into maturity at puberty, and their struggles for adult status during adolescence; and finally, their feelings and experiences of a sexual nature, and their adult patterns of living."[18]

The year before, Gundlach had been part of a research team in New York led by Dr. Irving Bieber that compared family dynamics between small groups of male homosexuals and male heterosexuals who had undergone psychotherapy. He became disillusioned with Bieber's perspective, a position he shared with a few other members of his profession as well as the Daughters. In "Research Through a Glass, Darkly: An Evaluation of the Bieber Study on Homosexuality," printed in *The Ladder* in 1966, Dr. Fritz Fluckiger questioned Bieber's basic assumption, that homosexuality was a form of mental illness, and stated his belief that "homosexual acts are, after all, deviations from prevalent *social* norms. But to define them as 'sick' on the ground that they deviate from a *biological* norm shows a thoughtless acceptance of the quasi-biological concepts in which psychoanalysis had its origins." Fluckiger rejected his colleagues' "moral judgments which are disguised as clinical observations."[19] In contrast to Bieber, Gundlach had convinced DOB members, notably Jaffy, that his efforts would be beneficial to them and that his intentions were to gather data to improve scientists' understanding of lesbianism, not to strengthen arguments against it.

Gundlach's experiences as a member of a despised minority in the late 1940s may have influenced his later interest in studying homosexual men and women. An associate professor of psychology at the University of Washington in Seattle in 1949, he was one of three professors who were fired following hearings by the Washington Legislature's Joint Fact-Finding Committee on Un-American Activities (the Canwell Committee) and the University of Washington Faculty Committee on Tenure and Academic Freedom. Gundlach and the others would not answer any questions from the committees, refusing to confer credibility. The University of Washington was the first school to fire tenured professors during the Cold War era.[20]

Gundlach, born in Kansas City, Missouri, in 1902 and educated at the University of Washington and the University of Illinois, was a progressive political activist who studied "social problems." He taught at the UW campus in Seattle throughout the 1930s and into the 1940s and was often controversial. Gundlach stated in 1948, "I have worked over many years with organizations whose aims and programs are democratic, humanitarian, charitable, peace-loving, friendly, forward-looking. I have taken those aims to be my aims and have worked to put them into effect. I am an anti-Fascist. I am not a Russian-hater, nor an anti-Communist." Although the Tenure

Committee voted against dismissal, UW's President Allen fired Gundlach; he was fined $250 and imprisoned for thirty days in 1949. Gundlach moved to New York in 1950; there he established a private therapeutic practice and consulted for the New York Medical College.[21]

Repeated articles and notices in *The Ladder* during the last half of 1963 about the Gundlach study, urging readers to cooperate, generated some negative reactions among DOB members. "F.I.B., California" (who identified her/himself as heterosexual) wrote to say that "the very nature of the study indicates bias in favor of environment's being the generally predisposing factor toward homosexuality," and argued that it promoted the idea that homosexuality was undesirable. "Homosexuality is a normal manifestation of human nature, not something to be cured like a disease. . . . What is wrong with homosexuality, what pushes the homosexual into unhealthy behavior and attitude patterns, is NOT homosexuality itself, but the way society feels about it and reacts to it."[22]

The disagreements over causes, cures, and whether and when to accommodate "the experts" only escalated. The pages of *The Ladder* soon filled with debates over the best ways to challenge society's continuing condemnations of homosexuality. Despite its initial focus on providing safety, proving normality, and winning acceptance, DOB was beginning to offer not just social events but critical social commentary.

In November 1963, Jaye Bell abruptly resigned from DOB. Encouraged by Phyllis Lyon and Del Martin, Cleo Bonner agreed to take on the role of acting president. She was the first and only African-American national leader of DOB, and the first woman of color to head a national gay organization. She had been elected to the national governing board two years before and was known mainly for her careful administrative work, first managing DOB's Book and Record Service with her partner and then tracking *The Ladder*'s circulation and sales. DOB founders Lyon and Martin threw their considerable weight behind her and actively organized support for their friend; many Daughters greeted her new role in the organization with applause. Given the significance of interracial activism to an organization dedicated to integration, Bonner's assumption of the leadership of the Daughters in late 1963 can be viewed as an organizational statement in favor of the larger issues of racial as well as sexual equality. But Bonner had a low profile for a DOB national president: there is very little, if anything, by or about her in *The Ladder*. This could be a result of Bonner's desire for privacy, or it could call into question just how much the symbolism of her position translated into widespread acceptance of her leadership.[23]

Soon after Bonner took over as DOB national president, America was shocked and stunned on November 22, at 12:30 P.M. Central Standard Time, by the sounds of gunfire erupting during a political parade. Six days before Thanksgiving on a sunny morning in Dallas, the assassination of President John F. Kennedy, who represented optimism and energetic engagement to many women and men, seemed to freeze time. The country, temporarily interrupted in its increasingly loud disagreements over the basic principles of its society and the recipients of its blessings, fell silent for a few days. It was a defining moment, one that no one who experienced it will ever forget. It was a portent of sudden change, a rupture with the past. It was the end of the 1950s.[24]

CHAPTER SIX

"A Conclave of Ladies with Crew Cuts"

From *The Ladder*, November 1964:

> Pants are proper! The running debate among top fashion
> designers on both sides of the Atlantic has at last subsided. With
> help from *Harper's, Vogue,* and the *New York Times,* the ayes
> have it! This season you can wear pants absolutely anywhere—
> which means dandy pants for town and fancy pants for evening.
> You can choose from knickers, britches, jumpsuits, pantsuits,
> pant-shifts, etc. Combine with a champion-swimmer hairdo
> sleeked back behind your ears and a cropped coat. An inside
> contact reports that fashion artists are being told to draw their
> panted women to 'look like lesbians.' But who can be sure what
> that means?[1]

She is shown seated, barefoot, dressed in a pale, short-sleeved blouse
and dark, knee-length tailored pants. Her right leg is folded under
her left as she poses on a low couch before a bamboo wall. Behind
her, on the wall, a painted scroll featuring an old man, also seated
cross-legged, provides a vivid backdrop to the delicate and beautiful
young woman. She is slender, light-skinned, in her mid-twenties,

unsmiling; she directs her gaze toward the photographer but does not look at the camera. Her short, curly, black hair and eyes are complemented by finely shaped brows and carefully darkened lips. She looks as if she is waiting for someone.

"Ger van Braam" was the first woman to be portrayed full-face on the cover of *The Ladder*. The credit given for the photo in the November 1964 issue is, simply, "Ger van B., by Rora." An Indonesian lesbian, van Braam found a copy of *The Ladder* at a friend's home in Jakarta early in 1964 and wrote to the editor. Her first letter, "Isolation in Indonesia," was printed in the June issue of *The Ladder*. Over the next few months, van Braam wrote a handful of letters and short stories, lamenting the lack of places to meet other women and the dearth of positive literature about homosexuality in her country. But in November, she wrote, "I am no longer alone, I have suddenly found friends!"

Rejoicing that she had met a woman, who was married and a mother, van Braam also echoed the difficult choices made by lesbians throughout the world. She wrote that she and her new lover were living together but it had meant her lover's painful decision to give up her son "because she doesn't think it wise to let him grow up among women only." She tells of her desire to "detect" what she trusts are "hundreds, thousands" of Indonesian lesbians, "who are not just bored upper-class dilettantes."[2]

In response to van Braam's comment about the scarcity in her country of novels or other works by and about lesbians, Barbara Gittings and Kay Lahusen came up with the idea of a book drive. They launched a Thanksgiving "Books for Ger" campaign, advertised it in *The Ladder,* and urged DOB members to send in copies of lesbian paperbacks, hardback originals, and other gay-themed works that would be boxed and mailed to her in Jakarta. After she learned of their plans, *The Ladder*'s new Jakarta correspondent wrote back to

Gittings and Lahusen immediately. "I just finished reading your letter for the *n*th time and I am still marveling at your ingenuity. I would never have hit upon something as original as your 'Books for Ger' campaign, and admire your spirit accordingly," van Braam was quoted in the December 1964 issue of *The Ladder*. "Rora is disturbing me and reminding me not to forget to tell you that we haven't read Simone de Beauvoir's THE SECOND SEX and would love to have it! I don't intend to keep all the books . . . I want to distribute them among our friends and the more we get the better!" By February 1965, Gittings reported, "[S]ome quality books have been gathered for shipment to subscriber Ger van B., half a world away. Donations of books and postage came from Massachusetts, New Jersey, Indiana, Missouri, Pennsylvania, and Virginia. As we go to press, the books are being packed for the long trip overseas . . ."[3]

DOB's efforts and influence were expanding, in large part through its little publication. Under Gittings's guidance, and with the funds provided by Shirley Willer's "angel," *The Ladder* was receiving favorable notice and even praise from some DOB members and from colleagues throughout the homophile movement. In a letter printed in the December 1964 issue, for example, "J.N., Australia" wrote, "[W]e have just seen several copies of THE LADDER and we were thunderstruck! The covers are beautiful! The content has improved 100%. We just look at each other and ask, 'Can this be THE LADDER?'" Still measuring 5 x 8 ½ inches, a digest of more than twenty-four typed pages, it was now printed on slick stock. The words "A Lesbian Review" were added to the cover in 1964, in a bold, unmistakable typeface, marking the first time the word "lesbian" was used as part of an ongoing magazine title.[4]

There were other breakthroughs achieved under Gittings's direction, such as the use of high-quality photographic portraits of lesbians like van Braam on the covers. Gittings's partner Kay Lahusen was one of the earliest photographers of homophile groups' activities and she created striking black-and-white portraits of attractive women for *The Ladder*. For the first time, a handful of lesbians were willing to be pictured on the front of a national gay publication: Esme Langley followed Ger van Braam on the cover in January 1965. Langley, a British lesbian activist, was one of the founders in 1963 of the DOB-styled Minorities Research Group in London. Founded by five women, MRG saw as its purpose "to investigate and report on the situation of the lesbian minority in general, and in particular in Great Britain."[5]

The beginnings of an international lesbian network were made possible by the exacting, ongoing work that DOB's magazine required. Each month, after editing *Ladder* copy, preparing a mockup and setting headlines, Gittings sent her work off to San Francisco for typing and printing. She then received a box of the finished magazine for distribution, as would DOB activists in San Francisco, Chicago, and Los Angeles. Chapter members delivered copies of *The Ladder* to about a dozen or so newsstands and bookstores: places like Lawrence Ferlinghetti's City Lights in San Francisco and a handful of spots around New York City, such as the 8th Street Bookshop, Harry Tobman's newsstand, The Paperback Gallery on Sixth Avenue in Greenwich Village, and a bookseller near Columbia University. Several bookstores in Philadelphia also sold it, including two in the vicinity of the University of Pennsylvania. *The Ladder* was found at bookstores in Los Angeles, Detroit, and Portland (Oregon); magazine distributors in Cleveland, Dallas, and Depew (New York) carried it as well. But Gittings and Lahusen remember that they were the only distributors in New York City; surprisingly, given the plethora of reading tastes in the nation's largest media market, "we tried but couldn't get a commercial distributor in the New York metropolitan area to carry *The Ladder*."[6]

While the Daughters did not realize greatly increased sales from placing *The Ladder* at selected newsstands, what they did accomplish in many ways is much more significant. Given that *The Ladder* featured portraits, line drawings, and photographs of women on its cover, it showcased "normal" lesbians to the world at a time when no such images existed.

We'll never know how many lesbians, perhaps too timid to purchase the magazine, surreptitiously looked *The Ladder* over and identified with the woman pictured on the cover. Or whether the curious heterosexual man or woman, glancing at the magazine, thought, "so *she's* a Lesbian." while purchasing their *Look* or *Life* or daily newspaper. DOB's promotion of attractive, young, neat, fit, generally white women on *The Ladder's* covers provided an alternative, albeit not an unproblematic one, to the mass-produced images of girlishly lascivious or mannishly straitlaced lesbians that were dominant in the popular culture at the time.

One of the few nonwhite women who was a lesbian leader in the mid-1960s traveled three thousand miles from home to take her place at the lectern. In June 1964, DOB's national president Cleo Bonner gave the welcoming address at the third DOB national convention, this time held in New York. On Saturday morning, June 20, after her introduction by the New York chapter's president Shirley Willer, she thanked attendees for being part of a DOB tradition. "As President of the Daughters of Bilitis, I must say that we've come a long way—we hold our convention every two years and that in itself is quite a world-shaking event. It now stands for six years. We have our struggles and disappointments, our financial difficulties—and when I say 'financial difficulties' it's a nice way of saying how broke we usually are. And when we feel despondent and sometimes say to ourselves, "Oh, who cares? What's the use?" we will get a letter or some person will call. Then we feel we should go on a little longer, to help where we can and do what we can." Bonner acknowledged the women from other regions as well as the local activists. "I must say I am very pleased to see all of you from the East, from the West, from Canada, and of course the New York people, to be up with us this morning and to come to our program. Thank you." Willer replied, after Bonner's remarks were met with applause, "We are very happy to have you here in New York—we've been wanting to meet you for a long time."[7]

One of the most important aspects of the biennial conventions was to allow the Daughters themselves to get together. Separated by miles and the expense of travel and telephone communication, the conventions provided the chance for them to put faces, bodies, and voices to the names of people they may have conducted DOB business with by mail or via *The Ladder.* In 1964, DOB had chapters in Chicago and New York as well as San Francisco, which also housed the national office; the Los Angeles chapter had become inactive a year earlier. For some Daughters—like Cleo Bonner—the convention doubled as a thrilling opportunity to travel far from home and enjoy the freedom of being openly lesbian. Phyllis Lyon remembers that she and Del Martin drove across the country with Bonner, first stopping in Chicago, where they met and stayed with local Daughters, then going on to New York. Lyon doesn't remember any problems associated with their interracial caravan. Instead, what she recalls is that their Greenwich Village hotel was a "real dive." "Cleo complained about the paper peeling from the walls" and refused to accept such tacky accommodations. The three women insisted that the management fix the problem and they ended up in the hotel's penthouse.[8]

Kicked off with a cocktail party held at the DOB chapter office at 441 West Twenty-eighth Street on Friday night, June 19, DOB's third conference—titled "The Threshold of the Future"—again featured speakers and panels throughout Saturday and a general assembly and sightseeing tour for Daughters on Sunday. Held at the Barbizon-Plaza on Central Park South, the convention fee included a special deal: half-price tickets to the 1964 World's Fair. Perhaps Daughters were able to use their World's Fair tickets on Monday, or skip the sightseeing tour on Sunday afternoon, because the convention weekend offered little or no unscheduled time. It was booked solid.

On Saturday, the meeting was packed with researchers, including Dr. Wardell B. Pomeroy, coauthor of both Kinsey reports, and the sociologist Dr. Sylvia Fava, the coeditor of an anthology of writings about the Kinsey reports. There were at least a half dozen others, as well as authors, an attorney, members of the clergy, a psychologist and a psychoanalyst, and fashion and fitness mavens.

One of the most provocative presentations at the '64 convention was the one given by Dr. Ralph Gundlach, who discussed preliminary findings of the survey he was then conducting with DOB's assistance. But his talk, titled "More Lesbians Than Non-Lesbians Report Rape—Why?" caused an uproar among some DOB members who felt that, once again, their sexuality was being pathologized. By contrast, Rev. Robert Wood, the much-beloved author of *Christ and the Homosexual*, took a more positive approach at Saturday's luncheon; he insisted that the church must open its doors to gay men and lesbians. Next came Donald Webster Cory (Edward Sagarin). As the decade progressed, Cory/Sagarin would increasingly advocate "curing" homosexuality; his remarks at the DOB convention pointed in that direction yet he was still politely received by the audience, perhaps in recognition of his groundbreaking work more than a decade earlier. He predicted accurately that he soon would be "displaced" by the next generation of gay activists and intellectuals.

But the high-minded and serious presentations at DOB's 1964 convention were upstaged by an inadvertently comical session on

"Femininity: What Is It?" The panel brought together Mrs. Lee Steiner, who featured Florence Jaffy on her local radio program in 1963; Florence DeSantis, the fashion editor for Bell Syndicated; and Adele Kenyon, an "authority on speedy ways to a trimmer figure." The three women discussed relationships, fashion, and fitness before a polite audience, but Kenyon caused quite a stir when she insisted that the convention participants join her in a "jounce in their seats" exercise session designed to "achieve that nice, narrow look in the beam."

With tongue firmly in cheek, DOB's *Ladder* reporter for this session, "NOLA," a New York writer whose work appeared in the *Village Voice* and the *New York Times*, deadpanned, "At the end of the exercise session, Miss Kenyon explained that 'the exterior look of femininity is built on a narrow base' and the look of masculinity was broad-based. This biologically revolutionary statement went unchallenged." NOLA concluded, "This rather surrealistic session gave a lift to things toward the close of the long afternoon." Taking aim at the high-fashion ladies, NOLA wrote, "Anyone seeing the triumphantly hatted panelists sashaying off the platform would have had to agree 'there's nothing like a dame.'"[9]

In addition to signaling a shift in who and what defined "femininity," DOB's 1964 national convention marked a change in the organization's visibility in the mainstream media. For the first time, reporters from the *New York Times* and the *Herald-Tribune* covered the speeches and ceremonies. The *Times* report appeared in the Sunday, June 21, edition and emphasized that some of DOB's speakers disagreed with the prevailing medical view of homosexuality. As Gittings wrote in *The Ladder*, "Thus, in a 5-inch, single column item tucked away on a back page, the *Times* made a rare departure from its usual touting of the disease and/or social menace theories. . . ." It was rumored that the new metropolitan editor, A. M. Rosenthal, had himself covered the DOB meeting.[10]

"The strangest postscript to the DOB convention," Gittings asserted, "was the most inaccurate and oblique press notice from Dorothy Kilgallen." Kilgallen, the popular New York columnist whose acerbic writings were widely syndicated, had described the Daughters' gathering "at a very proper East Side hotel" as "a conclave of ladies with crew cuts." Gittings archly responded, "Her comment was obviously not based on first-hand observation." Taking aim at Kilgallen's incorrect description both of their convention site and their participants, Gittings wrote in *The Ladder,* "If Miss Kilgallen looked for us on the East Side, that must be why she never showed up. Better luck next time!" And "ladies with crew cuts" were most definitely not in attendance. If they had been, the *Times* reporter covering the meeting—A. M. Rosenthal or someone else—surely would have mentioned them.[11]

"Homosexual Women Hear Psychologists" was the way the *Times* headlined their item. "The Daughters of Bilitis, a national organization of homosexual women, heard two psychologists take issue yesterday with the prevailing medical view that homosexuality is a disease," the unnamed reporter wrote. "About 100 persons, including representatives of male homosexual organizations, attended the opening session of a two-day biennial convention at the Barbizon-Plaza Hotel. Today's meeting will be limited to members of Bilitis, which takes its name from a fictional daughter of Sappho."

Despite its inaccuracies, such an item provided DOB with critically important publicity, especially appearing in the *New York Times*. A woman attracted by the headline would learn that a lesbian group existed, that they were a national membership organization, and the schedule and location for their conference, which was in town over the weekend. She would have rudimentary information about them and could make contact.[12]

However, not all media outlets were embracing coverage of the

Daughters. The same *Times* article reported that "[a] panel discussion of lesbianism that was to have been presented Friday night on the Les Crane television show on WABC-TV was ordered cancelled by the station's legal department. A spokesman for the show said that no reason had been given."

Despite the disappointments that went along with the excitement, the increased exposure made possible by DOB's biennial conventions helped chapter activists as well as national board members learn how to pursue relationships with radio, newspaper, and television outlets. By mid-1964, the Daughters were united in the belief that offering up their members as articulate, attractive examples of everyday, ordinary lesbians to reporters and photographers was an important part of their work.

From Chicago, in August 1964, DOB leader Del Shearer wrote to the DOB governing board to describe her meetings with the black journalist Balm Leavell, the editor of Chicago's *The New Crusader*. "While talking with him I learned of his rather close connection with Jimmy Hoffa, and for this reason Cleo and I thought it would be well that the board knew about this contact. . . . If you have objections about our using *The New Crusader* for publicity, please let me know immediately," she wrote. "I do feel that we should make use of public sources where we can. . . . It is true, however, that anyone trying to cut our throats as an organization might dig up facts like Leavell's connection with Hoffa." *The New Crusader* had already printed two informational articles about DOB's activities before Shearer's letter to the Board.[13]

Chicago DOBers had also worked to include lesbian representation in the electronic media. In April 1964, "Miss Shearer" was the only woman of five participants in a "lively two-hour exchange" televised on Chicago's WBKB. Shearer was identified simply as "President of the Chicago Chapter of Daughters of Bilitis," unlike the descriptions given Franklin Kameny ("physicist and astronomer in private industry, founder and president of the Mattachine Society of Washington, D.C."), Randolfe Wicker ("freelance writer, member of the Mattachine Society, Inc. of New York"), Father James Jones of Chicago's Episcopal Charities, and Dr. Jordan Scher, Director of the Chicago Psychiatric Foundation. Shearer articulated DOB's integrationist perspective but betrayed her own unquestioning use of then prevalent sexist language: "Sometimes a homosexual has a difficult time relating to people who are heterosexual simply because he is confronted with their heterosexuality. It stops him!" Shearer argued for a pragmatic approach. "If they are going to move in society and be a part of it, they have to be able to withstand the pressures of this heterosexual atmosphere."[14]

While most Daughters agreed on the importance of publicity—even if, like Cleo Bonner, they could only participate openly in public homophile events when they were many miles from home—now there were rumblings of dissent over the effectiveness of engaging in research. By 1965, heated disputes between DOB's Florence Jaffy (as Florence Conrad) and Mattachine's Franklin Kameny were appearing in the pages of *The Ladder*. The debate began after Jaffy wrote a long piece in the September 1964 issue of *The Ladder* explaining DOB's interest in cooperating with research efforts. She argued, "I think that what the public doesn't know about homosexuals is good, bad, and indifferent—but the good the public doesn't know (and the indifferent) is greater in amount than the bad, which is already very well known." She suggested that DOB adopt guidelines on which projects to join and that cooperation be limited to "persons with not only appropriate training but also research *experience*, and who are affiliated with a recognized institution of learning or research." She concluded that cooperation did not necessarily mean approval of methods or findings, and that the decision on whether to participate was an individual one. However, she hoped DOB members would agree that "research is a highly meaningful activity."[15]

In March 1965, the Mattachine Society of Washington became the first homophile organization to take the position that "in the absence of valid evidence to the contrary, homosexuality is not a sickness, disturbance, or other pathology in any sense, but is merely a preference, orientation, or propensity, on [a] par with, and not different in kind from, heterosexuality." This was a fresh perspective, a radical stand. *The Ladder*'s May 1965 issue contained an article by Franklin Kameny, "Does Research Into Homosexuality Matter?" His argument against homophile activists' engaging in research projects was that gay men and lesbians themselves were authorities on homosexuality and did not need to waste time with studies. "The Negro is not engrossed in questions about the origins of his skin color, nor the Jew in questions of the possibility of his conversion to Christianity," Kameny asserted. "Such questions are of academic, intellectual, scientific interest, but they are NOT—or ought not to be—burning ones for the homophile movement. Despite oft-made statements to the contrary, there is NO great need for research into homosexuality, and our movement is in no important way dependent upon such research or upon its findings."

This started a lengthy political debate between two articulate and opinionated homophile leaders. "As preliminary, I would ask where the Negro civil rights movement would be today, militant or not, if research into racial differences had not long ago supported the Negro's claim to equality of treatment?" Jaffy responded. She also emphasized the importance of Kinsey's work in establishing the normality of homosexuality. "Ours is a science-oriented society, and scientists are God to most people. In the long run, I do not think it can be seriously doubted that what science says *will* be important for the success of the homophile movement."

Kameny replied with "Emphasis on Research Has Had Its Day," indirectly complimenting those homophile activists—like Jaffy—who had preceded him by noting the evolution of the movement from "the formative years . . . when it was an extraordinary achievement even to have such a movement" to more recent forays "into the fight for civil liberties." "The differences between Miss Conrad [Jaffy] and me on research (as they often are when people acting in good faith have a common goal) are basically ones of emphasis. But I do recommend that Miss Conrad do some re-thinking about a formal position on homosexuality as sickness. There we do differ strongly."[16]

The two of them—and the organizations they represented—would continue to disagree about the significance of research for the homophile movement, but not for much longer. Their differing perspectives are symbolic of the currents of change swirling around the homophile movement at mid-decade. New forms of activism, which included organizing public protests and finding and cultivating new allies, were beginning to take shape for many of DOB's leaders. As Kay Lahusen remembers it, DOB leaders were beginning to define themselves and their cause differently. "In early 1964, when Marion [Glass] said that our movement was basically a civil rights movement, it was a revolutionary concept." The change in perspective meant a change in tactics and strategies; as always, however, geographic differences helped define the Daughters' responses.[17]

In San Francisco, meetings organized by Ted McIlvenna of Glide Church bore fruit with an early summer "live-in" at the White Memorial Retreat Center in the Marin County town of Mill Valley in 1964. *The Ladder* announced in May, "DOB members will join in the retreat-like meeting which aims at establishing better understanding between homosexuals and organized religion." McIlvenna brought together fifteen religious leaders from a number of Protestant denominations—Methodist, Lutheran, Episcopalian, United Church of Christ—with fifteen members of the homophile movement. DOB made sure that five of the delegates were women and that they were racially diverse. The Daughters' representatives at the retreat included Cleo Bonner and Pat "Dubby" Walker, as well as Lyon, Martin, and Billye Talmadge.

It was a difficult but life-changing experience for many of those involved. For once, gay men and lesbians had their chance to preach equality and inclusion to church leaders, and acquaint them with the realities of gay lives. The ministers listened; they also went on a "Gay Line" tour of bars and nightspots on Saturday night. Except for the bar tour, the thirty delegates spent the entire weekend at a remote retreat center high in the hills north of the Golden Gate Bridge. The strategy worked.[18]

As Del Martin wrote in *The Ladder*, "San Francisco was the setting for the historic birth of the United Nations in 1945. And again, in 1964, San Francisco provided the setting for the re-birth of Christian fellowship in the United States to include all human beings regardless of sexual proclivity." In December 1964, a new San Francisco coalition was formed, the Council on Religion and the Homosexual (CRH). It maintained a mix of (all male) religious leaders and (male and female) homophile activists as its directors. From DOB, Bonner, Lyon, and Martin agreed to continue their participation. Within a few months, the CRH created an ambitious program of education and public relations activities, and also developed plans to raise money to fund them.[19]

Because of CRH, San Francisco's gay rebellion started with a flash on New Year's Day 1965, nearly five years before New York's gay community erupted in rage over police repression at the now legendary Stonewall Inn in Greenwich Village. The Mardi Gras Ball—the first of its kind, organized by DOB and other San Francisco homophile groups as a fundraiser for CRH—would have been historic enough. It brought together disparate folks, many wearing colorful masks: gay men, some in full stage makeup and drag; white-collared clergy and their resplendent evening-gowned wives; and lesbians in assorted mufti, ranging from cocktail dresses to men's suits. The guests arrived joyfully at downtown San Francisco's California Hall the evening of January 1, only to be greeted by banks of bright spotlights and barricades, erected courtesy of the San Francisco Police Department. Despite advance negotiations, proper permits, and assurances from SFPD's representatives that guests would be able to attend the event without problems from officialdom, prominent Bay Area ministers, as well as local homosexuals, faced a horde of cameras outside the Hall.

Pat Lyon, then a graduate student in anthropology at UC Berkeley, had heard from her older sister Phyllis about the formation of CRH and the New Year's Day fund-raiser. Heterosexual but supportive, she had been involved with DOB since the early days. She had just returned home from doing field research in Peru and asked if she could help out. "They said yes, I could sell drink tickets. So there I was in a little booth, at California Hall, selling tickets," she said, "We didn't have a clue about the problems out front." The partygoers did not allow the threat of exposure to ruin the Ball, however: some five hundred San Francisco lesbians, gay men, and their friends braved the show of force that night, many proudly posing in their finery for the police photographers. But when participants began to protest the officers' presence and block further intrusions, they were arrested. Two gay men were charged with "disorderly conduct"; three attorneys and a housewife received lesser charges of obstructing the police.

Immediately afterward, Marshall Krause, an attorney from ACLU of Northern California, agreed to defend those arrested, and called a press conference. Ministers who were CRH members denounced the intimidation tactics they had experienced and were featured in news stories that went around the world, thus becoming identified as the first group of U.S. clergy to speak up for the rights of gay people.

After four days at trial, the judge ordered a verdict of "not guilty" on a technicality. It was the first time in San Francisco that gay men and lesbians had won in a confrontation with the local authorities. Continuing public outrage meant that the customary police harassment of gay men and lesbians would no longer be quietly tolerated. The New Year's Day Ball heralded a new era: the media, locally and internationally, gave extensive coverage both to the event and to the alliance of homophile activists and ministers. The City's officials responded to the embarrassing charges of police misconduct by designating Officer Elliot Blackstone the first liaison between SFPD and the gay and lesbian community, finally acknowledging that there was, in fact, a gay and lesbian community they needed to work with, not work over. It was, as Phyllis Lyon recalled, "our very first step into some kind of connectedness with the rest of the city."[20]

The CRH continued its high-profile activities in 1965. As a follow-up to the Ball, in June they published "A Brief of Injustices: An Indictment of Our Society in Its Treatment of the Homosexual" and distributed it widely within the religious and homophile communities, the press, and the general public. Written by CRH member Mark Forrester, the document was a clear and strong affirmation of lesbian and gay people, the first of its kind from a group of religious leaders. It listed ten areas in which gay people were denied their rights and their humanity, and ended with a call for self-definition, dignity, and justice for homosexuals. Unfortunately, the "Brief" used only male nouns, pronouns, and adjectives to describe "the homosexual": "[T]he homosexual is forced to perpetrate the last great injustice upon himself, that of failing to realize the best in himself and his part in cultivating the best in his society. Fear is the greatest obstacle which man must overcome."[21]

Working with open-minded members of the clergy was a historic shift for gay activists, and DOB leaders recognized that without Glide Memorial Methodist Church, none of the organizing of religious leaders would have been possible. The Church and its Foundation became centers for urban activism, racial and social justice organizing, and progressive politics in San Francisco for the next two decades. As Lyon and Martin have noted repeatedly over the years, "[I]t's the most unusual Methodist Church in the country." Not only did they launch the Council on Religion and the Homosexual, they also provided people like Phyllis Lyon with a job. "When I went to work for them in 1964, they had started what they called Glide Urban Center and it was a most amazing group of people," Lyon remembered. "There were four ministers: Cecil Williams; Louis Durham, the executive director; Don Kuhn; and Ted McIlvenna." Glide held training sessions for ministers from all over the country, usually but not exclusively Methodists, and taught them that the diversity of the city included gay men and lesbians. Lyon was hired as an administrative aide but rarely did clerical work. "I remember hearing ministers coming down the hall, and I heard someone say, 'I hear you have homosexuals around, I'd like to see one.' I kept saying that I wanted a sign on my desk: Here Sits the Token Lesbian. Mostly I was the gay and lesbian switchboard."[22]

In 1965, CRH organized another historic event, a Candidates' Night during which local politicians were quizzed on police misconduct and other issues of concern to gay and gay-friendly constituencies. It was the first time that "the gay vote" was courted in San Francisco, and it began a pattern of well-organized electoral activity among lesbians, gay men, and their allies that continues to this day. "It was remarkable," remembered Barbara Gittings recently. "That was something that the [gay] people in San Francisco were way ahead of the rest of the country in doing."[23]

But not everyone involved in DOB was as excited about the Council on Religion and the Homosexual as Bonner, Lyon, and Martin. The three women had been chafing at DOB's reluctance to see the potential in the new Council. Immediately after the 1964 retreat, they dutifully reported to DOB's national governing board on CRH's development, but no formal vote to affiliate was taken. They continued their involvement. When the Council decided to incorporate and seek not-for-profit status in December 1964, some of the DOB's governing board balked, citing one of DOB's original constitutional provisions—adopted at the height of the "Red Scare" in the mid-1950s—that prohibited them from joining any other organization.

Some governing board members objected to the fact that DOB leaders had moved from being representatives of DOB to active involvement in organizing the new coalition; others noted that members were acting outside the bounds of DOB's established procedures—the same argument that had been raised regarding the New York chapter's participation in ECHO (East Coast Homophile Organizations). Although Barbara Gittings and Kay Lahusen had been advocating that homophile groups needed to change their strategies from education and research to legislation and lobbying, Gittings questioned the "major and official commitment" DOB members were making on behalf of CRH without governing board approval. "So the project got launched without formalities and has snowballed without formalities," she wrote to Del Martin in January 1965. "Where is your respect for proper procedure?" Gittings noted, "DOB leaders have either insisted on the rules or evaded them—as it suited their aims of the moment." She went on to note all the internal DOB matters not receiving attention and urged Martin to "reveal the drama and glamour right in DOB's own central activities." Martin responded that "the irony of the situation is your own brief for legislative action. And yet you people are telling me that DOB cannot join in this community effort to accomplish what we have been working for the past 10 years? Surely you must be kidding!" She continued her CRH activism.[24]

The disputes over DOB's involvement in a coalition like CRH took place at the same time that direct action strategies were being adopted by the homophile movement. As women and men throughout the nation joined in ever-widening protests on a variety of issues, some DOB leaders and members took part in public homophile demonstrations even when the organization's official policies did not sanction them. "Gay activism took a different turn in the autumn of 1964 when [Randy] Wicker suggested to Craig Rodwell, the youngest member of New York Mattachine . . . that the time might be right to try a picket line," the historian John Loughery has noted.[25] On September 19, 1964, ten women and men (the majority of them heterosexual) picketed the U.S. Army's induction center on Whitehall Street. They held signs proclaiming, "We Don't Dodge the Draft—The Draft Dodges Us" and paraded on the narrow sidewalk in Lower Manhattan to protest the military's policies against gay men and lesbians.[26]

Two and a half months later, on December 2, Wicker and three other activists challenged Dr. Paul R. Dince of New York Medical College, scheduled to speak at Cooper Union on "Homosexuality, A Disease." Staking out the entrances to the hall and giving homophile literature to all who entered, the four wore signs reading WE REQUEST 10 MINUTES REBUTTAL TIME. They got it. During the question-and-answer session after Dince's talk, Wicker stated from the microphone in the audience that so-called experts didn't agree on homosexuality, betrayed their own biases and prejudices, and often began their studies from flawed assumptions. As reported in *The Ladder*, "He noted that those who call homosexuality a disease rarely warn their listeners about the unscrupulous therapists who charge exorbitant hourly fees and promise quick, easy cures to naïve homosexuals or their distraught parents."[27]

Wicker, Rodwell, and other activists with the Mattachine Societies of New York and Washington, eager for greater public visibility, were working to mobilize gay people to picket; they had agitated within the East Coast homophile coalition, ECHO, for it to sign on. It didn't take long. At their conference in the fall of 1964 in Washington, D.C., ECHO dedicated itself to "immediate action." "It was a gathering of men and women impatient to remedy the discrimination against the homosexual citizen in our society," Kay Lahusen and the homophile activist Jack Nichols wrote in their coverage of the conference for *The Ladder*. "Now there seems to be a militancy about the new groups and new leaders. There's a different mood." According to Lahusen and Nichols, the mood wasn't diminished by threats from the American Nazi Party to disrupt ECHO's conference, which the lone protestor on Sunday attempted but didn't accomplish. They also didn't let the Washington undercover cop who attended the entire conference—despite being recognized the first night by one of the local Mattachine activists—get in their way. In fact, the cop was put to work arresting the Nazi. *The Ladder* reported in January 1965 that "undercover officer Graham" was the same policeman who trapped Walter Jenkins, President Lyndon Johnson's close friend and top aide, in a gay sex sting at the YMCA men's room near the White House just days before the ECHO conference.[28]

Despite the realities of entrapment and arrest, however, the challenge—and thrill—of "going public" with gay issues was taking hold among some activists. When news broke in the spring of 1965 that Cuban President Fidel Castro's government would begin placing homosexuals in camps, Nichols suggested that, since there was no Cuban embassy, they picket the White House, as well as the Cuban Mission to the United Nations in New York. Ten gay rights picketers appeared in front of the White House on April 17 and twenty-nine appeared in front of the United Nations the next day. One of the signs pointed out the incongruity of American criticisms of Cuban political repression: "Cuba's Government Persecutes Homosexuals, U.S. Government Beat Them To It."[29]

A little more than one month later, the gay picketers were back again. Another White House protest—"Government Should Combat Prejudice, Not Submit to It and Promote It"—was held on May 29; it brought out thirteen people and led to interviews or reports by AP, UPI, Reuters, the *New York Times, Washington Star, Chicago Sun-Times,* Reuters, Agence France-Presse, and a number of TV stations.

The Memorial Day weekend event ushered in a summer of gay protest in the nation's capital. In June, when eighteen men and seven women picketed the Civil Service Commission to point out the unfairness of the federal ban on employment of gay people, there was a brief mention of the action in the *Washington Post.* On July 31, the Pentagon was the target: sixteen people protested the anti-gay policies of the U.S. armed forces. "Homosexuals Died for Their Country Too," read one sign; "Government Policy Creates Security Risk," another stated. CBS-TV covered the demonstration, which also was shown that evening on television in Washington. One month later, on August 28, fourteen people picketed the State Department, again protesting employment policies as well as security clearance issues. This time, there were reporters from CBS-TV, Agence France-Presse, and the *Kansas City Star;* a story ran the next day in the *Washington Post.* That autumn, activists ended the season of public gay actions with a third White House protest. It took place on October 23 and was the largest demonstration by homophiles yet; there were about

forty-five people circling the sidewalk to call attention to discriminatory federal policies.[30]

There were also public protests in other cities, among them
Philadelphia and San Francisco. In Philadelphia, known proudly as
William Penn's tolerant "City of Brotherly Love," pioneering picketers started a tradition of annual summertime gay and lesbian
demonstrations. On July 4, 1965, forty-four men and women joined
the first Philadelphia protest—called the "Reminder Day"—at Independence Hall. It was timed to viscerally remind the American public
that basic democratic rights were denied to many people in the
United States simply because of who they loved. The demonstration
again featured male and female homophile activists who quietly but
courageously used the anniversary of the country's Declaration of
Independence to question their status as second-class citizens. It was
an "Annual Reminder" that would be issued on July 4 for the rest of
the decade, a central feature of the organizing on the East Coast that
drew lesbians and gay men in ever-increasing numbers.[31]

By early fall, some of the gay folks on the West Coast got into the
picketing action. On September 26, thirty people—including Phyllis
Lyon and Del Martin—demonstrated in support of Rev. Canon Robert
W. Cromey, a minister who had his responsibilities "sharply curtailed"
due to his outspoken involvement in the new Coalition on Religion and
the Homosexual. His supporters assembled at Grace Cathedral, "the
masterpiece of the Episcopal Diocese of California, as worshippers
arrived for services on Sunday morning September 26," The Ladder
reported in the November 1965 issue. "Signs carried by the demonstra-
tors protested the 'removal of Bob Cromey.' Stories on the [diocesan]
council's decision [to downgrade his position] and the picketing
appeared in the Chronicle and the Examiner on September 27."[32]

The new media-conscious tactics of picketing and peaceful public
protest were a bold step for homophile activists in general and the

Daughters in particular. DOB had moved, in ten years' time, from assuring timid *Ladder* readers that "Your Name Is Safe" to publishing interviews and photographs of lesbian protesters. Kay Lahusen wrote "Picketing: The Impact & The Issues" for the September 1965 issue of *The Ladder*. "'We are not,' asserted one picketer, 'wild-eyed, dungareed radicals throwing ourselves beneath the wheels of police vans that have come to cart us away from a sit-in at the Blue Room of the White House.'" Instead, Lahusen emphasized that strict rules governed Reminder Day: "[T]he individual picketer serves merely to carry a sign or to increase the size of the demonstration; not he, but his sign should attract notice . . . Dress and appearance will be conservative and conventional.' And so they have been," she noted. "Women wear dresses; men wear business suits, white shirts and ties." On the first Reminder Day in 1965, what attracted notice was the group of ten women and thirty-four men who, as one observer reportedly commented to Lahusen, had "a lot of guts to stand up for your rights."[33]

Initially, however, even dignified protest tactics by the homophile groups had their detractors. The debate over picketing within DOB continued throughout the fall and into the next year; it centered on maintaining DOB's independence. "At this particular point we do not have confidence in the leadership as demonstrated by the Eastern Mattachine groups, who, under present circumstances, would be able to override DOB in any and all cases," members of the national governing board stated in June 1965. "And what DOB's participation would amount to is tacit support of the Mattachine program. We would prefer to hold DOB's identity as a separate organization intact and cooperate with the Eastern Mattachine groups in so far as we are able."[34]

• • •

By the mid-1960s, DOB was struggling to achieve a balance between its governing board and its activists, between institutional cohesion and local initiative, between the collective and the individual. It was not an easy balance to maintain. In both of the contested instances of DOB's involvement in "outside" coalitions, the initial response was one of adherence to established procedures. As a women's organization eager to protect its unique space in the homophile movement, many DOB activists were keenly aware of the tendency of the mostly male Mattachine members to dominate discussions and decisions. DOB leaders were determined to safeguard their autonomy.

Further, at least three of DOB's national officers at this time—Bonner, Lyon, and Martin—were very involved with the CRH. They were working closely with and were influenced by the perspectives of the ministers, some of whom were civil rights movement veterans, on the use of direct action tactics. In their June 7, 1965 letter to sister DOB officers Shearer, Gittings, and Marge McCann of Philadelphia, they quote the thinking of Cecil Williams, a black minister at Glide and the chair of the Social Action Committee of CRH, that "we should not engage in direct action until we have considered our strategy carefully and until we as individuals are committed to going to jail if necessary. Timing and strategy are of the utmost importance in direct action projects—as is proper training in techniques of non-violence." They felt that DOB's leadership had not yet had the necessary discussions about what adopting such tactics could mean for them individually or for their organization. They added that "it has been suggested that when we decide to adopt such a program we should be prepared to provide bail and attorneys' fees."[35]

For some DOB leaders, like Lyon and Martin, the issue was not a rejection of more militant approaches to homophile organizing. Rather, their concern was over the lack of planning that preceded actions like picketing and public demonstrations. There were other

Phyllis Lyon, co-founder of Daughters of Bilitis, in Seattle in 1950.

Phyllis Lyon and Del Martin, circa 1953.

Lisa Ben, circa 1948. She wrote, typed, and distributed the first known U.S. lesbian magazine, *VICE VERSA*, from 1947 to 1948 in Los Angeles.

Jane Kobuta and Stella Rush, circa 1946, in Los Angeles.

Stella Rush, 1955-1956.

Stella and Sandy at home: Waterloo Street in Los Angeles, 1958-1959.

Breakfast at Juanita's, Sausalito, September 1959. From left: Del Martin, Josie, Jan, Marge, Bev Hickok, and Phyllis Lyon.

"Griff" (P. D. Griffin), DOB's second president, circa 1955.

Barbara Gittings at the mimeograph machine, New York, circa 1959.

"Brock Harper" (Clara Brock), leader of the San Francisco DOB, circa 1960.

"Billie Tallmij" (Billye Talmadge), San Francisco DOB chapter leader, circa 1960.

The original back cover of *The Ladder*, November 1956.

The first cover of *The Ladder*, which debuted in November 1956.

Cover, *The Ladder*, October 1957. A depiction of a favorite theme of the Daughters: lesbians were encouraged to "take off the mask" and come out of hiding.

Lesbian paperback novelist and Chicago DOB activist Valerie Taylor on the cover of *Mattachine Review*, May 1961.

"Sten Russell" (Stella Rush) on the cover of *ONE*, June 1960.

The Ladder with unidentified cover girl, May 1964.

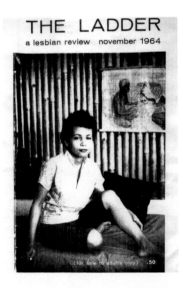

Cover, *The Ladder*, November 1964 featuring "Ger van Braam." Van Braam, who sent the photo and letters to *Ladder* editor Barbara Gittings from her home in Indonesia, was the first lesbian to be shown in a full-face portrait on the cover of *The Ladder*.

THE LADDER
A LESBIAN REVIEW

Jan. 1965

Cover, *The Ladder*, January 1965. Esme Langley, co-founder of the DOB-inspired Minorities Research Group in London, England, was the subject of the second *Ladder* lesbian cover portrait.

Cartoon by "Domino," *The Ladder*,
February 1962.

in this issue: EAST COAST
HOMOPHILE ORGANIZATIONS

Cover, *The Ladder*, December 1963. This sly
depiction of lesbian butch-femme styles was
one of the very few things about DOB and *The
Ladder* that Marijane Meaker remembers liking.

BAY AREA

NORTH BEACH BARS

1960 marked the first national lesbian convention. Sponsors Daughters of Bilitis mapped out the lesbian bars for the out-of-town women. Here you see a reprint, along with some additions* from earlier years which no longer existed. We've included the original "information" comments by the DOB.

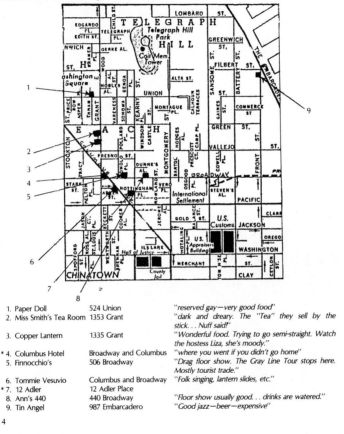

1. Paper Doll	524 Union	"reserved gay—very good food"
2. Miss Smith's Tea Room	1353 Grant	"dark and dreary. The "Tea" they sell by the stick. . . Nuff said!"
3. Copper Lantern	1335 Grant	"Wonderful food. Trying to go semi-straight. Watch the hostess Liza, she's moody."
* 4. Columbus Hotel	Broadway and Columbus	"where you went if you didn't go home"
5. Finnocchio's	506 Broadway	"Drag floor show. The Gray Line Tour stops here. Mostly tourist trade."
6. Tommie Vesuvio	Columbus and Broadway	"Folk singing, lantern slides, etc."
* 7. 12 Adler	12 Adler Place	
8. Ann's 440	440 Broadway	"Floor show usually good. . . drinks are watered."
9. Tin Angel	987 Embarcadero	"Good jazz—beer—expensive"

4

Map of Bay Area lesbian and gay bars, 1960. Created by DOB for their first National Convention and reprinted by the West Coast Lesbian Collections, Oakland, CA, spring 1984.

Phyllis Lyon picketing the Federal Building in San Francisco on Armed Forces Day, 1966.

Del Martin, Armed Forces Day protest in San Francisco, 1966.

"Cleo Glenn" (Cleo Bonner), DOB National President 1963–66.

Ernestine Eckstein, Greenwich Village, New York, winter 1966. Photographer and DOB New York activist Kay "Tobin" (Lahusen) posed Eckstein next to one of the newsstands that carried *The Ladder*.

Mattachine Society of Washington leader Lilly Vincenz on the cover of *The Ladder*, January 1966.

Ernestine Eckstein, vice president of New York DOB, on the cover of *The Ladder*, June 1966.

"The Changing Scene" as respresented on the cover of *The Ladder*, August 1968.

Cover, *The Ladder*, August/ September 1969. *Ladder* editor Barbara Grier ("Gene Damon") featured DOB leader Rita Laporte, the first and only DOB National President to have her photograph shown in the magazine.

Barbara Grier (left) and Robin Morgan,
The Ladder, April/May 1972.

Nina Kaiser, last president of
San Francisco DOB, circa 1977.

DOB San Francisco vice president Beth Elliot, circa 1971.

Front page of *Lesbian Tide*, 1973. The national lesbian feminist publication was originally the newsletter of the Los Angeles chapter of Daughters of Bilitis. Chapter leader Jeanne Cordova and other LA lesbian activists began to publish it as an independent magazine in 1972.

Del Martin and Phyllis Lyon, 1973, from
Lesbian Love and Liberation: The Yes Book of Sex.
Published by Multi Media Resource Center, San Francisco.

Gay Pride Rally, Boston, circa 1978. Boston DOB leaders Lois Johnson (left) and her lover Shari Barden helped to guide the local chapter for twenty-five years.

Gay Pride March, San Francisco, circa 1976. SF DOB president Nina Kaiser (second from right) holds banner next to Del Martin.

San Francisco chapter leader Pat "Dubby" Walker, circa 1997.

Kay Lahusen and Barbara Gittings (back), and Phyllis Lyon and Del Martin (front) at a 2001 event in San Francisco honoring Gittings's work with the American Library Association.

Daughters, however, such as Del Shearer, who expressed severe discomfort with this form of activism for gay men and lesbians. Another longtime DOB member and *Ladder* editor wrote, in reference to picketing, that "only dirty, unwashed rabble do that." But the Daughters included many strong and self-directed women who did not easily take no for an answer. The San Francisco DOB activists did not let the national DOB's reluctance to affiliate with CRH keep them from working with the new group, and some of DOB's leaders in New York and Philadelphia could not imagine not participating in the new direct action being organized on the East Coast.

Despite DOB's June 1965 policy against picketing, never printed in *The Ladder*, by mid-summer and fall of that year, Gittings, Lahusen, and a few other New York DOBers were among the first lesbians in the country to join the gay men and lesbians picketing important national public sites. Among them was the DOB leader Ernestine "Eckstein," a twenty-four-year-old African-American woman who had been active in the civil rights movement since her college days. In a photo taken at the October 23 White House protest, she wore white-rimmed sunglasses, a fitted white skirt and blouse, and white pumps. She held a sign that read "Denial of Equality of Opportunity Is Immoral."[36]

The 1965 demonstrations in Washington were significant because they marked the first time that a group of gay people openly took to the sidewalks of the nation's capital to demand their rights. Homophile activists had been influenced by the examples of countless civil rights protests, marches, pickets, and demonstrations that steadily increased in the first half of the 1960s. At that time within DOB, however, as Del Shearer's scorching letter to DOB's national governing board reveals, comparisons between the black civil rights struggle and the emerging gay rights movement were constantly asserted and highly contested.

The controversies over public protests had serious consequences: in 1965, Shearer—the founder and mainstay of the Chicago chapter and the vice president of DOB's national governing board—resigned. She took the opportunity to express her strong disagreement with the issue of picketing by homophile groups "at this time or in the very near future." She called it "ridiculous if not utter insanity," expressing her concern that homophile activists had not yet adequately influenced "the reflection of custom and public policy." She criticized Illinois's 1961 adoption of the American Law Institute's Model Penal Code as a "maneuver made at an opportune time," unsupported by public education and changes in popular opinion.

Shearer also addressed the connections linking the homophile cause to "the Negro Civil Rights issues." "The homosexual is not the Negro. If you look to that time when the Negro Civil Rights issues gained their greatest momentum, you will find there many factors which are totally and very apparently missing from the momentum of the homophile movement," she wrote. "You will find a history of suffering behind both causes. You will not find a century of subtle attack in the history of both. You will find an endless mass of literature concerned with the atrocities committed against Negroes, literature which has undoubtedly affected the general public and made them reflect upon issues which are near and dear to them." She argued that whites could accept black people's claims to equality more easily than heterosexuals could accept those of gay men and lesbians. "What issues can be so near and dear to them as voting power, integration, open-occupancy, equal employment opportunity, and property rights?" she asked. She asserted that the homophile cause was significantly different from the black civil rights struggle. "The antipathy is of a different nature." More work needed to be done to educate the public about homosexuals. "The literature directed at the general public which does exist is essentially antagonistic. While picketing has served the Negro cause, it has only done so because a large and significant population was already very much aware of the cause." Shearer also urged that DOB withdraw from ECHO to protect DOB's "separate identity." She ended her letter with "I would much prefer to see D.O.B. small and sound than great and vulnerable." She quit the organization, and the homophile movement, shortly thereafter. It was a significant loss: although Barbara McLean stepped in that summer and kept the Chicago chapter alive for the next year, she concentrated on local organizing and coalition work with a new chapter of Mattachine Midwest. Shearer had contributed to DOB at a formative stage of its growth on the local and national levels.[37]

Even the soon-to-be-inaugurated president of the Daughters was torn over the issue of picketing. "This split between those who wanted to make noise and those who wanted to do things quietly affected me very directly," Shirley Willer said in 1989. "During the second half of the 1960s, I was more and more at odds with the official position of DOB."

"Despite the objections of a lot of women in DOB, I supported public protests and went to them—in high heels!" This was a huge commitment for Willer, for whom even wearing a skirt was uncomfortable. "You see, I never wore heels because as a nurse you wore flat shoes. When I wasn't working, I wore penny loafers or something like that. And here I had to put these damn heels on and carry a sign and walk around and around in a circle. Walking in those heels took all the flesh off my ankles."[38]

Willer and her high-heeled comrades in 1965 not only sacrificed their personal comfort but surpassed their organization's reliance on education and "experts" to make their case for equality. Braving klieg lights and police barricades or walking in picket lines, they took a giant step forward to increase the visibility of lesbians in the mainstream media. As they did so, they began to change the image of "the lesbian" from aggressive vixen or passive victim to engaged citizen. The direct action tactics and strategies they borrowed from the black civil rights struggle helped advance their cause but it also cost them members who were not yet ready to forgo the patient approach of the 1950s. As the "Gay is Good" slogan began to surface—created by Kameny and influenced by the popularity of "Black is Beautiful"—the Daughters in the second half of the decade transformed themselves from female homophiles into lesbian rights activists.

CHAPTER SEVEN

Ten Days in August

It took place in New York in January: typically cold and gray. As they walked around Greenwich Village scouting locations for the shoot, Ernestine Eckstein kept her heavy sherpa coat with lamb's-wool collar buttoned up against the weather. In photographs taken that day, she is shown wearing a pin-striped button-down blouse and tailored wool slacks underneath her coat, leather gloves, and no hat. She must have felt good walking around her adopted city with her friends; she loved New York, and the winter weather didn't bother her. She was from Indiana, after all, where winter was brutally cold and seemed to last for eight months. New York had been the place she wanted to live after college; she thrived on its stimulating range of people, places, things to do. And now here she was, at twenty-five, making a life for herself in the Big City.

She was being photographed and interviewed for *The Ladder*. Even though being the object of so much attention made her uncomfortable, Ernestine liked Kay and Barbara, and wanted to be helpful to them. Besides, she had taken on leadership responsibilities for the local chapter and probably felt she had to go beyond her usual contributions as a mere member. She may have been convinced that her photo on the magazine's cover, and her opinions in its pages, would help to counter the prevailing stereotypes of homosexuals. As a young black woman who was not at all "mannish," hers was an image few people would associate with lesbianism. Perhaps still a bit nervous about appearing on the cover of a gay publication, however, she asked Kay to photograph her in profile.

The sun played hide-and-seek with the clouds as Kay posed her here and there—next to a newsstand on Sixth Avenue that carried *The Ladder*, near a tree in Washington Square Park. There were always small groups of teenagers in the park, sitting near the fountain wearing blue jeans, boots, and fringed suede jackets; they may have strummed guitars and sung "Like A Rolling Stone," oblivious to anyone but one another. "Once upon a time, you dressed so fine, you threw the bums a dime in your prime, didn't you? People'd call, say, 'Beware doll, you're bound to fall.' You thought they were all kiddin' you . . ."[1]

"How does it feel, how does it feel? To be on your own . . ." The chorus could have echoed in the air as Ernestine, Kay, and Barbara left the park and walked to the DOB office. It was a song they heard quite a bit around the DOB in those days—one of the new-generation New York Daughters, Deni Covello, was a big Bob Dylan fan. Eckstein had welcomed Covello and other younger lesbians into what she hoped would become a more activist DOB. Her plan was to reach out to women who saw the gay struggle as linked to other civil rights issues and hope that during her time as vice president of the local chapter she would help build a more social action–oriented group.[2]

Eckstein was feeling upbeat and positive. They had a good time during the interview: Barbara asked questions, Kay interrupted with comments. They debated where and how "the cause" should be advanced, the pros and cons of picketing and public demonstrations, the differences between the gay movement and the Negro civil rights movement, and whether homophile activists' involvement in other issues—like joining the growing opposition to the war in Vietnam—would help or harm the movement. And of course they gossiped about DOB.

When the magazine came out six months later, Eckstein was pleased with the portrait of her on its cover. Posed against a blank wall, her face turned away from the photographer, her smooth black hair framed her dark brown face and a slight smile played on her lips. Inside the magazine, her interview with Barbara and Kay had been edited but still took up eight pages and covered much of their conversation: "I think homosexual relationships can be very creative. People who are freed from family responsibilities can begin to take more responsibility toward society. They can be more productive. They can feel more at liberty to give of themselves to the outside world. And also, you can explore yourself more—which I think is very important."[3]

While Ernestine Eckstein allowed herself to be photographed in the park and profiled in *The Ladder*, she never used her real surname. Like many lesbians and gay men who lived in fear of losing their livelihoods and their families if they were known to be homosexual, Eckstein opted for the protection of a pseudonym. In this way, she balanced her desire for political visibility with personal caution. Born in 1941 and raised in South Bend, Indiana, Eckstein arrived in New York City in 1963. She moved East after graduation from Indiana University in Bloomington, where she had majored in journalism and also studied government and Russian. Yearbook pictures show a well-dressed, slender young woman who was often the only black person in a group picture. While at Bloomington, she was active in a variety of campus groups, including the daily student-produced newspaper.

In New York, Eckstein found employment as a social worker; for the first time she also found herself attracted to her female roommate.

After a brief period of soul-searching, she accepted herself as a lesbian and sought an organization to join. Her search for affiliation was in keeping with her college experiences: Eckstein had been actively involved with the Bloomington chapter of the NAACP while at Indiana University. Within two years of her arrival in New York, she joined not only the activist Congress of Racial Equality (CORE), but also the Mattachine Society and Daughters of Bilitis. By 1966, she was the vice president of the New York chapter of DOB.[4]

Eckstein urged DOB and the other homophile organizations to give more emphasis to public demonstrations and legal strategies. "My feeling is that there are certain broad, general problems that we all have as homosexuals, across the board so to speak, and we should concentrate on those—the discrimination by the government in employment and military service, the laws used against homosexuals, the rejection by the churches," she said in her interview with Gittings and Lahusen in the June 1966 issue of *The Ladder*. She drew parallels between the black civil rights and the homophile movements. "The homosexual has to call attention to the fact that he's been unjustly acted upon. This is what the Negro did," she said. "Demonstrations, as far as I'm concerned, are one of the very first steps toward changing society."[5]

"Changing society" was becoming more of a priority for many Daughters in 1966 than the old goal of "changing the variant." A new approach, and an embrace of public protests, increasingly was advocated within DOB by some of its leaders.

"I have carefully considered my actions and my decisions in participating in the Council. The time is now—and I am committed. There is no time to wait for the machinery of DOB to gear itself into action," Del Martin wrote in a January 1966 message to DOB leaders. It was appended to an article on the Council on Religion and the Homosexual she had written for *Challenge,* a magazine published by the San Francisco Theological Seminary.[6]

For Martin and Phyllis Lyon, the previous year's debates over picketing had led to a clear plan of action. In May 1966, timed to coincide with Armed Forces Day, they and San Francisco Daughter Barbara Deming joined ECHO picketers around the country in the first national protest over the exclusion of gay men and lesbians from the military. But DOB as an organization was lagging behind the new wave of public activism. As Del Martin wrote to Shirley Willer and Marion Glass in June 1966, "DOB here offered little support to the CRH Candidates Nights or to the Protest Day. As a consequence, Phyllis and I find ourselves moving in a direction that no longer encompasses DOB, and we have become more involved with CRH and Citizens Alert. This is an era of change, and both of these organizations represent action and change. We wish to be helpful to you, but cannot see our way clear to continued involvement with the S.F. chapter. We would prefer to remain inactive members."[7]

Their expanded activism, and their involvement with people from progressive church and community groups, led to organizing Citizens Alert in 1966. Citizens Alert (CA) was the first multi-issue police misconduct response network in San Francisco. Organizing CA brought the Daughters into collaboration with black civil rights groups and poor people's organizations, whose members were also subject to violence and harassment from the police. Lyon and Martin remember that after they had started having conversations with other gay activists about a Homophile Alert System to help those beaten or harassed by police, "Watts happened down in southern California and we realized it was a bigger problem than just for us. Other people were affected."

The southeast Los Angeles neighborhood of Watts—poor, black, marginalized, and neglected—erupted in August 1966 after a young African-American man, Marquette Fry, was chased and beaten by police. Simmering rage drove crowds into the area's streets and shops, and the authorities reacted with a ferocious show of force. Three days later, thirty-four people were dead and four thousand were wounded after one of the largest riots in the United States against racist police practices and unrelenting poverty. The Watts uprising inspired Lyon, Martin, and other activists in San Francisco to expand their network and create a new kind of coalition: one that would monitor law enforcement personnel and protest brutality. Glide's Cecil Williams convened the new group.[8]

In 1966, DOB founders Martin, who held no official position in the organization at this time, and Lyon, who was serving in the role of DOB public relations director, maintained their local involvement in DOB but focused their energies on the program and publicity for the upcoming DOB national convention. It was returning to San Francisco for the first time since DOB's historic inaugural conference in 1960. The changes in the social, political, and cultural climate in San Francisco for gay men and lesbians were unmistakable: in the six years between the first and fourth DOB national conventions, there were new leaders, alliances, and issues being addressed in the Bay Area.

DOB's fourth national convention followed their now well-established schedule. What was different was the media attention they received. "An unfortunate little spat between the Daughters of Bilitis and the San Francisco Convention and Visitors Bureau has ended happily," read the story in the *San Francisco Chronicle* under the headline "San Francisco Greets Daughters." When DOB's August 20 conference was left out of the weekly listing of conventions, Phyllis Lyon sent a letter charging discrimination and demanding "a public statement of apology." She sent copies to the two daily newspapers and the major TV and radio networks; many of San Francisco's major news outlets then provided coverage of the

DOB meeting. "On the hour news spots were broadcast on radio stations KEWB and KSFO. KDWB recorded two interviews with DOB members—one with Miss Lyon about the convention and one with Del Martin and Bobbi Deming about problems encountered by Lesbians in our society. Miss Lyon also appeared before the television cameras in a pre-convention news conference," *The Ladder* proudly noted in October 1966. "On August 20, the day of the public sessions of the convention program, a bevy of reporters were in the sound booth of the Jack Tar Hotel taping the speeches and discussion."[9] The Daughters were thrilled at the news media's interest. And this year, for those following the progress of the gay movement, there was even more to come.

The National Planning Conference of Homophile Organizations (NPCHO) was also meeting in San Francisco August 24 through 27 to launch a new effort to organize a national homophile coalition. The inaugural NPCHO conference in Kansas City in February resulted in the Armed Forces Day actions across the country. The group also agreed to hold its second planning meeting late that summer in San Francisco. DOB joined with local groups—the San Francisco Council on Religion and the Homosexual; the Mattachine Society; the Tavern Guild; the new homophile group Society for Individual Rights (SIR); and Guy Strait and Associates, publishers of the Bay Area gay newspaper *Citizen News*—to organize a full week and a half of homophile activities.

DOB publicized it as Ten Days in August and saw it as an opportunity to definitively put the movement "on the map" in the Bay Area. They planned for direct dialogue with city officials, from San Francisco Mayor John Shelley on down. "For the first time, representatives from city hall and the police department will sit down at a conference table with members of the homophile community and allied civic organizations . . . It is expected that in this face-to-face

confrontation, specific recommendations will be made to solve problems encountered by the homosexual minority in San Francisco."
From a Tavern Guild fishing trip to a special "Consultation on The-
ology and the Homosexual," the Ten Days featured a variety of discussions, trainings, and, of course, parties.[10]

DOB's convention started things off right. Speaking to the array
of civic officials and their representatives at DOB's opening session—
Mayor Shelley designated Dr. Ellis Sox, the director of Public Health
for the City and County of San Francisco, as his official liaison—
William Beardemphl, the president of the SIR, stated the hopes of the
homophile movement in simple terms that still resonate: "We ask no
special favor. We want only ordinary rights like every other citizen of
these United States—jobs, homes, friends, social lives, safety and
security." Drawing on allies from other San Francisco activist groups
with whom they had worked in the two years prior to the convention,
DOB presented an impressive array of speakers from the Mexican-
American Political Association; San Francisco Suicide Prevention;
Citizens Alert; Glide Foundation; and the Council on Religion and
the Homosexual.

CRH had continued its high-profile, groundbreaking work. Determined to take their message of religious tolerance to the public, the
Council reserved a booth at the California State Fair the month after
the Ten Days in August. This was a bold move into a public venue
known for its celebration of rural Americana, not alternative sexuality. When the fair's director discovered their application, he cancelled their exhibit space on the grounds that it would be "too
controversial." After unsuccessfully taking the fair's administrators
to court, members of CRH, DOB, SIR, and the Tavern Guild
handed out a pamphlet—with its hard-to-miss title, printed in big
black letters: *Every Tenth Person Is a Homosexual*—at the fair's

entrance gates. Lyon, Martin, and Martin's daughter, now a young woman, were among them.

Their pamphlet, and their presence, ensured that the crowds of Californians coming from all parts of the state to show off their livestock and prize-winning produce would also have the chance to meet real homosexuals, their families, and their supporters. "Twenty persons representing the Council on Religion and the Homosexual distributed about 8,000 pamphlets yesterday just outside the main entrance to the State Fair," the *Sacramento Bee*, the major newspaper in the state's capital, reported. "The group included men and women from San Francisco, San Rafael, Sacramento, the San Francisco Peninsula and other areas." No further problems were reported after State Fair police initially ordered the leafletters away from the gates. The police decided "not to make an issue of it." No doubt the respectable white-collared presence of Rev. Dr. Clarence A. Colwell, a United Church of Christ minister and president of the CRH, accompanied by his wife, Ruth, helped change the officers' minds. The fairgoers accepted pamphlets with "embarrassed amusement" and very few rejected or destroyed them. "Most were folded and tucked away in purses and pockets for future reading," *The Ladder* reported hopefully.[11]

As was customary at each national gathering, DOB members voted for their leaders at the 1966 conference; that year, for the first time, a Daughter from outside San Francisco was named national president. Shirley Willer prioritized organizing local DOB chapters and working in coalition with the other homophile groups. "As National DOB chair, I traveled back and forth across the country about 40 times," she remembered in 1987. Over the next two years, Willer—aided by her lover, NY DOB co-founder Marion Glass—helped establish new DOB groups in Boston, Cleveland, Philadelphia,

Phoenix, and Dallas. They were a formidable team: "Marion was the brains, Shirley was the mouthpiece," many Daughters remember.

Willer represented DOB at the opening of the National Planning Conference of Homophile Organizations and made a hard-hitting feminist speech asking that the delegates "affirm as a goal of such a conference to be as concerned about women's civil rights as male homosexuals' civil liberties." She then offered four "constructive steps" other homophile groups could take to ensure greater participation by lesbians: she urged homosexual men to appreciate the value of women as people, respect their abilities and not treat them as "show-pieces," and make consensual decisions at the planning conference after "consideration of all arguments." "Insofar as we do find trust and value in the male-oriented homophile organizations, we will find common ground upon which to work," she concluded.[12]

Willer's speech reflected an increased emphasis on women's rights among DOB leaders. While the organization had always addressed itself to the concerns of lesbians as women in a sexist society, by 1966 the greater militancy that was being embraced by the homophile groups in tactics was also being expressed by DOB in ideology. "The important difference between the male and female homosexual is that the Lesbian is discriminated against not only because she is a Lesbian, but because she is a woman. Although the Lesbian occupies a 'privileged' place among homosexuals, she occupies an under-privileged place in the world," Willer stated. She and other older Daughters, like Florence Jaffy, believed that lesbians were less likely than gay men to suffer police harassment, for example, or face hostile questions from neighbors or family members about their female "roommates." But they faced fewer economic opportunities in society due to sexism. She asked the mostly male homophile groups to "be open to new avenues of in-depth communication."[13]

• • •

The Daughters' growing emphasis on women's rights in the gay rights movement extended to criticisms of each other; another big change in leadership took place in August 1966. Initially pleased with Barbara Gittings's efforts as editor, and her expansion of *The Ladder*'s circulation and distribution, the DOB governing board members in San Francisco and the local chapter volunteers who worked to put *The Ladder* together every month started to grumble. The last straw came in the months preceding the national convention: some DOB leaders were furious that the Philadelphia-based Gittings did not provide enough lead time to write up and mail out *The Ladder,* their main vehicle for publicizing their meetings and related activities. But what was less articulated yet even more strongly felt by many of them was that their magazine—now widely admired—was no longer mainly focused on women despite its subtitle, "A Lesbian Review."[14]

Gittings and Lahusen had grown increasingly close to Franklin Kameny; they agreed with his perspectives on the gay movement and his ideas for activism, published his articles in *The Ladder,* and enjoyed working with him in ECHO. Gittings had also recruited the writer Leo Skir ("Leo Ebreo"), a New Yorker and contemporary of Allen Ginsberg, who contributed original fiction like "Beat Alice" to the magazine, as well as reviews of books and films. The increase in *Ladder* copy written by men or reflecting a gay, as opposed to lesbian, perspective, coupled with Gittings's difficulties in sending materials to San Francisco on schedule, caused hard feelings—most of them recorded in multipage, single-spaced, typed letters sent to and from members of the national governing board. Finally, Gittings was "fired" as editor (or "relieved of her duties," depending on who is telling the tale) immediately after the convention, which she did not attend. The August 1966 issue was the last to list Gittings as editor. She looks back on that time sadly. "I think no one likes being fired. It was a blunt rejection. And it came on top of an ugly clash I'd had with the DOB leadership that had nothing to do with my work on the magazine. I loved editing *The Ladder* and I regretted abandoning so much good material I had rounded up to publish." Typically, however, Gittings also finds the positive side of the situation. "On the other hand, I could now put my gay activist time and energy into other exciting ventures—and I did."[15]

Phyllis Lyon and Del Martin took over temporarily as acting editors. The September issue thanked Gittings, who was acknowledged as having "firmly established THE LADDER as a 'little magazine' with a big punch" and a leading homophile publication. Soon the control of DOB's "little magazine" would pass to a longtime West Coast Daughter.

"With this issue THE LADDER begins its second decade of publishing. Certain changes in editorial policy are anticipated," Helen Sandoz announced in November 1966. "To date emphasis has been on the Lesbian's role in the homophile movement. Her identity as a woman in our society has not yet been explored in depth. It is often stated in explaining 'Who is a Lesbian?' that she is a human being first, a woman secondly and a Lesbian only thirdly. The third aspect has been expounded at length. Now it is time to step up THE LADDER to the second rung."[16]

Sandoz returned *The Ladder* to its initial role as an organizational tool yet kept the focus on lesbian literature and reviews. She, too, agreed to take over temporarily. Under her leadership, in January 1967 DOB's Statement of Purpose was updated to remove references to "the variant."

She also helped Florence Jaffy publicize her new efforts, a DOB research project with a twist: Jaffy created a questionnaire to query psychiatrists, psychologists, and other mental health professionals on their opinions about their gay or lesbian clients. Working with Dr. Joel Fort of San Francisco's National Sex and Drug Forum, Jaffy

conceived and crafted the study—"Attitudes of Mental Health Professionals Toward Homosexuality and Its Treatment." It was
launched late in 1966. Del Martin recalls, "Results were published in
The Ladder but it took five more years to get them published in a
professional journal. One hundred and sixty-three professional therapists in the San Francisco Bay Area responded to the survey, which
investigated both techniques of treatment and opinions about homosexuality."[17]

Jaffy and her team also used the study to assess mental health professionals' opinions about government service for gay men and lesbians—ironically, the area of homophile activism to which Franklin
Kameny, with whom she debated the efficacy of research in the pages
of *The Ladder*, devoted much of his life. "Nearly all respondents
(98%) felt it was possible for homosexuals to function effectively.
Likewise, practically all (99%) opposed laws treating private homosexual acts between consenting adults as criminal." A majority of psychiatrists and social workers believed that homosexuality should
disqualify an individual from neither security-sensitive federal
employment nor the Armed Forces.[18]

The research into the attitudes of mental health professionals in
the San Francisco Bay Area was to be DOB's last official research
project. Despite the fact that the Mattachine Society had also prioritized participation in research projects when the organization began,
DOB's devotion to expanding the pool of knowledge about lesbians
had a gendered quality. As female homosexuals, they were often "the
invisible women," still largely ignored in popular culture, yet, when
noticed, routinely stereotyped as sick misfits or lost girls just in need
of a good man and good (heterosexual) sex.

But to some observers, like Jaffy and Shirley Willer, lesbians occu-
pied a somewhat more privileged status in society than other women
due to their rejection of the traditional female role and adoption of

more socially valued "masculine" characteristics like independence and self-direction. But lesbians were bound by strictures that severely limited all females' lives. The ability to earn a living wage, provide shelter and security for themselves, and create family and community were of paramount importance to lesbians, and heterosexual marriage was out of the question for most as a means to attain these goals. Women's lower economic and educational status in U.S. society in the 1950s and 1960s made independence an elusive goal, even when two women pooled their earnings. For example, when DOB was founded in 1955, women earned an average of 63 cents for every dollar earned by men.[19]

The Daughters' dedication to providing accurate information about themselves and other "normal" lesbians remained an important tactic as the rise of the women's liberation movement intensified demands for self-definition. DOB activists continued to rely on "experts" to define lesbian existence but by the late 1960s, most agreed with Del Martin and Phyllis Lyon that they were themselves the "experts" they'd been waiting for.[20]

Feminist ideology as a means of analysis and resistance was growing both among seasoned activists and for a new generation of lesbians, who would reject the "homophile" label just as surely as some of their older gay sisters would turn away from the "feminist" one. When some DOB members embraced women's liberation, they stoked the coals of difference that had always burned within DOB. Discussions about and disagreements over feminism, women's rights, and lesbianism within DOB were not new. They had been taking place for at least ten years. Rather, from 1966 on there was a seismic resurgence of these conflicts, ignited by feminist forces erupting throughout society.

Most if not all DOB activists had been talking, thinking, writing, and living feminist—or certainly woman-centered—lives for years.

From the organization's first discussions in 1955, many believed that discrimination against lesbians was grounded in their social status *as women* as well as in their choice of romantic or sexual partner. In the mid-1960s, it was as though American culture finally caught up with what they had been doing for decades: defining themselves as autonomous, resourceful people who did not need men to feel good about themselves. Del Martin established the importance of feminism for DOB in the inaugural issue of *The Ladder*. Ten years later, however, disagreements over lesbianism and lesbian-feminism were sharpened by the newly energized women's movement. Leaders like Gittings and Lahusen, who felt their primary commitment as activists was to gay rights, left DOB for involvement with mixed-gender groups like the Homophile Action League or new gay enterprises like the Oscar Wilde Memorial Bookstore in New York's Greenwich Village. Stella Rush and Helen Sandoz believed in women's equality but were increasingly "turned off" by the antimale rhetoric of the new breed of lesbian feminists. They felt uncomfortable in both movements but maintained their sometimes tenuous connections to local Daughters.[21]

Lyon and Martin found a new arena for activism in the National Organization for Women (NOW). A few months after hearing a radio broadcast featuring NOW organizer Inka O'Hanrahan in 1966, Lyon and Martin contacted her. O'Hanrahan was forming a Northern California chapter. "After all that had been going on [in the homophile/gay rights movement], some of the leadership of DOB was saying we really need to start with the women's organizations, and we didn't know how to go about it. We didn't know how to get connected." Lyon and Martin told O'Hanrahan that they wanted to join NOW—as a couple. "She said, 'oh that's wonderful' and put it up to their executive committee." While they were allowed to join as a couple initially, the "couples' membership" was quickly eliminated as an option by NOW's leadership; evidently, it had never been imagined that two women would claim it as applicable to them. Lyon and Martin blame NOW's founder, Betty Friedan, who was being challenged by lesbians within the organization on her antigay stance. It quickly became obvious that, just as they had challenged sexism in the homophile movement, they would now have to confront head-on the homophobia within the women's movement. Their years in DOB, working with lesbians in a women's organization, gave them ample organizing experience as well as important political credentials in the new women's liberation movement. Besides, they were enjoying their entry into a new world of women, straight and gay. It would provide a political and social center for Martin and Lyon much as DOB had ten years earlier.[22]

But DOB would still be a home base for some lesbians, especially those who wanted to be involved in gay rights activism through an all-female group. For Martha Shelley, it was crucial to join a women's organization in 1967. She was one of the women who gravitated to DOB specifically because, as a lesbian, she wanted to meet and work with women. "At DOB I was able to meet people who would relate to me in terms of my personality rather than, 'Here is a cute thing standing by a bar.'"

"Sometimes we'd have political discussions about what we could do to influence legislation or something . . . and there was the annual Fourth of July picketing at Independence Hall in Philadelphia," she said. Shelley remembered "walking around in my little white blouse and skirt and tourists standing there eating their ice cream cones and watching us like the zoo had opened." For Shelley and other new, younger Daughters, DOB in the late 1960s was not only a place where they could meet other lesbians, it provided a staging site for activism in the growing gay and women's liberation movements.[23]

CHAPTER EIGHT

Changing Times

Ada Bello remembers the night well. "On March 8, 1968, they raided Rusty's," she recalled. "And we at DOB had to do something about it." Rusty's was a popular women's bar in downtown Philadelphia; many members of the local chapter of DOB, organized the year before, were regulars. When news of the raid reached them, the Daughters wanted not only to counsel the women arrested but to protest the police harassment. DOB's rules were clear: the national board had to approve first. "It was difficult to get authorization from the administration of DOB," Bello said. "We couldn't find the president—remember, it was before cell phones and e-mail—and we felt that it was hampering our ability to react." As the pace quickened on the local scene, DOB's bureaucracy was increasingly frustrating. The Philadelphia DOB activists went ahead without the official OK and contacted the local ACLU. Together with Spencer Coxe, an ACLU lawyer, they held a meeting with Philadelphia police. "It was an all-time first," Bello remembers. When they left the meeting, "I drove the getaway car!"

Afterward, the leaders of DOB realized that "we were more interested in action than social gatherings. So we thought, 'Why not start another organization—one whose middle name is Action!'" The

Homophile Action League—or H.A.L.—was born on August 7, 1968. An organization of both lesbians and gay men, H.A.L. was active until the early 1970s in Philadelphia. Bello was a founder, one of the oldest and most experienced members.[1]

"I was born in Cuba—November 1933—and I lived there until I was twenty-five," Bello said in a recent interview. "I was going to the university in Havana when the struggle against Batista was happening—in fact the university was closed because too many students were being killed by the police. In 1958 I decided I couldn't wait anymore to finish my education, so I went to Louisiana State University and I got my degree in chemistry. And it was a big change in many ways—from a large, exciting urban campus to a place with rules and regulations worse than any convent."

Bello journeyed to New Orleans almost every weekend, where she found an active gay and lesbian scene. After graduation in 1961, she worked in Mississippi. "The tension was high—it was the time of the Freedom Riders. There was a lynching at nearby Poplarville," she remembers. When a good friend moved north to Philadelphia in 1962, she did, too. "It was Paradise," Bello said. "We went to a gay bar that very first night!" She found a position at the University of Pennsylvania—"a very open environment"—and she and her friend Lourdes began making the rounds of the local gay bars and met people involved in the gay and lesbian community. "Neither one of us were [U.S.] citizens," she noted. "We joined the local DOB under assumed names."[2]

The Philadelphia chapter of DOB was started in 1967, the result of Shirley Willer's organizing drive. Marc Stein, in *City of Sisterly and Brotherly Love,* noted that about twenty women were active in the chapter in its first few months. "Several months after DOB Philadelphia was established, *Philadelphia Magazine* featured Nancy Love's 'The Invisible Sorority,' which brought unprecedented attention to

the local lesbian community." DOB wrote to the magazine com-
mending the article for helping to 'keep before the public eye the
image of those of us who must make ourselves invisible.'"[3]

"It was the Rizzo years," Bello remembered, referring to the
brutal "law-and-order" police chief Frank Rizzo who would go on to
become Philadelphia's mayor in the 1970s. "He went after coffee
houses and bars" as well as hippies, students, blacks, and everyone
who challenged the established order. DOB, as usual, attracted many
women who thought it was primarily an alternative social space; the
local group struggled to define their work as political as well.

The Philadelphia chapter's inability to consult quickly with DOB
leaders after the Rusty's bar raid is a perfect example of what seemed
like a burdensome and unnecessary bureaucracy for such a small
organization. It is one concrete example of why two leaders in 1968
urged that significant organizational changes be made. "I felt like
DOB was the Catholic Church," Bello commented recently. "The
hierarchy always had to approve."[4]

Toward the end of the 1960s, as the pace and pattern of organizing for gay and lesbian rights accelerated and diversified, the growth
of the movement led to an emphasis on local activism rather than
national organizing. By 1968, DOB was the only homophile group
with area chapters and a strong and centralized governing structure.
Seven years earlier, in 1961, Mattachine decided to "get the Society
out of the branch office business" and revoked all local charters; the
national corporation in California allowed some local or regional
groups use of the name, but from then on, Mattachine groups functioned as autonomous organizations.[5]

In contrast, throughout the 1960s, and especially during the two
years that Shirley Willer was national president, DOB chapter organizing received a great deal more time and attention. Willer's encouragement of local DOB activism, however much it had the potential to

strengthen DOB's national network, also highlighted serious organizational weaknesses. As Bello noted, "the hierarchy always had to approve" yet the hierarchy was often unavailable or in disarray. As time drew near for DOB's fifth national convention, it was clear that the problems of the organization would be the main item on the agenda.

In April 1968, and then again in July, *Ladder* editor Helen Sandoz provided notice of the upcoming biennial meeting, and it was obvious that things would not proceed as usual. "It will be a very important meeting for all members of DOB and friends who may wish to come and help plan our course for the next two years." In a break from past conventions, there was no theme, no major speakers or topic panels, no gala event. In fact, what was noted was, "this is a jam-packed business meeting." Questions about the organization's goals, its magazine, its membership were all to be discussed; DOB's very existence was in question. *"Every member should come to this meeting."*[6]

For any longtime Daughter who was paying attention, this was a startling turn of events. In addition, many of them wondered, "Why Denver?" According to Shirley Willer, "It was halfway across country—and on nobody's home ground." Previous conventions were hosted by a local chapter, in San Francisco, Los Angeles, and New York; Denver seemed an odd choice, especially since Chicago would have been an obvious one. Although the DOB chapter there had weakened by 1968 due to the loss of two strong leaders in just three years, the Daughters still had many friends and quite a few members in the Chicago area. In addition, Mattachine Midwest was going strong and the North American Conference of Homophile Organizations (NACHO, newly transformed from the NPCHO: National Planning Conference of Homophile Organizations) was meeting in the Windy City in August. But DOB's national governing board vetoed Chicago as the site, so Shirley Willer selected Denver. She had recently visited and knew there were at least a few homophile activists she could call on to help organize the weekend meeting.[7]

At the center of this and other controversies erupting within DOB in 1968 were Willer and Marion Glass. In an effort to respond to mounting criticisms of Willer's leadership and DOB's cumbersome structure, they had spent two years drafting a new organizational constitution, which proposed a complete overhaul of who the Daughters were and how they operated. They sent their revolutionary proposal out to chapter leaders right before the Denver meeting.

Willer's busy DOB schedule since 1966, coupled with her connection to DOB's anonymous donor, had incurred from both national officers and chapter activists a complicated reaction to her leadership: they were irritated by her lack of accessibility as well as grateful for badly needed funding for their work. Increasingly, Willer held the purse strings that enabled *The Ladder* to survive and chapters to organize; she estimated in 1987 that "every chapter got at least $6,000" due to her friendship with "Pennsylvania." But she was frustrated by what she saw as intransigence on the part of the national governing board. She and Glass wanted to eliminate the board and the national office, replacing both with a representative body of chapter leaders.

In the Willer/Glass formulation, the renamed "United Daughters of Bilitis, Inc.," would be limited to "corporations and groups which have been authorized to conduct business as the Daughters of Bilitis in their localities." Each chapter would be autonomous, controlled and financed locally. Each chapter would also decide whether and how to support *The Ladder*, which would be the only remaining national project of the new federation.[8]

In an August 1968 article in *The Ladder* titled "Changing Times," Glass emphasized the "problem of reaching the appropriate balance between what should be saved to preserve continuity and what must be replaced to ensure vitality." Her main point was accountability: she felt that the governing body of DOB needed to be changed from "a few officers scattered across the continent who were neither elected by the Chapters exclusively, nor responsible to them." Glass urged that DOB's chapters "immediately undertake to be the effective nucleus of the Daughters in their areas." She also noted, "The revised structure establishes THE LADDER as a separate 'profit-making' corporation which will publish magazines when it has the funds to do so."[9]

Blessed with the perspective that twenty years brings, Willer explained in a 1989 interview that, through their travels around the country and their work with local groups, she and Glass had come to believe that DOB's bureaucracy was hampering its effectiveness. They thought that changing it into a federation similar to the Business and Professional Women would mean "DOB could last forever," Willer stated. During the 1960s, she emphasized, "things opened up a great deal—churches were supporting us, we were getting support from everywhere." It seemed like an optimal time to implement a vision of DOB's future that Willer and Glass shared. "She and I definitely had ideas about where we wanted the movement to go—we were headed toward dignity. Individually, we had it."[10]

But in 1968, their substantial reorganization plan set off a furor. And the dismal turnout of fewer than two dozen Daughters at the Denver convention in 1968 meant that no formal decision on the new constitution and the decentralization plan could be reached. Instead, the Daughters who did attend—minus Phyllis Lyon and Del Martin, who had not been actively involved with DOB since 1966—agreed that all pertinent materials should be disseminated to members via the existing chapters. They deferred any final decisions until the next convention, set for New York in 1970.

The few Daughters in attendance at the Denver meeting also voted for new officers: the San Francisco DOB activist Rita Laporte was elected national president and Barbara Grier was named the editor of *The Ladder*. And, for the last time, they named their favorite S.O.B.s at the convention's Saturday night banquet. "The list has grown over the years to where one wonders if there aren't about as many official S.O.B.'s as voting D.O.B.'s!!" wrote Stella Rush. That year, former San Francisco Mayor Willie Brown, then a California Assembly-member, received his official S.O.B. designation; so did Mattachine's founder, Harry Hay, and his partner, John Burnside; New York's John Lassoe; and ten other men. Rush commented that "all the above listed are now official S.O.B.'s, no matter what anyone's private opinion may have been before. Smile! That's a joke, son."[11]

But most Daughters weren't smiling, especially not the two women who had worked hardest to try to make changes in DOB's organizational culture. After all they had done to expand the group, Willer and Glass were furious that there hadn't even been a thoughtful discussion of their proposals. When their new constitution was shelved until 1970, Willer remembered in 1987, "I was totally crushed . . . We spent two years on it and, right before the '68 convention, we went to Denver to get ready. And I had my first heart attack." She and Glass appealed to local homophile activists for assistance. "We got help from guys connected to SIR and worked all night collating and putting together copies [of the new constitution]—the two men worked like dogs. One of them was the owner of the biggest porn shop in the area, he gave me a box of dildoes to give to the girls."

There is no record of whether the sex toys were ever delivered to the Daughters or, if they were, what the reactions were. But after the convention ended with the new constitution and reorganization plans put on hold, Willer recalled, "I quit the movement entirely."

• • •

Frustrated by the lack of support from her sisters in DOB ("Del and Phyllis didn't want to talk to me"), she and Glass "climbed into my camper—it was parked right outside [the convention hotel]—and we just started traveling. We went to Oregon for a while." Willer felt a huge sense of loss even twenty years later. "I started doing [homophile organizing] in my 20s, but everything for us stopped in '68." Their proposals, however, continued to cause a great deal of debate among women within the network.[12]

One of them argued forcefully that the Daughters should maintain their national structure as it was. While her main connection to the Daughters of Bilitis was via *The Ladder,* an involvement she had nurtured for a dozen years and in numerous essays, short stories, and poetry published in its pages, Jeannette Howard Foster paid attention to organizational issues as well. Before the '68 convention, when Willer and Glass circulated their proposal, Foster weighed in on the importance of maintaining DOB's governing board. By now she was revered for the groundbreaking lesbian bibliography she had published twelve years earlier, and her contributions to DOB and to the homophile cause were well recognized.

"As a member of D.O.B. and subscriber to THE LADDER almost from their birth, I have watched with keen interest the changing colors and temperatures of opinion within the organization and its published voice . . . I have heard repercussions of debates on group policy and action [and] some echoes have seemed mere healthy differences of opinion. Some have sounded dangerously close to civil war and secession. Thank heaven the latter has been averted." Foster went on to advance her theory that "a considerable number of the sisterhood have a strong need to dominate—even though some may look delicately feminine." She drew on her experiences in Indiana in the early 1950s. "During my service at the Kinsey Institute for Sex Research, I learned that homosexuals are homogeneous in nothing except their preference for their own sex. When one considers the geographical, racial, economic, intellectual, and social differences among the national members of D.O.B., what can be expected but sharp variations in interest and sympathy?"[13]

Despite differences, however, when battles over decentralization erupted within the organization, Foster urged DOB members to maintain the national structure, comparing it to the American Association of University Women and the National Association for the Advancement of Colored People. "May D.O.B. struggle along undivided, even though granted it is sure to have a struggle. And may its voice continue to be THE LADDER, perhaps more varied than it has been by spells in its history, but nevertheless our national magazine."

For the current editor, the best news to come out of the 1968 DOB convention was that she could finally hand things over to Barbara Grier. Both Helen Sandoz and her lover Stella Rush felt that it was time to take a break from DOB now that the constant pressures of editing *The Ladder*—and dealing with Grier—were done. They had spent the better part of the last decade—in fact, fifteen years for Rush, who joined ONE in 1953—intimately involved in homophile activism generally and DOB and *Ladder* leadership specifically. After a lull in chapter activity in the mid-1960s, LA DOB had started up again and now there were racial divisions erupting; as Rush has described it, "without a larger purpose to distract them from their petty differences, the thing just fell apart." Most of their old friends from DOB's early days had already moved on to other groups or parts of the country. "Denver was my final meeting," Rush remembers. "We huddled with Del and Phyllis afterward—they were trying to figure out what to do with the rest of their lives, too. Denver was the point at which I didn't want to do the work of [DOB] anymore." They felt like the organization was imploding; perhaps it had outlived its usefulness. But Rush also recognizes that it was an upsetting time in general: "1968, that's when everybody was getting killed—Martin Luther King Jr., Bobby Kennedy" and it was also when they left Los Angeles for a new home in Manhattan Beach. "We had always talked about, when we got to a certain point, we'd end." They had gotten to that point, where DOB no longer sustained them.[14]

The same could not be said for Barbara Grier; she had never been a DOB chapter activist or member of the national governing board. The Denver meeting was the first and only DOB convention she attended. From her home in Kansas City, she had been intimately involved with *The Ladder* since 1957 regardless of who or where the editor was: she wrote the monthly "Lesbiana" book review column, penned hundreds of letters to the editor, researched lesbian biographies. Now, finally, Grier thought, she would have her chance "to turn *The Ladder* into, at least, the *Atlantic Monthly* of Lesbian thought."

The August 1968 issue—the last one with Sandoz listed as editor—was radical in many respects. Its cover, by Elizabeth Chandler, announced the theme of the 1968 convention, "The Changing Scene," in the style of Janis Joplin or Jimi Hendrix concert posters then sprouting like daisies throughout San Francisco's Haight-Ashbury, New York's Greenwich Village, and other counterculture communities. Reflecting the bright, fresh fashion of the moment, and the increasingly militant tone of the times, the change in editorial direction was bold. In addition to a powerful personal and political reflection on the Vietnam War by the lesbian writer and expatriate Jane Rule ("My Country Wrong"), the August 1968 issue marks the first appearance of New York DOB activist Martha Shelley. Shelley wrote in her article "Homosexuality and Sexual Identity," "[T]o suggest that homosexuality is a disease because it involves guilt feelings, confusion about one's sexuality, and other psychological problems is again a sophistry. Going to bed with—and enjoying—one's own sex is not a disease. Prejudice is."[15]

With the next issue in September 1968, Grier put her particular mark on the magazine. She featured a stark geometric cover donated by the artist Jane Kogan, a member of the New York chapter. She dropped the subtitle "A Lesbian Review" and expanded every section, adding more fiction and poetry, cartoons and artwork. Then, starting with the October/November 1968 issue, she published news stories, essays, prose, and poetry about the burgeoning women's liberation movement; she also began issuing the magazine six times a year instead of monthly. *The Ladder* again printed contact information for the DOB national office and the San Francisco and New York chapters, as it had intermittently during the previous twelve years.

One year later, in the October/November 1969 issue, Grier as "Gene Damon" wrote about renewed DOB chapter organizing efforts. "Chapters provide all manner of recreation, an opportunity to work with those who may be less fortunate, a place to learn about our heritage and history, a place, a group with which to fight for our civil rights, a limitless tool to widen our horizons," she exhorted. She listed "growing groups" in Chicago, Boston, Miami, Cleveland, Denver, Portland (OR), and two Southern California chapters—a new one in San Diego and a reactivated one in Los Angeles. "If there is no group near enough," she invited readers, "start one of your own." Grier worked well with DOB president Rita Laporte and featured her one-woman DOB organizing roadshow in every issue of the magazine. Grier even put a picture of Laporte on the magazine's cover; it was the first time that a national president of the organization was featured.[16]

Through the regular column "Cross Currents" (inaugurated during Barbara Gittings's editorship from 1963 to 1966 as an expanded version of an earlier "Here and There" section of the magazine), Grier devoted space in the *Ladder*—from two to twelve pages out of a total of forty-six—to news tidbits she clipped or had sent to her. Many of them were segments from articles on women's liberation, reprinted from the *New York Times, Washington Post, Cleveland Plain Dealer,* and other daily newspapers, NOW newsletters, or chapter reports on DOB members' media appearances.

In addition, *The Ladder* reported on a DOB group organized in Melbourne by Marion Paull and Claudia Pearce in 1969. It was DOB's first "official" chapter outside the United States. The Melbourne DOB also was the first "openly homosexual political organization" in Australia. Rita Laporte reported that lesbians in several Scandinavian countries and in New Zealand had also contacted the organization about starting chapters. There are also many longer articles on feminism in *The Ladder* in 1969 and early 1970, like the one by Wilda Chase on "Lesbianism and Feminism"; Martha Shelley's "Confessions of a Pseudo-Male Chauvinist" (on internalized sexism, or "identifying with the male oppressor class"); feminist poetry from Elsa Gidlow; and reports on local and national women's liberation meetings and conferences.[17]

The Bay Area's homophile movement was slowly expanding; by the spring of 1969, there were at least ten gay or gay-friendly groups, and DOB members had helped organize many of them. New opportunities for activism were available for women who wanted to explore feminism as well, from small all-female groups discussing personal and political issues ("consciousness-raising groups," as both the mass media and many women dubbed them) to the local NOW chapter. Other early Daughters, like Barbara Deming in San Francisco, were devoting time to Citizens' Alert and monitoring complaints of police brutality throughout the City. Billye Talmadge was "helping people of all kinds—gay, straight, man, woman, old, young—to strip away the conditioned roles that imprisoned them" through her work as a leader in the Prosperos Society. Ernestine Eckstein dropped out of active involvement in the Daughters in 1968 and moved from New York to Northern California. She wanted to focus on social justice issues and joined Black Women Organized for Action, based in Oakland, in the early 1970s. When a friend of Lyon and Martin's who was also in the group learned of Eckstein's past connection to DOB, she gave her their phone number. Eckstein never contacted them. Barbara Gittings remembers that Eckstein had gotten tired of all the political wrangling and disagreements within DOB over strategies and tactics, as well as feeling that too much time and energy was devoted to members' intimate personal problems.[18]

In Los Angeles, although Helen Sandoz was now free of the burdens of editing *The Ladder,* she was still working on the magazine—an involvement that infuriated her partner. Stella Rush remembers that when she discovered Barbara Grier was still sending articles and assignments for Sandoz well after the transfer of responsibilities, she exploded. In 1969, "we had huge fights about that," she says. "After Denver, we had promised each other that it was our time for ourselves." They finally eased out of daily gay rights activism that summer.[19]

Despite the availability of a variety of activist and social opportunities, however, new leadership did emerge. In DOB's San Francisco chapter, Lois "Williams" (Beeby), for example, and a small group of DOB members maintained the group's mix of socializing and social action—from playing in softball tournaments to collaborating with civil rights groups. Beeby also was actively involved in Citizens' Alert.

In New York, one of the new generation of Daughters was escorting two others on a tour of the bars around Greenwich Village on a hot Friday night in late June 1969. Martha Shelley remembers, "They were going to start a DOB chapter in Boston. While we were walking around, we saw these people who looked younger than I was throwing things at cops. One of the women turned to me and said, 'What's going on here?' I said, 'Oh, it's a riot. These things happen in New York all the time.'"[20]

They had inadvertently stumbled on the beginnings of "Stonewall"—New York's gay uprising. Sparked in the early morning hours of Saturday, June 27 during a police raid at a Mafia-owned bar on Christopher Street, the Stonewall riots grew in intensity over the next few days and caught the attention of New York's alternative as well as mainstream media. "Stonewall" is often used to mark the beginnings of the gay liberation movement. However, the rage unleashed during a fortnight of street fighting in New York in the summer of 1969 had been building nationwide among gay men, lesbians, transvestites, butches, bar queens, fairies, and freaks for many years; other sporadic outbursts had erupted in cities, San Francisco among them, earlier in the 1960s.[21] But the Stonewall riots went on longer, and received more national and international media coverage, than any other gay protests up until that time.

Shelley was one of the first people to jump into the surge of street activism that followed Stonewall. She remembers that, at first, "I didn't know what that riot was about. Next day, I went to a DOB meeting and still didn't know." She soon found out. "It really struck me that we had to do something," she said. "I thought we should have a protest march." Shelley turned to DOB NY chapter chair Joan Kent. Kent said that if Dick Leitsch of the Mattachine Society was willing to sponsor it, then DOB would sign on. At a mass meeting called by Mattachine, the proposal for a march passed overwhelmingly.

DOB and Mattachine paid for a joint ad in the *Village Voice* to publicize the march. Shelley's job was to secure the necessary permit from the police. She was told that they needed a permit only if they planned to use a sound system. "I had been on the picket line for the service workers union and I thought, 'I can yell really loud. We don't need a sound system, so we don't need a permit.' The day of the protest, after we marched a few blocks and came back to Sheridan Square, Marty Robinson jumped up on this little water fountain and made a speech for the boys. I got up and made a speech for the girls." Shelley felt the energy and restlessness of the crowd. "I remember thinking, 'I've got all these people here, now what are we going to do with them?' So I said, 'This is just the beginning—go home peacefully today but keep in mind that this is just the beginning.'" The event heralded the start of a new era—and a new organization.[22]

The Gay Liberation Front (GLF) emerged from the planning meetings for the first protest march. "I remember we were out in the sun after the march, drinking beers, talking, all excited," Shelley recalled. People shouted out names for their new group and then heard "Gay Liberation Front." She banged her hand on the table, "[Y]es! That's it! That's it! We're the Gay Liberation Front!" Then, "I looked down at my hand and it was bleeding, I'd been banging so hard I broke the beer bottle."

Shelley maintained her personal connections with the Daughters after she became a leader in the new group. In less than a year, GLF splintered and Shelley joined several lesbian-feminist groups, beginning with Radicalesbians. She also continued publishing in *The Ladder*. Despite political differences between the generations, and disagreements among members of the same generation over tone, style, and involvement in "other causes," in the late 1960s it was often younger local activists who would team up with some of the older DOB members. They involved the organization and its resources in the marches and other mass actions, as well as the new groups and coalitions, which soon exploded throughout the nation. For both newcomers and veteran Daughters, feminism was often, although not always, a unifying ideology.

The young activists who were attracted to the gay and lesbian rights movement were children of the 1950s who came to political consciousness in the glare of television news stories and a popular culture that increasingly celebrated dissent: protests over racial injustice; antiwar mobilizations; and increasing uprisings against U.S. imperialism, at home and around the world, were daily fare. Many of them felt that all struggles were one and should be united. Shelley catalogued them: "The black civil rights movement, the struggle against the Vietnam War, the women's movement, feminist politics, socialist politics. Every ethnic group had its own civil rights cause. And, of course, the gay cause."[23]

Debates over DOB's involvement in "other struggles," including civil rights issues and antiwar protests, filled the pages of *The Ladder.* "S.C., New York City" wrote in early 1969, "I am pleased to see that *The Ladder* is going in more and more for women's rights in general, and for minority rights, rather than just sticking to the rights of Lesbians."[24] Six months earlier, Helen Sandoz, as "Helen Sanders," had written a long letter to *The Ladder* in response to an article by "Marilyn Barrow" that criticized homophile support for "taking up other banners, other causes." Barrow's insistence that Lesbians "have less civil rights than any other group" was too much for Sandoz. After detailing the many ways in which racial prejudice was alive and well in California at the end of 1968, and listing some of the privileges that she and her female partner, both white, enjoyed that blacks could not, Sandoz insisted, "I don't think we can win our objectives at the exclusion of other minorities' battles. . . . If I could not work in the field of civil rights for all people, I could not, in an honorable fashion, work for the civil rights of the homosexual." She added, "I cannot say to my Black sister that her problem is being homosexual. I have to say to her that I care about all of her problems . . . I cannot imagine anything more horrible than to be a 'free' Lesbian in society and find that my color still held me back from full and honorable participation in that society." Despite her years of experience in the homophile movement, Sandoz articulated a belief in individual and human rights that crossed generational, racial, and sexual lines.[25]

But real differences did exist in the late 1960s between Daughters then in their twenties and Daughters who first attended a DOB meeting ten years earlier, when they were in their thirties. An article printed in *The Ladder* in the April/May 1970 issue was headlined "Before the Gap becomes a Chasm." Written by Fen Gregory, it warned that the "generation gap has struck the homophile world" and must be understood so as not to allow the "rupture" of the movement. Gregory noted that, in the past, the homosexual and Lesbian minority group had fought their "battle for acceptance" by emphasizing similarity to the majority. "Now! Enter the young; the new morality; the belief that the individual has the RIGHT to be different. Basic to this attitude is the assertion that the larger society cannot legitimately dictate the life patterns or social habits of its individual members." Gregory summed up the "change in premise" between the "older, conformity oriented homophile community" and "young homosexuals and Lesbians" as "a vested interest in nonconformity rather than conformity. One's right to be different, indeed, rests with that of every other individual's." Of course, debates over conformity among lesbians had first been printed in *The Ladder* nearly fifteen years earlier but now they were attributed to generational differences.[26]

On the other hand, the following month's "Readers Respond" column featured a long letter from "R.B., New York," who wrote, "I have recently fallen into a bad humor with respect to radical activists and have made a step backward from radical to liberal . . . All the way from SDS to GLF one hardly sees anything but psychic and moral weaklings who seek to abandon all personal responsibility for their existence. . . . New York DOB itself got a faceful of their contempt recently." R.B. relayed the story of a recent break-in at DOB's New York office by "gay power" activists who needed to use their mimeograph machine. They wanted to protest immediately the death of a young man who leaped out of a second-story window during a police raid and impaled himself on the iron spike of a fence. "Their excuse was: dire circumstances justify dire means. An especially annoying fact is that they had every opportunity to ask for permission to use the machine and they didn't . . . In spite of real anger it was all the New York chapter could do to vote to censure the offenders, and there were many who proposed forgiveness on the grounds that we're all in the same 'thing.' What this 'thing' is that we're all in, I wish someone would tell me." The writer went on to insist, "Lesbians should tend their own garden and stop squandering their resources."[27]

The debates extended to working with the North American Conference of Homophile Organizations (NACHO), officially launched in August 1968 in Chicago just days before the city's law-and-order authorities—from the mayor down to the troops of police in riot gear—viciously attacked protestors at the Democratic National Convention. Shirley Willer had been DOB's main representative in these coalition efforts, as she pressed for women's rights in theory and practice and tried to guard the Daughters' autonomy within the larger group of mostly male homophile activists. When Willer abruptly left DOB, the sentiment shifted toward those Daughters who felt that being part of NACHO would not serve DOB well.

In the August/September 1969 issue of *The Ladder*, Del Martin and Rita Laporte argued against DOB's involvement in NACHO on the grounds that DOB's by-laws forbade membership in any other organizations. Ironically, this same provision had been used to argue against Martin's involvement in the Council on Religion and the Homosexual. Laporte took another tack: she emphasized in her article "Of What Use NACHO?" that "it needs to be said over and over again that the real gap within humanity is that between men and women, not that between homosexual and heterosexual. When all the homosexuals, male and female, have their rights as homosexuals, we Lesbians will have all the rights that *women* have." She emphasized that DOB had built an enviable reputation and "a fine image" with the public and had an excellent record of activism and education within the movement. Laporte quoted a recent review of *The Ladder* in *Library Journal* (published by the American Library Association) that cited it as a publication that is "serious in purpose." She ended by insisting, "[A]ll of our energies are needed in our work, our battle."[28]

Another article in the same issue, by Wilda Chase, announced "*Men* Are The Second Sex!" Chase argued that females' double X "sex chromosomes" as opposed to males' XY set (with the Y chromosome characterized as "non-functional and indisputably held to be a vestigial X chromosome") indicated "that the female is the first sex, the primal representative of the species, and that the male descended from the female through shriveling up of a chromosome. . . . [T]he male's chauvinistic sense of superiority over the female has its roots in an ineradicable and overpowering sense of inferiority."

She concluded, "Our minority status as women takes priority over our minority status as Lesbians. On considering the issue, it is hard to see how we could be Lesbians without being feminists."[29]

Grier also printed a letter in the same issue's "Readers Respond" column from Franklin Kameny, who took issue with *The Ladder*'s criticism of a recent article in *Sepia* magazine on homosexuality that the Daughters said ignored lesbians. He wrote, "You seem to forget that the Lesbian IS, first and foremost—subject to *all*—yes all—of the problems of the male homosexual and with *no* special problems as a Lesbian." He argued, "[T]hat the article does not deal with women's rights is, of course, understandable. That is a worthy cause, but one *totally* independent of the cause of the Lesbian (which cause—that of the female *homosexual*—is, after all, what DOB was set up for). I am dismayed by the increasing effort to mix the two causes—to the evident and obvious detriment of both."

Kameny's arguments in this letter capture the ongoing and escalating battles between women and men, and people of different races and religions. "If one is a Negro homosexual or a Jewish homosexual, one may well fight racism and anti-Semitism, as well as fighting anti-homosexuality. One's two battles are far better and far more effectively fought totally separately," he declared. Viewpoints like Kameny's were increasingly seen by many of the Daughters as either infuriatingly chauvinistic or irrelevant. It was to be Kameny's last letter published in *The Ladder*.[30]

The "changing times" at the end of the '60s for many Daughters meant a growing interest in feminism. The Stonewall riots were covered extensively in the "Cross Currents" section of the October/November issue of *The Ladder*, as was Martha Shelley's speech at the "Gay Power Vigil" on July 27. *The Ladder* gave the same attention to the Fifth Annual Reminder Day on July 4 at Philadelphia's Independence Hall. Grier reported that eight different homophile groups participated, and the crowd watching included the deputy mayor of Philadelphia and his wife and son. "The largest picket line ever turned out, with as many as 45 persons picketing at one time. . . . Another sign of change was that some of the rigidity in dress appeared to be relaxed, and some of the women had on slacks and some of the men, blue jeans."[31]

For many Daughters, however, the NOW summit meeting held in San Francisco the last weekend in June sparked a more significant, if underreported, feminist protest: national president Rita Laporte and DOB founder Del Martin joined a group of women who successfully integrated a men-only luncheon club. For many Daughters, 1969 was the beginning of a radical shift in their consciousness and behavior, especially regarding love for other women and a commitment to their liberation. No longer would they be dictated to, bullied, or ignored by men—gay or straight.

CHAPTER NINE

If That's All There Is

Like a good film noir story, it started with a murder and ended with a theft.

In the January 1957 issue of *The Ladder*, there was a somber, black-bannered piece. The headline screamed, "Ann Ferguson Is Dead." The murderer confessed: "I killed Ann Ferguson. Premeditatedly and with malice aforethought." She went on to explain: "We ran an article in the November issue of THE LADDER entitled 'Your Name is Safe.' Ann Ferguson wrote that article. Her words were true, her conclusions logical and documented—yet she was not practicing what she preached." As if to clear her conscience, the murderer admitted, "At the December public discussion meeting of the Daughters of Bilitis we got up—Ann Ferguson and I—and did away with Ann. Now there is only Phyllis Lyon." There is no indication that anyone mourned Ann Ferguson's demise.[1]

Thirteen years later, *The Ladder* was again the scene of a crime. This time, the perpetrator took DOB's most precious resource: the magazine's mailing list. In broad daylight, she went to their office in San Francisco; finding no one there, she took production tools, correspondence, and copies of every issue of *The Ladder*. The reac-

159

tion was swift. "Everybody thought it was the cops or the FBI. What lesbian would come and do a thing like this, you know, who would dare?"[2]

The answer came in the August/September 1970 issue: instead of the DOB's Statement of Purpose, there was a bold manifesto.

"THE LADDER, published by Lesbians and directed to ALL women seeking full human dignity, had its beginning in 1956. It was then the only Lesbian publication in the U.S. It is now the only women's magazine openly supporting Lesbians, a forceful minority within the women's liberation movement.

"Initially THE LADDER's goal was limited to achieving the rights accorded heterosexual women, that is, full second-class citizenship. In the 1950's women as a whole were as yet unaware of their oppression. The Lesbian knew. And she wondered silently when her sisters would realize that they too share many of the Lesbian's handicaps, those that pertained to being a woman."

On page 5, the perpetrator—Rita Laporte—proclaimed, "With this issue, *The Ladder*, now in its 14th year, is no longer a minority publication. It stands squarely with all women, that majority of human beings that has known oppression longer than anyone." Then came a statement of the magazine's new objectives: "To raise all women to full human status, with all of the rights and responsibilities this entails; to include ALL women, whether Lesbian or heterosexual. . . . OCCUPATIONS have no sex and must be opened to all qualified persons for the benefit of all. LIFE STYLES must be as numerous as human beings require for their personal happiness and fulfillment. ABILITY, AMBITION, TALENT—THESE ARE HUMAN QUALITIES."[3]

The Ladder no longer a lesbian review published by DOB? What had happened?

It all depends on who is doing the telling.

• • •

"It was Barbara's idea," Phyllis Lyon insists. She believes to this day that Barbara Grier convinced Rita Laporte to help her steal *The Ladder*. "Rita went to the place where the addressograph plates were made for mailing *The Ladder* to subscribers." The small business was one that she and Martin, along with three other friends, were partners in. One of them, Pat Durham, was there the day Laporte came in asking for the mailing materials. She knew Laporte was the president of DOB and so gave her the plates when asked. However, "she wondered, and later that same day called us," Lyon explained.[4] Without informing any of DOB's other leaders, Laporte took the address plates as well as files from DOB's office and transported all of it to her new home in Sparks, Nevada, near Reno. Although Grier still was editing the magazine from Kansas City, they began producing *The Ladder* from Nevada in early summer 1970—away from San Francisco and DOB's organizational center.

The realization that they had lost their beloved and well-respected magazine was a blow to longtime DOB members. Many of the women who had been involved from the beginning—Lyon, Martin, Gittings, Lahusen, Rush, Sandoz, and others—have always referred to the "theft" of *The Ladder* and it has been a sore spot between them and Grier ever since. Once the news started to spread among the Daughters, the reaction was often one of incredulousness. The "theft" being an inside job, done by "sisters," was unthinkable to many DOB members in 1970.[5]

Yet Grier insists that it was an act of lesbian feminist salvation. While she does not dispute the story of Laporte taking the mailing materials and back copies of the magazine to Nevada without authorization, she explains that they took *The Ladder* from DOB in order to save it. Both of them believed that the group's institutional weakness by 1970 put the magazine in jeopardy. "DOB was falling apart—we wanted *The Ladder* to survive."[6]

Just a few months earlier, no outward signs of disabling institutional weakness nor serious dissatisfactions were in evidence. Grier, as editor Gene Damon, reported in the December 1969/January 1970 issue, "DOB now has four fully active chapters and six groups in the process of becoming members." Overall DOB membership stood at about three hundred. She proclaimed 1969 "The Year of the Chapter," naming Boston, Cleveland, Denver, Portland, and San Diego as new DOB groups in addition to revitalized Chicago and Los Angeles chapters. She urged members to organize in areas like Miami, with one or two willing members, and wrote, "A strong DOB is essential to us all if we are to ever achieve our civil liberties."

The next month, she printed a letter from Rita Laporte responding to an article by Lesley Springvine, "Out From Under The Rocks—With Guns!" In the previous issue of *The Ladder*, Springvine urged lesbians to prioritize working for women's liberation. She suggested they join groups like NOW. Laporte strongly disagreed. "I would wish that every Lesbian understand that DOB is her best hope and that DOB welcomes ALL women. . . . Whether NOW will survive, whether heterosexual women in sufficient numbers can withstand all the temptations to give up, remains to be seen. The Lesbian, and by extension DOB, cannot and will not give up. DOB, however small and poorly publicized, is unquestionably in the lead." Laporte concluded: "all women's rights groups would do well to back DOB, for here is a force working for women that will not be stilled."[7]

The first hint of change came when the words "A Lesbian Review" no longer appeared on the cover of *The Ladder*'s April/May 1970 issue. There was an announcement of the "Sixth Biennial Convention and General Assembly of the Daughters of Bilitis, Inc.," set for July 10, 11, and 12 in New York City. The brief statement also noted that "the General Assembly meetings determine the next two years of life for DOB." A proxy ballot was included for members who could not attend. Also included was the notice in "Cross Currents" that "NOW WE ARE NINE." The item stated that "President Rita Laporte is happy to announce that as of March 15, 1970, there are NINE CHAPTERS OF DOB. . . . For those of you in the still-unchartered groups, it is encouraging to you (we hope) that the Reno, Nevada, chapter has been in the works for about a year-and-a-half . . . so don't be impatient—it just takes work and time."

The June/July 1970 issue, with its striking black-and-white cover photo of the author Jane Rule by Lynn Vardeman, showed clear signs of a shift in editorial control. Although the copyright was still given as "Daughters of Bilitis, Inc., San Francisco, California," there was no DOB Statement of Purpose printed in the magazine. Further, the masthead quietly announced an important change of address: "Published bi-monthly by the Daughters of Bilitis, Inc., a non-profit corporation, at P. O. Box 5025, Washington Station, Reno, Nevada 89503." Only two national officers for DOB were listed—President Rita Laporte and "Vice President, West" Jess K. Lane—but the list of *Ladder* staff included eight women.

On the inside front cover was a note from editor Grier—"ONCE MORE WITH FEELING." She wrote, "I have discovered my most unpleasant task as editor . . . having to remind you now and again of your duty as concerned reader. Not just reader, concerned reader. If you aren't—you ought to be."

She continued, "Those of you who have been around three or more years of our fifteen years know the strides DOB has made and the effort we are making to improve this magazine. To continue growing as an organization we need more women, women aware they are women as well as Lesbians." Grier offered to send a sample copy of *The Ladder* as well as DOB materials to anyone interested. The materials included a copy of the article written by the murdered "Ann Ferguson" in 1956, "Your Name Is Safe." Grier emphasized that the article "shows why NO ONE at any time in any way is ever jeopardized by belonging to DOB or by subscribing to *The Ladder*. You can send this to your friend(s) and thus, almost surely bring more people to help in the battle."[8]

An appeal for advertisers also appeared on the inside front cover. "A thousand adult readers regularly receive THE LADDER, a magazine circulated throughout this country featuring news and views of the homosexual and the homophile movement of particular interest to women. Most of our readers are women 21–45 years old who have devoted a major portion of their leisure time to assisting the Lesbian to become a more productive, secure citizen. . . . To these readers your advertisement places you on record as an ally in their personal area of deep concern." No ads, other than those for DOB-related projects or books and records they sold, were carried in *The Ladder* at that time and hadn't been since the late 1950s. For the first four years of *Ladder* publishing, a few San Francisco friends (like "Jeff Weiner, photographer" and "Dr. Vera H. Plunkett, Chiropractor") advertised their services from time to time, and there were some ads for other homophile publications; at other points, there were a few notices, such as one from a publisher seeking manuscripts "that deal in realistic and mature fashion with lesbianism." Advertising in *The Ladder* had been discussed and debated many times over the years but never aggressively pursued.[9]

Grier directed any potential advertisers to send copy ("and check in full") to the Reno address. (The inside cover went for $100 and a full-page ad was $80. Half-page ads were $45, and a quarter page cost $25.) Previously, all announcements in *The Ladder* about address changes, subscriptions, or payment directed readers to the DOB's headquarters. The fact that Grier could now be receiving advertising revenue independent of the national organization—even if it was highly unlikely that she would—should have caused quite a few Daughters in San Francisco to raise questioning eyebrows, yet it appears that no one challenged her actions. After all, she had been working with DOB on *The Ladder* almost since its beginnings. And then again, perhaps no one worried about it, as long as the magazine kept appearing in their mailboxes.

That is, until the August/September 1970 issue, when there was no mention of the Daughters of Bilitis at all. The only names listed were *Ladder* staff, with Rita Laporte listed as director of promotion. Instead of the DOB copyright was the notation "All rights reserved. No part of this periodical may be reproduced without the written consent of *The Ladder*." Contributions were requested because "we are a non-profit publication depending entirely upon subscriptions, donations and volunteer labor." Rita Laporte quoted from Lorraine Hansberry's May 1957 letter: "Women, like other oppressed groups of one kind or another, have particularly had to pay a price for the intellectual impoverishment that the second class status, imposed on us for centuries, created and sustained." The takeover was complete.

Grier insists today that increasingly fractious "tempests in teapots" were wracking DOB. "I did what I thought was important—I wanted *The Ladder* to get bigger," she insists. "When I took over [as editor] we were putting out a thousand or twelve hundred copies an issue and about eight hundred of them were paid for." She adds, "Rita made up her mind to do all of this" before the 1968 national convention, when she was elected DOB's national president. Grier disputes the suggestion that the Willer-Glass restructuring plan, which would have put *The Ladder* on shaky organizational ground, had anything to do with Laporte's actions. Instead, she insists that by 1970, "Rita wanted out of the political crap—her idea of how to run an organization was to tell people what to do as often and clearly as possible. The chapters didn't obey her—and most of them didn't do much."[10]

Grier describes Laporte as someone bold and forthright, a forceful public spokesperson and advocate, a graduate of UC Berkeley's Boalt Hall School of Law after she completed military service. "Rita was the strongest feminist I've ever known, but when she visited us [Grier and her partner at the time, Helen Bennett] in Kansas City, the tenth time we had to get up to get her something, Helen came into the kitchen with me and sang in my ear 'It's So Nice . . . To Have A Man . . . Around The House . . . !' She was the butchiest butch I've ever seen and the most demanding human being."

Laporte came from a wealthy white East Coast family. "They had lots of money and could pay for all her needs, all her life." Grier says that, after a scandal erupted over Laporte's involvement in a fight at a gay bar, her family provided a comfortable stipend so that she would keep her distance from them. "She was very bright and very handsome," Grier remembered. But her DOB organizing efforts didn't yield the results she hoped for. "Rita thought that all these people were going to form neat clusters and obey the rules and form happy little butch-femme relationships—and when it wasn't like that, it made her mad so she packed up all her toys and took her girlfriend to Sparks, Nevada."

Grier says that she and Laporte both felt strongly that *The Ladder* must survive. "It seemed like DOB was a dying organization," Grier remembers of that time. "I took the magazine because I thought it was good for the magazine." She insists that there was a strong division between organizationally minded women—who became chapter activists—and those who were more solitary and contributed to the lesbian movement via the magazine. "*The Ladder* was an entity of its own."[11]

Ultimately, however, what Grier and Laporte set in motion by seizing control of *The Ladder* doomed more than the magazine. In taking over the only fourteen-year-old lesbian publication in the world, they took away one of DOB's few organizational assets. In the name of advancing feminism, they stripped the only national lesbian network then in existence of its most effective means of communication and survival. Their actions in taking *The Ladder* from DOB hastened its collapse. As Rush put it, "without the glue that held us together, there was no reason to go on."[12]

From *The Ladder*, June/July 1970:

EPISODE
I have robbed the garrulous streets,
Thieved a fair girl from their blight,
I have taken her for a sacrifice
That I shall make to this fleeting night.

I have brought her, laughing
To my moon-enchanted garden.
For what will be done there
I ask no man's pardon.
—Elsa Gidlow[13]

During June of 1970, despite the anger and frustration that reverberated among the Daughters over the loss of *The Ladder*, members of the host New York chapter continued their preparations for the national convention in July. They knew that the Daughters would be facing big decisions during their business meeting—nothing less than the fate of the national organization was before them—and that discussions over governance and structure would be the centerpiece of the weekend. But they didn't want to eliminate completely the speakers or the parties that had always, except for the '68 gathering, been a big part of the DOB's conferences.

The business meeting was as dramatic as had been expected. Deciding what to do about the loss of their magazine was the first item on the agenda. The small group of Daughters in New York for the meeting included both founders and early members from the mid-1950s as well as brand-new lesbian sisters impatient for change. Many Daughters argued for abolishing the national governing board, adopting recommendations similar to those proposed two years before, with one big exception: *The Ladder* was already gone, operating as a separate, private enterprise under Grier and Laporte's direction.

Older DOB members had witnessed the wrenching battle ONE, Inc., had gone through in 1965, when the editor, Don Slater, took the magazine's mailing list and continued to publish it privately. He and ONE founder Dorr Legg had engaged in a paper duel for six months, each publishing a magazine using the name *ONE* until a court order gave Legg the rights to the name. Slater got the office equipment associated with the magazine. After consulting with their lawyer about what would be involved in bringing a lawsuit to regain *The Ladder*, the Daughters reluctantly opted to let their prize publication go rather than risk years of expensive litigation in federal court and a similar "punishing" struggle. "It literally would have been a federal case," Phyllis Lyon explains, "because Rita took everything across state lines, from California to Nevada."[14]

Barbara Gittings remembers traveling to New York from her apartment in Philadelphia to see Phyllis Lyon and Del Martin during the convention; she met them in the hotel lounge. "They were very upset about what Grier had done, and I agreed with them," she says today.

Gittings was also in New York to join DOB's public panel discussion on "The Lesbian and the Feminist Movement," the signature event of the convention weekend. DOB was weighing in on the hottest political debate in the lesbian and women's liberation movements at that time; Kay Lahusen was there to record the event.

"It represented a continuation of DOB's long flirtation with the feminist cause." Lahusen noted that Phyllis Lyon, the moderator, introduced the session by saying, "The lesbian's lot today is tied up with two movements: the feminist movement and the homophile movement. The lesbian's dilemma is that while she may offer her services and her loyalties to both, she is rarely truly accepted in either."

Featuring Minda Bikman ("a Radical Feminist and straight"), Carolyn Bird (author of the book *Born Female*), Barbara Gittings, Phyllis Lyon, Del Martin, and Mickey Zacuto ("a lesbian and a Radical Feminist"), the DOB panelists discussed the pros and cons of lesbian feminist activism. The feminist author Susan Brownmiller had agreed to speak "but at the last minute remembered a previous engagement" and sent a letter with her comments instead, which was read to the audience. Brownmiller wrote that "in her casual observations of lesbians' personal relationships, she often sees a playing out of the female stereotype that she finds intolerable." She acknowledged that being a lesbian didn't automatically imply "a commitment to women's liberation" and confessed that her own life included males: "Men are my enemy, but they're all I've got to work with. They must be won over." She then urged lesbians to join the feminist struggle "in the name of womanhood." Most of the speakers emphasized the importance of lesbians' involvement in the women's movement *as women* despite the work that was necessary to educate nonlesbian women about lesbians' lives. Only Barbara Gittings, representing Philadelphia's Homophile Action League, argued that the two causes ("the gay and the feminist") could not be fought together. While she acknowledged that women had feminist work to do with gay men to "turn their heads around" and insure equal treatment, she emphasized solidarity. "If gay men and women don't get together and fight the gay cause, nobody else is going to do it for us," she said.

The event ended with remarks from the audience. "One lesbian noted that the Brownmiller letter and other observations had led her to wonder 'how real is the understanding?' For this reason, some lesbians may shy away from the feminist movement." Lahusen noted that, "Another listener said DOB has a special place and a special obligation, to be an organizational home for lesbians, aside from their feminist concerns."[15]

At the close of the Daughters' last convention, the huge changes facing the organization were not seen as problematic. In fact, for many of DOB's younger members, it was an exciting moment. The demise of DOB as a national organization fit perfectly within and reflected the spirit of the late 1960s and early 1970s, when traditional ways of organizing were rejected in favor of new modes of activism.

For example, the recently reinvigorated Los Angeles chapter's newsletter of July 1970 is full of news about the convention. "Big old New York will never be the same!!" Bo Siewert and Carole Sheperd, the vice president and president, respectively, of the L.A. chapter of DOB, attended the biennial national convention of the Daughters. "L.A. took the town by storm, to say the very least!" They reported gleefully, "Old National DOB got pulled out of the closet and had a thorough washing and shaking out!! Ancient by-laws were abolished, stuffy closet queens were dethroned and Bo and Carole paved the way to a new, young and thriving organization that will more adequately serve the needs of *all* female homosexuals."

Willer and Glass's 1968 reorganization plan had, in effect, been adopted. "DOB chapters are now run on an independent, each city 'do your thing' basis with all monies staying in the local chapter for the good of our own girls, rather than being poured down a national level rathole. Things are indeed looking up for DOB of today and tomorrow. Yesterday has been thoroughly buried."[16]

Pat Rardin, in "A New Day Dawns," cheered DOB delegates from

Los Angeles, San Francisco, New York, Boston, and Melbourne, Australia. After the convention, "there are no longer any national officers. Each DOB chapter is now autonomous. A Governing Board now will run DOB . . . made up of various Chapter Presidents. All chapters who did not attend will be asked to join. However, right now and until we hear from the absentee chapters, those chapters who were represented at the convention are the *only* recognized chapters of DOB."

LA DOB offered explanations about the changes undertaken at the 1970 national convention, starting with the simple fact that many chapter members believed DOB activities were most effective on a local level. They also noted that "although the Ladder is no longer affiliated with DOB it is an excellent magazine for all women," and they provided the Reno, Nevada, mailing address.

By the late 1960s, after Sandoz and Rush curtailed their involvement, the Southern California DOB chapters—the original one in Los Angeles and a newer one in Manhattan Beach, started by Flo Fleischman—were relatively inactive. In 1970, however, Jeanne Cordova and other younger lesbian-feminist activists provided a new infusion of energy. Like Martha Shelley in New York, Cordova's interest in working in a specifically lesbian group is what drew her to DOB rather than one of the male-dominated gay liberation groups springing up across the country in the wake of the June 1969 Stonewall riots in New York.

Mexican-Irish by birth, raised in a suburban Catholic family in the 1950s and 1960s, Cordova entered the convent of the Immaculate Heart of Mary in Los Angeles at the age of seventeen. Following Pope John XXIII's radical changes to Roman Catholic practice, the IHM nuns were among the first to abandon their traditional dress and behaviors. They were encouraged to engage in encounter groups, move freely in the world, and take the gospel to the people.

Cordova quickly became disillusioned with the experimentation erupting within the order. She left the IHM, enrolled at UCLA, and received her master's degree in social work. She also started a quest for a female lover. "I was looking. . . . I knew dykes were baseball players, so I looked in the softball leagues for a while. But there was no one to talk to. I was 'the college kid' and really lonely.

"I saw a copy of *The Ladder* on my sister's coffee table. She said, 'Oh that's a gay thing . . . ' and I memorized the address and phone number!" Cordova recalled that the group met in either a church or an auditorium, and that there were twenty to twenty-five people there. "October 3, 1970—that's my political birthday as an activist. That's the day I went to my first DOB meeting."[17]

Cordova became president of the LA DOB within months of her first meeting; she soon met Barbara McLean, who had been very active in the revitalization of the Chicago chapter a few years earlier. Together, Cordova and McLean, and other new activists, introduced the homophile-era lesbians in Los Angeles to lesbian-feminist issues. "The [DOB] members were more conservative—they were into stereotypical butch/femme roles. I was comfortable with that. But we invited the group Women Against War to DOB—that caused a stir, but they listened," Cordova remembers.

But other longtime leaders were saddened by the loss of *The Ladder* and the demise of the national organization: they saw the end of an era. Stella Rush said that she and Helen Sandoz were uncomfortable with the younger activists, particularly some of the more separatist lesbians. "There was a lot of man-hating stuff, and Sandy and I just couldn't go along with that," Rush remembers. "I was more into human rights, and Sandy's thing had always been economic equity. We were turned off by their tone." They also never "followed Del and Phyllis into NOW," which Rush remembers discussing with their old friends at several points over the years.[18]

By 1970, Martin and Lyon were in the midst of another struggle over integration of lesbians, only this time it was with sisters in the feminist movement. After years of simmering internal struggles within NOW over same-sex sexuality, including "purges" of self-identified or accused lesbians from the local chapter, New York was the site of a historic confrontation over lesbianism in the women's movement that year.

It had been building for a while. New York NOW chapter president Ivy Bottini had worked hard to challenge the homophobia she experienced within the national NOW leadership and was finally driven from her post in 1969. The lesbian author and activist Rita Mae Brown also felt silenced in NOW. When DOB's name was omitted from a NOW press release listing the sponsors for the first national feminist Congress to Unite Women in 1969, she resigned and joined the newly formed Gay Liberation Front (GLF), where many "refugees" from the women's movement had hoped to find a home. Soon, a number of lesbian-feminist activists formed a collective within the GLF. After an article by Susan Brownmiller appeared in *The New York Times Magazine* that quoted Friedan's "lavender menace" comments about lesbians, they decided to stage a protest at the upcoming women's conference.[19]

At the second Congress to Unite Women, held in New York City on May 1, 1970, lesbian activists—such as Brown and Martha Shelley, as well as Karla Jay and over two dozen women—seized the moment. On the opening night of the Congress, while hundreds of people waited for the scheduled panel session to begin, the auditorium was suddenly plunged into darkness. When the lights were turned on again, seventeen women wearing purple T-shirts proclaiming themselves the "Lavender Menace" took over the stage after "decorating" the halls with such signs as "The Women's Movement is a Lesbian Plot." The group, who soon began calling themselves

Radicalesbians, also distributed a statement they had drafted titled "The Woman-Identified Woman."

Initially, the NOW audience was shocked by the protest but the Menaces got a resolution passed by the end of the weekend calling for the validation and affirmation of lesbians and lesbian sexuality. The Lavender Menace action created an opening for putting lesbian issues on NOW's agenda. In addition, within the next year new leadership emerged who would help open things up even more.

Aileen Hernandez, the seasoned San Francisco labor and civil rights activist who had been named by President Lyndon Johnson in 1965 as the only black woman member of the United States Equal Employment Opportunity Commission, was a founding member and the second national president of NOW. She was also Del Martin and Phyllis Lyon's friend and mentor in the women's liberation movement. She asked them to help organize educational programs on lesbianism for the next national NOW conference, scheduled for Los Angeles in 1971.

They agreed, and as the conference opened, they found in the official conference packets "a beautiful statement" from the host chapter about the importance of lesbians in NOW. There were many such statements of support from NOW chapters all over the country, from Atlanta to Detroit to Los Angeles, testifying to the crucial role lesbians had played in the organization at the local level. "They said lesbianism was pro-feminism and NOW couldn't throw out lesbians and still have a movement," Lyon and Martin have said. Friedan maintained her personal and public opposition; she continued to fight lesbian leadership in the organization and even questioned whether the Lavender Menace action was part of U.S. government agents' efforts to undermine the organization in the early 1970s. However, the NOW conference attendees produced a resolution affirming the importance of lesbian rights.[20]

As had happened with the American Civil Liberties Union and gay rights, it was local efforts by chapter activists, including some who had gained organizing skills through their work with the Daughters, that helped changed the thinking of NOW on lesbianism. Martin and Lyon were encouraged by the beginnings of activism in support of lesbians in the women's movement; they were also enjoying their involvement in a new political women's world. The same could not be said of their connection to the gay movement.

In the December 1970/January 1971 issue of *The Ladder,* Barbara Grier printed Martin's infamous "goodbye" to the homophile and gay liberation movements, "If That's All There Is." Martin and other DOB activists had gone to the NACHO meeting the previous August—on National Women's Strike Day, August 26, 1970—to confront the coalition on its irrelevance to women. The delegates had passed a resolution in support of women's liberation, but took no other actions on the women's complaints of exclusion and invisibility. "They would not address themselves to the underlying reason for the existence of separate women's organizations—that the female homosexual faces sex discrimination not only in the heterosexual world, but within the homophile community."

Martin remembers, "At a dinner for the entire community (but with few women present) Assembly Speaker Willie Brown gave a wonderful speech about the need for solidarity. The gay men ignored the women who were present, calling to the front only the men and pushing the women who had been at the head table out of the way."[21]

Martin's rage at her gay male comrades was huge. In her searing farewell, she wrote, "[F]ifteen years of masochism is enough. I will not be your 'nigger' any longer. Nor was I ever your mother. Those are stultifying roles you laid on me, and I shall no longer concern myself with your toilet training. As I bid you adieu, I leave each of you to your own device. Take care of it, stroke it gently, mouth it, and fondle it. As the center of your consciousness, it's really all you have."[22]

Not surprisingly, Martin's tirade caused controversy in the gay movement, not the least of which was among former Daughters with whom she had worked most closely over the years. Barbara Gittings and Kay Lahusen felt that her anger was misplaced and misdirected. "We didn't think the men were really sexist," Lahusen has commented. "And neither of us felt like we had been discriminated against because we were women. We were fighting for our rights as gay people."[23]

Gittings and Lahusen had turned their attention from DOB to a number of other gay rights fronts in the late 1960s and early 1970s. In 1971, Gittings was involved as a discussion leader at the American Psychiatric Association (APA) panel, which included Del Martin among six panelists, on "Life Styles of Non-Patient Homosexuals." The following year, she was the person responsible for the appearance of "Dr. H. Anonymous, the masked gay psychiatrist," who joined an official panel that she participated in with Franklin Kameny titled "Psychiatry: Friend or Foe to Homosexuals? A Dialogue." That year, and again in 1976 and 1978, she also organized and staffed gay exhibits at annual APA conferences. In addition, she worked with Kameny at gay people's security-clearance hearings. "The Defense Department administered security clearances both for military jobs and jobs in private industry; most of our cases were for civilian jobs with outside defense contractors." Always an avid bibliophile, she delighted in working with the gay caucus of the American Library Association to create gay-positive reading lists and book awards; boost the gay pamphlets, periodicals, audiovisuals, and books in libraries; and air issues of gay invisibility, censorship, and discrimination.

Lahusen was writing for Jack Nichols's newspaper *Gay* and was one of the founders of New York's Gay Activists Alliance in 1970 and the Gay Women's Alternative in 1973. Together they attended a few gay liberation meetings. Although she and Gittings disliked the insulting labels hurled at them by some younger radical gay liberationists, they welcomed the new militancy they saw emerging in the gay movement. "Later we actually went out and bought stuffed animals—dinosaurs—and put labels on them: 'Pre-Stonewall Activist.' We proudly took them with us to gay meetings and demonstrations," Lahusen has said. For both women, the gay cause was still the most important one and they prized their alliances and friendships with gay men.[24]

Ironically, it was Barbara Grier who applauded—and prominently displayed—Martin's indictment of gay men despite their personal and political rupture over Grier's "theft" of *The Ladder* six months earlier. In its "new" incorporation, *The Ladder* was now emphasizing gender over sexuality while still providing valuable information about the liberation struggles of both movements. It also continued its longstanding role of helping formulate new visual and verbal images of "the lesbian," although now she was unabashedly wearing the banner of feminism—or, rather, the martial-arts outfit of a woman arm-chopping a man in the face, under the headline "You've Come a Long Way, Baby," which appeared on the October/November 1970 cover.

From its first issue on, *The Ladder* had provided a place where women could create a multifaceted lesbian identity and advance lesbian visibility. Sometimes it was through the simple yet scary act of signing one's real name to an article or story, or being listed on the newsletter's masthead. It was a big step forward for Phyllis Lyon to "do away with Ann Ferguson" in 1957. It meant she was willing to drop her pen name and be identified as the editor of a lesbian magazine.

As Del Martin has often said, "We were fighting the church, the couch, and the courts." The DOB organized women and published a magazine during a time when lesbians and gay men were routinely viewed by the authorities as sinful, sick, and criminal. The Daughters of Bilitis and the other homophile groups worked hard to dispel their members' own feelings of inferiority and unease at being "outsiders" while insisting that the religious, medical, and legal institutions reform the policies and practices that pushed lesbians and gay men to the margins of society.

By the early 1970s, lesbians increasingly asserted their experiences of dual oppressions, based on both gender and sexual orientation. Disputes riddle *The Ladder*'s pages during these years about where gay women's loyalties should lie. As Rita Mae Brown wrote in "Say It Isn't So" in the June/July 1970 issue, "Our struggle is against the male power system which is a system of war and death. If in the process of that struggle we are forced to mutilate, murder, and massacre those men, then so it must be. But simultaneous with that struggle we must also struggle to build a culture of life and love."

Brown then emphasized that "to date, the women's movement has consistently rejected women who are trying to build a new way of life, a life of loving other women. If we can't love each other, if we can't learn to grow together, then we will only have a rebellion against the male death culture—a rebellion which may be successful. But I think we are capable of revolution. To love without role, without power plays, is revolution. I believe these are our goals."[25]

"I felt that DOB should change with the times, and that feminism was the determining factor for lesbians," Jeanne Cordova said recently. Beginning in January 1971, she took on the tasks associated with writing, producing, and mailing the monthly LA DOB publication, used mostly to communicate with local members, announce meetings and programs, and serve as publicity for the group. Most DOB chapters, starting with New York and Los Angeles in the late 1950s, produced brief newsletters if they had enough volunteers available to write, type, and mimeograph them. Many lasted for only a few months or a year, then shut down, and were started up again when a new infusion of activist energy was brought into the local group.

Soon Cordova, who was enjoying her work on the L.A. newsletter, began getting complaints from some members of the chapter who thought she was printing too many "radical" pieces about lesbian feminism. "There was a tension in the chapter between political activism and personal life," Cordova remembers. Along with a few other young activist lesbians, however, she continued to publish what they wanted to read.[26]

Barbara McLean remembers the excitement of working in the L.A. chapter in those days. A leader of Chicago DOB starting in 1966, McLean was employed by RCA Computer Systems as a computer programmer in the late 1960s. "I was hired in their Chicago office," she remembers. "And from the beginning I was honest with them. 'I'm gay,' I said. 'Okay, great, you're hired,' they said. They were tired of hiring women who would get married and quit and the company would have wasted money and training." She succeeded on the regional level and the company transferred her to Southern California in 1969. "I decided to look up DOB here and got connected in 1970." DOB's all-woman membership was appealing, to her and to other lesbians. "Men and women in their jobs were living a straight life; in their social life they wanted to get away from it." She emphasized the division that grew between gay men and lesbians in the 1970s and cites as an example the commemorative march that was organized in Los Angeles two years after New York's Stonewall riots. "For the 1971 gay pride march in L.A. we tried to create a coalition of all gay and lesbian organizations in the area—it was really tough. The women said, 'we're not working with men.'"[27]

In August, the LA DOB newsletter appeared as the newly renamed *Lesbian Tide*. By early winter, it was clear to Cordova and McLean that it should "graduate" from being a local DOB newsletter to a monthly national lesbian feminist magazine. In contrast to the steps taken by Grier and Laporte when they severed *The Ladder* from DOB, however, Cordova and McLean maintained their ties to the local organization while publishing the magazine on their own. They went to the L.A. chapter members and asked that the newsletter be released from the organization's control. Their wishes were granted, and *Lesbian Tide* became an independent publication in December 1971. As its masthead proclaimed in 1973, "The LESBIAN TIDE is an independent, feminist lesbian magazine. It is financially supported by the community it serves and is maintained by the pride, time, and efforts of a working collective of gay women."

It became known for its news and analysis, high production values, and not least, for its always sensual, sometimes sexually suggestive photographs of lesbians. Nancy Rosenblum is one of the many photographers and artists who created some of the powerful portraits that the magazine published. *Lesbian Tide* provided a start for other lesbian artists as well. In 1999, the singer-songwriter Margie Adam remembered, "The first invitation I ever received to perform in public was made by Jeanne Cordova of the *Lesbian Tide* magazine in Los Angeles after she heard me sing at an open mike at Kate Millett's Sacramento Women's Music Festival. I told her I wasn't a performer. I told her I wasn't political. She said just come and sing your songs at our benefit. I went to L.A. I sang songs about my life for this lesbian feminist magazine." That performance launched Adam as one of the most popular and influential lesbian musicians of the time.[28]

Lesbian Tide also helped fill the void when Barbara Grier stopped publishing *The Ladder* in 1972, despite a mailing list of 3,845 names. As Grier explains it today, "We ran out of money. It's that simple."

She says that DOB's regular $3,000 donations from its closeted
donor during the 1960s enabled the magazine to be printed and
mailed. "The minute the magazine was divorced from the organization, the subsidy dried up." Grier insists that she "never thought
about" how she would pay for the magazine without "Pennsylvania's" contributions but she soon realized that she was unable to
survive on subscriptions alone. Advertising revenue—except from
sources that the women who read the magazine wouldn't want, "like
sex services or porn distributors"—was not a viable option. "I created
the problem that caused it to have to fold," she admitted recently.
"We increased subscriptions to over three thousand and with the
money from that couldn't afford to print it and send it out even
though all the work was voluntary."[29]

In the August/September 1972 issue of *The Ladder*, Grier wrote
her final "Lesbiana" column. She noted that among many other new
books in 1972 there were new works by authors she had reviewed in
her column many times before: a volume of poetry by May Sarton
(*A Durable Fire*); John O'Hara's *The Ewings*; and the novel *An
Accidental Man*, by Iris Murdoch. Surprisingly, she failed to review
Phyllis Lyon and Del Martin's recently published *Lesbian/Woman*.
In 1972, they had pioneered once again, producing this instant
classic through the Glide Foundation. Through a mix of personal
histories, Lyon and Martin described lesbian lives in a positive way;
many women still remember the feeling of walking into a bookstore
or library and seeing a book with the word "Lesbian" in the title,
validating their existence.

Grier admitted to difficulty in evaluating *The Gay Crusaders* by Kay
Tobin (Lahusen) and Randy Wicker, which was also published in 1972.
They interviewed eleven gay and four lesbian activists during 1971 and
1972 and produced one of the earliest first-person accounts of 1950s
and 1960s gay activism. Grier wrote that "the disaffection between

male homosexuals and Lesbians is soft-pedaled to such an extent that one might imagine the two groups worked together congenially, which isn't and hasn't been so in many years." Grier's separatist sentiments reflect one of the strongest currents in the women's liberation movement of the early 1970s, especially among lesbian feminists.

Not all lesbians shared those views, however. In 1972, as had been true for at least twenty years, some gay men and lesbians were successfully "working together"—if not always "congenially." Within some mixed-gender organizations, personal and political work was done in the early 1970s to advance gay and lesbian rights; many activists—men and women—struggled together, most often over issues of sexism but also over questions of race and class, to form such organizations as the Gay Activists Alliance, the Gay Academic Union, and the National Gay Task Force.[30]

Shortly thereafter, using *The Ladder*'s mailing list to announce her new enterprise, Grier launched Naiad Press with three other women, including her partner, Donna McBride; Anyda Marchant (who wrote lesbian love stories under the pen name Sarah Aldridge); and Muriel Crawford. Their first book, published in 1974, was Aldridge's *The Latecomer*. For the next twenty-five years, Naiad successfully published lesbian literature, bringing back works that had been long out of print and launching new lesbian writers, such as Marchant, Katherine V. Forrest, Sheila Taylor Ortiz, and Jane Rule. In addition to fiction, Naiad published nonfiction such as Grier's *The Lesbian in Literature: A Bibliography* and Rosemary Curb and Nancy Manahan's *Lesbian Nuns: Breaking Silence*, which included Jeanne Cordova's account of convent life.

The Ladder's demise came about during the groundswell of lesbian and feminist publications in the early 1970s: one of the most significant and long-lasting actions taken by lesbians and feminists was the proliferation of writings and images expressing their new worldviews. Veterans of 1950s and 1960s movements—civil rights, homophile, antiwar, among others—lesbians and feminists had learned the lesson that "the power of the press" belonged to the person who owned one. They not only produced newsletters, books, and magazines but soon created all-women feminist printing businesses and bookstores as well.

"In 1970, fourteen years into its existence, The Ladder was joined by the first of a new generation of alternative publications devoted to reporting and theorizing about gay and lesbian existence: in that year, the new organization New York Gay Liberation Front (GLF) began publishing *Come Out!* and in 1971, *Gay Community News* began publishing in Boston," the lesbian scholar Kate Adams wrote in 1998.[31] The feminist newsjournal *off our backs* also started publishing in 1970, joining an avalanche of new women's newspapers, magazines, and journals, including *Lesbian Tide*.

The very year that Grier took *The Ladder* away from DOB and began to publish it privately, it was no longer the only source of information about lesbians. But it was still the only lesbian feminist magazine that had a fourteen-year track record. And few activists knew that Grier's actions had cost DOB its most valuable asset. Most lesbians continued to support, value, and subscribe to the magazine; it was like an old friend that helped one stay connected and "on the alert." And Grier reaped a good deal of lesbian feminist goodwill, if not financial riches, because *The Ladder* was still the model, publishing exciting and provocative art, fiction, essays, poetry, and news from around the world.

The explosion in lesbian and feminist liberation media didn't come from out of nowhere. In part because the Daughters had prioritized the development of chapter newsletters as well as a monthly national lesbian magazine, there were already publications in place when lesbian feminism seized the minds and hearts of a new generation of "woman-loving women." Former Daughters who were committed to the new women's movement—among them Barbara Grier, Rita Laporte, Phyllis Lyon, and Del Martin—passed on their experience and knowledge. Others, like Jeanne Cordova and Barbara McLean, were at the forefront of creating new vehicles for lesbian feminist thought. Still other Daughters, like Kay Lahusen, continued to contribute their artistry to the newspapers and books being created by gay liberation activists.

They all benefited—as did the social change movements to which they contributed their time and talents—from the existence of the Daughters of Bilitis. The experience of engaging in education, research, and social action, as well as publishing, gave many lesbians practical political skills and valuable organizing strategies in the heady if contentious days of 1970s lesbian and feminist liberation.

CHAPTER TEN

Lesbos Arise!

A SMALL CONTRADICTION

It is politically incorrect
to demand monogamous
relationships—

It's emotionally insecure
to seek
ownership of
another's soul—
or body &
damaging to one's psyche
to restrict the giving and
taking of love.

Me, I am
totally opposed to
monogamous relationships
unless

i'm
in love.

—Pat Parker[1]

By 1973, the combination of lesbian identity and feminist ideology was a powerful force. "The lesbian" went from being maligned in the mid-1950s to exalted by the mid-1970s, at least among those women who found love and friendship in women-centered events and organizations. The new lesbian feminism was nurtured by the proliferation of women's newspapers, magazines, bars, and businesses. "Feminism is the theory, lesbianism is the practice" had become gospel in many women's circles, and for some the mission was the creation not only of separate lesbian sites but specifically lesbian-feminist lifestyles and values. As Lillian Faderman wrote in her 1991 history of American lesbian life in the twentieth century, *Odd Girls and Twilight Lovers,* "radical feminism had helped redefine lesbianism to make it almost a categorical imperative for all women truly interested in the welfare and progress of other women."[2]

The creation of all-woman spaces, services, and groups was familiar to anyone who had gone to a DOB meeting in the 1960s or received *The Ladder,* but the definitions of who a lesbian was and how she should live her life were complicated and contradictory in the early 1970s. With boundless energy and enthusiasm, radical lesbian feminists experimented with ways to reclaim women's freedom. For example, many proclaimed that all lesbian relationships should be open, free, and nonmonogamous . . . until, of course, as the black poet and activist Pat Parker famously admitted, "i'm in love."

The quickly shifting boundaries could be confusing; opinions on what constituted "correct" lesbian feminist behavior changed rapidly and diverged wildly. The West Coast Lesbian Conference, held in Los Angeles in 1973, was one of the first large lesbian feminist gatherings to create a special "women's space" and it highlighted many of the challenges of a brand-new culture.

"It was the biggest lesbian conference in the world!" Thirty years

later, Jeanne Cordova can still summon up the intensity and excitement she felt in April 1973. "That conference was like giving
birth—always messy, the contractions don't proceed as expected,"
she says. "It birthed *Lesbian Nation*." Drawing inspiration from
other radical movements of the late 1960s, the *Village Voice* columnist and radical lesbian Jill Johnston articulated the lesbian separatist
rationale in her 1973 book *Lesbian Nation: The Feminist Solution*.
"Historically the lesbian had two choices: being criminal or going
straight. The present revolutionary project is the creation of a legitimate state defined by women."[3]

For many members of the integrationist DOB, the growing separatism was jarring. That is one reason the formation of a new
group—L.A.W., or Lesbian Activist Women—was necessary when
Cordova, Barbara McLean, and other Daughters joined with L.A.
activists in November 1972 to organize a weekend conference for the
following April. In 1971, a small lesbian conference had been held in
Los Angeles; now the organizers set their sights on producing a big
event that would bring hundreds of lesbians together from around
the country. To their amazement, they got all that, and more.

The West Coast Lesbian Conference was held at UCLA April 13
to 15, 1973. UCLA staff member Sheila Kuehl—who played Zelda
in the television sitcom *The Many Loves of Dobie Gillis* in the 1960s
and went on to become an openly lesbian Assembly member, then
state Senator, in California—secured the site.[4] Despite the fact that
Kuehl had reserved a 700-seat auditorium for them, the sheer numbers of women who attended the conference overwhelmed the
organizers. On that sunny Southern California spring weekend, fifteen hundred women—nearly twice as many as they had expected,
more than double what the room could hold—converged on the
UCLA campus. They came from over two hundred U.S. cities and
twenty-six states, as well as Canada, Denmark, France, and Sweden.

In addition to meeting space, approximately one-third of them also needed free community housing.

The dozen or so women who were on the conference planning committee scrambled to find beds, couches, pillows, or floors; they also had to arrange for child care and host the speakers and musicians. There seemed to be a constant barrage of questions from UCLA officials, the media, and the participants. The whole scene was chaotic and controversial. It was also unprecedented.

In Barbara McLean's "Diary of a Mad Organizer," printed in the June 1973 special *Lesbian Tide* commemorative issue, she tracked the organizers from eager beginnings to exhausted end. She described the initial missteps: "[A]fter scheduling it for April 20 to 22 at UCLA, some sister points out that that is the Easter weekend. How could we have MISSED that? By using an anarchist calendar!"[5]

McLean detailed the complaints as well as some of the inadvertently comical conversations:

> *"Hi, Barbara. I'm calling from the Women's Resource Center. We, ah, just received one of those forms about housing."*

> "Oh, really, from who?"

> *"Uh . . . well, it's from someone named Hummingbird."*

> "Hummingbird?"

> *"Yes, Hummingbird. And the message is that housing is needed for sixty mountain dykes from Tucson, Oregon, and Albuquerque."*

> "Did you say *sixty?*"

"Yes, sixty."

"Mountain dykes?"

"Yes, from Tucson, Oregon, and Albuquerque."

"How did Oregon get in there?"

"Friends of Hummingbird, I suppose . . . it was addressed 'UCLA, Women's Resource Center, c/o The Dykes'."

"Well, uh, it got to the right place, didn't it?"

McLean spelled out the goals of the organizers. "I think we mostly want what everyone wants: the experience of standing in the center of a sea of lesbians, the experience of looking around and seeing, as far as the eye can see, LESBIANS." Throughout the weekend, however, there were disagreements over almost everything, from child care to radical politics. The essential arguments were over what constituted authentic "lesbian culture" and who could claim lesbian identity. "'Happiness is meeting your mother at a lesbian conference,' somebody said. Well, I ran into my mother at the conference, and let me tell you it was scary as hell," Alice Bloch wrote in "Dem Ol' Conference Crazies." "My mother died a long time ago and now here I was, a lesbian surrounded by lesbians, all of us fighting like jealous lovers, and I knew I'd come home."[6]

The conference exploded on opening night—"Friday the 13th—that's another thing we hadn't thought of." The young singer-songwriter scheduled to provide the evening's entertainment was one of DOB's most active members on the West Coast; she was a leader in the San Francisco chapter and had been part of the

organizing team for the conference. She had written some new lesbian feminist songs and was excited about performing at Friday's
opening session. But her appearance shattered any illusion of sisterhood within the gathering and set off a firestorm over whether
transsexual women were welcome in the lesbian feminist movement. It foreshadowed debates that would continue for the next
three decades.

Transsexualism was not a new issue for DOB. The first time that it
was aired in *The Ladder* was July 1958, when Phyllis Lyon published
a letter to DOB from "Lady Kay, New York, N.Y." who suggested
using the term "femmen" for "females in male bodies." But in 1973
it literally jumped to center stage. Beth Elliott was a preoperative
MTF (male-to-female) transsexual who joined DOB in San Francisco
in 1971. She was honest about her transition and, after heated controversy and disagreements among the members, was accepted, even
becoming vice president of the local chapter. As she tells the story, a
former friend "outted" her by screaming, "There's a man on stage!"
as she prepared to start her set on opening night. It was an orches-
trated ambush that had been planned well ahead of time. "I got a
threatening phone call one night during the week leading up the conference," Elliott said recently. She took the stage anyway. The
resulting furor threatened to tear the conference apart.[7]

As one conference participant, Ann Forfreedom, put it, "Though
men attempted to disrupt the conference several times during the
weekend, only one being-with-a-penis actually succeeded." She
recounted the scene that erupted when a handful of San Francisco
women tried to shout Elliott from the stage. Other women in the
audience and on stage defended Elliott's appearance; the debates
over her participation raged for the rest of the night and the next two
days. Was she a lesbian? Did she belong in "women-only space?"
Who had the right, the responsibility, to decide?

When Robin Morgan, the keynote speaker, claimed that she, Morgan, was a lesbian despite her involvement in a heterosexual relationship, she captured another controversy over authentic lesbianism. In the post-conference *Lesbian Tide,* L.A. activist Pat Buchanan rejected Morgan's definition of lesbianism as based solely on "woman-loving." She quoted Morgan's statement that she lived with a man (a "faggot effeminist") and they were raising their child together. Buchanan responded, "It seems strange to me that a woman (and I will not call her sister) with such a high consciousness level & who attacks men so radically, can continue in her own lifestyle." She added, "Many women attack Betty Friedan for her anti-Lesbian stand. At least give Friedan the dubious honor of saying honestly what she thinks & not aligning herself falsely."8

Conference organizers worked feverishly to get things back on track after Friday night's melee, and Saturday's sessions proceeded as planned. But another controversy erupted over the issue of children. While groups at the UCLA conference were meeting in support of lesbian mothers, for example, sharing child care responsibilities during the weekend sorely tested the limits of "sisterhood." Despite the volunteer energies of Morris Kight, a gay male activist in L.A., and a small team from the Gay Community Services Center, the child care facilities and staffing were inadequate, causing a confrontation on Saturday afternoon led by women who had brought their children with them. "Although there seemed [to be] little concern for child care on the part of the majority of gay women, a few of the mothers themselves seemed just as unconcerned," one "non-mother" wrote in response. "Gay mothers, can you submerge your own hang-ups to concentrate on your children's best interests? Non-mothers, can you turn your back on your sisters' children? Can any of us afford to pass the buck any longer?"9

Afterward, Ann Forfreedom described a weekend that "gave me a new pride, a new definition of myself and of Lesbianism." She applauded the "female culture" at the conference. Beth Elliott called her conference experience "an emotional battering" that caused her great distress. After being heckled and threatened, she left the conference but stayed connected with L.A.W. and the Orange County Dyke Patrol in Southern California, as well as the Alice B. Toklas Memorial Democratic Club, which she had helped start, in San Francisco. She also continued her work with the California Committee for Sexual Law Reform "until we got California's sodomy laws repealed in 1975. Then I had the delayed reaction crash and burn." Although Elliott didn't return to SF DOB, she still acknowledges that it had been her home. "Being welcome there had inspired me to do my best for my sisters," she said recently.[10]

While some Daughters were in the eye of the lesbian feminist storm in Los Angeles in 1973, others utilized DOB as a refuge from often intense political collectives and coalitions. Because of the organization's consistent emphasis on providing social space for women, DOB provided a home for lesbians who needed a low-key, accepting environment. There was space not only for the lesbian misfit—who didn't feel comfortable in androgynous crunchy-granola flannel shirts and jeans, or dress-for-success suits as well as the woman just beginning to explore her sexual desires and emotional feelings for other women.

The establishment of chapters in the mid- to late 1960s, pushed by DOB's last two national presidents Shirley Willer and Rita Laporte, meant that, by the mid-1970s, there were small DOB groups in twenty metropolitan areas. While some floundered and could not sustain themselves for more than a year or two, groups of Daughters could be found from Cleveland to Tampa, New Hampshire to New Orleans. Daughters in San Francisco and New York (now renamed

the "New York/New Jersey" chapter) continued their social, educational, and legislative activities. But it was in Boston that new DOB
activists organized a group with staying power. "In 1965 an article
appeared in the *Mid-Town Journal* announcing an appearance by the
president of DOB's New York chapter at a hotel in Brookline to discuss the formation of a Boston chapter. The Boston branch was
eventually formed in 1969."[11] In 1974, despite controversy over
their involvement in feminist issues, the Daughters in Boston celebrated their fifth anniversary by planning another Thanksgiving
extravaganza.

Lois Johnson and her lover, Shari Barden, were two white women
in their thirties; they were introduced to the newly formed DOB in
1969 by a local organizer, Jan Chase. They became actively involved
soon thereafter. According to Barbara Grier, early leaders of the DOB
in Boston were Pat Peterson and her lover, Annette; women listed in
Ladder announcements as representing the chapter in numerous
speaking engagements and media appearances in 1969 and 1970 were
Terry Andot, Kim Stabinski, Ann Haley, Marty Kelly, and Laura Robin.
In February 1970, the new chapter's newsletter, *Maiden Voyage*, was
unveiled. By April of that year, eighteen months after growing gay
activism in Boston finally put the city on the homophile map, a number
of groups had been organized, including DOB, the Homophile Union
of Boston, the Council on Religion and the Homosexual, and the
Harvard Graduate Student Homophile Association.[12]

In 1971 the Daughters began offering "rap" sessions. The small-
group discussions may have been renamed to reflect more current
terminology but they were similar to the "Gab 'n' Java" gatherings
DOB members had organized fifteen years earlier in San Francisco,
Los Angeles, and New York. "I well remember the combination of
excitement and apprehension with which I tentatively entered my
first 'rap.' My eyes bugged open. There must have been twenty-five

women in the room," Johnson reminisced. "It was an exhilarating experience for someone who had been gay for ten to twelve years but had not really know many women except her lovers." Johnson assumed the role of Boston DOB president in 1975 and led the group for the next twenty years.[13]

"The Arlington Community Church was the first place to allow us to rent space," Shari Barden remembered in 2002. They had monthly potlucks to raise money for such chapter projects as the upgrade of the monthly newsletter into a professionally printed magazine edited by Barden, telephone service with answering machine, and ads recruiting members. Their first office was located at 419 Boylston Street—"Bay Village on South Bay was a gay neighborhood"—and they shared the building with the Homophile Union of Boston (HUB) and the Homophile Community Health Service. Barden remembers that DOB members helped plan the early Gay Pride marches in Boston. For some, however, fear of being identified as gay combined with a flare for the dramatic: they marched wearing paper bags over their heads.[14]

The next three years were busy ones for DOB Boston. Their newsletter was transformed and renamed *Focus*. In addition, they worked with HUB to organize "the first New England Gay Conference," which was followed by several others attracting gay men and lesbians from throughout the Northeast.

For the athletically inclined, Boston DOB had a softball team. "There were pick-up games every Sunday near the BU [Boston University] bridge; we also had brunches at various places like the Saints, which was a women's bar downtown."

But perhaps owing to the holiday's familial significance, it was DOB's Thanksgiving dinners that were the organization's annual triumphs. "St. John's Episcopal Church on Beacon Street allowed us to rent their basement. We had the first Thanksgiving dinner for

Daughters in the early 1970s." Johnson explained that lesbians often faced difficult personal choices at holidays, such as being unable to return home with their lovers or pretending to be straight for the sake of family harmony. DOB presented a warm, inviting alternative. "It was held the Sunday before Thanksgiving—kids were ok—and it was a home-cooked Thanksgiving dinner," Johnson said. Barden did most of the cooking. There were regularly seventy to one hundred and fifty people enjoying the feast with lovers and friends.

Barden was the president of Boston DOB in 1974 when controversy erupted over "taking stands" on women's liberation issues. "Some lesbians wanted a feminist political action group—we were adamant against them—and it was a tooth and nail fight." The group voted to continue as the Daughters of Bilitis but lost many younger activist members. They reemphasized personal and social support for the individual lesbian, education of the public, and reform of laws barring lesbians from enjoyment of their "full civil and human rights." Despite the lesbian feminism being embraced in other chapters, Boston DOB was typecast as a group of "conservative old ladies," according to Barden, and it was not seen as a place for discussing emerging political questions.

Although DOB had the reputation of being stodgy in the increasingly radicalized lesbian feminist and gay liberation movements in Boston, it was valued as a safe space for some lesbians, especially those in the early stages of acknowledging their same-sex desires. "There are still women who clip out our advertisement, put it on their wall, look at it every day for months, and then finally feel courageous enough to come to a meeting," Johnson noted.[15]

Jewelle Gomez was one of them. She recently reminisced about how, as a young black lesbian living in Boston, she would agonize over her desire to attend a DOB meeting but could not work up the nerve to go. "If I had, I would have met Diane years earlier." Her current partner, Diane Sabin, was a member of Boston DOB at the same time; the two met later in San Francisco when Sabin produced a feminist poetry reading.[16]

The explosion of new opportunities in the 1970s for women's voices far surpassed what DOB could provide through its network. In 1975, three years after she stopped producing *The Ladder*, Barbara Grier delivered a complete set of issues to Arno Press. Sixteen years' worth of writing about lesbian, feminist, homophile, and human rights issues were bound into eight orange volumes as part of the series *Homosexuality: Lesbians and Gay Men in Society, History and Literature*. The series editor was the pioneering gay historian Jonathan Ned Katz, author of *Gay American History* and *Gay and Lesbian Almanac*; Barbara Gittings served on the editorial board. The eight volumes containing *The Ladder* are "reprinted from copies in the library of Barbara Grier." They include an Introduction written by Grier, still using the pseudonym Gene Damon, titled "*The Ladder*, Rung by Rung."

In her Introduction, she recounts the magazine's history, its role in the emerging gay and lesbian rights movement, and the "growing procession of well-known writers" whose work first appeared in its pages. She ended on a celebratory note that reflects both the heady optimism of the mid-1970s and her personal stake in the magazine. "There is much more in these pages. There is a history of very oppressed people who did not wish to stay oppressed and who worked to do something about it," she wrote. "What they have accomplished is visible in today's much less restrictive, much freer atmosphere. No one associated with *The Ladder* feels that the magazine was all by itself responsible for these changes, but we all feel we helped."[17]

The following year, Grier and her partner, Donna McBride,

attended the first Women in Print conference, held in Omaha, Nebraska. Grier remembers a room with a hundred and fifty women, each of whom introduced herself and the publication, store, or organization she worked with. When it came to Grier's turn, she recounted, "Charlotte Bunch was moderating and she leaned over and said, 'You're next, Barbara, try to keep it short,' because it was taking a long time to get through everybody," Grier remembered recently. She gave her name and announced that she was representing Naiad Press and *The Ladder*. "Every woman in the room stood up and stomped and screamed and applauded at the mention of the magazine. It went on for fifteen minutes. . . . That was the very first time I knew how much *The Ladder* meant to all those women. . . . I never had any idea."[18] Most of the women in attendance probably had no idea of the story behind Grier's takeover of *The Ladder*; what they did know was that she was the magazine's last editor and the one most closely associated with ensuring its legacy. *The Ladder* was revered as a small gem of lesbian and feminist expression that had thrived during a time when nothing else like it existed.

But its importance to the DOB was never in doubt. Six years after "the theft," anger over Grier's actions still infuriated some Daughters. In 1976, Del Martin wrote a letter to Coletta Reid of Diana Press in Baltimore about Diana's plans to publish three *Ladder* anthologies. She asked Reid why DOB had not been contacted directly and noted that Barbara Grier would be entitled to republish any articles written by her "under her various pseudonyms" but had no authorization to publish any other articles that had appeared in the magazine before 1970. DOB would be "open to negotiations" if Diana wanted to publish materials from *The Ladder* that appeared during the time the organization published the magazine. "As a feminist press you will, of course, wish to protect the rights of all sisters involved."[19]

In one of the three anthologies of *Ladder* writings that Diana Press published in 1976, *The Lavender Herring: Lesbian Essays from The Ladder*, the first page read, "We respectfully dedicate these anthologies to *The Ladder* women. They know who they are!" Grier made it clear in the Introduction that all but one of the essays appeared in the magazine between 1968 and 1972, the four years when she was the editor; she explained "the theft" by stating, "In 1970, *The Ladder* was divorced from DOB and became an independent Lesbian/feminist publication."[20]

In Chicago that same year, Marie Kuda, a lesbian activist and founder of Womanpress, published a book of poetry by Jeannette Howard Foster and Valerie Taylor. Titled *Two Women,* it expanded the scope and availability of the work—created over five decades by the pioneering midwestern authors—and introduced them to a new generation of readers. Foster's magnum opus, *Sex Variant Women in Literature,* received the 1974 Gay Book Award, given by the American Library Association's Gay Task Force, which was part of the Social Responsibilities Round Table. In 1975, it was reissued by Diana Press.[21]

In addition to maintaining some limited involvement in DOB, both in San Francisco and in chapters across the country, Del Martin had focused her energies increasingly on violence against women. In 1976, she published the groundbreaking book *Battered Wives,* one of the first to detail the extent of spousal and family abuse in the United States. Martin's work on exposing domestic violence led her to join with other San Francisco activists to start the first battered women's shelter in the city, La Casa de las Madres. Phyllis Lyon continued her work at the Glide Foundation and with the National Sex Forum; she presented workshops and wrote and distributed lesbian-positive sex education materials.[22]

But the growth in feminist books, newspapers, groups, and businesses in the mid-1970s also brought significant challenges to the women's liberation movement. Foremost among them were the critiques offered by women of color, who were increasingly resistant to the universalizing notions of feminism.

Barbara Smith and other black feminists in Boston started the Combahee River Collective in 1974, naming it after Harriet Tubman's 1863 guerrilla action in the Port Royal region of South Carolina to free more than 750 slaves. They played a crucial role in bringing issues of race, class, sexuality, and gender to the forefront of American consciousness. Three years later, Barbara Smith, her sister Beverly Smith, and Demita Frazier published "The Combahee River Collective Statement" in Zillah Eisenstein's anthology *Capitalist Patriarchy and the Case for Socialist Feminism.*

"A combined anti-racist and anti-sexist position drew us together initially, and as we developed politically we addressed ourselves to heterosexism and economic oppression under capitalism," they wrote. "We realize that the only people who care enough about us to work consistently for our liberation are us. Our politics evolve from a healthy love for ourselves, our sisters and our community which allows us to continue our struggle and work." They and other feminist women of color like Gloria Anzaldua, Barbara Cameron, Audre Lorde, Cherrie Moraga, and Merle Woo challenged white feminism's unwillingness to confront head-on the continuing reality of U.S. racism and American colonialist legacies around the globe, and created new women's organizations centered on racial and ethnic identities, as well as gender and sexuality.[23]

WHO SAID IT WAS SIMPLE

There are so many roots to the tree of anger
that sometimes the branches shatter
before they bear.

Sitting in Nedicks
the women rally before they march
discussing the problematic girls
they hire to make them free.
An almost white counterman passes
a waiting brother to serve them first
and the ladies neither notice nor reject
the slighter pleasures of their slavery.
But I who am bound by my mirror
as well as my bed
see causes in color
as well as sex

and sit here wondering
which me will survive
all these liberations.

—Audre Lorde[24]

"You know, Barbara, we have to do something about *publishing*," the black lesbian feminist poet and activist Audre Lorde said to Smith in the late 1970s; in 1981 in New York they founded Kitchen Table: Women of Color Press, the first U.S. publisher for women of color. It remained a vital resource until 1995. Lorde's words show the continuing importance of women's control over their ideas and images; they also signify the necessity of developing specific publishing outlets to insure the inclusion of *all* women. For Lorde, embracing differences among people was necessary and empowering. "When you are a member of an out-group, and you challenge others with whom you share this outsider position to examine some aspect of their lives that distorts differences between you, then there can be a great deal of pain," Lorde wrote in 1983. "In other words, when people of a group share an oppression, there are certain strengths that they build together. But there are also certain vulnerabilities. For instance, talking about racism to the women's movement results in 'Huh, don't bother us with that. Look, we're all sisters, please don't rock the boat.' Talking to the black community about sexism results in pretty much the same thing. You get a 'Wait, wait . . . wait a minute: we're all black together. Don't rock the boat.' In our work and in our living, we must recognize that difference is a reason for celebration and growth, rather than a reason for destruction."[25]

The recognition of the liberating power of difference, and the need to engage multiple sites of struggle, personal and political, energized some women but made others hunger for escape. In a poem published in *The Ladder* in 1962, Pat "Dubby" Walker wrote, "I seek the sanctum of an oasis / where in the cool of sheltering shade / by a pool of life-giving water I may be revived once more." Del Martin quoted Walker's poem in her essay on Dubby for Vern Bullough's 2002 book, *Before Stonewall: Activists for Gay and Lesbian Civil Rights in Historical Context*. Martin wrote, "In her later years, Pat Walker found her beloved 'sanctum' near Lake Elsinore." She had inherited property in Los Angeles from an aunt and the sale of it enabled Walker to purchase five acres in the desert, where she usually lived alone and functioned well despite her impaired vision. "It did not matter to her that she had to walk five miles to get groceries. She had a dog and two cockatiels. She could listen to her records. She could play her musical instruments (sax, piano, flute, piccolo, and guitar) as loud and as long as she wanted without interruption," Martin noted. She enjoyed her solitude.[26]

Besides, Walker said in 1988, after DOB she had no interest in gay or women's organizations. "If you're there because you want to be with women, and then politics make you enemies, it splits you," she said in an interview. "I never have belonged to another group. It bothered me more than I even realized to be on the outs with people I care about because of stupid politics. To me, emotions are much more important than politics." Walker "lived her dream" until 1999, when she died in her desert home, surrounded by friends and family.[27]

For other former DOB leaders, relocation was also a way of rejuvenating themselves. After a number of months, Shirley Willer and Marion Glass finally stopped traveling after taking off from the 1968 DOB convention; they eventually settled at the southernmost tip of Florida. In Key West, they became avid mineral collectors and "rock hounds." According to Phyllis Lyon and Del Martin, they also become involved with the local gay and lesbian community in the last years of their lives.[28]

By the late 1970s, Billye Talmadge, another early Daughter, had moved from the Bay Area to New Orleans, where there was a DOB chapter. "I called—it was listed in the phone book—but it was strictly a social group," she said recently. She continued across the country with her lover, Marcia, and settled in Maryland, where Marcia found a position as an ethnomusicologist with the University of Maryland. Wherever she went, Talmadge continued her interest and involvement in alternative spiritualities, but she had little to do with the gay and lesbian movement.[29]

In addition to losing friends and former Daughters to both physical and emotional distance, by 1978 Lyon and Martin also had word of the deaths of two former DOB national presidents. Cleo Bonner and Rita Laporte both died of cancer before the age of sixty.[30]

The year 1978 also saw the demise of the original DOB group in San Francisco. Nina Kaiser and the few other San Francisco Daughters who were still active gave up their struggle to keep it going. The possibilities for lesbians in the Bay Area who were interested in social and political activities had quadrupled, and declining interest in DOB plagued the local chapter. After four years of fits and starts—calling special meetings, organizing events like a lesbian erotica film festival, plus hosting the usual dances and parties—they tired of begging women to assume leadership. Kaiser resigned as president in July and they turned once more to Lyon and Martin. They agreed to turn the remaining treasury over to the San Francisco Women's Centers, which was raising money at that time to purchase a building, and to the Bay Area Feminist Federal Credit Union.[31]

DOB's files—local and national—were cleared out of their last office at 330 Grove Street. Lyon remembers, "I got a guy with a truck and we took all of it back to my office at the Institute for Advanced Study of Human Sexuality." Later, it went to Martin's office in the Glide Building and eventually was turned over to the Gay, Lesbian, Bisexual, Transgender (GLBT) Historical Society.[32]

"It" included twenty-three years of letters and cards from around the world; address lists for twenty chapters; *Ladder* sales and circulation records; names of delegates to every national convention; newspaper and magazine clippings; and DOB detritus of all sorts. The remnants of their first foray into activism joined Lyon and Martin's current collection of books, papers, and "to do" lists on women's liberation, human rights, and the growing lesbian and gay rights movements, all of which were suddenly facing an increasingly well-organized, well-funded conservative backlash that had been growing in strength throughout the decade.

It started in 1972. The same year that American citizens were granted the right to vote on their eighteenth birthday—unless they were in prison or had already fled the country—President Richard "I Am Not a Crook" Nixon was overwhelmingly reelected; only Massachusetts voted for his Democratic challenger, Senator George McGovern. It signaled to many people that even corrupt and deceitful practices at the top would not necessarily bring down an administration. Two years later, under threat of impeachment for lying about dirty tricks that included a bungled break-in at Democratic campaign headquarters in the Watergate apartment complex in Washington, Nixon resigned. In many ways it was a hollow victory for those who worked hard for his ouster.

In 1973, a woman's right to choose whether and when to bear a child was validated by the U.S. Supreme Court, unless she was one of the millions who relied on the federal government for health care. That same year, the American Psychiatric Association finally succumbed to pressure from within its ranks—as well as repeated loud protests and quiet lobbying from those outside—and, deciding that gays weren't sick after all, removed "homosexuality" from the lists of mental illnesses in its Diagnostic and Statistical Manual. Both victories were the result of years of grassroots activism and a shift in the American social and cultural climate. However, the effectiveness of government surveillance and infiltration efforts like the Counterintelligence Program, or COINTELPRO, in disrupting social action groups; the murder or incarceration of many liberal and radical leaders; and the end of the Vietnam War all helped to defuse the revolutionary ideologies and impulses of many who had been activists in the 1960s. The climate of fear so widespread in the 1950s may have changed, but the Cold War had not ended.

As a major economic recession hit people's pocketbooks, gas shortages meant long lines and short drives, and even financial capitals like New York came close to declaring bankruptcy. The 1970s were erroneously nicknamed "the Me Decade"—the "Why Me? Decade" would have been more apt. Struggles over court-ordered busing to desegregate city schools erupted in street fights in Boston and other northern cities: simmering class resentments and a rising white ethnic rage cast an ugly shadow over the civil rights victories of the 1960s. When the U.S. Supreme Court sided in 1978 with Allen Bakke, a white student who had not been accepted by the UC medical school, over his challenge to their affirmative action policies, battles over access to public education and housing further split neighbors and friends.[33]

Paradoxically, for many gay men and lesbians the late 1970s were a time of celebrating newfound freedom and creating separate communities. But politics—electoral politics—increasingly were demanding their collective attention, in California and throughout the country. Early in November 1978, California activists enjoyed a heady victory at the polls when voters decisively rejected the Briggs Initiative, which would have banned gay topics and teachers from California's public schools. State Senator John Briggs drafted and circulated the measure bearing his name to help promote his candidacy for governor; it appeared as Proposition 6 on California's November 1978 ballot. The Briggs Initiative was fueled by and aided the surge in right-wing organizing that produced the presidencies of Ronald Reagan, George H. W. Bush, and George W. Bush.

Campaigns like Anita Bryant's "Save Our Children" in Florida in 1977 mobilized religious and political reactionaries to stop the passage of modest civil rights legislation for lesbians and gay men. California's rejection of the Briggs Initiative was one of the few victories during this period; by contrast, gay rights measures were repealed in St. Paul, Minnesota; Wichita, Kansas; Eugene, Oregon; and Dade County, Florida. Aggressive organizing in lesbian and gay communities, as well as strong alliances with teachers at all levels and most liberal politicians and Democratic clubs, kept Senator Briggs and his right-wing backers from victory in California.[34]

The jubilation of defeating the homophobic measure was cut short by the discovery a few weeks later of the mass suicide of the members of the People's Temple in Jonestown, Guyana; many of Jim Jones's followers were San Franciscans. Then, within days of that tragedy, San Francisco Supervisor Dan White murdered Mayor George Moscone and Supervisor Harvey Milk at City Hall. Grief turned to rage. Local gay and lesbian leaders quickly surfaced to organize peaceful protests; they included the black activists Pat Norman and Gwenn Craig and white educators like Sally Gearhart. The next year, Dan White's claim of diminished capacity—made famous by a psychiatrist's reference to his indulgence in junk food and embraced by media pundits as the "Twinkie defense"—was accepted by the jury; he was found guilty only of two counts of manslaughter. San Francisco erupted in violence; gay men and lesbians stormed City Hall, smashing its ornate front doors and setting police cars on fire. The San Francisco Police Department responded by invading the City's main gay neighborhood, the Castro, and brutalizing bystanders and bar patrons in reprisal for the "White Night" riots.[35]

When the smoke cleared, a sense of sorrow swept the City along with demands for change. The growing anger and frustration of many activists came from the realization that, despite the hard-won victories of more than twenty-five years of education, research, lobbying, and public protests, they were still vulnerable. Just a few years later, new issues—including a horrifying "gay disease" and bitter disputes among lesbians over images and expressions of sexuality—would further expose deep levels of fear, hate, resistance, and renewal.

Epilogue

"Hello, Marcie? This is Del Martin." The low, no-nonsense voice on the phone instantly made my heart pound. "I need you to get me an analysis of all the bills in Sacramento dealing with censorship—by Friday." I gulped and lied, "Uh, okay, sure. No problem."

It was Wednesday. I was already swamped. But I couldn't say no—it was *Del Martin* calling. I begged help from my friend and coworker Donna Hitchens, then a staff attorney at the ACLU of Northern California (ACLU-NC). Hitchens, now a San Francisco Superior Court judge, founded the nation's first legal group for lesbians, the Lesbian Rights Project, in 1977; today, renamed the National Center for Lesbian Rights, it is one of the largest advocates for lesbians and other sexually nonconforming people fighting for basic employment and family rights. Hitchens was also DOB's lawyer in the 1970s. Because she knew Lyon and Martin well, she didn't hesitate to jump in. We got them the requested summaries of over a dozen bills, and they brought the information to their political networks. Along with activists from other women's and civil rights organizations, we were able to defeat the pro-censorship bills in Sacramento that year.[1]

I first worked with Lyon and Martin in 1985 as part of my field organizing responsibilities for the ACLU-NC. It was an exciting campaign: we helped create the Bay Area Feminist Anti-Censorship Task Force (BAFACT) as a response to the political alignment of some feminists with right-wing politicians who hoped to ban pornography by equating it with violence against women. Lyon and Martin were among the initial organizers of the group.[2]

In 1983, the feminist author Andrea Dworkin and the legal scholar Catherine MacKinnon drafted a model local ordinance aimed at giving women the right to take producers, distributors, sellers and/or exhibitors of pornography to court. The ordinances were adopted in Indianapolis, Cambridge, and Cincinnati, among other cities, and inspired similar legislation at the state level throughout the country, including California. The Dworkin/MacKinnon approach differed from other previous attempts to suppress pornography in that they focused on sex discrimination and equated pornography with the cultural and legal subordination of women. Pro–sexual expression and anticensorship women in New York like Nan Hunter organized the Feminist Anti-Censorship Task Force (FACT) in 1984 to fight the ordinances, and some local chapters of FACT were established. FACT activists, who included liberal and radical lesbians and feminists, argued that government censorship only harmed women's sexual and political freedom. After a two-year court battle, the U.S. Supreme Court let stand a lower court decision that declared the Dworkin/MacKinnon antipornography ordinance an unconstitutional violation of the First Amendment.[3]

A few years later, in 1990, Lyon and Martin received the ACLU of Northern California's highest award for courageous advocacy on behalf of civil liberties. The night of the awards ceremony at a hotel in downtown San Francisco, not far from where DOB's first office had been located, they joined the activist African-American law professor Derrick Bell on the dais and talked about their lifelong membership in the ACLU and their essential commitment to the protection and expansion of constitutional rights for all people. Never ones to forget early friends in the homophile struggle, they acknowledged the work undertaken by the ACLU-NC's first director, Ernest Besig, with the Daughters of Bilitis thirty-five years earlier.

Remembering that night, I also remember my earliest friends in the gay and lesbian rights struggle. Lyon and Martin shared the ACLU-NC's honors in 1990 with my dear friend Doug Warner, who was recognized posthumously for his passion and devotion to civil liberties, gay rights, and the ACLU. Doug died on Valentine's Day that year of complications due to AIDS—one more among the legions of beautiful, brilliant men, women, and children who were taken too soon and too painfully by the disease that ravaged our neighborhoods and our hearts in San Francisco, throughout the country, and increasingly around the world in the 1980s and 1990s.

Our intense relationship was not an uncommon one among gay men and lesbians in those days. In the dozen short years that I knew him, Doug and I shared a love for partying, dancing, gardening, and our families, both those we were born into and those we created. He taught me more than I ever wanted to know about gay male life and introduced me to gay rights activism in the time that we were running buddies. We talked constantly: we debated whether closing the bathhouses would prevent the spread of AIDS or just limit the distribution of condoms; we agreed that both abortion and gay rights should be at the top of the ACLU's agenda; we disagreed over many issues that sparked debate among gay men and lesbians at that time, like the ethics of man-boy sex and the effects of monogamy. Sometimes he made me want to weep with frustration, then laugh ecstatically, and I suspect he would not have mellowed with age. In this way, I am reminded of him whenever I talk with Phyllis Lyon and Del Martin.

In 2004, the two women blazed a trail yet again and got married. All of a sudden, the newlyweds, celebrating more than half a century of same-sex passion and partnership, became international news. From as nearby as the East Bay and as far away as Scandinavia, the flowers, calls, letters, e-mails, and cards of congratulations poured in to the already overflowing house. "We can't believe all this," Lyon said. As the *USA Today* story put it, "The pair never felt the need to get married, but they did it for the same reason they became domestic partners: to speak out." The act catapulted them into worldwide celebrity; the photograph of them in pink and green pantsuits, gently embracing while behind them a small semicircle of women and men smile, weep, and celebrate, was circulated on wire services and Web sites almost instantly.[4]

Convinced that the action would advance the cause of lesbian and gay rights, they agreed to go to San Francisco City Hall on February 12—two days before their fifty-first anniversary as a couple—and be part of the new mayor's efforts to challenge what he saw as an archaic, discriminatory law. It was completely in keeping with everything else Lyon and Martin had done in their lives.

Fifty years earlier, they were among eight lesbians in San Francisco who faced a basic human need—to be loved and accepted—and answered it without any gay rights organization to turn to for support, in fact without any medical or religious or legal authority anywhere telling them that what they wanted was right and natural and legitimate. They intended first and foremost to build the self-confidence necessary for lesbians to claim their place in society, but they never saw that society as flawless. The very idea that they could form a group—and then incorporate it under both California and federal laws—for women to explore the "problem" of "the female variant" was a radical one. The program of education, research, and legislative reform they adopted for themselves had never before been attempted. What they did was extraordinary.

And it is finally being celebrated. On November 10, 2005, my lover Ann and I joined over two hundred women and men gathered in San Francisco's downtown South-of-Market neighborhood (SoMa) at the high-ceilinged headquarters of Olivia, the successful women's travel company established by feminist and lesbian singers and musicians in the mid-1970s. We were there to celebrate the fiftieth anniversary of the Daughters of Bilitis and the eighty-first birthday of one of its founders, Phyllis Lyon. The upbeat crowd of Bay Area lesbians and friends—artists and activists spanning at least six decades—was festive and celebratory. The rooms were full of the sounds of happy reunions; quick catch-ups and compliments—"you look GREAT!"—could be overheard repeatedly between allies and comrades from years past, most of whom really did. The event sparkled. When Ruth Mahaney, the emcee, herself a well-respected longtime progressive lesbian activist in San Francisco, invited all former Daughters in the crowd to join Lyon and Martin in the spotlight, nine women stepped forward.

Former DOB friends and members ranged from Charlotte Coleman, the owner of The Front, one of the oldest and longest-running gay bars in San Francisco, to Clara Brock, who faced Dubby Walker at the chessboard in 1960. One of the "new generation" of lesbian feminist DOB leaders in the 1970s, Nina Kaiser, also stepped forward, as did Beth Elliott, the transsexual lesbian vice president of SF DOB in the early 1970s, and "Vee Vee," or Venice Ostwald, an early member and leader of the Los Angeles chapter. All of them spoke of DOB's significance in their lives. Former Boston DOB member Diane Sabin was there with her partner and event host Jewelle Gomez, both of whom today are celebrated members of San Francisco's lesbian communities. The theme of the evening, Jewelle and I agreed as we divided up our host duties, was "DOB saved my life." All of us talked about DOB's importance, the examples set by Lyon and Martin, and the personal circumstances that enabled each one of us to take part, unashamed and proud, at a public event in 2005 celebrating fifty years of lesbian activism.

Each woman who stepped forward that night to claim her part in DOB's history helped create a brightly colored tableau of generational lesbian activism. The image blazed before my eyes against the background of soft guitar music offered by a talented young female guitarist. The event was fueled by an open bar and delicious appetizers, plenty of humor, and good-looking guests of all ages, genders, and sexual orientations. It was a prime example of one variety of twenty-first-century American Sapphic celebration—the fundraiser for a community cause or institution, in this case the Gay, Lesbian, Bisexual, Transgender Historical Society, the home of the largest collection of DOB organizational files.

Within the warmth of the party that night, what was electrifying was not a feeling of nostalgia; it was a sense of lasting connection. Seen from a larger perspective, what the DOB birthday party also revealed was two of DOB's achievements during the last five decades: the growth of lesbian visibility and the development of lesbian and LGBT organizations and institutions. The very space in which the party took place was testimony to their work: a women's business like Olivia, which caters specifically to lesbians, would not have been possible without them.

The DOB fiftieth birthday party also coincided with the 2005 Creating Change conference of the National Gay and Lesbian Task Force, held in Oakland, California. There, three thousand lesbians, gay men, bisexuals, gender-different, queer, and sexually nonconforming people gathered to talk, flirt, debate, dance, and strategize about how to advance a progressive LGBT agenda in the face of

ever-increasing fundamentalist worldwide power grabs. Little could
Barbara Gittings have imagined in the early 1970s, when she was one
of the first board members of the National Gay Task Force, that their
efforts would result in a well-established, multimillion-dollar organization with annual conferences drawing thousands of activists from
throughout the United States and around the world.[5]

Since the Daughters first began their work, and despite continued
attacks on our rights and our existence since, sexual minorities have
become a highly visible part of the national and international land-
scape. From the tiny groups who met in California in the early part
of the 1950s have come the current proliferation of academic and
community centers, associations, books, businesses, clubs, classes,
university departments, and organizations of all sorts. Instead of the
handful of helpful heterosexuals, there are thousands of LGBT
accountants, doctors, filmmakers, journalists, judges, lawyers, musicians, politicians, teachers, and therapists. The few local radio programs that earnestly discussed how to "cure" homosexuality back
then are drowned out today by gay and lesbian cable television networks, programming, films, comedy shows, and musical and dramatic
theater. In 2005, the former site of gay Annual Reminder protests in
Philadelphia was adorned with a historic marker recognizing that
"Annual public demonstrations for gay and lesbian equality were held
at Independence Hall. These peaceful protests and New York's
Stonewall riots in 1969 & Pride Parade in 1970 transformed a small
national campaign into a civil rights movement." Former Daughters
Ada Bello, Barbara Gittings, and Kay Lahusen, as well as gay leaders
Franklin Kameny and William Kelley, were there to witness it.[6]

The women who organized the Daughters of Bilitis in 1955 could
not have envisioned the varieties of lesbian and queer communities
that exist today, just as those born after the 1970s have a difficult time
understanding the secretive, sexually charged homosexual subcultures

of a half century ago. When the *Lawrence v. Texas* decision decriminalizing private consensual sexual conduct was announced by the U.S. Supreme Court in June 2003, I called Phyllis Lyon for her reaction. She quietly said to me, "It's incredible. We never thought we'd see this in our lifetime." The Daughters—those who have survived to tell their tales and those who have left behind their stories—provide a vital link between yesterday and today, when a widening acceptance of sexual nonconformity inspires an increasingly vicious assault.

As the writer Jean Rhys said in 1975:

> Listen to me. All of writing is a huge lake. There are rivers that feed the lake, like Tolstoy and Dostoyevsky. And there are mere trickles, like Jean Rhys. All that matters is feeding the lake. I don't matter. The lake matters.[7]

I hope that, with *Different Daughters,* we have been able to provide a tiny trickle of knowledge, to "feed the lake" of understanding about what it meant to challenge U.S. gender and sexual mores in the mid-twentieth century and what it might teach us about activism, social justice, and liberation in the twenty-first. From the standpoint of yet another repressive period in U.S. history, it seems that finally, today, we may be able to appreciate the complicated women who wore, decorated, and then discarded the mask of conformity a half century ago.

Appendix: Oral History Interviews

All interviews were conducted by the author.

Ada Bello, Philadelphia, PA; September 17, 2003.

Lois Beeby (Williams), Sunnyvale, CA; May 27, 2002.

Clara Brock (Brock Harper), San Jose, CA; May 17, 2002.

Patti Brown, New York, NY; May 10, 1996 and July 20, 2002 (e-mail).

Jeanne Cordova, Los Angeles, CA; September 7, 2002.

Beth Elliott, Oakland, CA; March 12 & 13, 2002; January 5, 2006 (e-mail); July 10, 2006 (e-mail).

Sandra Fields, Sacramento, CA; May 28, 2002.

Florence Fleischman, Los Angeles, CA; September 6, 2002.

Eva Freund, Washington, D.C.; March 21, 2002 (e-mail).

Barbara Gittings and Kay Lahusen (Tobin), Wilmington, DE; April 23 and 30, 2002; September 20, 2002; August 23, 2003; November 8, 2003; January 30, 2004; July 3, 2004; October 15, 2005; December 22, 2005; May 20 – 25, 2006 (e-mail).

Barbara Grier (Gene Damon), Alligator Point, FL; December 29, 2003; August 15, 2005 (e-mail); August 28, 2005 (telephone); September 12, 2005 (e-mail).

P. D. Griffin, Fairfax, CA; May 30, 2002.

Sue Handley, Willows, CA; May 14, 2002.

Beverly Hickok, Berkeley, CA. March 14, 2002 (telephone); May 13, 2002.

Lois Johnson and Shari Barden, Boston, MA; March 19, 2002 (telephone); June 10, 2002.

Nina Kaiser, San Francisco, CA; September 9, 2002.

William Kelley, Chicago, IL; October 16, 2002.

Shirley Kelly, Oakland, CA; May 15, 2002.

Marie Kuda, Oak Park, IL; October 17, 2002 (telephone).

Natalie Lando, Oakland, CA; May 15, 2002.

Patricia Lyon, Berkeley, CA; May 17, 2002.

Phyllis Lyon and Del Martin, San Francisco, CA; February 18, 1997; April 25, 1997; May 11, 1998; March 1, 1999; March 6, 2002; May 15, 2002; June 10, 2003; February 13, 2004; November 10, 2005; January 5–14, 2006 (e-mail).

Marijane Meaker, Sag Harbor, NY; July 12, 2005 (telephone).

Marjorie McCann, Philadelphia, PA; September 17, 2003.

Barbara McLean, Portland, ME; August 21, 2003 (telephone).

Venice Ostwald (Vostwald), Henderson, NV and San Jose, CA; May 26, 2002; September 5, 2002.

Tracy Rappaport, San Francisco, CA; March 30, 2002.

Audrey Rose, Sonoma, CA, March 26, 2002.

Stella Rush (Sten Russell), Westminster, CA; May 2, 2002 (telephone); May 21 and 22, 2002; May 27, 2002 (telephone); September 14, 2002; September 16, 2003; February 16, 2004; November 6, 2005; December 29, 2005 (mail); May 5, 2006.

Karen Ryer (Wells), Guerneville, CA; May 30, 2002.

Pat Sax, San Francisco, CA; February 23, 2000.

Martha Shelley, Oakland, CA; February 16, 2004.

Billye Talmadge (Billie Tallmij), Chevy Chase, MD; March 30, 2002.

Carol Vorvolakis (Wilson), Oakland, CA; May 15, 2002.

Bibliography

I. PRIMARY SOURCES:

ARCHIVAL SOURCES AND COLLECTIONS

Gay, Lesbian, Bisexual, Transgender Historical Society
San Francisco, CA
    Phyllis Lyon and Del Martin Papers, 1954–2000 #93–13
    Florence Jaffy Papers
    Don Lucas Papers
    San Francisco Women's Building Records
    Lesbian and Gay Advisory Committee to SF Human Rights Commission,
        1990–1992
    GLBTHS Periodical Collection
    GLBTHS Vertical Files, including Clippings File
    GLBTHS Ephemera Files—Organizations

Gerber/Hart Library and Archives
Chicago, IL
    Valerie Taylor Papers
    City of Chicago Lesbian and Gay Hall of Fame
    Mattachine Midwest Collection

June L. Mazer Lesbian Archives
West Hollywood, CA
    Daughters of Bilitis Papers
    Marion Zimmer Bradley Papers
    Vice Versa Collection
    West Coast Women's Collection

Lesbian Herstory Archives
Brooklyn, NY
    Daughters of Bilitis Video Project
    Daughters of Bilitis Organizational Files
    Julie Lee Papers
    Alma Routsong Papers
    Shirley Willer Papers
    Periodicals Files

New York Public Library
New York, NY
    "Becoming Visible: The Legacy of Stonewall," an exhibition on the history of
        New York's lesbian and gay communities; June 18–September 24, 1994
    International Gay and Lesbian Collection: Daughters of Bilitis; audiotapes of
        interviews with Lisa Ben et al. (John D'Emilio)

ONE Institute and Archives
University of Southern California
Los Angeles, CA
    Lesbian History Project: Lesbians of Color Collection (Yolanda Retter)

William Way Lesbian, Gay, Bisexual, Transgender Community Center and Archives
Philadelphia, PA

PRIVATE COLLECTIONS
Barbara Gittings and Kay Tobin Lahusen Collection

    Clara Brock; San Jose, CA
    Beth Elliott; Oakland, CA

Barbara Gittings and Kay Lahusen; Wilmington, DE

P.D. Griffen; Fairfax, CA

Beverly Hickok; Berkeley, CA

Lois Johnson and Shari Barden; Boston, MA

Nina Kaiser; Oakland, CA

Bill Kelley; Chicago, IL

Shirley Kelley, Oakland CA

Phyllis Lyon and Del Martin; San Francisco, CA

Stella Rush; Westminster, CA

PERIODICALS CONSULTED

Chrysalis

Gay City News

Gay Community News

glq: A Journal of Lesbian and Gay Studies

Journal of Homosexuality

Journal of the History of Sexuality

Journal of Women's History

Lambda Literary Report

Lesbian Tide

Mattachine Review

Off Our Backs

On Our Backs

ONE

OUT/Look

Radical History Review

Signs

Sisters

Socialist Review

The Advocate

The Harvard Gay and Lesbian Review (now *The Gay and Lesbian Review Worldwide*)

The Ladder

The Women's Review of Books

PUBLISHED PRIMARY SOURCES

Adelman, Marcy, ed. *Long Time Passing: Lives of Older Lesbians*. Boston: Alyson, 1986.

Bullough, Vern L. *Before Stonewall: Activists for Gay and Lesbian Rights in Historical Context*. New York: Haworth Press, 2002.

Cain, Paul. *Leading the Parade: Conversations with America's Most Influential Lesbians and Gay Men*. Lanham, MD: The Scarecrow Press.

Cordova, Jeanne. *Kicking the Habit: A Lesbian Nun Story*. Los Angeles: Multiple Dimensions, 1990.

Cutler, Marvin. *Homosexuals Today: A Handbook of Organizations and Publications*. Los Angeles: ONE Press, Inc., 1956.

Gidlow, Elsa. *Elsa: I Come With My Songs*. San Francisco: Bootlegger Press, 1991.

Grier, Barbara, and Coletta Reid, eds. *The Lavender Herring: Lesbian Essays from The Ladder*. Baltimore, MD: Diana Press, 1976.

Jay, Karla. *Tales of the Lavender Menace: A Memoir of Liberation*. New York: Basic Books, 1999.

Jay, Karla, and Allen Young, eds. *Out of the Closets: Voices of Gay Liberation*. New York: Harcourt Brace Jovanovich, 1972; 1977.

Kepner, Jim. *Rough News—Daring Views: 1950s Pioneer Gay Press Journalism*. New York: Haworth Press, Inc., 1998.

Martin, Del, and Phyllis Lyon, *Lesbian/Woman*. Volcano, CA: Volcano Press, 1972, 1991.

Meaker, Marijane. *Highsmith: A Romance of the 1950s*. San Francisco: Cleis Press, 2003.

Tobin, Kay, and Randy Wicker, eds. *The Gay Crusaders*. New York: Paperback Library, 1972.

VIDEOCASSETTES

Before Stonewall: The Making of a Gay and Lesbian Community. Dirs. Greta Schiller and Robert Rosenberg. Cinema Guild, 1986.

Forbidden Loves. Dirs. Aerlyn Weissman and Lynne Fernie. National Film Board of Canada, 1992.

Gay Pioneers. Dir. Glenn Holsten. WHYY and Equality Forum, 2004.

Last Call at Maud's. Dir. Paris Poirier. The Maud's Project, 1993.

No Secret Anymore: The Times of Del Martin and Phyllis Lyon. Dir. Joan E. Biren
(JEB). Moonforce Media, 2003.

Paragraph 175. Dirs. Rob Epstein and Jeffrey Friedman. Reflective Image, Inc., 2000.

A Question of Equality, Part I. A Show of Force Production, 1995.

Screaming Queens: The Riot at Compton's Cafeteria. Dir. Susan Stryker, in association
with ITVS and KQED Public Television, 2005.

Word Is Out: Stories of Some of Our Lives. Dirs. Nancy Adair and Casey Adair. Mariposa
Film Group, 1977.

II. SECONDARY SOURCES:

Abelove, Henry, Michele Aina Barale, and David M. Halperin, eds. *The Lesbian and
Gay Studies Reader.* New York: Routledge, 1993.

Adam, Barry. *The Rise of a Gay and Lesbian Movement.* Boston: Twayne, 1987.

Adams, Kate. "Making the World Safe for the Missionary Position: Images of the
Lesbian in Post-World War II America." Karla Jay and Joanne Glasgow, eds.,
Lesbian Texts and Contexts: Radical Revisions. New York: New York University
Press, 1990.

_____. "Built Out of Books: Lesbian Energy and Feminist Ideology in Alternative
Publishing." *Journal of Homosexuality,* Vol. 34, Issue 3/4, 1998.

Abbott, Sidney, and Barbara Love. *Sappho Was a Right-on Woman.* New York: Stein
and Day, 1972; 1993.

Alarcon, Norma, Ana Castillo, and Cherrie Moraga, eds. *Third Woman: The Sexuality
of Latinas.* Berkeley: Third Woman Press, 1986.

Aldrich, Ann. *Carol in a Thousand Cities.* New York: Fawcett/Gold Medal, 1960.

_____. *We, Too, Must Love.* New York: Fawcett/Gold Medal, 1958.

_____. *We Walk Alone.* New York: Fawcett/Gold Medal, 1958.

Allison, Dorothy. "A Personal History of Lesbian Porn," *New York Native,* May 24–
June 6, 1982.

_____. *Bastard Out of Carolina.* New York: Dutton/Penguin Books, 1992.

Altman, Dennis. *Homosexual Oppression and Liberation.* New York: Dutton/Outer-
bridge and Denstrey, 1971.

_____. *The Homosexualization of America.* Boston: Beacon Press, 1982.

Anderson, Bonnie. *Joyous Greetings: The First International Women's Movement,
1830–1860.* New York: Oxford University Press, 2000.

Anderson, Kelly P. "Out in the Fifties: The Daughters of Bilitis and the Politics of Identity." Master's thesis, Sarah Lawrence College, 1994.

Anderson, Michael. "'Education of Another Kind'—Lorraine Hansberry in the Fifties," Toni Lester, ed., *Gender Nonconformity, Race, and Sexuality: Charting the Connections*. Madison: University of Wisconsin Press, 2002.

Anzaldua, Gloria. *Borderlands/La Frontera: The New Mestiza*. San Francisco: Spinsters/Aunt Lute, 1987.

Aptheker, Bettina. *Woman's Legacy: Essays on Race, Sex, and Class in American History*. Amherst: The University of Massachusetts Press, 1982.

Armstrong, Elizabeth A. *Forging Gay Identities: Organizing Sexuality in San Francisco, 1950–1994*. Chicago: University of Chicago Press, 2002.

Baldwin, James. *Another Country*. New York: Dell Publishing Co., 1962.

_____. *Giovanni's Room*. New York: Dell Publishing Co., 1956.

Bannon, Ann. *Beebo Brinker*. New York: Fawcett/Gold Medal, 1962; reissued by Naiad Press, 1983, and by Cleis Press, 2001.

_____. *I Am a Woman*. New York: Fawcett/Gold Medal, 1959; reissued by Naiad Press, 1983, and by Cleis Press, 2002.

_____. *Journey to a Woman*. New York: Fawcett/Gold Medal, 1960; reissued by Naiad Press, 1983, and by Cleis Press, 2003.

_____. *Odd Girl Out*. New York: Fawcett/Gold Medal, 1957; reissued by Naiad Press, 1983, and by Cleis Press, 2001.

_____. *Women in the Shadows*. New York: Fawcett/Gold Medal, 1959; reissued by Naiad Press, 1983, and by Cleis Press, 2002.

Beam, Joseph, ed. *In the Life: A Black Gay Anthology*. Boston: Alyson Publications, Inc., 1986.

Beinart, Peter. "The Rehabilitation of the Cold War Liberal," *New York Times,* April 30, 2006.

Berube, Allan. *Coming Out Under Fire*. New York: The Free Press/Macmillan, Inc., 1990.

Berube, Allan, and John D'Emilio. "The Military and Lesbians During the McCarthy Years." Estelle Freedman et al., eds., *The Lesbian Issue: Essays from Signs*. Chicago: University of Chicago Press, 1985.

Boyd, Nan Alamilla. *Wide Open Town: A History of Queer San Francisco to 1965*. Berkeley: University of California Press, 2003.

Branch, Taylor. *Parting the Waters: America in the King Years, 1954–1963*. New York: Simon & Schuster, 1988.

Bronski, Michael, ed. *Pulp Friction: Uncovering the Golden Age of Gay Male Pulps.* New York: St. Martin's Griffin, 2003.

Brook, James, Chris Carlsson, and Nancy J. Peters, eds. *Reclaiming San Francisco: History, Politics, Culture.* San Francisco: City Lights Books, 1998.

Brooten, Bernadette J. *Love Between Women: Early Christian Responses to Female Homoeroticism.* Chicago: University of Chicago Press, 1996.

Bullough, Vern. "Lesbianism, Homosexuality, and the American Civil Liberties Union." *Journal of Homosexuality,* Vol. 13(1), Fall 1986.

Burner, David. *Making Peace with the Sixties.* Princeton: Princeton University Press, 1996.

Capsuto, Steven. *Alternate Channels: The Uncensorsed Story of Gay and Lesbian Images on Radio and Television: 1930s to the Present.* New York: Ballantine Books, 2000.

Carson, Rachel. *The Sea Around Us.* Oxford: Oxford University Press, 1951, 1991.

Carter, David. *Stonewall: The Riots That Sparked the Gay Revolution.* New York: St. Martin's Press, 2004.

Cavin, Susan. *Lesbian Origins.* San Francisco: ism press, 1985.

Center for Lesbian and Gay Studies. *Queer Ideas: The David R. Kessler Lectures in Lesbian and Gay Studies.* New York: The Feminist Press of the City University of New York, 2003.

Chafe, William H. *The American Woman: Her Changing Social, Economic, and Political Roles, 1920–1970.* New York: Oxford University Press, 1972.

_____. *The Paradox of Change: American Women in the 20th Century.* New York: Oxford University Press, 1991.

Chauncey, George Jr. *Gay New York: Gender, Urban Culture, and the Making of the Gay Male World, 1890–1940.* New York: Basic Books, 1994.

Clendinen, Dudley and Adam Nagourney. *Out for Good: The Struggle to Build a Gay Rights Movement in America.* New York: Simon & Schuster, 1999.

Cook, Blanche Wiesen. "Female Support Networks and Political Activism." *Chrysalis* 3 (Autumn 1977): 43–61.

_____. "The Historical Denial of Lesbianism," *Radical History Review* 20 (1979): 60–65.

_____. *Eleanor Roosevelt: Vol. I, 1884–1933.* New York: Viking, 1992.

Coontz, Stephanie. *The Way We Never Were.* New York: Basic Books, 1992.

Corber, Robert J. *Homosexuality in Cold War America: Resistance and the Crisis of Masculinity.* Durham: Duke University Press, 1997.

Corinne, Tee. *Valerie Taylor: A Resource Book*. Published by the estate of Valerie Taylor, 1999. Gerber/Hart Library, Chicago, IL.

Cory, Donald Webster. *The Homosexual in America: A Subjective Approach*. New York: Greenberg, 1951.

———. *Homosexuality. A Cross Cultural Approach*. New York: Julian, 1956.

Costello, John. *Virtue Under Fire: How World War II Changed Our Social and Sexual Attitudes*. Boston: Little, Brown, 1985.

Cruikshank, Margaret, ed. *The Lesbian Path*. Tallahassee, FL: Naiad Press, 1981.

Cuordileone, K. A. "'Politics in an Age of Anxiety': Cold War Political Culture and the Crisis in American Masculinity, 1949 to 1960." *The Journal of American History*, September 2000.

Davis, Angela Y. *Blues Legacies and Black Feminism*. New York: Vintage Books, 1998.

de Beauvoir, Simone. *The Second Sex*. New York: Penguin, 1949; 1972.

D'Emilio, John. *Lost Prophet: The Life and Times of Bayard Rustin*. New York: Free Press, 2003.

———. *Making Trouble: Essays on Gay History, Politics, and the University*. New York: Routledge, 1992.

———. *Sexual Politics, Sexual Communties: The Making of a Homosexual Minority in the United States, 1940–1970*. Chicago: University of Chicago Press, 1983.

———. *The World Turned: Essays on Gay History, Politics, and Culture*. Durham: Duke University Press, 2002.

D'Emilio, John, and Estelle Freedman. *Intimate Matters: A History of Sexuality in America*. New York: Harper & Row, 1988.

Diamond, Irene, and Lee Quinby. *Feminism & Foucault: Reflections on Resistance*. Boston: Northeastern University Press, 1988.

Doan, Laura. *Fashioning Sapphism: The Origins of a Modern English Lesbian Culture*. New York: Columbia University Press, 2001.

Douglas, Susan J. *Where the Girls Are: Growing Up Female with the Mass Media*. New York: Times Books/Random House, 1994.

Dower, John. *War Without Mercy: Race and Power in the Pacific War*. New York: Pantheon, 1986.

Duberman, Martin. *About Time: Exploring the Gay Past*. New York: Penguin Books, 1986; 1991.

———. *Cures: A Gay Man's Odyssey*. New York: Dutton/Plume, 1991.

———. *Haymarket*. New York: Seven Stories Press, 2003.

_____. *Left Out: The Politics of Exclusion—Essays 1964–2002*. Boston: South End Press, 2002.

_____. *Midlife Queer: Autobiography of a Decade, 1971–1981*. New York: Scribner, 1996.

_____. *Stonewall*. New York: Penguin Books, 1993.

_____. "The 'Father of the Homophile Movement': The Life and Times of Donald Webster Cory." *The Harvard Gay and Lesbian Review*, Volume IV, Number 4 Fall 1997.

Duberman, Martin, Martha Vicinus, and George Chauncey Jr., eds. *Hidden From History: Reclaiming the Gay and Lesbian Past*. New York: Penguin Books, 1989.

Duggan, Lisa. *Sapphic Slashers: Sex, Violence and American Modernity*. Durham: Duke University Press, 2000.

Echols, Alice. *Daring to Be Bad: Radical Feminism in America 1967–1975*. Minneapolis: University of Minnesota Press, 1989.

Ehrenstein, David. *Open Secret (Gay Hollywood 1928–1998)*. New York: William Morrow and Company, Inc., 1998.

Emblidge, David, ed. *My Day: The Best of Eleanor Roosevelt's Acclaimed Newspaper Columns, 1936–1962*. New York: Da Capo Press, 2001.

Escoffier, Jeffrey. "Homosexuality and the Sociological Imagination: The 1950s And 1960s," Martin Duberman, ed., A *Queer World: The Center for Lesbian and Gay Studies Reader*, New York: New York University Press, 1997.

Evans, Sara. *Personal Politics: The Roots of Women's Liberation in the Civil Rights Movement and the Left*. New York: Penguin, 1979.

_____. *Tidal Wave: How Women Changed America at Century's End*. New York: The Free Press, 2004.

F.A.C.T. [Feminist Anticensorship Task Force]. *Caught Looking: Feminism, Pornography, and Censorship*. Seattle: The Real Comet Press, 1988.

Faderman, Lillian. *Odd Girls and Twilight Lovers., A History of Lesbian Life in Twentieth Century America*. New York: Columbia University Press, 1991.

_____. *Surpassing the Love of Men*. New York: William Morrow and Co., Inc., 1981.

_____. *To Believe in Women*. Boston: Houghton Mifflin Company, 1999.

Fairclough, Adam. *To Redeem the Soul of America: The Southern Christian Leadership Conference and Martin Luther King, Jr.* Athens, GA: University of Georgia Press, 1987.

Feinberg, Leslie. *Stone Butch Blues*. Ithaca: Firebrand Books, 1993.

Firestone, Shulamith. *The Dialectic of Sex: The Case for Feminist Revolution*. New York: Bantam, 1971.

Foner, Eric. *The Story of American Freedom*. New York: W. W. Norton & Company, Inc., 1998.

Formisano. Ronald P. *Boston Against Busing: Race, Class, and Ethnicity in the 1960s and 1970s*. Chapel Hill: University of North Carolina Press, 1991.

Forrest, Katherine V., ed. *Lesbian Pulp Fiction: The Sexually Intrepid World of Lesbian Paperback Novels 1950–1965*. San Francisco: Cleis Press, 2005.

Foucault, Michel. *The History of Sexuality: An Introduction*. Vol. 1. New York: Vintage Books/Random House, 1990.

Fraser, Steve, and Gary Gerstle, eds. *The Rise and Fall of the New Deal Order, 1930–1980*. Princeton: Princeton University Press, 1989.

Freeman, Joshua B. *Working-Class New York*. New York: The New Press, 2000.

Freedman, Estelle B. *No Turning Back: The History of Feminism and the Future of Women*. New York: Ballantine Books, 2002.

_____. "Separatism Revisited: Women's Institutions, Social Reform, and the Career of Miriam Van Waters." In Linda Kerber, Alice Kessler-Harris, and Kathryn Kish Sklar, eds., *U.S. History As Women's History: New Feminist Essays*. Chapel Hill: University of North Carolina Press, 1995.

Friedan, Betty. *The Feminine Mystique*. New York: Dell Publishing, 1963.

Gartrell, Nanette, and Esther D. Rothblum, eds. *Everyday Mutinies: Funding Lesbian Activism*. New York: Haworth Press, 2001.

Giddings, Paula. *When and Where I Enter: The Impact of Black Women on Race and Sex in America*. New York: Bantam Books, 1984.

Glick, Brian. *War At Home: Covert Action Against U.S. Activists and What We Can Do About It*. Boston: South End Press, 1989.

Goldstein, Richard. "Liberation vs. 'Progress': A Challenge to Queer People & Their Allies." *Guild Practitioner*, Vol. 60, No. 2. New York: National Lawyers' Guild, 2003.

Gorman, Phyllis. "The Daughters of Bilitis: A Description and Analysis of a Female Homophile Social Movement Organization 1955–1963." Master's thesis, Ohio State University, 1985.

Gornick, Vivian, and Barbara K. Moran. *Woman in Sexist Society: Studies in Power and Powerlessness*. New York: Basic Books/New American Library, 1971.

Halberstam, David. *The Fifties*. New York: Villard, 1993.

Hall, Radclyffe. *The Well of Loneliness*. Garden City, NY: Blue Ribbon Books, 1928.

Halperin, David M. *How to Do the History of Homosexuality.* Chicago: University of Chicago Press, 2001.

Hamer, Emily. *Brittania's Glory. A History of Twentieth-Century Lesbians.* London: Cassell, 1996.

Hansberry, Lorraine. *A Raisin in the Sun.* New York: Signet Books, 1961.

_____. *To Be Young, Gifted and Black: Lorraine Hansberry in Her Own Words.* Robert Nemiroff, ed. New York: Vintage, 1995.

Hardisty, Jean. *Mobilizing Resentment: Conservative Resurgence from the John Birch Society to the Promise Keepers.* Boston: Beacon Press, 1999.

Harris, Paisley. "Gatekeeping and Remaking: The Politics of Respectability in African American Women's History and Black Feminism." *Journal of Women's History,* Vol. 15, No. 1 (Spring 2003): 212–219.

Harris, Virginia. "A Pearl of Great Price." *Common Lives/Lesbian Lives* 2 (Spring 1987): 3–10.

Harvey, Brett. *The Fifties: A Women's Oral History.* New York: Harper, 1994.

Hellman, Lillian. *Scoundrel Time.* New York: Little Brown & Co., 1976.

Herman, Ellen. "All In The Family: Lesbian Motherhood Meets Popular Psychology in a Dysfunctional Era." in Ellen Lewin, ed., *Inventing Lesbian Cultures in America,* Boston: Beacon Press, 1996.

Hewitt, Nancy. *Women's Activism and Social Change: Rochester, New York 1822–1871.* Ithaca: Cornell University Press, 1984.

History Project, The. *Improper Bostonians: Lesbian and Gay History from the Puritans to Playland.* Boston: Beacon Press, 1998.

Hogan, Steve, and Lee Hudson, eds. *Completely Queer: The Gay and Lesbian Encyclopedia.* New York: Henry Holt and Company, 1998.

Horne, Gerald. *Fire This Time: The Watts Uprising and the 1960s.* New York: Da Capo Press, 1997.

Howard, John, ed. *Carryin' On in the Lesbian and Gay South.* New York: New York University Press, 1997.

Hunter, Nan, Courtney Joslin, and Sharon McGowan. *Rights of Lesbians, Gay Men, Bisexuals, and Transgendered People.* New York: NYU Press, 2004.

Jay, Karla, and Joanne Glasgow, eds. *Lesbian Texts and Contexts: Radical Revisions.* New York: New York University Press, 1990.

Jennings, Kevin, ed. *Becoming Visible.* Boston: Alyson Publications, Inc., 1994.

Johnson, David K. *The Lavender Scare: The Cold War Persecution of Gays and Lesbians in the Federal Government.* Chicago: University of Chicago Press, 2004.

Johnston, Jill. *Lesbian Nation: The Feminist Solution.* New York: Simon & Schuster, 1973.

Katz, Jonathan Ned. *Gay American History: Lesbians & Gay Men in the U.S.A.* New York: Penguin Books, 1976; 1992.

_____. *Government vs. Homosexuals.* New York: Arno Press, 1975.

_____. *The Invention of Heterosexuality.* New York: Dutton/Penguin Books, 1995.

Kinsey, Alfred C., Wardell B. Pomeroy, and Clyde E. Martin. *Sexual Behavior in the Human Male.* Philadelphia: Saunders, 1948.

Kinsey, Alfred C., Wardell B. Pomeroy, Clyde E. Martin, and Paul H. Gebhard. *Sexual Behavior in the Human Female.* Philadelphia: Saunders, 1953.

Kennedy, Elizabeth Lapovsky, and Madeline D. Davis. *Boots of Leather, Slippers of Gold: The History of a Lesbian Community.* New York: Penguin Books, 1994.

Klatch, Rebecca. *A Generation Divided: The New Left, the New Right, and the 1960s.* Berkeley: University of California Press, 1999.

Kuda, Marie J., "Kinsey: Sex by the Numbers," *Windy City Times,* Chicago, IL, August 27, 2003.

_____, ed. *Two Women: The Poetry of Jeannette Foster and Valerie Taylor.* Chicago: Womanpress, 1976.

Kushner, Tony. *Angels in America: Perestroika* (I) and *The Millenium Approaches* (II). New York: Theater Communications Group, 1995.

Lassell, Michael, and Elena Georgiou. *The World in Us: Lesbian and Gay Poetry of the Next Wave.* New York: St. Martin's Press, 2000.

Lauritsen, John, and David Thorstad. *The Early Homosexual Rights Movement (1864–1935).* Novato, CA: Times Change Press, 1974; 1995.

Lester, Toni, ed. *Gender Nonconformity, Race, and Sexuality: Charting the Connections.* Madison: University of Wisconsin, 2002.

Licata, Salvadore J. "The Homosexual Rights Movement in the United States: A Traditionally Overlooked Area of American History." *Journal of Homosexuality* 6, Fall/Winter 1980/81.

Lorde, Audre. *Zami: A New Spelling of My Name.* Watertown, MA: Persephone Press, 1982.

_____. "Who Said It Was Simple," *Chosen Poems, Old and New.* New York: W. W. Norton, 1982.

Loughery, John. *The Other Side of Silence: Men's Lives and Gay Identities: A Twentieth-Century History.* New York: Henry Holt and Company, Inc., 1998.

Louys, Pierre. *The Collected Works of Pierre Louys.* New York: Avon Publications, Inc. 1955.

Luker, Kristin. *Abortion and the Politics of Motherhood.* Berkeley: University of California Press, 1984.

Manahan, Nancy, and Rosemary Curb. *Lesbian Nuns: Breaking Silence.* New York: Warner Books, 1985.

Marcus, Eric. *Making History: The Struggle for Gay and Lesbian Equal Rights, 1945–1990—An Oral History.* New York: Harper/Collins, 1992.

———. *Making Gay History: The Half-Century Fight for Lesbian and Gay Equal Rights.* New York: HarperCollins, 2002.

Marotta, Toby. *The Politics of Homosexuality: How Lesbians and Gay Men Have Made Themselves a Political and Social Force in Modern America.* Boston: Houghton Mifflin, 1981.

May, Elaine Tyler. *Homeward Bound: American Families in the Cold War Era.* New York: Basic Books/HarperCollins, 1988.

———. "Pushing the Limits, 1940–1960." In Nancy Cott, ed., *No Small Courage: A History of Women in the United States,* Oxford: Oxford University Press, 2000. McGirr, Lisa. *Suburban Warriors: The Origins of the New American Right.* Princeton, NJ: Princeton University Press, 2001.

Meeker, Martin Dennis, Jr. "Behind the Mask of Respectability: Reconsidering the Mattachine Society and Male Homophile Practice, 1950s and 1960s." *Journal of the History of Sexuality,* Vol. 10, No. 1, January 2001.

———. *Contacts Desired: Gay and Lesbian Communications and Community, 1940s–1970s.* Chicago: University of Chicago Press, 2006.

Meyerowitz, Joanne, ed. *Not June Cleaver: Women and Gender in Postwar America, 1945–1960.* Philadelphia: Temple University Press, 1994.

———. "Women, Cheesecake, and Borderline Material: Responses to Girlie Pictures in the Mid-Twentieth Century U.S." *Journal of Women's History,* Vol. 8, No. 3, 1996.

Miller, Neil. *Out of the Past: Gay and Lesbian History From 1869 to the Present.* New York: Vintage Books/Random House, 1995.

———. *Sex Crime Panic: A Journey to the Paranoid Heart of the 1950s.* Los Angeles: Alyson Books, 2002.

Mixner, David, and Dennis Bailey. *Brave Journeys: Profiles in Gay and Lesbian Courage.* New York: Bantam Books, 2000.

Moody, Anne. *Coming of Age in Mississippi.* New York: Dell Publishing, 1968.

Moraga, Cherrie, and Gloria Anzaldua, eds. *This Bridge Called My Back. Writings by Radical Women of Color.* New York: Kitchen Table: Women of Color Press, 1981.

Morgan, Claire. *The Price of Salt.* Tallahassee: Naiad Press, 1984.

Morgan, Robin, ed. *Sisterhood is Powerful: An Anthology of Writings from the Women's Liberation Movement.* New York: Random House/Vintage Books, 1970.

Morone, James A. *Hellfire Nation: The Politics of Sin in American History.* New Haven: Yale University Press, 2003.

Nakatani, Robert. "1960's-Era Judge Sparked Gay Rights Battle that Continues Today," *Daily Journal,* June 13, 2006.

Navasky, Victor. *Naming Names.* New York: Penguin Books, 1980.

Nestle, Joan. A *Restricted Country.* Ithaca, NY: Firebrand, 1987.

_____. *The Persistent Desire.* Boston: Alyson Publications, Inc., 1992.

Newton, Esther. *Cherry Grove, Fire Island: Sixty Years in America's First Gay and Lesbian Town.* Boston: Beacon Press, 1993.

Norton, Rictor. "The Nature of Lesbian History," *Lesbian History* (August 2003), http://www.infopt.demon.co.uk/lesbians.htm

Parker, Pat. *Pit Stop.* Oakland, CA: The Women's Press Collective, 1973/1975.

Patterson, James T. *Brown v. Board of Education: A Civil Rights Milestone and Its Troubled Legacy.* New York: Oxford University Press, 2001.

Payne, Charles M. *I've Got the Light of Freedom: The Organizing Tradition and the Mississippi Freedom Struggle.* Berkeley: University of California Press, 1995.

Perkins, Laura. "Bad Times and Good: Gays and San Francisco share a long—and sometimes tumultuous—past," *San Francisco Chronicle,* June 23, 2000.

Plant, Richard. *The Pink Triangle.* New York: New Republic Books/Henry Holt and Company, 1986.

Plante, David. "Jean Rhys: A Remembrance," *The Paris Review,* No. 76 Fall 1979.

Pogash, Carol. "The Myth of the 'Twinkie Defense:' The verdict in the Dan White case wasn't based on his ingestion of junk food," *San Francisco Chronicle,* November 23, 2003.

Poling, John. "Mattachine Midwest." Master's thesis, University of Iowa, 2002.

Ransby, Barbara. *Ella Baker & the Black Freedom Movement: A Radical Democratic Vision.* Chapel Hill: University of North California Press, 2003.

Renault, Mary. *The Friendly Young Ladies.* London: Longmann, Green & Co., 1944; Virago Press, 1984.

Retter, Yolanda. *Lesbian (Feminist) Los Angeles, 1970–1990: An Exploratory*

Ethnohistory, 1995; Lesbian History Project, Univeristy of Southern California. www.lib.usc.edu.

Ridinger, Robert B. Marks, ed. *The Gay and Lesbian Movement References and Resources.* New York: G.K. Hall & Co., Simon & Schuster Macmillan, 1996.

Robson, Ruthann. *Lesbian (Out)Law: Survival Under the Rule of Law.* Ithaca: Firebrand Books, 1992.

Rodgers, Bruce. *The Queens' Vernacular.* San Francisco: Straight Arrow Books, 1972.

Rosen, Ruth. *The World Split Open: How the Modern Women's Movement Changed America.* New York: Viking Penguin, 2000.

Ruiz, Vicki, and Ellen Carol DuBois, eds. *Unequal Sisters: A Multicultural Reader in U.S. Women's History.* New York: Routledge, 1990.

Rupp, Leila. *A Desired Past: A Short History of Same-Sex Love in America.* Chicago: University of Chicago Press, 1999.

_____. *Worlds of Women: The Making of an International Women's Movement.* Princeton: Princeton University Press, 1997.

Sarton, May. *Faithful are the Wounds.* New York: W.W. Norton & Company, 1955.

Sayre, Nora. *Previous Convictions: A Journey Through the 1950s.* New Brunswick, NJ: Rutgers University Press, 1995.

Schrecker, Ellen. *Many Are The Crimes: McCarthyism in America.* Boston: Little, Brown and Company, 1998.

Shilts, Randy. *The Mayor of Castro Street.* New York: St. Martin's Press, 1982.

_____. *Conduct Unbecoming.* New York: St. Martin's Press, 1993.

Shockley, Ann. *Loving Her.* New York: Avon Books, 1978.

Smith, Barbara, ed. *Home Girls: A Black Feminist Anthology.* New York: Kitchen Table: Women of Color Press, 1983.

Smith, Barbara, Gloria Steinem, Gwendolyn Mink, Marysa Navarro, and Wilma Mankiller, eds. *The Reader's Companion to U.S. Women's History.* Boston: Houghton Mifflin Publishing, Inc., 1998.

Smith-Rosenberg, Carroll. *Disorderly Conduct: Visions of Gender in Victorian America.* New York: Knopf, 1985.

Snitow, Ann, Christine Stansell, and Sharon Thompson, eds. *Powers of Desire: The Politics of Sexuality.* New York: Monthly Review Press, 1983.

Soares, Manuela. "The Purloined *Ladder:* Its Place in Lesbian History." *Journal of Homosexuality,* Vol. 34, No. 3/4, Winter 1998: 27–49.

Stein, Marc. *City of Sisterly and Brotherly Love: Making Lesbian and Gay History in Philadelphia, 1945–1972.* Chicago: University of Chicago Press, 2000.

Streitmatter, Rodger. *Unspeakable: The Rise of the Gay and Lesbian Press in America*. Boston: Faber and Faber, 1995.

Stryker, Susan. *Lesbian Pulp Address Book*. San Francisco: Chronicle Books, 2000.

Stryker, Susan, and Jim Van Buskirk. *Gay by the Bay: A History of Queer Culture in the San Francisco Bay Area*. San Francisco: Chronicle Books, 1996.

Sugrue, Thomas J. *The Origins of the Urban Crisis: Race and Inequality in Postwar Detroit*. Princeton: Princeton University Press, 1996.

Sweet, Roxanne Thayer. "Political and Social Action in Homophile Organizations." Ph.D. Dissertation, University of California, Berkeley, 1968.

Swerdlow, Amy. *Women Strike for Peace*. Chicago: University of Chicago Press, 1993.

Takaki, Ronald. *A Different Mirror: A History of Multicultural America*. Boston: Little, Brown & Co., 1993.

Tate, Claudia. *Black Women Writers At Work*. New York: Continuum, 1984.

Taylor, Valerie. *A World Without Men*. New York: Midwood Tower, 1963; reissued by Naiad Press, 1982.

_____. *Journey to Fulfillment*. New York: Midwood Tower, 1964; reissued by Naiad Press, 1982.

_____. *Stranger on Lesbos*. New York: Fawcett/Crest, 1960.

_____. *The Girls in 3–B*. New York: Fawcett/Gold Medal, 1959.

_____. *Whisper Their Love*. New York: Fawcett/Crest, 1957.

Terry, Jennifer. *An American Obsession: Science, Medicine, and Homosexuality in Modern Society*. Chicago: University of Chicago Press, 1999.

Timmons, Stuart. *The Trouble with Harry Hay*. Boston: Alyson Publications, 1990.

Tobias, Sheila. *Faces of Feminism: An Activist's Reflections on the Women's Movement*. Boulder: Westview Press/HarperCollins, 1997.

Torres, Tereska. *Women's Barracks*. New York: Fawcett Publications, 1950.

Trend, David, ed. "Queer Subjects." *Socialist Review*, Vol. 25, No. 1 (1995).

Vance, Carole S., ed. *Pleasure and Danger: Exploring Female Sexuality*. New York: Pandora/HarperCollins, 1989.

Van De Carr, Paul. "Death of Dreams: Harvey Milk & Jonestown: 25 Years Later," *The Advocate* (November 2003), 32–36.

Vicinus, Martha, ed. *Lesbian Subjects: A Feminist Studies Reader*. Bloomington: Indiana University Press, 1996.

_____. *Intimate Friends: Women Who Loved Women, 1778–1928*. Chicago: University of Chicago Press, 2005.

Walker, Samuel. *In Defense of American Liberties: A History of the ACLU*. New York: Oxford University Press, 1990.

Warner, Michael. *Fear of a Queer Planet: Queer Politics and Social Theory*. Minneapolis: Minnesota University Press, 1993.

Weston, Kath. *Families We Choose: Lesbians, Gays, and Kinship*. New York: Columbia University Press, 1991.

Weitz, Rose. "The Development of Tertiary Deviance in the Lesbian World." Master's thesis, Arizona State University, 1982.

White, E. Frances. *Dark Continent of Our Bodies: Black Feminism and the Politics of Respectability*. Philadelphia: Temple University Press, 2001.

Willett, Graham. *Living Out Loud: A History of Gay and Lesbian Activism in Australia*. St. Leonards, Australia: Allen & Unwin, 2000.

Wolcott, Victoria W. *Remaking Respectability: African American Women in Interwar Detroit*. Chapel Hill: University of North Carolina Press, 2001.

Zimet, Jaye. *Strange Sisters: The Art of Lesbian Pulp Fiction, 1949–1969*. New York: Viking/Penguin, 1999.

Endnotes

PROLOGUE

1. COINTELPRO refers to a series of FBI counterintelligence programs that operated from 1956 to 1971. According to Brian Glick, author of *War At Home: Covert Action Against U.S. Activists and What We Can Do About It* (Boston: South End Press, 1989), "Though the name stands for 'Counterintelligence Program,' the targets were not enemy spies. The FBI set out to eliminate 'radical' political opposition inside the U.S." After the illegal program was revealed in 1971, committees of the U.S. Senate and House of Representatives held lengthy investigations which uncovered extensive covert counterintelligence programs involving the FBI, CIA, U.S. Army intelligence, the White House, the Attorney General, and local and state law enforcement. Many opponents—liberal as well as radical—of government domestic and foreign policy were targeted, especially black liberation or civil rights groups; pacifists and antinuclear weapons activists; independence movements; socialist or communist organizations; and New Left, feminist, and gay and lesbian groups. In "Spying on the Protestors," John S. Friedman's article in *The Nation*, September 1, 2005, he noted that "scattered evidence accumulating around the country suggests that the domestic surveillance that occurred during the Vietnam War may be returning, involving a more coordinated federal effort through the National Guard as well as the Joint Terrorism Task Force, teams of state and local police, and federal agents, led by the FBI."

2. Tom Eastham, "More CIA Bay Area drug tests," *San Francisco Examiner*, September 20, 1977.

3. Phyllis Lyon, interview with author, August 10, 2005.

4. Glennda Chui, "How FBI Spied on S.F. Gays," *San Francisco Chronicle*, September 9, 1982.

5. FBI and CIA Correspondence and Related Materials, Boxes 16/17–17/3, Del Martin and Phyllis Lyon Papers, 1954–2000, 93–13, the Gay, Lesbian, Bisexual, Transgender Historical Society, San Francisco, CA. Hereinafter referred to as "Martin and Lyon Papers, GLBTHS."

6. Eleanor Roosevelt's "My Day" was a nationally syndicated, six-days-a-week newspaper column on issues of wide-ranging social and political import. For examples, see David Emblidge, ed., *My Day: The Best of Eleanor Roosevelt's Acclaimed Newspaper Columns, 1936–1962* (New York: Da Capo Press, 2001).

7. From the FBI's erroneous description in 1956 on, commentators on the homophile and gay rights movements regularly referred to the Daughters of Bilitis as being a subsidiary or "sister organization" of one of the mostly-male gay groups, such as the Mattachine Society. Although early gay historians like Jonathan Ned Katz, John D'Emilio, and Martin Duberman were careful to discuss DOB and Mattachine, ONE, etc., as independent, autonomous, sometimes antagonistic groups, other writers erred in stating their affiliations. As recently as 2003, an article titled "Liberation vs. 'Progress': A Challenge to Queer People & Their Allies," by long-time gay journalist Richard Goldstein, referred to DOB as "a sororal organization to the Mattachines," in *Guild Practitioner* (Vol. 60, No. 2), published by the National Lawyers Guild.

8. Kay Lahusen, interview with author, April 23, 2002.

9. Billye Talmadge, interview with author, March 30, 2002. See also Del Martin and Phyllis Lyon, *Lesbian/Woman* (Volcano, CA: Volcano Press, Inc., 1972; 1991).

10. Stella Rush, conversation with author, May 20, 2005; Martin Duberman, *Stonewall* (New York: Penguin Books USA, Inc., 1994), 234.

11. Stella Rush, interviews with author, March 26 and 27, 2002.

12. Ibid.

13. For evocative recreations of the post–World War II American culture of fear, from a variety of time periods and perspectives, see May Sarton, *Faithful Are the Wounds* (New York: W. W. Norton, 1955); Victor Navasky, *Naming Names* (New York: Penguin, 1980); David Halberstam, *The Fifties* (New York: Villard, 1993); Ellen Schrecker, *Many Are The Crimes: McCarthyism in America* (Boston: Little, Brown and Company, 1998); and Peter Beinart, "The Rehabilitation of the Cold War Liberal," *New York Times,* April 30, 2006.

14. See John D'Emilio, *Sexual Politics, Sexual Communities: The Making of a Homosexual Minority in the United States, 1940–1970* (Chicago: University of Chicago Press, 1983; 1998); Elaine Tyler May, *Homeward Bound: American Families in the Cold War Era* (New York: Basic Books/HarperCollins, 1988); and K. A. Cuordileone, "'Politics in an Age of Anxiety': Cold War Political Culture and the

Crisis in American Masculinity, 1949 to 1960," *The Journal of American History*, September 2000.

15. James A. Morone, *Hellfire Nation: The Politics of Sin in American History* (New Haven: Yale University Press, 2003), 391; see also John D'Emilio, *Sexual Politics, Sexual Communities*.

16. John Loughery, *The Other Side of Silence: Men's Lives and Gay Identities: A Twentieth-Century History* (New York: Henry Holt and Company, 1998), 199–204.

17. Robert Corber, *Homosexuality in Cold War America: Resistance and the Crisis of Masculinity* (Durham: Duke University Press, 1997), 10; David K. Johnson, *The Lavender Scare: The Cold War Persecution of Gays and Lesbians in the Federal Government* (Chicago: University of Chicago Press, 2004).

18. James Morone, *Hellfire Nation: The Politics of Sin in American History*, 392.

19. See Tony Kushner, *Angels in America: Perestroika* (I) and *The Millenium Approaches* (II) (New York: Theater Communications Group, 1995); John Loughery, *The Other Side of Silence: Men's Lives and Gay Identities: A Twentieth-Century History*, Lillian Hellman, *Scoundrel Time* (New York: Little Brown & Co., 1976).

20. Nora Sayre, *Previous Convictions: A Journey through the 1950s* (New Brunswick, NJ: Rutgers University Press, 1995), 274. "The Committee" is a reference to the House Committee on Un-American Activities, popularly known by the acronym HUAC.

21. Greta Schiller and Robert Rosenberg, dirs., *Before Stonewall: the Making of a Gay and Lesbian Community* (Cinema Guild, 1986). See also Randy Shilts, *Conduct Unbecoming*, 107-108.

22. Audre Lorde, *Zami: A New Spelling of My Name* (New York: Persephone Press, 1982); 172.

23. For examples of social change organizing in the 1950s and early 1960s see Stephanie Coontz, *The Way We Never Were: American Families and the Nostalgia Trap* (New York: Basic Books, 1992; 2000); Thomas J. Sugrue, *The Origins of the Urban Crisis: Race and Inequality in Postwar Detroit* (Princeton, NJ: Princeton University Press, 1996); Charles M. Payne, *I've Got the Light of Freedom: The Organizing Tradition and the Mississippi Freedom Struggle* (Berkeley: University of California Press, 1995); Amy Swerdlow, *Women Strike for Peace* (Chicago: University of Chicago Press, 1993); Ronald Takaki, *A Different Mirror: A History of Multicultural America* (Boston: Little, Brown & Co., 1993); Adam Fairclough, *To Redeem the Soul of America: The Southern Christian Leadership Conference and Martin Luther King, Jr.* (Athens, GA: University of Georgia Press, 1987).

24. Foundational books on American gay and lesbian histories include the following,

listed chronologically: Jonathan Ned Katz, *Gay American History: Lesbians & Gay Men in the U.S.A.* (New York: Penguin Books, 1976); Lillian Faderman, *Surpassing the Love of Men* (New York: William Morrow and Co., Inc., 1981); Toby Marotta, *The Politics of Homosexuality: How Lesbians and Gay Men Have Made Themselves a Political and Social Force in Modern America* (Boston: Houghton Mifflin, 1981); John D'Emilio, *Sexual Politics, Sexual Communities;* Carroll Smith-Rosenberg, *Disorderly Conduct: Visions of Gender in Victorian America* (New York: Knopf, 1985); Martin Duberman, *About Time: Exploring the Gay Past* (New York: Penguin Books, 1986); Martin Duberman, Martha Vicinus, and George Chauncey, Jr., eds., *Hidden From History: Reclaiming the Gay and Lesbian Past* (New York: Penguin Books, 1989); Allan Berube, *Coming Out Under Fire: The History of Gay Men and Lesbians in World War II* (New York: The Free Press, 1990); Lillian Faderman, *Odd Girls and Twilight Lovers: A History of Lesbian Life in Twentieth-Century America* (New York: Columbia University Press, 1991); Martin Duberman, *Stonewall;* Elizabeth Lapovsky Kennedy and Madeline D. Davis, *Boots of Leather, Slippers of Gold: The History of a Lesbian Community* (New York: Penguin Books, 1994); George Chauncey, Jr., *Gay New York: Gender, Urban Culture, and the Making of the Gay Male World* (New York: Basic Books, 1994).

Lesbian and gay histories published since the late 1990s and in the early years of the twenty-first century which not only reconstruct the homosexual past but help to deepen knowledge of the homophile movement include, among others, John Loughery, *The Other Side of Silence: Men's Lives and Gay Identities: A Twentieth-Century History* (1998); Lillian Faderman, *To Believe in Women* (Boston: Houghton Mifflin Company, 1999); Leila Rupp, *A Desired Past: A Short History of Same-Sex Love in America* (Chicago: University of Chicago Press, 1999); Jennifer Terry, *An American Obsession: Science, Medicine, and Homosexuality in Modern Society* (Chicago: University of Chicago Press, 1999); Marc Stein, *City of Sisterly and Brotherly Love: Making Lesbian and Gay History in Philadelphia, 1945–1972* (Chicago: University of Chicago Press, 2000); Steven Capsuto, *Alternate Channels: The Uncensored Story of Gay and Lesbian Images on Radio and Television, 1930s to the Present* (New York: Ballantine Books, 2000); John D'Emilio, *The World Turned: Essays on Gay History, Politics, and Culture* (Durham: Duke University Press, 2002); Nan Alamilla Boyd, *Wide Open Town: A History of Queer San Francisco to 1965* (Berkeley: University of California Press, 2003); and Martin Meeker, *Contacts Desired: Gay and Lesbian Communications and Community, 1940s–1970s* (Chicago: University of Chicago Press, 2006).

25. Elaine Tyler May, "Pushing the Limits." In Nancy Cott, ed., *No Small Courage: A History of Women in the United States* (Oxford: Oxford University Press, 2000),

504–505. See also Estelle Freedman, *No Turning Back: The History of Feminism and the Future of Women* (New York: Ballantine Books, 2002).

26. Lillian Faderman, *To Believe in Women.*

27. Marie J. Kuda, "Kinsey: Sex by the Numbers," *Windy City Times,* Chicago, IL, August 27, 2003.

28. Steve Hogan and Lee Hudson, *Completely Queer: The Gay and Lesbian Encyclopedia* (New York: Henry Holt and Company, 1998), 79, 559.

29. Florine Fleischman with Susan Bullough, "Lisa Ben (1921)." In Vern L. Bullough, ed., *Before Stonewall: Activists for Gay and Lesbian Rights in Historical Context* (New York: Haworth Press, 2002), 63–65.

30. Paul Cain, "Lisa Ben," *Leading the Parade: Conversations with America's Most Influential Lesbians and Gay Men* (Lanham, MD: Scarecrow Press, 2002), 15.

31. Stuart Timmons, *The Trouble with Harry Hay* (Boston: Alyson Publications, 1990); Barbara Gittings, correspondence with author, May 25, 2006.

32. Edward Sagarin (Donald Webster Cory) took his pseudonymous surname from Andre Gide's classic novel *Corydon*. Greenberg Press published his book *The Homosexual in America* in 1951; five years later it had gone through six reprintings. See also Martin Duberman, "The 'Father of the Homophile Movement.'"

33. Jim Kepner, *Rough News—Daring Views: 1950s' Pioneer Gay Press Journalism* (New York: Haworth Press, 1998), 3; Stella Rush, discussion with author, May 4, 2006.

34. Stella Rush, interviews with author, May 21 and 22, 2002; June 29, 2002.

35. Stella Rush, interviews with author, March 15 through 19, 2002.

36. Judith M. Saunders, "Stella Rush a.k.a. Sten Russell (1925–)," *Before Stonewall,* 135–144.

37. Sten Russell, "Letter to a Newcomer," *ONE,* February 1954.

38. Lillian Faderman, *Odd Girls and Twilight Lovers,* 140; John D'Emilio, *Sexual Politics, Sexual Communities,* 36–37.

39. By the time of her death in 1981, Dr. Jeannette Howard Foster had gained some acclaim for her groundbreaking work in lesbian and gay circles. In October 1998, she was inducted into the City of Chicago's Gay and Lesbian Hall of Fame. See Marie Kuda, "A personal reflection," http://www.queertheory.com/histories; see also Gerber/Hart Library, Chicago, IL.

40. Boyd, *Wide Open Town,* 92, 131–133.

41. Allan Berube, "Resorts for Sex Perverts," unpublished paper for slide show, author's copy; Boyd, 137; Elizabeth A. Armstrong, *Forging Gay Identities: Organizing Sexuality in San Francisco, 1950–1994* (Chicago: University of Chicago Press, 2002), 35; Susan Stryker and Jim Van Buskirk, *Gay by the Bay: A History of*

Queer Culture in the San Francisco Bay Area (San Francisco: Chronicle Books, 1996), 30.

42. Boyd, 93, 134–35. See also John Loughery, 241–243; and Neil Miller, *Sex Crime Panic: A Journey to the Paranoid Heart of the 1950s* (Los Angeles: Alyson Books, 2002).

43. Boyd, *Wide Open Town*, 150.

44. Phyllis Lyon, interviews with author, May 11, 1998; June 10, 2003; August 10, 2005; and May 15, 2006. See also Del Martin and Phyllis Lyon, *Lesbian/Woman* (Volcano, CA: Volcano Press, Inc., 1972) and Del Martin, "Phyllis Lyon (1924–)," *Before Stonewall*, 169–177.

45. Del Martin, interviews with author, May 11, 1998; June 10, 2003; August 10, 2005; and May 15, 2006. See also Phyllis Lyon, "Del Martin (1921–), *Before Stonewall*, 160–168; and Del Martin and Phyllis Lyon, *Lesbian/Woman*.

46. Phyllis Lyon and Del Martin, interview dated August 27, 1996, KQED Television, San Francisco, CA, Box 40/26, Martin and Lyon Papers, GLBTHS.

47. Ernest Lenn, "State Fights Bar Hangouts of Deviates," *San Francisco Examiner,* May 25, 1955. Clippings File, GLBTHS, San Francisco, CA.

CHAPTER ONE

1. Phyllis Lyon and Del Martin, interview dated August 27, 1996, KQED Television, San Francisco, CA; Box 40/26, Martin and Lyon Papers, GLBTHS.

2. Phyllis Lyon, interview with author, June 10, 2003. There are numerous "official" accounts of DOB's founding, including annual organizational histories published in *The Ladder;* presentations to homophile conferences throughout the 1950s and 1960s; and pamphlets published by DOB in the late 1960s and 1970s. See Box 9/2, Martin and Lyon Papers, GLBTHS. See also Del Martin and Phyllis Lyon, *Lesbian/Woman*, pp. 219–255.

3. Pierre Louys, *The Songs of Bilitis* (Chicago: Argus Books, 1931, first U.S. edition). The poems were reissued in paperback in the United States in 1955 by Avon Publications, Inc., in *The Collected Works of Pierre Louys*. Phyllis Lyon and Martin, interviews with author, May 11, 1998, and June 10, 2003. See also Susan Cavin, *Lesbian Origins* (San Francisco: ism press, 1985); Laura Doan, *Fashioning Sapphism: The Origins of a Modern English Lesbian Culture* (New York: Columbia University Press, 2001); Rictor Norton, "The Nature of Lesbian History," *Lesbian History* (August 2003), www.infopt.demon.co.uk/lesbians.htm; Martha Vicinus, *Intimate Friends: Women Who Loved Women, 1778–1928* (Chicago: University of Chicago Press, 2005).

4. Phyllis Lyon, interview with author, February 18, 1997; and correspondence with author, January 5, 2006.

5. "Resume of First Meeting," dated September 21, 1955, Box 2/2, Martin and Lyon Papers, GLBTHS.

6. "Rules for Membership," n.d., Box 2/2, Martin and Lyon Papers, GLBTHS.

7. Neither Phyllis Lyon nor Del Martin remembers any discussion among DOB's founders about choosing a triangle as the club's insignia. The choice is striking because the inverted pink triangle became a popular symbol of gay liberation in the U.S. in the late 1960s and early 1970s. By that time, American activists had learned about its use by the Nazis as a way to mark and persecute homosexuals, and they reclaimed it as a symbol of resistance to repression. However, it is not known whether any of the original members of the Daughters of Bilitis were aware of the triangle's significance to gay people when they made it their club pin. In 1958, they received a letter from "Miss B," a German subscriber to *The Ladder* whose long letter was published in the June issue. She wrote, "I do not know if it is known to you that homosexuals have been in concentration camps. Their backs were marked with a *pink triangle.* Because of this I was amazed when I saw the triangle—you use it as a sign. (The boys here, too.)" There is no record of a response to Miss B, nor any discussion in the pages of *The Ladder.* See Erwin J. Haeberle, "Swastika, Pink Triangle, and Yellow Star: The Destruction of Sexology and the Persecution of Homosexuals in Nazi Germany," *Hidden from History: Reclaiming the Gay and Lesbian Past,* Duberman et al., 365–379; see also Richard Plant, *The Pink Triangle* (New York: New Republic Books, Henry Holt and Company, Inc., 1986).

8. "Minutes," October 5, 1955, Box 2/2, Martin and Lyon Papers, GLBTHS.

9. Phyllis Lyon, interview with author, September 10, 1998.

10. Del Martin and Phyllis Lyon, *Lesbian/Woman,* 220–221.

11. Ibid.

12. On the Daughters' early use of the term "sex variant," Phyllis Lyon has commented, "At least it's better than 'pervert.'" Phyllis Lyon, correspondence with author, March 15, 2004. Lesbian bibliographer Jeanette Howard Foster thought so, too, and used "Female Variant" in the title of her 1956 study of literary references to lesbianism. According to Bruce Rodgers, author of the quirky *The Queens' Vernacular,* the term dates from the 1930s; in the 1950s it was less "loaded" than "female homosexual." He says that "Lesbian" in that time period was more of a "dirty word." *The Queens' Vernacular* (San Francisco: Straight Arrow Books, 1972), 125. "Rules for Membership," November 16, 1955, Box 2/2, Martin and Lyon Papers, GLBTHS.

13. "Minutes," January 4, 1956, and January 18, 1956, Box 2/2, Martin and Lyon Papers, GLBTHS.

14. The first club Frey started after DOB was named Quatrefoil. According to Martin

and Lyon, when she tried to enforce the same strict rules she proposed for DOB and her leadership was challenged again, she established Hale Aikane; both "lesbian sororities" lasted for a few years. Frey stayed friendly with DOB members; at one point she and Hale Aikane shared office space with the Daughters. Del Martin and Phyllis Lyon, *Lesbian/Woman*, 222.

15. Billye Talmadge, interview with author, March 30, 2002.

16. Phyllis Lyon, interview with author, March 6, 2002; Stella Rush, interview with author, May 22, 2002.

17. "Minutes," June 14, 1956, Box 2/2, Martin and Lyon Papers, GLBTHS.

18. Barbara Gittings, interview with author, June 25, 2002.

19. Kay Lahusen, "Barbara Gittings...," *Before Stonewall*, 242. See also Paul Cain, 60; Neil Miller, *Out of the Past* (New York: Vintage Books, 1995), 340; Kay Tobin and Randy Wicker, *The Gay Crusaders* (New York: Paperback Library, 1972), 208.

20. Phyllis Lyon, interview with author, March 6, 2002.

21. "Minutes," July 4, 1956, Box 2/2, Martin and Lyon Papers, GLBTHS.

22. Policy of the ACLU National Governing Board, January 17, 1957. Reported in *The Ladder*, Vol. 1, No. 5 (February 1957): 5.

23. There were strong connections between the civil liberties watchdog and the homophile groups. Many of the Daughters interviewed—such as Barbara Gittings, Phyllis Lyon, Del Martin, and Stella Rush—cite their longtime membership in the ACLU as important to them. Also, examples of interaction with local ACLU offices and officials abound in homophile newsletters and programs of the 1950s and 1960s. For example, in his essay in *Before Stonewall* (2002), the heterosexual homophile activist and scholar Vern Bullough recounted that when he moved to Los Angeles in 1959, he immediately joined the ACLU there and began meeting with the director of the LA office, Eason Monroe, to change national ACLU policy regarding gay men and lesbians. Bullough was also the author of "Lesbianism, Homosexuality, and the American Civil Liberties Union" (*Journal of Homosexuality*, Vol. 13[1], Fall 1986, 23–33), which traces the Southern California ACLU affiliate's efforts on behalf of gay men and women in the 1950s and 1960s. John D'Emilio's *Sexual Politics, Sexual Communities* also highlights the importance of activists' involvement with ACLU affiliates, as does John Loughery's *The Other Side of Silence* and David Johnson's *The Lavender Scare*.

24. Robert Nakatani, "1960's-Era Judge Sparked Gay Rights Battle that Continues Today," *Daily Journal*, June 13, 2006, and ACLU Annual Report (New York: American Civil Liberties Union, 132 Broad Street, New York, NY; 2003). For a general history of the ACLU, see Samuel Walker, *In Defense of American Liberties: A History of the ACLU* (New York: Oxford University Press, 1990).

25. Eric Marcus, "The Teacher—Billie Tallmij,"*Making History: The Struggle for Gay and Lesbian Rights 1945–1990* (New York: HarperCollins Publishers, 1992), 76–77. On Daughters' opinions of gay male sexual practices, see, for example, the exchange of letters in *The Ladder*, Vol. 5, No. 10 (June 1961): 23–26. One writer stated, "Somehow I find it a little difficult to take up the banner in a 'crusade for cruising' or do battle to make legal latrine lechery and passion in our public parks. If the Lesbian recognizes the bounds of good taste and common courtesy, so be it. If the male refuses to, then let him assume the responsibility for his actions."

26. See Del Martin's editorial in the January 1962 *Ladder* insisting that reform of "our outmoded sex laws" was a high priority for homophile activists "and may draw homosexuals together," Vol. 6, No. 4, 4–5. Also see David Mixner and Dennis Bailey, *Brave Journeys*, 32.

27. Many speeches to DOB meetings and conventions, as well as essays and letters in *The Ladder*, address this issue, especially in the years 1956 through 1965. One of the earliest was "A Plea for Integration," written by Barbara Stephens for *The Ladder* in Vol. 1, No. 8 (May 1957): 17–18.

28. Paula Giddings, *When and Where I Enter: The Impact of Black Women on Race and Sex in America* (New York: Bantam Books, 1985), 81–82, and E. Frances White, *Dark Continent of Our Bodies: Black Feminism and the Politics of Respectability* (Philadelphia: Temple University Press, 2001), 14, 33.

In addition, see Sara M. Evans, *Tidal Wave: How Women Changed America at Century's End* (New York: Free Press, 2003); Estelle Freedman, *No Turning Back: The History of Feminism and the Future of Women*, op. cit., 257–261; Elaine Tyler May, "Pushing the Limits 1940–1961," *No Small Courage*, 473–526; Joanne Meyerowitz, ed., *Not June Cleaver: Women and Gender in Postwar America, 1945–1960* (Philadelphia: Temple University Press, 1994); Ruth Rosen, *The World Split Open: How The Modern Women's Movement Changed America* (New York: Penguin Putnam USA, Inc., 2000); Vicki Ruiz and Ellen Carol DuBois, eds., *Unequal Sisters: A Multicultural Reader in U.S. Women's History* (New York: Routledge, 1990).

29. Paisley Harris, "Gatekeeping and Remaking: The Politics of Respectability in African American Women's History and Black Feminism," *Journal of Women's History*, Vol. 15, No. 1 (Spring 2003): 212–219.

30. White, *Dark Continent of Our Bodies*, 35.

31. Phyllis Lyon, correspondence with author, January 5, 2006.

CHAPTER TWO

1. Portion of a letter signed by "L.H.N., New York, N.Y." in "Readers Respond," *The Ladder*, Vol. 1, No. 8 (May 1957): 26–28.

2. Ibid.

3. Ibid.

4. Michael Anderson, "'Education of Another Kind'—Lorraine Hansberry in the Fifties," Toni Lester, ed., *Gender Nonconformity, Race, and Sexuality: Charting the Connections* (Madison: University of Wisconsin Press, 2002), 211; Lorraine Hansberry, *To Be Young, Gifted and Black: Lorraine Hansberry in Her Own Words,* adapted by Robert Nemiroff (New York: Vintage, 1995), 73–74; Neil Miller, "Lorraine Hansberry," *Out of the Past,* op. cit., 328–332.

5. "A.C., New York, N.Y.," in "Readers Respond," *The Ladder,* Vol. 1, No. 10 (July 1957): 27–28.

6. "B.S., San Leandro," in "Readers Respond," *The Ladder,* Vol. 1, No. 10, (July 1957): 28–29.

7. Stella Rush, correspondence with author, March 13, 2004; Billye Talmadge, interview with author, March 25, 2002.

8. Minutes, July 24, 1956, Box 2/2, Martin and Lyon Papers, GLBTHS.

9. *The Ladder,* Vol. 1, No. 9 (June 1957) and Vol. 1 No. 10 (July 1957).

10. *The Ladder,* Vol. 1, No. 1 (November 1956).

11. *The Ladder,* Vol. 1, No. 2 (December 1956).

12. Del Martin, "The Positive Approach, *The Ladder,* Vol. 1, No. 2 (November 1956): 8–9.

13. Ann Ferguson, "Your Name Is Safe!" *The Ladder,* Vol. 1, No. 2 (November 1956): 10–12.

14. "J.M., Cleveland, Ohio," in "Readers Respond," *The Ladder,* Vol. 1, No. 2 (November 1956): 14.

15. Book Review: *Homosexuals Today—1956, The Ladder,* Vol. 1, No. 3 (December 1956): 5–6.

16. *The Ladder,* Vol. 1 No. 4 (January 1957): 6, 9–10.

17. "ONE's Annual Midwinter Institute Impressive," *The Ladder,* Vol. 1, No. 5 (February 1957): 3–6.

18. "B.D.H., Washington, D.C.," in "Readers Respond," *The Ladder,* Vol. 1, No. 8, (April 1957): 22–24.

19. "D.B., Long Beach, Calif.," in "Readers Respond," *The Ladder,* Vol. 1, No. 3 (December 1956): 13; Del Martin, "Why A Chapter In Your Area?" *The Ladder,* Vol. 1, No. 5 (February 1957), 7.

20. Stella Rush, interviews with author, May 27, 2002, and September 8, 2002; interview with Helen Sandoz and Stella Rush, May 15, 1987; #DV20, DOB Video Project, Lesbian Herstory Archives.

21. Barbara Grier, interview with author, December 29, 2003. Also see Victoria A.

Brownworth, "Barbara Grier (1933–): Climbing the Ladder," *Before Stonewall*, 253–264.

22. Marion Zimmer Bradley, "Variant Women in Literature," *The Ladder*, Vol. 1, No. 8 (May 1957): 8–10. See also Virginia Elwood-Akers, "Jeannette Howard Foster," *Before Stonewall*, 50.

CHAPTER THREE

1. Natalie Lando, interview with author, May 22, 2002.

2. "G.M., Orange, New Jersey," in "Readers Respond," *The Ladder*, Vol. 2, No. 2 (November 1957): 23–24.

3. "C.H. Pasadena, Calif.," in "Readers Respond," *The Ladder*, Vol. 2, No. 6 (March 1958): 20–21.

4. Phyllis Lyon, "Growing Pains," *The Ladder*, Vol. 4, No. 1 (October 1959): 4, 21.

5. Kay Lahusen, interview with author, June 25, 2002; Kay Tobin Lahusen, "Barbara Gittings, (1932–): Independent Spirit," *Before Stonewall*, 243; Stella Rush, "Helen Sandoz a.k.a. Helen Sanders a.k.a. Ben Cat (1920–1987), *Before Stonewall*, 146.

6. Kay Lahusen, "Barbara Gittings," *Before Stonewall*, 243.

7. Kay Lahusen, interview with author, January 31, 2004.

8. Phyllis Lyon, discussion with author, April 9, 2004; Del Martin, correspondence with author, January 5, 2006.

9. DOB New York chapter newsletter, November 1959; DOB Chapter Files, Lesbian Herstory Project.

10. Stella Rush, interview with author, September 16, 2003.

11. Venice Ostwald, interview with author, May 26, 2002.

12. Sten Russell, "ONE Symposium–Homosexuality, A Way of Life," *The Ladder*, Vol. 2, No. 5 (February 1958), 7–8.

13. Venice Ostwald, interview with author, September 5, 2002.

14. Del Martin and Phyllis Lyon, "Workshop Words," *Gay and Lesbian Outreach to Elders Newsletter* (February 1986). Florence Jaffy Papers, 97–23, GLBTHS.

15. Jennifer Terry, *An American Obsession*, 355–356.

16. Michael Bronski, *Pulp Fiction: Uncovering the Golden Age of Gay Male Pulps* (New York: St. Martin's Griffin, 2003), 25–30. See also Katherine V. Forrest, ed., *Lesbian Pulp Fiction: The Sexually Intrepid World of Lesbian Paperback Novels 1950–1965* (San Francisco: Cleis Press, 2005), x.

17. Florence Conrad and Ev Howe, "DOB Questionnaire Reveals Some Facts About Lesbians," *The Ladder*, Vol. 3, No. 12 (September 1959), 4–5.

18. Vern Bullough, "Berry Berryman (1901–1972)," *Before Stonewall*, 66–68. See also *Signs*, 2 (1977), 895–904.

19. "DOB Questionnaire," *The Ladder*, Vol. 3, No. 12 (September 1959): 6–7.

20. Ibid., 7–8; Phyllis Lyon, interview with author, March 1, 1999.

21. Ibid., 18.

22. Ibid., 23.

23. Ibid., 25.

24. *Some Comparisons Between Male & Female Homosexuals*, pamphlet published by *The Ladder*/Daughters of Bilitis, San Francisco, CA, 1961, 1–14.

25. Ibid.

26. "R.L., California," in "Readers Respond," *The Ladder*, Vol. 5, No. 2 (November 1960): 21–22.

CHAPTER FOUR

1. Clara Brock, interview with author, May 17, 2002; Phyllis Lyon, interview with author, May 15, 2002.

2. Pat Walker, October 1988, #MV46, DOB Video Project, Lesbian Herstory Archives.

3. Ibid.

4. Del Martin with assistance from Leslie Warren, "Pat Walker (1938–1999)," *Before Stonewall*, 191–192.

5. Del Martin and Phyllis Lyon, "Cleo Glenn (Bonner) (Dates Unknown)," *Before Stonewall*, 189–190.

6. "Beginning—DOB Book Service," *The Ladder*, Vol. 4, No. 8 (May 1960): 9.

7. "Here and There," *The Ladder*, Vol. 4, No. 6 (March 1960): 26; and "'Organized Homosexuals' Issue in S.F. Election," *The Ladder*, Vol. 4, No. 3 (December 1959): 5–9. In referencing Russ Wolden, Herb Caen was reminding his readers of the attempts by the recently defeated San Francisco mayoral candidate to inject hysteria over homosexuality into the 1959 campaign. Wolden, the city assessor, had charged that his opponent, incumbent Mayor George Christopher, had created a lax climate wherein "Sex Deviates Make S.F. Headquarters," as the headline in a free daily newspaper, the *San Francisco Progress*, charged in October. One of Wolden's supporters, William Brandhove, had joined the Mattachine Society and introduced a resolution at its annual convention in September 1959, praising Christopher and his Police Chief, Thomas Cahill, for their "enlightened and just City government and Police Force." It passed unanimously. The *Progress* article used the resolution to charge that San Francisco "has become the national headquarters of the organized homosexuals in the United States" and named Mattachine, ONE, and DOB (again relegated to the status of "sort of a woman's auxiliary to Mattachine"). Such an "endorsement" from the homophile groups was considered the kiss of death to a politician at that

time, especially one like Christopher who had claimed to give San Franciscans a
"clean city." Mattachine responded by filing a $1 million slander suit against Wolden
for "wrongfully and maliciously" declaring them to be "organized homosexuals."

Wolden was exposed and denounced by the mainstream media for his smear
tactics, but not before Brandhove's undercover work as a member of Mattachine was
detailed in a homophobic pamphlet printed and distributed "door to door in areas
of San Francisco." In it, he warned "you parents of daughters—do not sit back com-
placently feeling that because you have no boys in your family, everything is all right
as far as you are concerned. To enlighten you to the existence of a Lesbian organization composed of homosexual women, whose purposes are the same as the Mattachine Society, the male counterpart, make yourselves acquainted with the name
'Daughters of Bilitis.'" DOB's address and telephone number were included.
8. Del Martin, interview with author, June 10, 2003, and Phyllis Lyon, correspondence with author, January 5, 2006.
9. "II—Impressions by Helen Sanders," *The Ladder,* Vol. 4, No. 9 (June 1960): 6.
10. Del Martin and Phyllis Lyon, *Lesbian/Woman,* 237–238.
11. Stella Rush, correspondence with author, January 14, 2006.
12. "II—Impressions by Helen Sanders," *The Ladder,* Vol. 4, No. 9 (June 1960): 6.
13. Stella Rush, correspondence with author, January 14, 2006 and Sten Russell,
"DOB Convention," *The Ladder,* Vol. 4, No. 10 (July 1960): 16–22.
14. Del Martin and Phyllis Lyon, *Lesbian/Woman,* 234; "Directive No. 2" and
"Directive No. 3," National Daughters of Bilitis Governing Board Correspondence,
Box 6/1, Martin and Lyon Papers, GLBTHS. For discussions of DOB members'
patronage of gay bars which challenges older notions of their disapproval of and
estrangement from such places, see *No Secret Anymore: The Times of Del Martin and
Phyllis Lyon,* documentary film by Joan E. Biren (JEB), Moonforce Media, 2003;
Last Call at Maud's, documentary film by Paris Poirier, The Maud's Project, Venice,
CA, 1993; Kelly P. Anderson, "Out in the Fifties: The Daughters of Bilitis and the
Politics of Identity"(Master's thesis, Sarah Lawrence College, 1994), and Nan
Alamilla Boyd, *Wide Open Town,* op. cit.
15. "Bay Area 1945–1960: North Beach Bars," reprint of DOB map, West Coast
Lesbian Collections Newsletter, 1983. The West Coast Lesbian Collections, founded
by Lynn Fonfa, Waverly Lowell, and other lesbian activists and archivists in Oakland,
California, in 1981, moved to Los Angeles in 1987. It was renamed the June L.
Mazer Lesbian Archives.
16. Del Martin and Phyllis Lyon, *Lesbian/Woman,* 235.
17. As the years went on, S.O.B. awards were fewer. In 1962, they were given to
Thane Walker, Prosperos Society founder and leader, Henry Foster, Bob Burke, and

Fred Bunyan; in 1964, researchers Ralph H. Gundlach and Wardell B. Pomeroy, and Rev. Robert Wood were named "S.O.B.s." In 1966, Dr. Clay Colwell, president of the San Francisco Council on Religion and the Homosexual, was the lone man so honored. Only in 1968—the last year the awards were given—did "S.O.B.s" include a significant number of men again, such as Mattachine founder Harry Hay and former San Francisco Mayor Willie Brown, then a member of the California state Assembly.

18. "II—Impressions by Helen Sanders," *The Ladder,* Vol. 4, No. 9 (June 1960): 25. "Ex–CIA Shrink Reveals Exotic Bay Area Tests," *San Francisco Examiner,* September 20. 1977.

19. Phyllis Lyon, "Au Revoir," *The Ladder,* Vol. 4, No. 9 (June 1960): 4.

20. Marijane Meaker, interview with author, July 12, 2005.

21. Ibid.

22. Del Martin, "Open Letter to Ann Aldrich," *The Ladder,* Vol. 2, No. 7 (April 1958): 4–6; Marijane Meaker, interview with author, July 12, 2005.

23. Gene Damon, "An Evening's Reading," *The Ladder,* Vol. 4, No. 11 (August 1960): 7.

24. Jeannette Howard Foster, "Ann of 10,000 Words Plus," *The Ladder,* Vol. 4, No. 11 (August 1960): 8–9.

25. Del Martin, "Readers Respond," *The Ladder,* Vol. 5, No. 1 (October 1960): 19–21. In this issue, DOB also offered "the complete story" of Aldrich's "indictment" of DOB and *The Ladder,* as well as her book *Carol In A Thousand Cities,* through their Book Service.

26. Len Evans, *Gay Chronicles: California,* http://www.geocities.com.

27. "D.S., Illinois" ("Del Shearer"), in "Readers Respond," *The Ladder,* Vol. 5, No. 7 (April 1961): 23.

28. William Kelley, interview with author, October 16, 2002; Eric Marcus, "Shirley Willer," *Making Gay History: The Half-Century Fight for Lesbian and Gay Equal Rights* (New York: HarperCollins, 2002), 12–13. John Poling, "Mattachine Midwest," (Master's thesis, University of Iowa, 2002).

29. "Daughters of Bilitis, Chicago Chapter, August 17, 1963, Special Meeting" minutes list, "Velma Tate," Box 15/11, Martin and Lyon Papers, GLBTHS. Taylor also discussed her DOB involvement in an undated interview for *Windy City Times,* Chicago's gay newspaper; transcript at Gerber/Hart Library, Chicago, IL. Thanks to Karen Sendziak for this reference.

30. Tee Corinne, *Valerie Taylor: A Resource Book* (published by the estate of Valerie Taylor, 1999), 3–7. Valerie Taylor, *Journey to Fulfillment* (New York: Midwood-Tower, 1964; republished Tallahassee FL: Naiad Press, 1982).

31. Michael Bronski, *Pulp Friction: Uncovering the Golden Age of Gay Male Pulps,* 17.

32. Marion Zimmer Bradley, "Lesbian Stereotypes in the Commercial Novel," *The Ladder*, Vol. 8, No. 12 (September 1964): 14–19; Dorothy Allison, "A Personal History of Lesbian Porn," *New York Native* (May 24–June 6, 1982): 22–23; Kate Adams, "Making the World Safe for the Missionary Position: Images of the Lesbian in post-World War II America," *Lesbian Texts and Contexts: Radical Revisions*, Karla Jay and Joanne Glasgow, eds. (New York: New York University Press, 1990), 255–274. See also Jaye Zimet, *Strange Sisters: The Art of Lesbian Pulp Fiction, 1949–1969* (New York: Penguin, 1999); and especially Katherine V. Forrest, ed., *Lesbian Pulp Fiction*.

33. Jaye Bell, "DOB's Anniversary Message From the President," *The Ladder*, Vol. 6, No. 1 (October 1961): 9.

34. "DOB on New York Radio in September," *The Ladder*, Vol. 5, No. 11 (August 1961): 7.

35. Kay Lahusen in Marcus, *Making Gay History*, 15–16, 84–87; Kay Lahusen, interview with author, January 31, 2004; correspondence with author, May 24, 2006.

CHAPTER FIVE

1. Valerie Taylor, *Return to Lesbos* (New York: Midwood Tower, 1963).

2. Stella Rush, interview with author, September 16, 2003.

3. Stella Rush, interview with author, September 8, 2002.

4. Billye Talmadge, Stella Rush, Helen Sanders, Del Martin, and Phyllis Lyon have acknowledged and discussed their involvement in the Prosperos Society in interviews with the author in 2002 and 2003; Rush continues to be connected to the group today, although much less so. Also, three profiles in *Before Stonewall* mention homophile activists' involvement in the Prosperos: for Lyon's discussion of Martin's involvement, see pp. 164–165; see also William Fennie, "Billye Talmadge," 186–187; and James T. Sears, "Hal Call," 154.

5. Kay Lahusen, interview with author, June 15, 2003.

6. "A Report on DOB's Second National Convention (Part I)," *The Ladder*, Vol. 6, No. 10 (July 1962): 4.

7. Steven Capsuto, *Alternate Channels*, 43–44.

8. "Paul Coates Interviews," *The Ladder*, Vol. 6, No. 10 (July 1962): 15, 26.

9. "L.L., California," in Readers Respond, *The Ladder*, Vol. 7, No. 2 (November 1962): 26.

10. Kay Lahusen, interview with author, January 31, 2004; Barbara Gittings, interview with author, August 23, 2003.

11. Shirley Willer, July 12, 1989, #MV24, DOB Video Project, Lesbian Herstory Archives; Phyllis Lyon and Del Martin, interview with author, June 2000; Del

Martin and Phyllis Lyon, "The Daughters of Bilitis and the Ladder That Teetered," *Everyday Mutinies: Funding Lesbian Activism*, Nanette K. Gartrell and Esther D. Rothblum, eds.; *Journal of Lesbian Studies*, Vol. 5, No. 3 (2001): 113–118.

12. "Another Year," *The Ladder*, Vol. 7, No. 1 (October 1962): 4. One early recipient of a DOB scholarship was lesbian poet Judy Grahn.

13. Del Martin and Phyllis Lyon, interview with author, March 1, 1999. See also David Mixner, *Brave Journeys*, 35; Martin Duberman, *Stonewall*, 99–100.

14. Del Martin and Phyllis Lyon, *Lesbian/Woman*, 238–240.

15. John D'Emilio, *Lost Prophet*.

16. "Cross Currents," *The Ladder*, Vol. 7, No. 7 (April 1963): 15.

17. Florence Conrad, "New Research on Lesbians to Begin This Fall," *The Ladder*, Vol. 7, No. 9 (June 1963): 4–5.

18. Dr. Ralph H. Gundlach, New York City, "Why is a Lesbian?" *The Ladder*, Vol. 7, No. 12 (September 1963): 4.

19. Fritz A. Fluckiger, Ph.D., "An Evaluation of the Bieber Study on Homosexuality," Barbara Gittings/Kay Tobin Lahusen Archives, Wilmington, DE; copy given to author September 2003; published in three parts as "Research Through a Glass, Darkly" in *The Ladder*, Vol. 10, No. 10 (July 1966): 16–26; Vol. 10, No. 11 (August 1966): 18–26; and Vol. 10, No. 12 (September 1966): 22–26.

20. John Ruhland, "Un-Americanism in Seattle: The University of Washington, possibly the birthplace of McCarthyism, now shows some remorse," *Washington Free Press*, Seattle History, #33, May/June 1998.

21. Biography, University of Washington Libraries, Ralph H. Gundlach Papers, Accession No. 686–3; Ralph Gundlach's Statement to the Tenure Committee (1948), University of Washington Libraries, Ralph H. Gundlach Papers, Accession #686–70–21, folder 1/11. According to his "Biography," after his dismissal from UW, "Gundlach continued to be a recognized leader in his field. Shortly after his firing from the University, he received scholarly endorsements from various professional organizations, including the Society for the Psychological Study of Social Issues, the Consumers Union, and the American Psychological Association. He prospered as a private psychotherapist in New York City and worked as a consultant to the New York Medical College. Gundlach continued to publish extensively in psychology journals and, in his own words, continued working for 'lost causes,' such as Julius and Ethel Rosenberg's appeal to the U.S. Supreme Court." It is interesting that none of Gundlach's research work on lesbians and gay men in the 1960s is mentioned. He died in Great Britain in 1978.

22. "F.I.B., California," "Readers Respond," *The Ladder*, Vol. 8, No. 2 (November 1963): 23–24.

23. Phyllis Lyon and Del Martin, "Cleo Glenn (Bonner)," *Before Stonewall,* 189–190.

24. "Kennedy Is Killed by Sniper as He Rides In Car In Dallas; Johnson Sworn In On Plane; Gov. Connally Shot, Mrs. Kennedy Safe," Tom Wicker, *New York Times,* Saturday, November 23, 1963, 1.

CHAPTER SIX

1. Melanie, "focus on fashion," *The Ladder,* Vol. 9, No. 2 (November 1964): 16–17.

2. Ger van B., "Thanksgiving from Indonesia," *The Ladder,* Vol. 9, No. 2 (November 1964): 9–11.

3. "Special Notices," *The Ladder,* Vol. 9, Nos. 5 and 6 (February-March 1965): 6–7.

4. "J.N., Australia," in "Readers Respond," *The Ladder,* Vol. 9, No. 3 (December 1964): 26.

5. *The Ladder,* Vol. 9, No. 4 (January 1965); on page 23 of this issue, Gittings wrote a "Salute to ARENA THREE," the magazine published by Minorities Research Group, recognizing it as "one of the liveliest and most sophisticated homophile publications."

6. Letter from Barbara Gittings to "Dear Cleo," August 21, 1964; copy given to the author by Barbara Gittings from the Gittings-Lahusen personal collection, November 2002. See also Cleo Glenn, "Memo to All Chapters Re: Newsstand Distribution," n.d. (probably 1964), Box 12/7, Martin and Lyon Papers, GLBTHS.

7. Cleo Glenn, "Address of Welcome," DOB National Convention; introduced by Shirley Willer, June 20, 1964. Audiotape of convention proceedings, DOB Collection, William Way Lesbian, Gay, Bisexual, Transgender Community Center and Archives, Philadelphia, PA. Thanks to Steven Capsuto for providing this important collection of speeches.

8. Phyllis Lyon, interview with author, May 15, 2002; see also Phyllis Lyon and Del Martin, "Cleo Glenn (Bonner)," *Before Stonewall,* 190.

9. Barbara Gittings, interview with author, November 8, 2003.

10. "Report Round-Up, Part One," *The Ladder,* Vol. 8, No. 10 (July 1964): 7–16 and "Report Round-Up, Part Two," *The Ladder,* Vol. 8, No. 11 (August 1964): 11–21. "NOLA" was the DOB pen name of Elenore Lester.

11. Barbara Gittings, *The Ladder,* Vol. 9, No. 2 (November 1964): 23.

12. "Homosexual Women Hear Psychologists," *New York Times,* Sunday, June 21, 1964.

13. Del Shearer, Letter to Governing Board, August 15, 1964; Box 15/12, Martin and Lyon Papers, GLBTHS.

14. W. Mitchell, "Special Report—'Off The Cuff,'" *The Ladder,* Vol. 9, No. 1 (October 1964): 9–12.

15. F. Conrad, "How Much Research—and Why?" *The Ladder*, Vol. 8, No. 12 (September 1964): 20–24.

16. Dr. Franklin E. Kameny, "Does Research Into Homosexuality Matter?" *The Ladder*, Vol. 10, No. 1 (May 1965): 14–20; Florence Conrad, "Research Is Here to Stay," *The Ladder*, Vol. 9, Nos. 10 and 11 (July/August 1965): 15–21; Dr. Franklin E. Kameny, "Emphasis on Research Has Had Its Day," Vol. 10, No. 1 (October 1965): 10–14, 23–26.

17. Kay Lahusen, interview with author, January 31, 2004.

18. "Cross-currents," *The Ladder*, Vol. 8, No. 8 (May 1964), 11. See also David Mixner, 35.

19. Del Martin, "The Church and the Homosexual: A New Rapport," *The Ladder*, Vol. 8, No. 12 (September 1964): 9–13.

20. Del Martin & Phyllis Lyon, interview with author, March 1, 1999; Patricia Lyon, interview with author, May 17, 2002; Del Martin, correspondence to Barbara Gittings, January 4, 1965, Box 6/10, Martin and Lyon Papers, GLBTHS; Herb Donaldson and Evander Smith in Eric Marcus, *Making Gay History*, 99–104. For other accounts of the New Year's Ball, see Nan Alamilla Boyd, *Wide Open Town*, 231–234; John D'Emilio, *Sexual Politics, Sexual Communities*, 202; John Loughery, *The Other Side of Silence*, 286–287; Martin Duberman, *Stonewall*, 99–100.

21. "A Brief of Injustices: An Indictment of Our Society in Its Treatment of the Homosexual," the Council on Religion and the Homosexual (published by Glide Memorial Methodist Church, 1965), Box 17/8, Martin and Lyon Papers, GLBTHS. Issuance of the Brief brought CRH front-page coverage in the San Francisco press: "Council Issues Brief on Homosexuals," *San Francisco Chronicle*, September 25, 1965, 1. Phyllis Lyon, correspondence with author, January 5, 2006.

22. Phyllis Lyon, interview with author, June 10, 2003. See also Del Martin and Phyllis Lyon, *Lesbian/Woman*, 238–240.

23. Barbara Gittings, interview with author, January 31, 2004. "Cross Currents," *The Ladder*, Vol. 10, No. 1 (October 1965): 19; "Homosexual Voting Bloc Puts Pizazz in Politics," *The Ladder*, Vol. 10, No. 2 (November 1965): 13–14.

24. Correspondence between Barbara Gittings and Del Martin, January 1965; Box 6/5, Martin and Lyon Papers, GLBTHS.

25. John Loughery, *The Other Side of Silence*, 269–272.

26. From "Gay Picketing—Chronology" flyer accompanying the photo exhibit titled "Standing Tall Before Stonewall," curated by Kay Tobin Lahusen, William Way Lesbian, Gay, Bisexual, Transgender Community Center, Philadelphia, PA, June–July, 2000.

27. "'Expert' Challenged," *The Ladder*, Vol. 9, Nos. 5 and 6 (February–March 1965): 18.

28. Warren D. Atkins (Jack Nichols) and Kay Tobin (Lahusen), "ECHO Report '64, Part One: Sidelights of ECHO," *The Ladder,* Vol. 9, No. 4 (January 1965): 4; Al Weisel, "LBJ's Sex Scandal," *Out,* December 1999, 76–131.

29. Kay Lahusen, "Gay Picketing–Chronology."

30. "Rusk Probed on Picketing," *The Ladder,* Vol. 10, No. 1 (October 1965), 18.

31. Martin Duberman, *Stonewall,* 111–114; Barbara Gittings and Kay Lahusen, interviews with author, June 25, 2002, and November 8, 2003. By 1970, the Reminder Day fell out of favor, replaced by marches in New York and Los Angeles to mark the June 1969 riots at the Stonewall Inn in Greenwich Village. By the first decade of the twenty-first century, activists throughout the world had added million-dollar corporate-sponsored festivals and parties to annual "Gay Pride" parades.

32. "A Brief of Injustices," *The Ladder,* Vol. 10, No. 2 (November 1965): 4–5.

33. Kay Tobin, "Picketing: The Impact and The Issues," *The Ladder,* Vol. 9, No. 12 (September 1965): 4–8.

34. Letter to Marge McCann, Del Shearer, and Barbara Gittings signed by Cleo Glenn (Bonner), President; Phyllis Leon (Lyon), Public Relations Director; and Del Martin, Treasurer; June 7, 1965, Box 6/10, Martin and Lyon Papers, GLBTHS.

35. Ibid.

36. Correspondence between Barbara Gittings and Del Martin, August 1965, Box 6/12, Martin and Lyon Papers, GLBTHS. Photo by Kay Tobin, October 23, 1965, *The Ladder,* Vol. 10, No. 9 (June 1966): back cover. See also "Standing Tall Before Stonewall: The First Gay Pickets," curated by Kay Tobin Lahusen.

37. "Letter to The Governing Board from Del Shearer RE: Daughters of Bilitis, Inc. Participation in ECHO and Specifically Picketing, June 10, 1965," Box 6/12, Martin and Lyon Papers, GLBTHS.

38. Eric Marcus, "Shirley Willer—One Angry Nurse," *Making History,* 134.

CHAPTER SEVEN

1. Bob Dylan, "Like A Rolling Stone," *Highway 61 Revisited,* Columbia Records, released August 30, 1965.

2. Barbara Gittings and Kay Lahusen, interviews with author; August 23 and November 8, 2003; see also Toby Marotta, *The Politics of Homosexuality.*

3. Barbara Gittings, "Interview with Ernestine," *The Ladder,* Vol. 10, No. 9 (June 1966): 4–11.

4. *The Arbutus* Yearbooks, 1960–1963, Main Library, Bloomington campus, University of Indiana. "Interview with Ernestine Eckstein," audiotape recorded by Barbara Gittings and Kay Tobin, William Way LGBT Center and Archives, Philadelphia, PA.

5. Ibid.

6. Del Martin, "Report on Council on Religion and the Homosexual Activities in San Francisco: Opening of an Article to be submitted to *Challenge,* a magazine published by the San Francisco Theological Seminar," January 14, 1965, Box 18/6, Martin and Lyon Papers, GLBTHS.

7. Del Martin, Letter to "Shirley & Marion," June 2, 1966, Box 6/10, Martin and Lyon Papers, GLBTHS.

8. For specific comments on organizing a broad-based community response network to charges of police brutality, see Lyon and Martin, Talk to San Francisco State University women's studies class, March 25, 1998, General Files, GLBTHS. On the impact of Watts, see Gerald Horne, *Fire This Time: The Watts Uprising and the 1960s* (New York: Da Capo Press, 1997).

9. "S.F. Greets Daughters," *The Ladder,* Vol. 11, No. 1 (October 1966): 4. See also "S.F. Greets 'Daughters,'" *San Francisco Chronicle,* August 17, 1966 4; Maitland Zane, "Life in a World of Sexual Hostility," *San Francisco Chronicle,* August 20, 1966, 12; DOB General Clippings, Martin and Lyon Papers, GLBTHS.

10. "DOB Puts San Francisco On The Spot," *The Ladder,* Vol. 10, No. 11 (August 1966): 4; "A Challenge to San Francisco," *The Ladder,* Vol. 11, No. 1 (October 1966): 15. See also John D'Emilio, *Sexual Politics, Sexual Communities,* 203.

11. "Court Backs Fair Board: No Booth on Homosexuals," *The Sacramento Bee,* Friday, September 2, 1966, 12; "Homosexual Council Hands Out Pamphlets," *The Sacramento Bee,* September 5, 1966, 8. "EVERY TENTH PERSON IS A HOMO-SEXUAL!" *The Ladder,* Vol. 11, No. 1 (October 1966): 21–22.

12. Shirley Willer, "What Concrete Steps...," *The Ladder,* Vol. 11, No. 2 (November 1966): 17–18.

13. Ibid.

14. Correspondence between Del Martin and Barbara Gittings, Box 6/12, Martin and Lyon Papers, GLBTHS; Barbara Gittings, interview with author, January 29, 2004.

15. Barbara Gittings, correspondence with author, May 29, 2006.

16. Del Martin, Acting Editor, *The Ladder,* Vol. 11, No. 1 (October 1966): 24; *The Ladder,* Vol. 11, No. 4 (January 1967): 1.

17. Ibid.

18. Joel Fort, Claude M. Steiner, and Florence Conrad, "Attitudes of Mental Health Professionals Toward Homosexuality and Its Treatment," *Psychological Reports,* 29 (1971): 347–350.

19. In addition, the number of women in the workforce had jumped from 8.5 million in 1947 to almost 13 million in 1956. *Feminist Chronicles* (published by the Feminist Majority Foundation, 2000), www.feminist.org.

20. Del Martin and Phyllis Lyon, *Lesbian/Woman*, 282–283.

21. Del Martin, "President's Message," *The Ladder*, Vol. 1, No. 1 (October 1956): 7; Barbara Gittings and Kay Lahusen, interviews with author, January 31, 2004, and June 14, 2005; Stella Rush, interview with author, December 2003; Helen Sandoz and Stella Rush, May 15, 1987, #DV-20, DOB Video Project, Lesbian Herstory Archives.

22. Lyon and Martin, talk to San Francisco State University women's studies class, March 25, 1998, General Files, GLBTHS. See also Martin and Lyon, *Lesbian/Woman*, 261–263.

23. Martha Shelley, interview with author, February 16, 2004; Eric Marcus, "The Radical Activist—Martha Shelley," *Making History*, 176.

CHAPTER EIGHT

1. Ada Bello, interview with author, September 17, 2003.

2. Ibid.

3. Marc Stein, *City of Sisterly and Brotherly Love*, 229-235, 253.

4. Ada Bello, interview with author, September 17, 2003.

5. "There's Been Some Changes Made," *The Ladder*, Vol. 5, No. 9 (June 1961): 13.

6. "BI-ENNIAL ASSEMBLY AND CONVENTION OF THE DAUGHTERS OF BILITIS," *The Ladder*, Vol. 12, No. 9 (July 1968): 30.

7. Shirley Willer, October 1989, #DV 15, DOB Video Project, Lesbian Herstory Archives.

8. "Amended Articles of Incorporation—United Daughters of Bilitis, Incorporated," Box 7/2, Martin and Lyon Papers, GLBTHS; Meredith Grey, "Changing Times," *The Ladder*, Vol. 12, No. 10 (August 1968): 19–22.

9. Ibid.

10. Shirley Willer, July 1987, #MV24; DOB Video Project, Lesbian Herstory Archives.

11. Rita Laporte, "Arguments in Opposition to Corporate Reorganization," n.d., Box 7/2, Martin and Lyon Papers, GLBTHS. See also Sten Russell, "Report of General Assembly," *The Ladder*, Vol. 12, No. 11 and 12 (September 1968): 14.

12. Shirley Willer, July 1987, #MV24, DOB Videotape Project, Lesbian Herstory Archives.

13. Jeannette Howard Foster, "Dominance," *The Ladder*, Vol. 13, No. 1 and 2 (October/November 1968): 17–18.

14. Stella Rush, interviews with author, September 16, 2003, and February 16, 2004.

15. Martha Shelley, "Homosexuality and Sexual Identity," *The Ladder*, Vol. 12, No. 10 (August 1968): 6–7.

16. Gene Damon, "Three Ways to Serve," *The Ladder*, Vol. 14, No. 1 and 2 (October/November 1969): 4; Rita Laporte, cover portrait, *The Ladder*, Vol. 13, No. 11 and 12 (August/September 1969).

17. See, for example, *The Ladder* issues in late 1969 and the early months of 1970: Vol. 14, No. 3 and 4, 13–16; Vol. 14, No. 7 and 8, 4–6; Vol. 14, No. 9 and 10, 23–25. See also Graham Willett, *Living Out Loud: A History of Gay and Lesbian Activism in Australia* (St. Leonards: Allen & Unwin, 2000), 36–37.

18. Phyllis Lyon, interview with author, May 15, 2002. No additional information about Eckstein is known at this time. Gittings and Lahusen have surmised that by the time she left DOB, Eckstein was "tired of all the personal issues—she wanted a more political organization." Barbara Gittings and Kay Lahusen, interview with author, June 25, 2002. William Fennie, "Billye Talmadge," *Before Stonewall*, 186.

In addition to DOB and Mattachine, the Tavern Guild, SIR (Society for Individual Rights), the Council on Religion and the Homosexual, Citizens Alert, the Imperial Court System, Guy Strait's *Citizen News*, Vanguard (for young gays), and the Committee for Homosexual Freedom were all organizing in the Bay area. Susan Stryker and Jim Van Buskirk, *Gay by the Bay*, 44–53.

19. Stella Rush, interview with author, September 16, 2003.

20. Lois Beeby, interview with author, May 27, 2002; Martha Shelley, interview with author, February 16, 2004; Martha Shelley in Marcus, *Making Gay History*, 130.

21. Susan Stryker and Jim van Buskirk, *Gay By the Bay*; Susan Stryker, dir., *Screaming Queens: The Riot at Compton's Cafeteria*, ITVS and KQED Public Television, 2005.

22. Martha Shelley in Marcus, *Making Gay History*; Martha Shelley, interview with author, February 16, 2004. See also Martin Duberman, *Stonewall*.

23. Ibid.

24. "S.C., New York City," in "Readers Respond," *The Ladder*, Vol. 13, No. 7 and 8 (April–May 1969): 44.

25. Helen Sanders, Los Angeles, in "Readers Respond," *The Ladder*, Vol. 13, No. 3 and 4 (December–January 1968–69): 39–40.

26. Fen Gregory, "Before the Gap Becomes a Chasm," *The Ladder*, Vol. 14, No. 7 and 8 (April/May, 1970): 27–28.

27. "R.B., New York," in "Readers Respond," *The Ladder*, Vol. 14, No. 9 and 10 (June/July, 1970): 46.

28. Del Martin, "No to Nacho," and Rita Laporte, "Of What Use Nacho" *The Ladder*, Vol. 13, No. 11 and 12 (August/September, 1969): 16, 18–19.

29. Wilda Chase, "Men are the Second Sex," *The Ladder*, Vol. 13, No. 11 and 12 (August/September, 1969): 33–34.

30. Franklin Kameny, "Readers Respond," *The Ladder,* Vol. 13, No. 11 and 12 (August/September, 1969): 47.

31. "Cross Currents," *The Ladder,* Vol. 14, No. 1 and 2 (October/November 1969): 39.

CHAPTER NINE

1. "Ann Ferguson Is Dead," *The Ladder,* Vol. 1, No. 4 (January 1957): 7.

2. Manuela Soares, "The Purloined *Ladder:* Its Place in Lesbian History," *Journal of Homosexuality* (New York: Haworth Press, Inc., 1998), 27–49.

3. *The Ladder,* Vol. 14, No. 11 and 12 (August/September 1970): 2.

4. Phyllis Lyon, interview with author, May 11, 1998, and correspondence with author, January 13, 2006.

5. All five women mentioned Grier and Laporte's "theft" at least two or three times in our interviews. In the DOB Video Project tapes of Helen Sandoz and Shirley Willer, they also refer to Grier "stealing" *The Ladder* (DV15 and MV24, Lesbian Herstory Archives). On the other hand, some other Daughters—such as Jeanne Cordova and Martha Shelley—told me that they found Grier to be "very helpful" and kind to them as they were getting started in lesbian activism and publishing.

6. Barbara Grier, interview with author, December 29, 2003. Rita Laporte died in the early 1970s. To my knowledge, she never told her side of *The Ladder* story.

7. Rita Laporte, "Readers Respond," *The Ladder,* Vol. 14, No. 5 and 6 (February/March 1970): 43–44.

8. Gene Damon, "Once More With Feeling," *The Ladder,* Vol. 14, No. 9 and 10 (June/July 1970), 2–3. Membership numbers have been difficult to quantify for DOB due to incomplete records, but listings for 1960 show thirty-five New York members, forty-four LA members, sixty-one SF members, and twenty-six National members. In 1966, listings of those members "eligible to vote" in the upcoming convention show seventy-one New York members, seventy-nine SF members, and fourteen LA members. Martin and Lyon Papers, DOB Box 4-10-4-13, GLBTHS, San Francisco.

In the April-May 1969 issue of *The Ladder,* editor Barbara Grier noted that 1100–1200 copies of the magazine were sent to paid subscribers and DOB members every issue; she also quoted uncited membership figures of "100 in San Francisco, 100 in New York, with probably 10 to 20 in each of the other major cities of the country." *The Ladder,* Vol. 13, No. 7 and 8 (April–May 1969).

9. See, for example, "An Invitation to Readers of the Ladder," *The Ladder,* Vol. 9, No. 1 (October 1964): 20.

10. Barbara Grier, interview with author, December 29, 2003.

11. Ibid.

12. Stella Rush, interview with author, September 8, 2002.

13. Elsa Gidlow, "Episode," *The Ladder,* Vol. 14, No. 9 and 10 (June/July 1970): 23.

14. Phyllis Lyon, interview with author, June 10, 2003. See also Martin Duberman, *Stonewall*, 160. For more information on the battle over *ONE* magazine, see Rodger Streitmatter, *Unspeakable: The Rise of the Gay and Lesbian Press in America*, 145; Wayne Dynes, "W. Dorr Legg (1904–1994)," *Before Stonewall*, 99–100.

15. Kay Lahusen, "Daughters of Bilitis Confronts Feminist Issues," Lesbian Resource Center, Minneapolis, MN. DOB Chapter Files: New York Chapter, Lesbian Herstory Archives.

16. W.C.S., "DOB Convention," *LA DOB*, July 1970, Box 15/6 Los Angeles Chapter File, Martin and Lyon Papers, GLBTHS.

17. Jeanne Cordova, interview with author, September 10, 2003. See also Jeanne Cordova, *Kicking the Habit—A Lesbian Nun Story* (Los Angeles: Multiple Dimensions, 1990); "My Immaculate Heart," *Lesbian Nuns: Breaking Silence*, Nancy Manahan and Rosemary Curb, eds. (New York: Warner Books, 1985); Jeanne Cordova, "Butches, Lies & Feminism," *Persistent Desire: A Femme Butch Reader,* Joan Nestle, ed. (Boston: Alyson Publications, 1992).

18. Judith M. Saunders, "Stella Rush," *Before Stonewall,* 143; Stella Rush, interview with author, September 10, 2002.

19. Del Martin and Phyllis Lyon, *Lesbian/Woman*, 266; see also Karla Jay, *Tales of the Lavender Menace* (New York: Basic Books, 1999).

20. At the National NOW Conference in September, members "passed historic resolutions on lesbianism 'as a legitimate concern of feminism,' voluntarism, and the double oppression of minority women." (09/03–06/71) *Feminist Chronicles–1971*, Feminist Majority Foundation, 2000, http://www.feminist.org

21. Del Martin, correspondence with author, January 10, 2006.

22. Del Martin, "Is That All There is?" *The Ladder*, Vol. 15, No. 3 and 4 (December 1970–January 1971): 4–6.

23. Kay Lahusen, interview with author, November 8, 2003.

24. Kay Tobin Lahusen, interviews with author, March 12, 2004, and May 14, 2006.

25. Rita Mae Brown, "Say It Isn't So," *The Ladder,* Vol. 14, No. 9 and 10 (June/July 1970): 29–30.

26. Jeanne Cordova, interview with author, September 7, 2002.

27. Barbara McLean, interview with author, September 10, 2003.

28. Margie Adam, twenty-fifth National Women's Music Festival Speech, 1999, www.margieadam.com.

29. Barbara Grier, interview with author, December 29, 2003.

30. See Martin Duberman, *Cures: A Gay Man's Odyssey* (New York: Dutton Books, 1991), 275–277; John Loughery, *The Other Side of Silence*, 344–345.

31. Kate Adams, "Built Out of Books: Lesbian Energy and Feminist Ideology in Alternative Publishing,," *Journal of Homosexuality* Vol. 34, Issue 3/4, 1998.

CHAPTER TEN

1. Pat Parker, *Pit Stop* (Oakland, CA: The Women's Press Collective, 1973/1975).

2. Lillian Faderman, *Odd Girls and Twilight Lovers*, 207.

3. Jill Johnston, *Lesbian Nation: The Feminist Solution* (New York: Simon & Schuster, 1973): 277.

4. Yolanda Retter, Lesbian History Project; ONE Institute, University of Southern California; Jesse McKinley, "From TV Role in 'Dobie Gillis' to Rights Fight in Legislature," *New York Times*, May 14, 2006.

5. Barbara McLean, "Diary of a Mad Organizer, " *Lesbian Tide*, Vol. 2, No. 10/11 (June 1973), 16–17; 28–29.

6. *Lesbian Tide*, June 1973: 4–5.

7. Beth Elliott, interviews with author, May 12 and 13, 2002; correspondence with author, January 3 and 24, 2006. "Lady Kay, New York, N.Y." in "Readers Respond," *The Ladder*, Vol. 2, No. 10 (July 1958): 26.

8. *Lesbian Tide*, June 1973: 1–18.

9. Ibid.

10. Beth Elliott, correspondence with author, January 3, 2006.

11. The History Project, *Improper Bostonians: Lesbian and Gay History from the Puritans to Playland* (Boston: Beacon Press, 1998): 198.

12. Barbara Grier, interview with author, December 30, 2003; Shari Barden and Lois Johnson, interviews with author, June 10, 2002.

13. Lois Johnson, "History of DOB," *Gay Community News*, October 1978.

14. Shari Barden and Lois Johnson, interviews with author, June 10, 2002.

15. Ibid.

16. Jewelle Gomez and Diane Sabin, discussion with author, November 10, 2005.

17. Manuela Soares, "The Purloined *Ladder*," 27–29. Gene Damon, "The Ladder, Rung By Rung," *The Ladder*, Vols. 1–2 (New York: Arno Press, 1975).

18. Barbara Grier, interview with author, December 30, 2003.

19. Del Martin, letter to Coletta Reid of Diana Press, Box 12/14, Martin and Lyon Papers, GLBTHS.

20. Barbara Grier and Coletta Reid, eds., *The Lavender Herring: Lesbian Essays from The Ladder* (Baltimore, MD: Diana Press, 1976).

21. *Two Women: The Poetry of Jeannette Foster and Valerie Taylor* (Chicago: Woman-press, 1976).

22. Phyllis Lyon and Del Martin, interviews with author, May 15, 2002 and June 10, 2003.

23. Combahee River Collective, "The Combahee River Collective Statement," reprinted in Barbara Smith, ed., *Home Girls: A Black Feminist Anthology* (New York: Kitchen Table: Women of Color Press, 1983), 272–275. See also Cherie Moraga, "La Guera"; Barbara Cameron, "You Don't Look Like An Indian From the Reservation"; and other essays in *This Bridge Called My Back: Writings by Radical Women of Color*, Gloria Anzaldua and Cherrie Moraga, eds. (New York: Kitchen Table: Women of Color Press, 1981).

24. Audre Lorde, "Who Said It Was Simple," *Chosen Poems, Old and New* (New York: W. W. Norton, 1982).

25. Audre Lorde in Claudia Tate, *Black Women Writers At Work* (New York: Continuum, 1984).

26. Del Martin, with assistance from Leslie Warren, "Pat Walker (1938–1999)," *Before Stonewall*, 191–92.

27. Pat Walker, October 1988, #MV46; DOB Video Project, Lesbian Herstory Archives.

28. Del Martin and Phyllis Lyon, "Shirley Willer (1922–1999)," *Before Stonewall*, 203–204. Shirley Willer, July 1987, #MV24, Lesbian Herstory Archives.

29. Billie Talmadge, interview with author, May 2002, College Park, MD.

30. Phyllis Lyon and Del Martin, interviews with author, May 15, 2002 and June 10, 2003.

31. Nina Kaiser, interview with author, September 9, 2002; "Daughters of Bilitis—News Brief," January 1978, and "What Happened to D.O.B.?" memorandum dated July 1978, Box 4/8, Martin and Lyon Papers, GLBTHS.

32. Phyllis Lyon, correspondence with author, January 6, 2006.

33. See Jean Hardisty, *Mobilizing Resentment: Conservative Resurgence from the John Birch Society to the Promise Keepers* (Boston: Beacon Press, 1999). See also Ronald P Formisano, *Boston Against Busing: Race, Class, and Ethnicity in the 1960s and 1970s* (Chapel Hill: University of North Carolina Press, 1991); Rebecca Klatch, *A Generation Divided: The New Left, the New Right, and the 1960s* (Berkeley: University of California Press, 1999); Kristin Luker, *Abortion and the Politics of Motherhood* (Berkeley: University of California Press, 1984); Lisa McGirr, *Suburban Warriors: The Origins of the New American Right* (Princeton, NJ: Princeton University Press, 2001).

34. *Daughters of Bilitis Newsletter*, San Francisco Chapter, May 1978, Box 2/1, Del Martin and Phyllis Lyon Papers, GLBTHS; Dudley Clendinen and Adam

Nagourney. *Out for Good: The Struggle to Build a Gay Rights Movement in America* (New York: Simon & Schuster, 1999); Randy Shilts, *The Mayor of Castro Street: The Life and Times of Harvey Milk* (New York: St. Martin's Press, 1982).

35. Carol Pogash, "The Myth of the 'Twinkie Defense:' The verdict in the Dan White case wasn't based on his ingestion of junk food," *San Francisco Chronicle*, November 23, 2003; Paul Van De Carr, "Death of Dreams: Harvey Milk & Jonestown: 25 Years Later," *The Advocate* (November 25, 2003): 32–36; Laura Perkins, "Bad Times and Good: Gays and San Francisco share a long—and sometimes tumultuous—past," *San Francisco Chronicle*, June 23, 2000.

EPILOGUE

1. ACLU of Northern California, Annual Report 1985 (1663 Mission Street, San Francisco, CA 94103; www.aclunc.org). Information about the National Center for Lesbian Rights can be found at www.nclr.org.

2. F.A.C.T. [Feminist Anticensorship Task Force], *Caught Looking: Feminism, Pornography, and Censorship* (Seattle: The Real Comet Press, 1988).

3. For a good summary of the history of American "porn wars," see Joanne Meyerowitz, "Women, Cheesecake, and Borderline Material: Responses to Girlie Pictures in the Mid-Twentieth Century U.S.," *Journal of Women's History*, Vol. 8, No. 3, 1996.

4. Janet Kornblum, *USA Today* (printed in *The News Journal*, Wilmington, DE), Monday, March 8, 2004, E2.

5. John D'Emilio, "Interpreting the NGLTF Story," *The World Turned*, op. cit. For more information about the history and current programs of the National Gay and Lesbian Task Force, and its annual Creating Change conference, see www.thetaskforce.org.

6. Barbara Gittings, co-author of text for commemorative plaque at Independence Hall, Philadelphia, PA; placed July 4, 2005.

7. David Plante, "Jean Rhys: A Remembrance," *The Paris Review*, No. 76 (Fall 1979): 247. Thanks to Gerry Gomez Pearlberg for sharing this quote.

Index